PRAISE FOR RHIANNON HELD'S *SILVER*

"Andrew Dare's job as the enforcer for the Roanoke pack of werewolves requires him to work solo. But when a strange and disturbing scent leads him to a rogue werewolf, a female called Silver, he ends up joining forces with her. . . . Held's urban fantasy debut presents a different view of werewolves that takes into account not only their dual nature, but their struggle to exist within a world that does not understand the closeness and loyalty of a pack. Verdict: Held's characters are believable, and her compelling story begs for further development in future novels." —*Library Journal*
(SF/Fantasy Debut of the Month, starred review)

"Wow. What an amazing read! Held has taken a completely new and utterly believable look at werewolves and pack-based society and spun an engrossing tale that was so engaging I stayed up until 3 A.M. to finish it. She writes with the assurance and subtlety of an old hand while bringing something completely new to urban fantasy. I loved the characters and the marvelous twists of the story. *Silver* is a remarkable debut; I'm blown away."
—Kat Richardson,
bestselling author of *Greywalker,* on *Silver*

"Interesting twists, smooth writing, and genuine chemistry between the leads." —*Publishers Weekly*

TOR BOOKS BY RHIANNON HELD

Silver
Tarnished
*Reflected**

*forthcoming

Tarnished

Rhiannon Held

TOR®
fantasy

A TOM DOHERTY ASSOCIATES BOOK
NEW YORK

This is a work of fiction. All of the characters, organizations, and events portrayed in this novel are either products of the author's imagination or are used fictitiously.

TARNISHED

A Tor Book
Published by Tom Doherty Associates, LLC
175 Fifth Avenue
New York, NY 10010

www.tor-forge.com

Tor® is a registered trademark of Tom Doherty Associates, LLC.

ISBN 978-0-7653-6816-4

Tor books may be purchased for educational, business, or promotional use. For information on bulk purchases, please contact Macmillan Corporate and Premium Sales Department at 1-800-221-7945, extension 5442, or write specialmarkets@macmillan.com.

First Edition: May 2013
First Mass Market Edition: January 2014

Printed in the United States of America

0 9 8 7 6 5 4 3 2 1

This one's for Mum
For taking all the phone calls, and reminding me:
Life is a spiral. When you think you're falling
back into the bad times, look down . . .
And see how far, slowly but surely, you've climbed.

ACKNOWLEDGMENTS

Here we are, back for the second book, and no one seems to have learned their lesson the first time and avoided getting sucked into the whole crazy process. Fortunately for me!

The Fairwood Writers nursed this novel through several, often rough, incarnations. Renee Stern, David Silas, Corry Lee, Christopher Bodan, Erin Tidwell, and Kim Ritchie, I couldn't have done it without you.

My agent, Cameron McClure, and my editor, Beth Meacham, have been wonderful to work with, as well as Melissa Frain, Aisha Cloud, and the whole team at Tor. John Pitts has been my author mentor, and the sister continues to be my brainstormer extraordinaire.

Chris Vincent is the director of the Market Street Singers community choir, and shares his joy in singing with us every practice. The music in this book is for all of you.

Last but not least, I enjoyed amazing and unstinting support from my family and the many communities to which I belong. Fellow archaeologists, choir members, gamers, and writers: thank you.

Tarnished

1

Just thinking about the challenge he was planning made restlessness twist under Andrew Dare's skin as he drove through Snoqualmie Pass toward Seattle. In the afternoon sunlight, scrubby brown foothills gradually greened and sharpened into evergreen-covered slopes, then grew increasingly dusted with snow. He wanted to shift and run something down on four feet, breathe the rich variety of smells with a lupine nose. But he saw nowhere to pull off where he wouldn't be visible from the road. Andrew passed the ski resort with annoyance, holding down the need to run and chase until the highway signs turned brown to indicate exits into the national forest.

Beside him, Silver dozed, strands of her pure white hair wisping out of her messy braid to form a soft cloud around her face. She looked much healthier now than when he'd first met her. Her body had smooth curves rather than sharp angles, but her left arm, scarred from when she had been injected with silver nitrate, remained thin from lack of use. She had it tucked away under her now. He took a brown-signed exit at random and the change of speed made her open her eyes and look up, but she kept her arm hidden.

Perhaps it wasn't right to say she hid her bad arm, but she certainly did whatever she could to minimize its impression on people. Andrew supposed he couldn't blame her. His silver injuries were now fully healed, the reason he was heading back to Seattle to set the challenge in motion, but he'd done everything he could to hide his limp during the long, frustrating healing process.

A stretch of wide, graveled shoulder suggested a trailhead and Andrew pulled his battered compact off the road. He tucked it against a tall patch of sword ferns, tire on a line of stubborn snow. That the line survived after probably a week or more above freezing was a testament to how high the plowed mound must have been to start with.

The lack of other cars suggested they'd have the trail to themselves, not surprising with the bite to the wind even now in April. He shucked his jacket and shirt onto the driver's seat and came around to open Silver's door. She managed her seat belt for herself. Something must be on her mind to distract her. When she focused on a task in the modern world, she tended to lose her unconscious skills.

"Seemed like a nice place for us to run," Andrew said. He dumped his wallet and phone on the seat, locked the car, and handed the keys to her for safekeeping. He hated that the silver nitrate lingering in her veins prevented her from shifting along with him as much as she did—or maybe more, sometimes. But they were used to it by now. It did make keeping track of their possessions more convenient.

Silver slipped the keys into the back pocket of her jeans without looking. She cupped his cheek with her good hand and gave him a dry smile. "Don't go pulling a muscle because you're so happy to be healed." She pressed a quick kiss to his lips and stepped back with a snort of amusement. "Go ahead and circle back. I'm not going to bother trying to keep up with you when you're in this mood."

Andrew hesitated, trying to read her. She'd stepped downwind, so he had only her expression to help him. So far as he could tell, her offer was sincere. She had to know by now that he'd always wait for her. "Call me back sooner if you get bored." He stepped deeper into the comparatively clear space beneath the old trees. Young vine maples tangled with blackberry in the greater light at the road's edge made a good shield in case a car should pass. He pulled off his shoes, jeans, and underwear and shifted.

The Lady was just past full, meaning the tipping point into wolf came quickly, but he could feel the effort increasing again. His body sense stretched and twisted and reshaped. He shook himself to settle his fur and steady his perceptions. He lifted his nose to the wind. Now to find something warm-blooded to chase, and imagine it was his former alpha, Rory, running from him.

Rory wasn't going to give up power without a fight, of course. Andrew's allies said Rory's campaigning against him had grown more polished lately. It would be much easier to leave the man be. Being alpha could be a thankless job. But Rory had put their pack in danger with his incompetence, and Andrew couldn't stand by and let that happen again. He needed to take the responsibility away from Rory, to keep everyone safe. Having made that decision, Andrew couldn't shake the restlessness.

After living out among sagebrush and poplars east of the pass, Andrew found the mingled scents of damp growing things distracting, and the spring wind carried the promise of more drizzle. Rather than search for a trail he settled into an easy lope, running until his nose acclimated.

Nothing could camouflage the scent of another werewolf when he encountered it about half an hour later, though. Andrew skidded to a stop with his nose lifted high to pinpoint the source. Not too close yet, but even in wolf form, geography would tend to funnel other Were into the pass rather than the sides of the Cascade mountains surrounding it. Was it one of Seattle's people? At this distance, Andrew could only tell it was a man and not someone he knew well, but that didn't necessarily mean anything. Seattle oversaw too much territory to guard it all constantly, but he'd have people out walking the periphery periodically. Still, the scent's unfamiliarity was worrisome enough to investigate.

Silver met him about halfway back, his underwear, jeans, and shoes tucked up under her good arm. Andrew looked up at her, panting. A shift back so soon would be a pain, so he hoped she might be able to answer his question without him voicing it.

"Not one of Seattle's," Silver said, interpreting his look. "And he mentioned no one new when last we talked. I thought you might want these." She set down his clothes and buried her fingers in his ruff as his hackles rose. As a guest on Seattle's territory with no status of his own, an intruder was none of his business, but instinct still made him bristle.

He could hardly call Seattle in wolf form, though. Andrew stepped back from Silver's hand and shoved his muscles back through the twisting process, ignoring the tiredness that lingered from the first time. He had to pant for several breaths before standing and taking his underwear and jeans to pull them on.

"Smells like he's closing quickly," Silver said with a tinge of warning in her voice. Andrew jammed on his shoes and straightened to get his nose back into the wind. She was right.

Andrew glanced back toward the car. "Well, I suppose this is the point when we call Seattle and then drive off like good little guests." He flexed his hands with frustration. Back in his days as enforcer for the Roanoke pack, he'd escorted plenty of lones and Were from neighboring packs out of Roanoke territory. The impulse was ingrained now and it was hard to leave. But he needed Seattle on his side. Once he challenged to be Roanoke himself, he'd be back on the East Coast and out of Seattle's territory, but until then he needed somewhere to stay. With a sigh and clenched fists, Andrew headed for the car and let the scent fall away downwind. Silver gave him a twisted smile of sympathy and followed.

The scent returned with a rush as they approached the car about fifteen minutes later. Andrew stopped briefly in surprise. The Were must have cut across to the road to find their exit point rather than tracking them directly. So much for Andrew leaving this to Seattle.

They cleared the last of the trees to see the stranger leaning against the car. His disarranged clothes and a bag with a wolf-slobbered handle at his feet suggested he'd recently shifted back himself. He was young, probably younger than he wanted anyone to realize, but solidly muscled. His bleached hair had brown roots, and he had several gold rings in the top of each ear. Andrew gave a mental snort at the vanity that must have prompted the man to carry the jewelry with him and put it in quickly. Too dangerous to leave them on in wolf. People noticed wild animals with piercings.

"Andrew Dare," the man said, not quite a question, but Andrew nodded anyway. "My alpha wants to talk to you."

Andrew sized the Were up. Like many werewolves, the stranger had a slight advantage on him in sheer size. Young meant inexperienced, but also faster reflexes, and Andrew was already operating at some unknown disadvantage because of his past injuries. They'd healed, but he'd had no chance to test himself in a real fight since then.

"Well, you're not part of the Seattle pack, and you're not part of the Roanoke pack, so I don't particularly see why I should want to talk to him," Andrew said. The second conclusion was more of a stretch: the Roanoke pack was formed of sub-packs and encompassed the entire eastern half of the continent out to the Mississippi River. On the other hand, in his time as enforcer, Andrew had known every single Were in his territory by smell, if not name. If this man had joined in the months Andrew had been gone, he wouldn't have earned the status to be sent on this kind of mission yet.

"Sacramento said you'd be cowardly enough I'd have to encourage you a little." The young man pushed away from the car and sauntered close.

Andrew stood his ground as he thought furiously. He'd stayed well out of Sacramento's reach since he'd had to execute the man's son for his crimes. There was being a coward and then there was avoiding fights with vengeful, grieving parents. "I especially have nothing I wish to talk with Sacramento about. He aired his grievance in front of the Convocation and they ruled in my favor." Not that he expected Sacramento's thug to care about that, but one had to follow the formalities.

In answer, the young man smirked and cracked his knuckles. Andrew resisted the urge to roll his eyes. Why settle for the language of intimidation of humans in movies when Were methods worked so much better? Andrew caught his gaze, pushing the shared look past the sort of dominance assessment everyone did when they met a stranger, and into a full struggle. As he'd suspected, the young man chickened out and broke the gaze to throw a punch before he could lose.

He hauled back so far Andrew saw it coming a mile away and stepped out of reach. He did the same with the next punch. "How'd you find me?"

The blond man ignored the question and seemed to figure out what Andrew was doing. This time he charged before he drew back, bringing him into range fast enough that Andrew had to back up to avoid it. Time to take him out quickly, before his greater strength allowed him to catch Andrew in a hold he couldn't break.

Andrew used the warning the man's next draw back gave him to step forward, blocking the blow with one arm as he drove the other elbow into the man's throat. While the man was still stunned, gasping, he followed up with a knee to the groin that doubled the man over in agony.

Andrew stepped back again, crossing his arms to add a little intimidation for good measure. "How'd you find me?"

"We knew you couldn't hide at the edge of Seattle territory

forever. Set up a net around the city for when you finally came back in," the man wheezed out. "My alpha *is* going to talk to you, one way or another." Despite his pain, he managed a certain sort of glee, like Andrew should be cowering in his den now he knew Sacramento was coming for him.

Andrew bared his teeth in a snarl. That was what he was afraid of. He didn't have time for the distraction of dealing with Sacramento's hissy fits. "I don't know what Nate's told you, but his son was in Roanoke territory when he decided to continue his little game of raping human women. I executed him lawfully." Once, he'd have pretended it was his alpha's decision, but no more.

The blond man growled with discomfort when Andrew used Sacramento's name rather than his title, as Andrew had intended, but shook it off after a second. "Humans." He sneered and pulled himself up straight using the car. Andrew braced himself for another attack, but the man just snarled at him. The bruise on his throat modulated from blue to yellow as it healed with a werewolf's speed.

"Oh, and you have no human blood anywhere among your ancestors?" Silver made a show of draping herself over Andrew's shoulder, but he felt her hand spread over his back, probably checking his muscles for the telltale shake of exhaustion. Dammit, he was healed. She worried too much. "You'd allow someone like your grandmother to be raped, someone like your great-aunt to be violated?"

Andrew shook his head at Silver, meaning both that he was fine, and that she shouldn't waste her time trying to reason with the man. She made a noise of acknowledgment and stepped back out of the way as the man launched himself at Andrew one more time. She snorted with dark amusement.

Andrew's heart sped with a moment of worry that the man might have learned his lesson, but he still telegraphed his punches. Like many Were, the blond man had never bothered to learn any of the nuances of fighting in human and treated it like a fight in wolf: a lot of lunges with as much power as possible behind them.

Andrew ducked the punch and kicked out the man's knee. He heard the squishy pop sound he'd been hoping for and the man went down clutching the joint. That was something else unique to werewolf fighting. If the man didn't stop immediately to pop the joint into its proper place, it would heal dislocated and have to be reset with even more pain later. The man gritted his teeth, yanked, and gasped.

"If Sacramento wants to talk to me, he can call and get permission to enter Seattle's territory like a civilized Were," Andrew told him, looming ready to kick again and start the process over. "Understand?" He didn't step back until the man nodded.

The man growled something incomprehensible as he got to his feet. He snatched up his bag and stomped off into the trees.

Andrew waited a few minutes to see if the man would return, though he doubted it. He got the keys from Silver, unlocked the car, and took his time about pulling on the rest of his clothes. Silver hitched her ass on the trunk, giving a distracting angle and length to her legs, and watched him. "Word gets around, it seems."

"I've been out here for—" Andrew frowned, counting. "Lady, seven months, I think it comes to. I'm sure every one of the

Western packs knows that the infamous Butcher of Barcelona is off his leash and prowling the West by now. I just didn't realize that good old Nate's grudge was so strong he'd trespass to get to me."

Silver cocked her head, listening in the direction of an empty patch of ground. Andrew was so used to it by this point he didn't even bother reacting. If Silver's hallucination of Death conveyed something important, she'd mention it. If she didn't, Andrew didn't care what Death thought. He did avoid looking too closely at the spot, though. Ever since Andrew had hallucinated Death himself in the midst of excruciating pain, he caught imagined glimpses of the wolf-shaped patch of darkness at the edge of his vision every so often.

"You're not going to get off this easy, though," Silver said. She came to stand in front of him, meeting his eyes. With her, the match of dominance was almost a caress, rather than a struggle.

"I know." Andrew frowned off into the trees. "But the Convocation's in two weeks, and once I've challenged Rory we'll either be out of reach beyond the Mississippi, or we'll have to join the Alaska pack or something. Run around in the ice and the snow with those nutjobs."

Silver's muscles tensed and her expression chilled. "They spend nearly all of their time in wolf. I can't."

Andrew winced. He hadn't even thought about that before he made the stupid joke. Dammit. "I'll just have to win then, won't I?" He tried for a weak laugh. That was what *he* was trying not to think about: he had no wish to join the Alaska pack either, but if Rory beat him, he'd have few choices.

Silver laughed suddenly too, her timing suggesting Death had said something. "Oh, enough gloom," she said, and yanked

Andrew's head down for a deep kiss. He grabbed her ass to pull her closer to him and she wiggled away, laughing brightly. She ran a few steps into the trees and turned back to grin at him.

Andrew checked the wind to make sure Sacramento's thug was well gone, then grinned right back and followed. Now this was the kind of chase he could get into. John could wait a little for his call about a trespasser on his territory.

2

Susan gave her son a last gentle push on the park swing and then stepped back to let his father have a turn. Edmond laughed and slapped his little hands on the top edge of the swing's basket. John let the baby's momentum wind down before pushing again.

Susan leaned the side of her forehead against the metal bar of the swing set. The sun warmed the back of her dark peacoat, left over from work clothes though she'd shucked the bank-appropriate blouse and slacks the moment she got home. The metal was cool in contrast, part of the mixture of chill and warmth she loved about spring. Though spring also meant mud, of course. No matter the quantities of wood chips dumped on this playground, little feet always dragged bare streaks down to mud under the swings.

"You going to see that romantic comedy this evening? Whatever it's called, I forget." John wobbled the swing side to side with a grin, and Edmond shrieked with delight. They both had the same smile, which drew one from Susan. She suspected that Edmond would someday grow into his father's rugged looks. John reminded her of an old-time cowboy, if one had survived into the twenty-first century, and got a job at a software firm. He was a little clean-cut for a cowboy today, though, brown hair combed into order for once. Not for work, since he'd had Edmond today while he telecommuted, so it must be for whatever thing he had tonight.

"I might hang around my apartment. Much as I hate to waste an evening off." Susan slid into the next swing over. That one was the style for older children, wide and bendy enough to allow an adult's hips. She pushed herself only a few inches back before falling forward, conscious of not stressing the structure. However hard it was to wrap her head around the idea of the father of her child being a werewolf, his pack made good babysitters. Usually, that balanced out the hassle of John wanting her to keep her own place rather than move in with them. "Besides, why would I want to go alone when I could subject you to the sap later?"

John stepped sideways and gave her a sudden shove. Susan shrieked in surprise herself and tried not to fall off, laughing. John caught her against him on the way back and kissed the side of her head. "Cruel."

Susan leaned her head back into his warm solidity. His muscles moved as his phone rang and he reached down to slide it from the holster on his belt and answer it. On seeing who it was, John pulled back so quickly Susan almost fell backward. She twisted to frown at him as he answered with a curt greeting.

"You ran into who?" John listened for a moment. "Lady."

Edmond started to fuss so Susan stood and pulled him out of the swing. The diaper bag was at John's feet, but when Susan stepped over to collect it, he startled back and strode out of earshot. Susan glared after him, juggling the weight of Edmond on her hip and the bag on her opposite shoulder. She assumed the call was about werewolf stuff. Had to be. She'd noticed lately that John avoided touching her when anyone from that other world of his could see. This reaction to a phone call was a little much, though.

John strode back a moment later. "We'd better get home. My guests just came over the pass."

Susan pushed the diaper bag at him. "Which means they're not going to be here for another forty-five minutes at least. What's wrong?"

"He hasn't even arrived, and Dare has already collected trouble to bring with him." John sighed, scrubbed at his face, and accepted the bag. "Lady. It's never his *fault*, but . . ."

"I've known people like that." Susan smiled, but John didn't laugh at the humor. It seemed he'd stepped fully into what she thought of as his alpha persona before they even got back to the house. Or maybe this was the real John, and the relaxed, playful guy he was when they were alone was the persona, but Susan somehow doubted it. She mentally cursed the phone call for making him switch over sooner.

John slid the bag onto his shoulder. He started to step away, but he reconsidered a second later and pressed a hand to the small of her back as he kissed her hair. "We'd better get back. I have some stuff to take care of before they get here."

Susan sat on her curiosity and didn't ask what that stuff was. She knew he wouldn't answer, and it was easier to not have that stubborn silence become reality. She'd decided he was worth it, alpha persona and all, so there was no point picking at it, however much she was dying to know.

As they neared Seattle's den, the land opened up for Silver to look ahead of them, the view no longer blocked by the nearest mountainside. A river curled, branched, and branched again through the tallest of trees, not wide but very deep and churning, always fighting on its way to the sea. By now, she was familiar enough with what the poison had done to her mind to look harder. Not river, not trees, but something else with a heavy weight of meaning she could sense but couldn't touch. With time to spare in their journey, Silver pushed and struggled to touch that weight.

Paths. It came to her like blinking away tears so the world sharpened and ceased refracting at the edges. She was seeing paths, much traveled by humans, not rivers. Refraction remained, an uncertain sense she was still missing something, but Silver relaxed and let it slide away again. She trusted Dare to navigate for them both.

As they drew up at the den, Silver's other worries tightened around her. Death must have sensed this, because he returned just as her hand started to feel empty, loose by her side. She buried her fingers in the warm fur of his ruff. She always caught herself expecting that it would be chill, chill as the sky of a night in the new without the Lady's light or warmth. Death was as black as that sky, without even the points of stars to fill him, but warm anyway.

"You're practically shaking like a doe," Death said with her mother's voice, exasperated. Silver lifted her hand in surprise, and found it steady. Death was just being a cat. She smacked at Death's ears, but he danced out of the way. "Why do you fear your mother's pack, your birth pack?" He returned to his favorite male voice, presumably that of a Were dead generations ago. Death had no voice of his own.

Silver looked ahead, but Dare had enough distance that he could pretend he didn't hear her talking to Death, and she could pretend she didn't notice him pretending. "I don't fear them. I'm not looking forward to dealing with them, that's all." Silver clenched her hand. They'd undoubtedly be as pitying as they had been on other visits, when Dare's pack nature had gotten to be too much and he'd made some excuse to see other Were. Pity, pity the poor cripple. Scarred by the silver, unable to use her arm, unable to shift. Barred from the Lady forever. Pity her.

"You're as pack by personality as he is," Death said, not looking back as he paced ahead over the dozens of paw prints leading to the den's entrance. Silver hurried to catch up. "You want to claim you're not lonely, just the two of you, no other wolves?"

Silver said nothing and kept going past Death to catch up with Dare as he clasped hands with her cousin, Seattle, both measuring their strength while pretending they weren't. If she tried to defend herself against Death's too-perceptive questions, he only came up with even more infuriating ones.

"Seattle," Dare said as they released their grip. "It's good to see you. Sorry to have apparently brought trouble, but I hope to be able to get off your territory quite soon."

Silver heard a hint of gritted teeth in Dare's voice when he used her cousin's title. This was no romp through a field for

Dare either, meeting another alpha while he had no status of his own. She saw his discomfort even more clearly in his wild self. When Were's tame selves were ascendant, their wild selves usually followed quietly at their heels. Dare's wild self exchanged snaps of teeth with Seattle's before they both settled back behind their tame selves and their polite masks.

"I've sent people out to deal with that trouble. I appreciate the warning. Welcome." Seattle stepped aside and gestured into the den with more of that politeness that none of them believed.

Silver let Dare go first. As she passed her cousin, she stooped to ruffle his wild self's ears while checking it for new scars. At the back of her mind, Silver knew that she was the only one who could see wild selves, but that gave her all the more reason to check, since no one else could.

Tame selves did not form scars, except for injuries caused with silver, but wild selves did. Silver glanced ahead at the band of roughed, bleached fur over the back of Dare's wild self. In contrast, Seattle's wild self looked weak with his pretty fur and muscles that flexed without the catch of scar tissue.

Seen together, the men's tame selves formed a different contrast. Seattle was broad-shouldered and muscled where Dare was lean; Seattle still looked young, while Dare was silver-marked in the locks of white hair among the dark at his temples.

Seattle pulled her out of her thoughts with a squeeze of her shoulder that he extended into an arm across her back, guiding her inside like a child. "Are you hungry? Can I get you anything?"

Silver punched him in the side and he let go immediately. At least he learned. Sort of. He was family, so the smothering was a little easier to take from him. "I've yet to shatter into pieces since you saw me last, cousin."

Seattle muttered an apology and hurried inside to get them drinks anyway. Silver ignored hers when he offered it. Something was amiss in the den. Dare and Seattle started making strained, meaningless conversation while they drank, all about the things she couldn't see, so Silver slipped away, Death padding beside her. His tongue lolled out in a self-satisfied expression, so she guessed he approved of her curiosity. No wonder. Curiosity often led to trouble, and Death loved to see people off-balance.

The smell of one of the rooms caught Silver's attention. Seattle's human lover looked up as Silver approached, wariness written across her body in the awkward way of humans: they didn't know what they were doing so they couldn't hide their emotions, but neither could they choose to make a clear statement of a few emotions rather than always a muddled mess of several.

The human pushed to her feet. "Hello." She laughed, mere awkwardness, not warmth. "I know we've met before, but I've forgotten your name. Are you here to talk business? Should I be out of the house already?"

"Silver." Silver frowned, trying to suppress the sharp flash of frustration when the human woman's name slipped out of her mental grasp. Names, at least, she'd been working on, trying to strengthen her memory for them through practice. She frowned at the woman, trying to find the name by studying her. She was shorter than Silver, more curved, especially in the hips, and her short hair was an undistinguished brown. Without a Were's wild self to provide the rest of the appearance, it was a little like trying to recognize someone with half her face covered. Humans always looked so lonely.

Like Silver herself, she supposed.

Death butted his shoulder into the side of her knee as he passed to investigate the woman. Silver half-smiled. At least she did have someone to walk with her in place of a wild self.

"Susan," the woman said finally. Her eyes had been on Silver's injured arm in the pause and Silver realized that she'd forgotten to tuck it into her pocket when she and Dare arrived. The snakes inscribed there were dead now, only the diamond-backed white lines of their shed skins remaining. Silver traced them with her fingertip, thinking of when they had hissed and bitten her with every movement, before Dare had killed them.

"I suppose Seattle told you the story of what happened to me?"

Susan shook her head. "Seattle—that's some kind of title, isn't it? I've heard the others call him that."

Silver winced. Her cousin was keeping his lover in staggering ignorance. Clearly, she was intelligent enough to begin to put things together without his help. "He hasn't told you anything?"

"Some things, about how our son will grow up." Susan shrugged, expression tightening. "I know I'm not supposed to know about you guys *at all,* but now I do, I don't see that it matters how much more I find out. But he clearly wants to keep me . . ." Susan hesitated. "Separate from that part of his life somehow, including making sure I know as little about it as possible."

Silver smiled, thin-lipped. "To protect you, probably. I understand about people trying to protect me by keeping things from me."

"And what are you going to do about it?" Death said, brushing past Susan's legs, first on one side, then the other.

Silver grinned, a quick flash that seemed to take the human woman aback a little. "Maybe I'll have to tell you myself."

Susan's baby began to cry from somewhere deeper in the den and Susan reacted to the sound like she had werewolf hearing. A mystery of motherhood, perhaps. She pushed right past Death but hesitated halfway out of the room, desperate curiosity warring with the maternal instincts in her body language. "I do want to hear about you guys, I'm sorry, I just have to—"

"We can talk later," Silver assured her and Susan disappeared with a nod.

Death came up beside her and yawned, white teeth stark against all of his blackness. "You might want to be careful. Her safety now is in being unseen. Knowing too much might give her the tools to put herself in danger."

"Life is more than safety." Silver rubbed her bad arm. "But you're right. I should make sure she understands the risks and give her a choice before I continue."

"And if you're both extremely lucky, any choice she makes will even matter." Death wandered off through the den in the direction of Dare and Seattle. After a moment, Silver followed.

3

Andrew stuck to small talk with John, waiting for Silver to get back before he got to the real point of the visit. As his mate she was as concerned with a challenge for alpha as he was.

Silver pushed through the door of a downstairs bedroom a moment after John's human girlfriend jogged upstairs in response to the baby crying. Silver joined him in the kitchen, where he stood awkwardly opposite John, both with barely touched beers. She pressed up against Andrew, her bad side closest. He touched her bad wrist, and when she tipped her chin in a tiny nod, he tucked it into her front jeans pocket for her. It gave her a slightly more natural look she liked.

John offered her another open beer and Silver accepted it with a dry smile. "Talking to Susan?" he asked.

"I was quite interested to find out how little you'd seen fit to tell her."

Andrew looked down at Silver in surprise at the sharpness in her voice. What was that all about? Of course John had told Susan as little as possible. He shouldn't have told her about Were in the first place. He was only trying to keep her safe.

"You should tell Silver that," a male voice said behind him.

Andrew swallowed hard when he heard that familiar voice. Death was a manifestation of his unconscious. Nothing more. No black wolf hulked at the edge of his vision in the doorway to the kitchen, and that black wolf didn't laugh when he caught Andrew turning his head to avoid seeing him. "Better yet, tell her that you're going to do something to keep *her* safe," Death said.

Andrew suppressed a wince. If he ever did that, Silver would hand him his own balls on a platter. He looked up the stairs after the human woman. He hadn't ever considered Susan in that light. Perhaps he should drop a word in John's ear about the care and feeding of strong-minded mates.

"So you're going to challenge at the Convocation?" John asked Andrew, sounding desperate to change the subject. "I assume, at least, given your timing. I invited Portland over like you asked, so she'll be here to discuss it later tonight."

"Yeah. I quit my job in Ellensburg and moved out of the apartment. Maybe it's a little early, but I was going insane." Andrew rubbed his temple. The last time he'd been in the human workforce and not on Rory's payroll as enforcer, it had seemed much simpler, but since then he'd grown accustomed to holding more authority as a Were. He had a tough time giving it up among the humans.

John raised his eyebrows. "You were working at the university? College students?"

"The work-study types were about as intelligent as the paper clips, but that wasn't the only problem. The department was underfunded and didn't have a clear place in the university hierarchy. Add in an absentee head—" Andrew waggled his hand, and John nodded in understanding. Few Were liked dealing with the mushy undefined structure so many humans pretended they wanted.

John tipped back his beer. His scent soured, and Andrew wondered if he was stalling to avoid something.

"Silver and I are going to crash at one of those extended-stay hotels," Andrew said. No alpha would want another dominant Were in his house for too long. Did John fear that he was inviting himself in for the couple weeks until the Convocation? It was so frustrating not to know anyone he could stay with on this coast. He hadn't been able to go home since he broke with Rory, so all of his and Silver's belongings were packed in the trunk of the car. "I plan to avoid Sacramento until the challenge is settled, but if he comes looking for trouble again, he'll come looking there."

John gestured generously with his bottle. "The basement here is all yours if you want it. I'm sure we can survive a few weeks." He grinned briefly, Silver snorted, and Andrew chuckled his agreement. "Survive" was the operative word, but it was good of John to make the offer. "The thing is—speaking of Sacramento, I think maybe you should reevaluate your chances of even getting to the point of the challenge."

He hesitated and Andrew let his questioning silence grow heavier. John needed to just spit it out.

"Sacramento's been talking to a lot of people. I told him to go bite his own tail, but I've heard from Portland and Billings that he approached both of them. You can probably figure he talked to all of the Western alphas."

Andrew clenched a fist, then forced himself to relax the muscles. "If I need to address the question of his son again, I will. The Convocation upheld my decision to execute him at the time. He was a disgusting little shit, even leaving aside the rapes. I doubt anyone besides his father has much sympathy for him."

John shook his head. "It's not just that. He's aiming wider, and leaving his son out of it for the most part. He claims Rory is saying that you're power hungry enough to want all of North America, and that was your goal when you challenged me before."

"Do you believe that?" Silver asked. She unconsciously tipped her chin up to put her nose at a better angle to read him. John swirled his beer, probably to try to swamp his scent with that of the alcohol.

"If any Were in North America could pull it off, it would be you," John said at length.

"But no one can." Andrew snorted. He doubted John actually believed he could accomplish that impossible task, but it was worrisome if he thought Andrew would want to. He wasn't power hungry. He'd explained his reasons for challenging John at the time. He'd needed the ability to chase Silver's attacker without wasting time talking John into every single step. John should have smelled the truth of that on him. "So that's not an answer, Seattle."

"No. I don't believe it." John sighed. "However much you seem to attract trouble by nature, it's not like you're going out and picking fights to get it. But it sounds plenty plausible, and the kind of thing Rory would say."

Andrew snorted. "He probably did say it. But he's running scared. A lot of Were saw the danger he put his pack in when he let the man who hurt Silver get too close. The Roanoke sub-packs will have heard all about it, and they'll remember all the other times he let his obsession with hanging on to power drive him to bad decisions. The Western alphas don't know him like we do."

John spread his hands, one open, one tilting the beer bottle. "I'm just saying, you might want to watch out."

Silver cocked her head like Death was saying something. Her frown afterward didn't reassure Andrew. Was Sacramento really going to be such a problem? "Well, there's an easy way to find out what the Roanoke packs' reactions to Sacramento's shit are. I'll call Boston, see what he thinks," Andrew said. He pulled out his phone and rubbed a hand down Silver's back as he nodded questioningly to the front door. He'd go outside to avoid anyone listening in, and she might want to join him.

"I'll stay here. If Seattle doesn't get to feed me something soon, I think he'll explode from worry," Silver said. She brushed imaginary John-bits off her shirt. "Not worth the mess."

Under the humor, Andrew caught an edged note to her voice. It could be her usual frustration with being patronized by any-one, but he made a mental note to follow up later to make sure. He gave her a quick peck on the lips.

John stiffened with frustrated protectiveness, then wrestled it back under control. Andrew gritted his teeth. John's mistaken concern about Silver being in a relationship given her mental state apparently wasn't going to die either. After Andrew and Silver first made love, John had accused Andrew of taking advantage of someone who couldn't give consent, until Silver verbally kicked his ass. Given his previous reaction, maybe silence was progress. Fine. Let John stew, Andrew wasn't going to dignify his issues by defending himself.

Outside, Andrew eyed the suburban street and the neighbors' manicured front yards and crossed instead to the side gate to let himself into the backyard. It matched the sprawling house in size, conspicuous consumption for most humans, but necessary for a pack living together. The pack had landscaped it with dense bushes and trees along the fence to prevent anyone peering through or over the wooden slats. They'd left most of the rest of the space wild and grassy.

Boston answered after two rings, and Andrew's tone warmed automatically for his greeting. "Benjamin. How is everyone?"

"Dare." Benjamin's voice, in contrast, held a lurking frustration. Andrew thought at first it might be directed at him, but then Boston blew out a sigh. "All of us in the Roanoke pack need you more than ever, but I fear you may have missed your window."

Andrew slipped a hand under the hem of his shirt, feeling the ugly ridges of scar tissue along the small of his back. He hadn't wanted to wait this long. There were a lot of good people in the Roanoke pack who needed his protection. "John tried to tell me something similar, but I hadn't realized it was so bad. Sacramento's been winning people over?"

"With Rory's help. You'll remember I said Rory sounded too polished. Well, recently Sacramento has started talking to people directly. It's rather well planned. Must have been Sacramento's idea." Benjamin's tone was as withering as only the experience of over a century could make it. "Rory doesn't campaign too obviously against you, but the same things get said."

"Empire building?" Andrew rubbed his temple again. Who in their right mind would want such power? Especially since the Europeans might stop squabbling among themselves long enough to sit up and feel threatened. In Andrew's experience, the Europeans could manage to feel threatened by the most innocent of events, never mind a continent uniting behind one leader.

"And the events in Spain grow no less lurid for repetition, especially since you haven't told the story yourself to squash the exaggerations."

Andrew waited for the familiar rush of anger, the impulse to beat whoever asked a question about his history until they withdrew it. It didn't come. He'd told Silver the story, and she was still with him. She'd helped to center him more than he realized. "Wouldn't admitting what I did cement it in everyone's minds? I killed seven of the Barcelona pack. That's not an exaggeration. But if you think that's what we need to do, the Convocation's good for that, I suppose. A platform for telling stories."

He pinched the bridge of his nose, trying to think strategically. "Maybe Silver could back me up. When I told her about how I'd ripped out their throats to keep their voices from the Lady in the depths of the rage, she said that Death said I was a fool to think their voices rested only in a chunk of muscle."

Silence greeted that, and Andrew silently swore at himself. He needed to be careful about making Silver seem crazy before people got a chance to meet her for themselves. "She's completely lucid, Benjamin, even if she still sees some of her own world. She sees plenty of this one too. She just has a different perspective."

"That wasn't what I was thinking." Benjamin's voice held a

gentle note of correction. "I was thinking that I'm very much looking forward to meeting this mate of yours. I assume from your twitterpated tone that those rumors are correct, at least?"

Andrew had to laugh. "I'm sure the rumors are wrong somehow, but we're together now."

"Is she dominant?"

To avoid teasing, Andrew tried to keep the desire out of his voice, but found it impossible. "Yes."

Benjamin laughed, the sound suffused with the warmth that had been missing at the beginning of the conversation. "My advice is to use that, then. I can't think of the last time a North American pack had a mated pair of true alphas, and I've been keeping track longer than most."

Andrew stared below one of the bushes where a starling was poking around. Brave bird, by a house of predators. He hadn't thought of using Silver's dominance as an argument for his challenge. "Silver can take some getting used to." He laughed. "Then again, I know she'd kick the ass of anyone who underestimated her."

"I *definitely* need to meet her." Benjamin's laughter trailed back into seriousness. "I don't know what contacts you have out there, Dare, but it wouldn't hurt to start courting the Western alphas. Talk to them, remind them that you're not a slavering monster. I'll do what I can over here in Roanoke until you can pick it up yourself when everyone's gathered at the Convocation."

"Thanks," Andrew said. He ended the call with a quick goodbye. Hopefully he'd have some luck with Portland when she arrived tonight. She'd been helpful when he'd visited while searching for Silver's attacker. He also suspected she'd understand about having to sell herself, since she was the only female North American alpha at the moment.

Andrew headed in through the back door. Time he learned a bit about selling himself too, it seemed. If he could learn it fast enough.

4

When Susan got Edmond settled, she came downstairs to find Silver busy talking with her boyfriend and John over drinks. Rather than hover too obviously, Susan snagged her laptop and joined some of the pack's youngsters in the living room. They'd commandeered the couch to watch one of their modeling reality shows, but Susan managed to claim a chair that allowed her a sideways view of the kitchen doorway as well as the TV.

Her personal e-mail offered nothing in particular to hold her attention, mostly forwards from her brother and mother. She read the former, dumb jokes and PhotoShopped pictures, good for a groan, and deleted the latter. She appreciated the importance of keeping a professional-looking home that the articles trumpeted, but imaginative window treatments were the least of her worries when she spent most of her time in a house full of werewolves.

Tracy, fourteen but already sporting bleached hair and plenty of eye shadow, shrieked. "Susan, look at what she's wearing!" The girl pointed melodramatically at the screen, where the model looked as if she'd been swathed in taffeta and then attacked by a rabid badger. "She could hunt just by scaring the prey to death."

"The length is terrible, too. Makes her legs look stumpy." The length was the least of the dress's worries, but Tracy burst into giggles as Susan had intended. She got the sense she was the only one in the house who knew enough about fashion to converse with Tracy about it beyond "that looks stupid." Susan had developed most of her knowledge out of necessity when accumulating her professional wardrobe, rather than true interest, but she was happy enough to put it to use talking to the girl.

The kids flipped to another show during the commercials and Susan returned her attention to her computer screen, looking up every so often to watch for Silver. Such a strange name. There must be some kind of obscure werewolf irony she was missing. Another thing to ask her when she got the chance.

Dare left the kitchen first. For several months, Susan had actually thought that was his first name, since John rarely used anything else. She wondered if he had some kind of status, since she hadn't heard John call any of the others by their last names. Susan kept her head down and watched from the corner of her eye as John and Silver followed.

Susan waited for John to go into his office or upstairs, but he came over to her instead. She set her laptop on the chair as she rose, and John gave her a quick peck on the lips. She wished he'd have let her deepen it, but she knew better than that.

"You'd better get going," he said, head hanging.

Susan craned to see over his shoulder. Silver disappeared up the stairs. "I know. Soon. I just want to talk to Silver first . . ." She detoured around John but he stopped her with a firm grip on her upper arm.

"Susan. It's getting late." He used what Susan thought of as his werewolf voice, since he used it giving orders to the others, but not to her. Usually. She glared at him. The voice belonged to a stressed-out, cold person, not the person she'd fallen in love with. She'd been willing to compromise about these nights off, and accept the free babysitting and time to herself, but what did a few minutes matter? Someone had finally offered her some information and John was trying to prevent her getting it.

"So? I won't be long." Susan jerked her arm out of his grasp. "Silver already knows about me, and I want a chance to ask someone questions for once." She jogged up the stairs before he had a chance to plan his next objection. He looked surprised at her resistance, which made Susan even more determined to see this through. She'd accepted the status quo, because he was worth it when they were alone, but if his werewolf persona was going to start bleeding over, she was going to reevaluate.

The only open door on the second floor was the nursery. Susan headed to it, but stopped at John's room on the way to grab her peacoat from where she'd dumped it over a chair. Another petty, pricking annoyance of not living here: having no space of her own to keep her things.

Silver stood just inside the nursery doorway. She didn't look up when Susan came in. She had the air most of the werewolves did of having known you were there all along. She tipped her chin to Edmond's crib. "He's gotten so big since I saw him last. I'm afraid I've forgotten his name."

"Edmond. Nine months old now. He's a healthy boy." Susan leaned over the crib rail and ran a fingertip over her son's soft hair. "I think. Hell if I know how werewolves calculate milestones. He only has one word, and it's not mama or dada, but then he rolled over—and sat up, all those things—a month or two early."

"Were," Silver corrected absently, "is the people. Werewolf is the species. What's the word? Wolf?"

Susan blinked at her. "Well. More like 'woof.' But I think so. So that's normal?"

The other woman came to stand by the crib. Only one of her hands went to the rail, the other stayed tucked into the hip pocket of her jeans. The angle hid the scars a little, but Susan still could see the branching white lines along her upper arm. At this moment, Silver, more than any of the other werewolves, seemed somehow Other to Susan. Maybe it was something about the way she stood, or maybe it was her hair. The pure white on a woman in her twenties demanded your attention no matter how many times you'd seen it before.

"If knowing all about us would put you in danger, what would you choose? Information or safer ignorance?"

Susan froze. "What danger?" John had never said anything about her being in danger. No one could know about her, sure, but she'd assumed that was because John would get in trouble and they'd demand she and John split up. Where did the danger come in?

Silver blew out a breath. She leaned back, holding herself in balance with the hand on the crib. "By Were custom, you should have been killed for knowing as much as you've already been told. The more I tell you, the worse it would look if someone found out. And the more you know, the likelier you are to let something small slip around another Were."

Susan rocked back a step from Silver, then another, heart fluttering. That explained what John had been trying to keep her away from. But shouldn't she have expected something like this? After all, they were half wolves. Predators. Did they even think the same way about killing someone as a human would? Even taking into account only their human sides, they were organized in tight-knit family packs like the mob. And here Susan was, breaking a mob's laws.

She'd seen John as a wolf only once. She'd been so overwhelmed she hadn't taken in the sight properly. He'd been so damn big. So much power in those muscles. Wolves weren't like that in pictures or on the other side of a fence a long way away at the zoo. But even then, she hadn't thought to make the jump to considering whether he could kill in that form. But he must kill all the time. The pack was forever going off to hunt.

Silver held out her one hand, palm up and nonthreatening. "I'm not going to hurt you. Neither is Dare. But that's what Seattle's been trying to protect you from. I think there are better ways to protect you than what he's chosen, but you deserve to make your own decision in this."

She tipped her fingers to indicate Edmond behind her. "You could still walk away. My father was the wandering type, and my mother died just after my Lady ceremony. My brother and I were raised by the pack. It's a loving way to grow up."

Susan swallowed convulsively. However strong her burst of fear had been, her anger now was stronger. No way in hell would she ever abandon Edmond, no matter what happened, no matter the part of her that whispered that he'd grow up to be one of the killers himself. All the more reason why he needed his mother to steer him away from that. "You think I'd up and leave my son? Are you insane?"

The corner of Silver's lips twitched up. "Yes. But not in this case. I just wanted you to know your options. It wouldn't scar him, if that's what you need to do." She stepped away from the crib, and Susan darted in to pick up her son, asleep or not. She cradled him against her and he murmured sleepily.

"Relax. I'm not saying you should, just that you can. In your place, I wouldn't leave." Silver looked at the back of Edmond's head, and Susan recognized the expression. It was the ticking biological clock look. She'd seen it on plenty of her coworkers. But this was the most naked, longing form she'd ever seen.

Susan heard footsteps in the hall. The lingering wash of adrenaline from what Silver had said made her wonder whether John was walking heavily on purpose, to make her feel better, to make him seem less of a predator. He looked in the door. "Susan?"

"I'm going," Susan snapped, and tried to put Edmond back down. Now fully awake, he clung on and started to cry. Susan took a deep breath, trying to draw in patience, and handed him to his father. Holding her coat to her like a shield, she pushed by John before he could say anything else. Maybe it was good that she'd have some time to think.

5

Andrew nursed a beer at the dark wood dining table while he waited for Michelle to arrive. He mostly managed not to listen to Susan's argument with John, though he could hear it perfectly. Her conversation with Silver upstairs was much easier not to hear. Eventually, she thumped down the stairs and out to her car, leaving behind a tendril of sweaty fear that twisted into his nose. What had Silver said to her? Andrew considered staying out of it, but John would be pissed, and Andrew needed John's undistracted help as well as Silver's when Michelle got there.

The baby wailed in earnest, almost covering the sound of Susan's car pulling away, as Andrew reached the head of the stairs. He followed the wail to the nursery. John bounced his son desperately, talking to him, while Silver watched longingly. After a few moments, she made an exasperated noise and smiled at the boy. After a suspicious look, he stopped crying, though he didn't quite smile back.

"I have to go get ready for Michelle," John muttered in frustration, and Silver held out her arm. When John opened his mouth to object, Andrew coughed. The man was holding the boy mostly with one arm himself. If he thought Silver wasn't well practiced in doing things one-handed, he hadn't been paying attention. John shot Andrew a glare, but after another moment's dithering, he helped Silver settle the baby against her shoulder and clumped down the stairs.

"Edmond," Silver introduced the boy, clearly quite proud of remembering the name.

Andrew came closer and gave the boy a quick smile too. Curiosity about the new people and situation had overcome his crying and he focused on Andrew. "Woof," he said, solemnly.

"I am," Andrew agreed. He put out his hand as if to shake, one finger extended. Edmond grabbed on. It wasn't quite the tiny grip, it wasn't quite the familiar mangling of "wolf," but some combination of everything brought his daughter to mind. He jerked his hand away. She was a teenager by now, he reminded himself. A teenager raised by his in-laws, who'd made their opinion of him clear. She'd likely share it by now.

"His name is Edmond," Silver said sharply, breaking Andrew out of his thoughts. "Another baby. Different. You can't spend your whole life flinching from children."

"Later, Silver," Andrew said, rolling his shoulders to stop the tension before it got any worse. He didn't have time right now to worry about things he couldn't change. He'd fought years ago to get access to his daughter, fought hard, and he'd lost. Now, he needed to concentrate on battles he actually had a chance of winning. "What did you say to Susan, anyway?"

"Seattle never told her she could be killed for knowing about us."

Andrew slid a finger under Silver's chin, tilting her head up from the baby so he could see her expression. She was concentrating hard, attention miles away. "That's a lot to spring on her." Earlier, he'd compared Susan to Silver, but the fear he'd smelled suggested the flaw in that line of thinking. Susan was probably no coward, in human terms. The trouble was, many humans didn't deal with the idea of killing up front in this day and age. At least Were hunted. "Are you sure she needs you interfering?"

Silver rolled her working shoulder muscles on her bad side as if she wanted to smack Andrew. He smiled, dropped his hand, and acted as if she'd succeeded, rocking back a step. "I'm going to interfere until people realize she's capable of making her own choices. Like I am," Silver said.

"But she's not you." Andrew put a hand on her bad shoulder. "No one here assumes you can't think for yourself, or are as clueless as a human."

"Want to bet?" Anything further from Silver was cut off by a car pulling into the driveway. The smooth purr of Michelle's BMW was a contrast to whatever gutless gas-efficient compact Susan had been driving. The sound of John opening the door followed soon after. Andrew took his time helping Silver return Edmond to his crib. It wasn't his place to welcome anyone to another alpha's house, so better he stall a bit to arrive after the greetings were over.

When a new male voice joined Michelle's downstairs in the foyer, Andrew stopped screwing around and headed to the stairs. If Michelle had brought her prickly beta, this meeting would be more difficult . . .

"Dare!" The official greetings apparently over, a lanky young man with dirty-blond hair bounded to meet Andrew at the foot of the stairs like an oversized puppy. Tom must have been twenty or so by now, but he still had the same grin. Andrew remembered that grin from when he was busting the kid for mischief as a teenager back in Roanoke territory. Tom slammed into Andrew's chest. Andrew rocked with the impact and smacked a fist into the young man's shoulder.

"Ass. What are you doing here?" He stepped back to examine Tom's face. "You didn't get yourself kicked out, did you?" Andrew looked up to catch Michelle's smile of amusement.

"He joined for love, but young love is fleeting." Michelle accepted the beer John held out to her and followed him toward the dining room. John put out another couple coasters at the end of the dining table. Michelle rested her hand on the back of a chair in front of one of the coasters and laughed at Tom's hangdog look. "I think he wants to transfer."

"You're going to be Roanoke soon, aren't you? Can't I come back with you?" Tom made his eyes huge with pleading.

Andrew squashed a twinge of guilt. Tom was out here, safe, not back East anymore, but what about all the other Roanoke pack members Andrew had taken care of when he was Rory's enforcer? Seeing the trust in Tom's eyes only served to make the guilt twist in more sharply.

He sighed. "It's a lot more complicated than that. I might not pull it off, and even if I do, it won't be until the Convocation. You'd do better to stay in Portland for the moment or head back East yourself."

Tom pulled a face. "It's so weird with Emily now. Besides, I want to be in *your* pack, not any old pack. Can't I stay up here with you?" He turned his pleading eyes on John. "Permission to stay temporarily . . ."

John suppressed a grin that had sprung up out of Tom's sight. "You can stick around for a hunt. I want to see how you get along with everyone else before I say for sure."

"Thank you, sir." Tom bounced down to one knee and back up. It exasperated Andrew to see that limberness when he thought of all the trouble he'd had getting his legs up to strength after his back healed.

"Most of the pack are downstairs." John stepped out of the dining room and pointed around the corner to the basement door, as if Tom couldn't already smell them down there. Having everyone out of the way helped prevent eavesdropping on the alpha's private business.

Tom nodded and wandered down, leaving them in peace. When Silver came into the room Michelle set down her beer and examined her. They formed a study in contrasts. Portland had black hair and a Latina skin tone, and while she was several inches shorter than Silver, she packed a sense of concentrated power into her petite frame. Silver's dominance flowed much deeper below the surface, leaving her easier to underestimate.

Michelle seemed surprised after her study, like she'd expected Silver to start weeping or ranting or to fall into a seizure. Though that was how Portland had seen her last, Andrew supposed. Until he'd bled most of the silver nitrate out of her system, Silver had been prone to the latter two at least.

Silver met Michelle's attention steadily, though without direct eye contact, for several seconds until Michelle turned uncomfortably away to Andrew. "Seattle said you wanted to talk to me about something before the Convocation?" She pulled out her chair and sat. Everyone else followed her lead.

Andrew saw Silver frown at the conversation being so clearly directed away from her, but she didn't say anything. He wasn't sure of the best course of action himself. Given that he wanted to sweet-talk Michelle, it didn't seem politic to make demands of her, like acknowledging Silver as an alpha dominant.

"With an old enemy campaigning against Dare, we could use the support of anyone who knows he's not some bloodthirsty killer," Silver said.

Michelle raised her eyebrows. " 'We,' huh?"

Andrew stiffened. That tone was too far. But Silver put a fore-stalling hand on his knee. "Let me." Suppressed anger filled her voice.

Silver pushed her chair out so she was facing Michelle straight on, legs set wide. She leaned over them with false casualness. "Because I'm crazy?" Michelle sought first John's, then Andrew's, gaze in confusion. Silver snapped her fingers. "Look at *me,* not them. They're not my caretakers." Silver waited until Michelle met her eyes, then nodded. "It's true, I can no longer shift. It's true, some aspects of your world I can no longer quite . . . see. That doesn't mean I'm still as you saw me last. My mind works."

Silver stood in a sudden smooth movement, holding the eye contact. Michelle stood too, rather than break it. Silver walked closer until they were locked into more than a casual gaze. It wasn't a challenge, where one would win and one would lose, but rather a measuring of strength.

It was always strange to watch such struggles from the out-side. There was no external sign of what the women were thinking, but Andrew had participated in such contests often enough to fill in the feeling from memory. Contests with Silver, especially. Silver was surprising when you came up against her dominance for the first time.

Michelle made a choking noise and broke the stare first. "A mated pair of alphas. That's . . . unusual. Impossible, I'd have said. I assumed dominants didn't get along well enough long-term."

Her expression twisted, apology mixing with instinctive hostility toward another dominant Were. "I'm sorry. I know what it's like to be constantly underestimated as a female alpha. I should know better."

"Not your fault," Silver murmured. "But now you see why I'm part of the planning." She dragged her chair back so she was leaning against Andrew's side again, and he obligingly slid his arm around her.

"Silver's something of a switch, I've found," Andrew said. Silver snorted at the term, but didn't object. Any Were could try to act like one of a higher or lower status, but it was a rare one who could make anyone believe it. When Silver decided a stranger shouldn't notice her, she was damn convincing. "So it would have been surprising if you'd read her dominance when you first met." He squeezed his hand on Silver's arm. "Boston suggested we use it to win people over: that we're a pair of alphas."

Michelle started to look away and then changed her mind and looked at him, though they both avoided direct eye contact. The reluctance her initial look suggested didn't reassure Andrew. Her scent was neutral, at least. "It's going to be a tough battle. You know that, right? Your reputation is tarnished, to say the least. Sacramento has a lot of ammunition."

"That's why we need support," Andrew said. He pretended

relaxation he didn't feel and sipped his beer. "You can be a character witness, since you know differently."

"Do I?" Michelle sighed. "No one knows what really happened in Barcelona. Sacramento's chasing that one hard. Everyone knows why, too, because most people hated his little shit of a son and didn't shed any tears over his execution. But he does have a point about the Barcelona massacre."

Andrew took a deep breath. All right. Time to practice in front of people ostensibly his allies before he had to do it in front of his enemies. He took Silver's hand under the table, and she laced her fingers with his and squeezed tightly back. He could do this.

"The thing about Europe is that everyone has long memories, and there's not much space." Andrew tapped fingertips on the tabletop in lines corresponding to the territory divisions on the map in his mind. "They squabble over inches of land. Inches. Skirmish and it goes to Madrid, skirmish and it goes back to Barcelona. When I was there, it was popular to burn the other pack's houses. That forced the noncombatants to pick up and move farther toward the center of the territory. Supposedly, the idea wasn't to kill anyone, but they made a mistake with my wife. She'd forgotten something and returned to the house to get it. Barcelona thought we were out for the evening."

Andrew saw John and Michelle's attention sharpen as he left the generalities of Europe, but their expressions still suggested they expected some kind of redirection at the end. "So while Madrid and my in-laws sifted through the ashes, planning their retaliation, what house they would burn, what utterly pointless fight they would pick, I went to Barcelona. I found the beta out running with some others on their hunting grounds. He thought I was *funny*, coming out to chastise him all by myself."

Andrew drew in a shuddering breath and brought Silver's hand to his chest where he could clasp it with his other. Silver gave him a thin-lipped smile of encouragement, and the two alphas stared in shock at getting real details. Andrew's satisfaction at shoving them off-balance was a dim thing in the face of the crushing pressure of the memories, but he clung to it anyway.

"Really, the only reason I managed to kill the beta was because he let his guard down, underestimating me that way. Then the others were so shocked, they were easier. Some may have surrendered at the end. I don't remember. I don't think I was able to hear them at that point. Then I set the hunting grounds on fire, so the remaining pack would remember what it was about." Andrew took another breath. Just breathe. "I honestly can't tell you much about my reasoning at the time. I wish I could. That would mean there was more to it than falling into blind, berserker rage and being like Were used to be, combining the worst of human and animal."

Frozen silence fell for several moments. Michelle was the first to speak. "The rumors say their throats—"

"Death says he took their voices to the Lady regardless," Silver broke in, making Michelle start. "I see no particular reason to believe otherwise." She tugged on her hand until Andrew dropped it from his chest so she could scoot forward in her chair. She leaned in as if sharing a confidence. "Now, you're thinking, 'See, he's admitted it, he did kill all those Were, he did tear out their throats so Death couldn't take their voices to the Lady to give them their rest with Her. Why should we trust this man to be a leader?'"

Michelle nodded with a jerk. Andrew wanted to flinch. Why had Silver laid it out so starkly? Said like that, he wondered how he ever could convince someone differently.

Silver freed her hand and held it against her core. "You should trust him because he's found that place inside himself, and now he knows where it is. You have that place, no matter that you may think you don't. With the Lady's grace you'll never have cause to find it. But if you should stumble onto it unexpectedly, you'll no more be able to control it than he could. None of his pack would ever need to worry he'd stumble, because he knows, and he'll control it."

Andrew turned to stare at Silver. She'd never said that to him before, but she smelled of absolute sincerity and belief in him.

Michelle put her hand out to her beer bottle, but didn't drink. "But someone who has killed before might find it easier next time." Her inflection trailed almost into a question at the end.

"Someone's who's killed before knows the cost," Andrew said, and hesitated, choosing his words. "The madman who injected Silver and killed her whole pack, including the children, should I have let him walk away? Locked him up to escape again someday?"

"He deserved to die for his crimes." John thumped his bottle on the table for emphasis.

"And who do you want to judge that? Someone who knows the cost, or someone like Rory, who was such a pussy that he demanded I run back to Virginia to protect him instead of tracking the killer down?"

Michelle turned her head away to hide her expression and her scent muddied. She seemed less sure than she had been at the beginning of the conversation. Less sure in what direction, Andrew didn't know. He hoped she hadn't revised her opinion downward.

"At the end of the hunt, what does it matter to me who controls Roanoke? The Mississippi's a long way from my eastern border," Michelle said.

"Because we help keep you safer," Andrew said. He was on firm ground here. He'd thought this about the Western packs for years, and now he had the perfect example to back him up. "If a threat comes in through the East, we take care of it. We track lones, watch out for people, *communicate*. We caught a lot of problems and dealt with them before they ever got to the West because there was no way for people to slip between the cracks when they passed from one territory to another. Especially when two alphas happened to be in a snit and not talking that week."

Andrew eyed Seattle and Portland, and they both looked guilty. "You'll notice it wasn't one of the Roanoke sub-packs that madman managed to get to. Better if all the packs had more cooperation, but at least Roanoke catches threats within a reasonably large area. And without an enforcer shoring him up, Rory's too weak to hold what his father built, so the continent will lose that safety."

"You're such a philanthropist," John said, ostensibly a joke, but Andrew could hear the edge buried in the words.

"What, you think I want power for power's sake?" Andrew changed position in his chair, trying to ease muscles in his back that were aching from all the tension in the air. Did he need to show them the scars there? Would that make them understand that everything he did, he did to keep Were safe? To prevent what had happened to Silver, to Silver's pack, to him, from happening to someone else?

"You're the one talking about how great being together in one big pack is. Maybe you do want to take over all of North America for everyone's own good." Michelle raised her eyebrows. "You took over Seattle days after arriving."

"And then gave it back."

"When you were too hurt to hold it."

Andrew slammed a fist on the table. "Because it wasn't really mine! I needed to be able to track the madman without having to stop and persuade John into every step. But I didn't really deserve it. John takes care of his people. I'm only going after Roanoke because someone needs to take care of *them*." He looked at Silver, one of the stories she'd told once drifting into his mind.

"Sometimes someone has to be the one to get something done, even if people hate him for it at the time," Silver said, obviously thinking in the same direction.

"And there's a difference between holding something together and being the first to unite it," Andrew said. "One prevents upset, the other creates it. I'm trying to preserve the safety that already exists in Roanoke. Since I don't want the power for power's sake, there's no way in the Lady's name I'd want *more* of it." Andrew let tense silence settle to see if Michelle would come up with any arguments he needed to counter, but she seemed content to consider his words, lips thin.

"He's telling the truth about when he challenged me." John didn't sound happy about it, but he was saying it. "I think he would have handed control back even if he hadn't been injured. Nothing was easy or straightforward about dealing with that situation."

Andrew gave him a slow nod of thanks. A little less grudging would have been nice, but he'd take what he could get. Silence fell. Andrew finished his beer and started to peel off the label. Michelle's scent was still too conflicted for him to pick out any one emotion.

"I'll think about it," she said finally. "But it comes down to this, Dare. Sacramento's on my border. If I support you, he's going to make my life absolute hell. My people have jobs to go to, even if I could lock them in the house to keep them from being harassed by Sacramento's bullies while going about their daily lives. If you can get him to give up his grudge about his son, in front of everyone, fine. I'm with you. But otherwise I can't afford to."

"I understand," Andrew said, his voice as neutral as he could make it. He did understand, after all. Borders in this day and age were always more a product of common agreement than something fought for and enforced. No patrol could keep someone from driving past on the freeway, smell contained by the car. You could only try to cover enough territory to notice when anyone left a vehicle. He didn't blame Michelle but frustration still twisted his muscles. His problems kept circling around to Sacramento. It was clear he had to deal with the man somehow, but how?

"Maybe you should think about taking over Sacramento's territory," Silver told Michelle. Michelle eyed her and Silver laughed. A moment later the other woman joined in. The joke broke the tension, though Andrew wasn't entirely sure it had been a joke.

Michelle lounged back in her chair and let the conversation lull long enough to make an obvious break between business and small talk. "Well, I'd ask if there were any exciting new additions to the pack lately, but it smells like you're still with that same human woman?"

John stopped with his bottle halfway to his lips, and Andrew stepped in to fill the silence. "Less work than a bunch of different ones." If John wasn't careful, he'd give Susan away with his jumpiness alone.

"If it gives me a rest from the attention of one of the male alphas surrounding me, I'm not going to argue." Michelle toasted the idea. "Hey, baby, wanna join territories?"

John sputtered. "I was never that bad."

"You were." Michelle shared a look of feminine communication with Silver and both grinned.

The topics stayed lighter after that, and Andrew mostly remained silent, drinking his second beer, since he wasn't familiar with a lot of the people they gossiped about. He listened, though. You never knew when something might be useful to know later.

After about an hour, Michelle pushed to her feet. John followed. "We're going hunting tonight, if you don't want to drive back so soon?" he offered.

Michelle shook out her thick black curls and tried to finger-comb them into some kind of order. She pointedly drew in a breath of the charged atmosphere of the dining room. "Four dominants, one hunt?" She smiled and shook her head. "I'll take permission to run in a park down nearer your border and head out, I think, before any wrestling matches break out."

Andrew said his good-byes still sitting, and let John be the one to show her to the door. When the front door shut, Seattle and Portland's voices continuing toward the driveway, he looked at Silver, who looked as frustrated as he felt. "If she's an ally, I hate to think what the others are going to say," he said, and she nodded.

6

Susan stalled in the coffee shop for a whole ten minutes after John called her with the all clear, staring at the same page in her book. She'd grabbed one of her favorite paperback spy thrillers for a reread, but she hadn't made it past the first chapter. She read whole paragraphs several times without remembering what they said, as a campy movie delivery of "If I told you, I'd have to kill you" looped in her mind. Now that it was real for her, she couldn't imagine why she'd once thought it would be exciting, in the days when she and her brother would chase each other around the house with water pistols when their parents weren't home. Susan finally gave up and shut her book with a snap.

The stubborn feeling that flooded her at the thought of giving in and letting her brother declare himself winner hadn't changed, though. She wasn't going to leave her son, but she also wasn't going to abandon what she had with John so easily. So they were dangerous people. So what. She couldn't let them bully her and John both. Susan left the coffee shop feeling slightly more settled.

She arrived back at the house to a scene of chaos in the foyer. A hunt, she realized, pausing to watch with her hand on the shoe cubby. Predators, out to kill something. She didn't remove her shoes yet. Better to wait until the pack was out of the way. Even without considering their true natures, they were an intimidating bunch. Around fifteen adults lived in the house, though of course not all of them were gathered here tonight. Teens made up the difference in numbers from anyone still at work. It sometimes seemed a physics anomaly to Susan that they all fit, especially with memories at the surface of her mind of rattling around with her brother in their parents' big, showy home.

Watching the werewolves get ready to go out was like watching any other set of people in reverse. Rather than collecting possessions and coats, they shed them, getting rid of everything they could and still be decent. Men emptied their pockets, women who were built small enough wriggled out of their bras. Several were still in business clothes from the workday, and seeing the maneuvers done with slacks and crisp shirts and blouses made them seem even more surreal. They also looked likely to get awfully cold. It must have been in the fifties outside, but Susan supposed that didn't matter with fur.

Tracy waved at her from the foot of the stairs, clearly bursting with something she wanted to tell her friend. Susan hesitated a beat, then started nudging through the crowd. She'd decided she wasn't going to let them get to her, after all. Most people were polite enough to edge out of her way, but the beta stayed a stubborn obstacle and eyed her, arms crossed, as she detoured past. Susan was used to that from him by now. The feeling was mutual.

Dare came down the staircase as Tracy chattered in Susan's ear about the dress that had won in the program after Susan left. He looked regal, standing above the throng with the white streaks in his hair. "Silver," he called back over his shoulder. "Coming along?" Heads in the foyer turned to her as she came to the top of the stairs. Several of the people's expressions surprised Susan. They looked annoyed, like Dare had invited his bimbo of a girlfriend along on an important mob hit. But Silver was a werewolf like the rest of them.

Silver's back stiffened. "I'll stay and help with the cubs."

Dare shot everyone a look, but by then they all looked innocent. "Are you sure? I could stay, and we could drive out later to catch the end of it." Even Susan could tell he wasn't wild about missing most of the hunt.

"I was going out too." Susan wanted to wince under the pressure of all the eyes that switched to her. Predators. She pushed back through the crowd toward the door without looking at anyone. "Just shopping. But if you wanted to get out for a while, Silver?"

John frowned, and drew Susan aside into the doorway to the kitchen. "That's probably not a great idea," he said, leaning in and lowering his voice. Susan frowned at him, trying to formulate her question. Whatever disqualified Silver from a hunt shouldn't have anything to do with a simple shopping trip.

"Thank you." Silver said it loud enough to cut John off even from the stairs. "I'd love to." She followed the remains of Susan's path through the crowd, Dare on her heels.

When John reached out to stop Silver, Dare got there first, blocking the man with his body. He pulled out his wallet, and extended a folded twenty to Silver. "If you find something you want." Silver eyed him as if she had expected him to try to stop her too. When he just nodded to her, she smiled at him in a quick flash and took the bill. She turned it over in her fingers and examined it with concentration for a moment like it was some cryptic puzzle that had to be unlocked before use.

Did she even understand what it was? Susan had bristled at Dare's attitude, but she lost the feeling to confusion now. Silver grimaced at the money a final time in incomprehension and shoved it into her pocket. She tugged on Susan's arm.

Since she still had her coat on, Susan let Silver propel them both outside without protest. "I don't actually need anything. I thought I'd wander around the store when I can do it without calibrating the timing between feedings and naps." Back when she was single and grocery shopping alone, she'd actually rather enjoyed it. She wondered what John would think of her old comparison of it to the thrill of the hunt, discovering what new items the store held that day.

"I might pick up some ice cream to eat before we get back. Food enters this house and it's gone before I blink, never mind eat any. I don't know how interesting it will be for you." Susan gave Silver an apologetic shrug.

Silver nodded but didn't answer as they got into the car. Susan let silence reign for as long as she could stand as they drove through darkness. Light slipped and slid off the dampness on every surface from drizzle earlier in the day.

The trouble was, she saw no good way to work what she wanted to ask Silver into a casual conversation. Every time she thought of an opening, the question filled her mind again, choking out the innocuous comment.

Silver turned away from staring out the window, a smile banishing her residual frown. "Please don't explode," she said.

Susan blinked. "What?"

"There's something you're pent up about. I can smell it a mile away. Was there something you wanted to ask me?" Silver smoothed some flyaway strands of her fine hair down to her head, then gave Susan her full attention.

"Have you ever killed anyone?" Susan blurted it out and immediately regretted it. If the werewolves were that dangerous, pissing one off with rude questions was a bad idea. But no matter how she tried to think of predators, she couldn't reconcile the idea of a secret society of stone-cold killers with Tracy's delight in modeling shows. "I don't mean— But you talked about them killing me, and you're the only one who seems halfway . . . well, someone I could ask—"

"Halfway safe?" Silver smiled as she interrupted and saved Susan from digging herself deeper. She didn't seem offended. "You'll find many Were will automatically consider you weak too. I make it a policy to take the assumption and use it against them. You might want to do the same." She looked out the window. "As to your question—yes and no."

Susan swallowed convulsively, trying to imagine how one could only sort of kill someone. Fortunately, Silver continued before she had time to come up with anything graphic. "The man who did this to me." She took the wrist of her bad arm and laid it over her lap. In the uncertain light, the raised texture of the scars extending upward from the elbow showed better than the color. "Poured the fire into my blood and killed all my pack. Dare and I killed him together when he returned for me."

Susan picked a side street and pulled over in front of a house. Only the upstairs lights were on at this time of night. She shoved the car into park and allowed herself two breaths of openly staring at the scars. The scars themselves didn't look so bad, but the limp stillness of the arm itself was upsetting on a subconscious level. "You're serious?" she demanded. "This is how Weres— Were?—live?"

"No more than most humans live that way." Silver scooted in her seat and tucked one leg up. Despite the relaxed position, Susan got the sense that she wasn't entirely comfortable talking about that incident. "If not for the monster, I wouldn't have killed anyone. Dare would, but that's his job. To do that kind of thing so others can keep their hands clean."

"So is he the one—"

Silver growled and took Susan's chin in a strong grip. "No one is planning to kill you at the moment, I swear upon the Lady. Dare has too much honor for it. If someone else tries, defend yourself. I'll show you how. You have no wild self for me to see the sharpness of her teeth or strength of her jaw, but humans have that spark. They just keep it somewhere hidden." Silver released Susan's chin and tapped a fingertip somewhere around her solar plexus. "But I think Death sees it. He hasn't said I should stop wasting my time on you, which is telling."

Susan choked a little. "Death?" Half of that hadn't made any sense, and she was starting to doubt her choice of source for Were information. Wild self? Was this werewolf stuff, or was this Silver?

Silver looked away as if embarrassed. "Death walks with me. We were lonely, he and I. Me without my wild self, and Death without the Lady. You don't need to worry. He doesn't deal with humans."

Susan turned off the engine to avoid wasting fuel and turned on the dome light to supplement the watery orange glow of the streetlight down the street. Crazy or not, this woman was offering to protect her—teach her to protect herself, even. Teach a man to fish and all that. Something in Susan's gut-level read of Silver told her to accept. All right, then. Fair enough. The first thing to do seemed to be to start collecting information.

Susan tried to formulate her next question. What Silver had said about Death made her sound like a morbid goth teenager. If anyone looked the opposite of goth, though, it was Silver, with her fine features and soft white hair. "By 'the lady,' you mean the moon, right?" The other werewolves mentioned a lady often enough, but Susan knew nothing besides her connection with the moon.

Silver's lips thinned. "Your mate is a fool. I can't imagine what harm he thinks you'd do with that information. The Lady is our goddess. She made us as Her children, as your human gods made you. It's Her light that calls us to ourselves." Silver pointed upward. "That's why we call it our Lady ceremony after we shift for the first time. It's the time when a cub first truly meets the Lady."

Susan's attention sharpened. That, at least, John had talked to her about, given that it concerned her son directly. "That's at puberty, isn't it?"

Silver nodded. "For girls, it's soon after the first blood. For boys, it's harder to predict." She smiled suddenly. "Though it's easy enough for everyone but the cubs to tell when they're getting close. It's the itchiest feeling, and you're cranky and restless for weeks. Unmistakable. Then when the Lady is near full, it builds and builds until it almost hurts and then you fall into your wild self, and it doesn't hurt anymore." Silver drew in a jagged breath, and her muscles spasmed. "Oh, Lady—" she gasped. "That's a memory it does no good to call."

"Are you all right?" Susan frowned.

"My wild self is dead. It builds, but there's nowhere for me to go—" Silver held her breath and clenched her hand for a moment, and then collapsed. "Lady, that hurts." She curled up, pressing her cheek into the seat. Silence fell, until she broke it again unexpectedly. "That's why they don't want me to run with them, because I can't keep up with human legs. Dare will run with me anyway, but they won't."

Susan remembered her earlier analogy. The bimbo girlfriend screwing things up indeed. What was a werewolf who couldn't turn into a wolf? Back when she'd been a lowly teller at the bank, she'd had laryngitis for a week. Her supervisor had tried to find her clerical work to fill her hours, but Susan remembered the feeling of watching her coworkers chat with customers while she waited to struggle her way through communicating something simple and silly to one of them. She couldn't imagine the sheer frustration of being stuck with that forever. "I'm sorry."

"Sometimes things happen, and eventually you have to get up and keep hunting." Silver straightened herself out in her seat, and Susan started the car.

They reached the twenty-four-hour grocery about two minutes later. It was still reasonably busy with people picking up a bottle of wine or late-night snacks. Silver trailed behind Susan, watching the people and examining the food with the same casual curiosity. She only broke away once in the produce section after sniffing the air. She returned with a couple of pears, surprisingly ripe for grocery store produce, held in her good hand rather than bagged.

After all the trouble of carting them around half the store, Silver set the pears down on a display table in the bakery area. Susan switched her basket to the other hand, but Silver grabbed her wrist before she could pick them up.

"He shouldn't be here. Dare warned him once already." Silver's voice was difficult to hear. Susan leaned in only to be jerked up as Silver dragged her toward an emergency exit door. Where was the danger? Susan scanned the bakery and the sections of aisles she could see, but no one looked threatening.

"We have to pay." Susan braced her feet and hefted her basket to illustrate. Silver pulled the basket from her, slid it beneath another display table, and kept dragging. Susan resisted the urge to suck the skin of her fingers that had been burned by the basket handles. Silver was *strong*. "Where are we going?"

"You may say that, but attacking Dare at the edge of Seattle's territory is one thing. Showing up in the center is another," Silver snapped at an empty patch of air. Susan pressed her lips together. Silver had seemed not quite all there before, and now she was talking to the air. It wasn't that much of a stretch to assume that their pursuer might be just as imaginary. Maybe she should call John. But she couldn't reach her purse while she was being pulled along like this, so she went along with Silver without protest. None of the woman's crazy moments had lasted very long so far.

An emergency exit buzzer sounded briefly as they pushed

through the doors. A man stepped away from the side of the building as they turned toward the main parking lot. Silver jerked to a stop when it became clear that the man would reach them before they reached the corner of the building.

"You must be Silver," the man said. "I've heard so much about you."

Susan took a couple steps back. One piece of advice had always stuck with her, from a self-defense class she'd taken in college. Trust your instincts, your fear, about whether a person or situation is dangerous. There wasn't anything about the man she would point to—he had a sharp face, gelled black hair, and had his hands in the pockets of expensive slacks—but she wanted to get away from him. The atmosphere out here didn't help. Most of the light was only spillover from the streetlights covering the front parking lot and the delivery bays in the back.

"You have the advantage of me." Silver gave him a dangerous smile of her own. Susan had to look away when her fingers fumbled too much to find her cell phone by feel. "I have permission to be here. Do you? I know your underling doesn't." Silver nodded to the store.

The man turned a blinding smile on Susan. "Silver here and I are old friends. Why don't you let us catch up, hm? I'll give her a ride home when we're done."

Susan froze when the man looked at her, phone halfway out of her purse. Like hell she was going to leave Silver alone with him. He smirked over her shoulder, and Susan whirled. A bleached-blond man with multiple gold rings along the tops of his ears swaggered around the side of the building from the front doors. He must not have wanted to set the emergency alarm off a second time by using the same side door as them.

"Hurry up," the sharp-faced man behind Susan said. Leaving Silver alone looked like the lesser of two evils now. She needed to get help. Susan started to run past the blond to the light and people and safety, but he moved so *fast*. One breath he was at the corner of the building, the next his hand was on Susan's shoulder as he slammed her into the gray-painted cinder blocks of the store wall. Agony bloomed up from her temple, making it hard to see for a moment. Her phone fell with a distant clatter. Tears stung her eyes from the unexpected force of the pain. Susan mentally screamed at herself to move, to do something when the man stepped away from her. Instead she continued to hug the wall, waiting for the throbbing pain to fade enough for her thoughts to move again.

With Susan taken care of, the underling caught Silver's good wrist and twisted her arm, forcing her into the wall. She whimpered, and let him. Time to play wounded little thing. She had a weapon of her own, but if she used it too soon, they could still rush her, two against one. Better to draw them in close and let them relax.

"You do stink of silver, just like the gossip said," the alpha murmured with mocking casualness. "Is there really some still in your blood?"

"Watch what you say," Silver said, twisting to get at least her cheek away from the wall. "The human—" Of all the people who might discover Susan knew about the Were, this man had to be one of the worst. Everyone knew not to reveal themselves in front of the humans, though. If she could get the alpha to play along with that, he'd never have the opportunity to notice that Susan was much less surprised than she should have been.

"Is stunned, poor thing." The alpha leaned in so close Silver could feel his breath on her cheek, smell his satisfaction with her weakness. "Even if she could hear this far."

"Call for your lover." Silver raised her voice so Susan could hear. "Leave anyone else out of this." The last thing they needed was more humans. A beat later, the underling slammed a fist into her back. Apparently the alpha didn't approve of her order to Susan. Silver closed her eyes to weather the surge of pain.

"This party is for Dare. No need to be inviting others. Unless your mate happens to have a human piece on the side." Some anger sneaked into the alpha's tone, but he was back to mocking by the end.

The underling pulled Silver back and slammed her into the wall again. She went limp and managed to lead with her shoulder. Pain clawed at her, but only enough force reached her temple to scrape it. The smell of her own blood fogged her nose. She rolled her other shoulder, but it only pulled her bad hand free to hang dead and useless. "Dare will be coming, don't worry."

The alpha laughed. "Oh, good. I'm looking forward to talking to him." He looked pityingly at Silver. "I didn't think it would be so easy."

"If you have never learned the lesson that once in a while a cowering enemy bites all the harder when you least expect it, I think you are about to," Death said. He stood proud and tall silhouetted against the Lady's piercing light, and the underling's sandy-colored wild self showed its belly. The alpha's wild self was gray and built low to the ground, probably perfect for a lifetime of hugging the shadows before jumping out to attack. He didn't even seem to notice Death, more fool he.

Silver tested the underling's hold, and he smashed another punch into the same place on her back for her trouble. Shadows sucked in her vision for a moment. She whimpered for effect, though if she was honest, it wasn't far from the truth. The blood trail down her cheek turned from warm to chill. "Why hurt me, if it's my mate you want? Why anger Seattle with this trespass?"

"I'm doing Seattle a favor, getting the Butcher out of his territory for him. He should be grateful." The alpha touched a fingertip to her chin and then rocked back. "You're my message. Since Dare doesn't wish to listen to what I have to say."

Silver ignored the alpha for a moment to gather her thoughts, though she was careful to leave her muscles limp. She didn't want to give the underling any warning. Then she smashed her head back and heard the satisfying snap of the underling's nose. He didn't drop her, but his grip loosened enough for Silver to pull free.

The underling was back on her a moment later, but a moment was all Silver needed. She wormed her fingers into her pocket and found the comforting chill of her necklace chain. She pulled the silver metal out and the underling flinched back.

The alpha hissed in shock. "Lady, how can you *touch*—" He fell silent and stared at her fingertips, as if searching for burns that didn't exist.

Into the silence of the fragile stalemate, Susan spoke. "John. You have to get here right now." Her voice stretched high and thin until it broke. She spoke more, details of their location Silver couldn't make herself follow at the moment. It was enough to know help would arrive soon. For now, she needed information.

She planted her feet and let the chain trickle from her hand until she had only a single loop over her fingers. She waited a beat, letting them second-guess their instincts about the danger she posed, letting them relax. Then she lashed out with it. The underling, smarter, flinched faster. She caught the alpha across the cheek, smelled the sizzle-burn of his skin under the metal, and showed him her teeth.

"And you call me a drama queen," Death said, but his tone approved.

"What was your name again?" Silver dimly recalled it from Dare's discussions with her cousin, but she wanted to force the man to give it to her in his own voice. To give her some shade of Death's power over him.

"Sacramento. You crazy cat." The man put fingertips to his cheek, disbelief sharpening into rage, and hissed in surprised pain. The silver-made wound hadn't healed as a normal one would have.

"What's your plan?" Silver let the chain hang loose. Not a weapon to be overused. Just the threat of it held the underling back. "You could challenge Dare to a fight in revenge for your son's death this moment. But instead you talk, you attack me, you attack a human under Seattle's protection. Why? Are you so certain you'd lose?"

Sacramento tried to sneer but it caught at wounded muscles and he stopped with a gasp. "Death in a fight is short, pussy. The world holds far more painful and fitting punishments for what he did to my son."

"Short?" Death used the voice of the one who'd killed Silver's pack, jagged with his madness. She had to suppress a shiver. "Only if you ask me nicely."

Silver stepped back. "How very human of you. They're the ones who invented—" She hesitated, not finding the saying she wanted among the more slippery of her former memories.

"An eye for an eye," Death supplied, and Silver repeated it. With that prompting, the rest followed.

"And the whole world goes blind." Silver stepped to Susan's side.

Sacramento ignored her and gestured his underling to circle around behind Susan. The underling herded her, and by extension Silver, even farther from where other humans hurried back and forth. "Perhaps Seattle will be crashing our party this time, but I'm still staying to make sure Dare receives my message properly. Get comfortable."

7

Andrew beat everyone out of the pack's minivan. John had to slam it into park before his feet hit the asphalt a second later. The rest of his Were followed shortly. John had said Susan was garbled on the phone about their exact location, but the scents came starkly clear from the side of the store. Andrew ran. John followed, the limp he'd picked up hunting hardly slowing him down.

Silver was first in his mind, but strangely Andrew couldn't stop thinking of his wife as well. Something was wrong, and he was running to her, but would he get there soon enough this time? He had to. He refused to believe otherwise, but his heart still pounded in his ears, rabbit-fast.

"Susan? Selene?" John called as they all turned the corner. Silver stood beside Susan, confident and patient in her waiting stance, her silver chain in hand. The rush of relief was so great,

Andrew didn't bother to correct John about using the wrong name for Silver.

Sacramento had a fresh silver burn on his cheek. The bleached-blond man who had attacked Andrew at the pass blocked the women's path to the parking lot, but he skittered aside on seeing Andrew, as if the silver metal had weakened his confidence.

Under the stink of Sacramento's burn, Andrew smelled blood. When he spotted it on Silver's temple, panic changed to rage as easily as shifting in the full. Sacramento would pay for that blood. Andrew could imagine the feeling of the man's throat in his teeth even now.

John crossed immediately to his girlfriend and enfolded her in a tight embrace. He drew her away from Sacramento and toward the pack's fighters massed near the minivan, waiting for orders. Andrew would have loved to do the same to Silver, but he knew better than to imply she needed such reassurance in front of an enemy. He came to stand behind her and she backed up to create contact between their bodies without his hands touching her. She was all right, he reminded himself to try to slow his heart. Hurt, but all right.

"Hello, Nate. Long time no see."

Sacramento snorted at the borderline insult. Technically, Andrew was out of line to drop Sacramento's title when he didn't have a personal relationship with the man, or wasn't another alpha. The years since Andrew had seen him had sharpened his face, especially since he'd shaved the beard that once softened his jaw. Maybe he'd want to grow it back now, to hide the scar, Andrew reflected with satisfaction. "I hear we have a problem."

"You should discipline your mate." Sacramento mustered a sneer through the pain of the burn. Andrew rubbed at the ridges along his back through his shirt, and felt not an ounce of sympathy. "Using silver on her own kind. Is that what her leash on you is made of?" He nodded to John. "Like whatever that human has on Seattle. What is she, his fuck-toy? I had no idea he was into that kind of thing." Sacramento pointedly kept his voice below Susan's threshold of hearing at her distance.

"You're trespassing, Sacramento." John growled, full-throated and threatening. Sacramento's voice carried fine to werewolf hearing. He left Susan to join them. "And attacking those under my protection. You have an hour to make it beyond the border, or I'll throw you out myself."

Sacramento held up his hands. "I've delivered my message. I have no beef with you, Seattle. I'll be waiting on the other side of your southern border tomorrow morning. I'd suggest you send Dare to face the Lady's clear gaze." He pressed a hand to his cheek and walked with pointed insouciance toward a truck dimly visible in a parking lot adjoining the back of the store's lot. The blond hurried after. Sacramento turned over his shoulder to blow a kiss from his fingertips to Silver. "You and me, babe. I look forward to the rematch soon."

Silver lifted her chin as she watched him go. "I've found Death tends to punish those who assume he'll come at their call like some kind of domesticated pet. Watch out for him yourself." Sacramento laughed in the slightly awkward way of someone who didn't understand the joke.

John's beta, Pierce, came up behind him to bolster Seattle's appearance of strength, and all of them watched until the taillights of Sacramento's truck disappeared onto the road beyond. "No point following them on foot," John told the rest of the pack over his shoulder. "And we need the van to take Susan and Silver home. Do a quick sweep now to make sure they're really gone. Then I want you all on extra patrols near the house."

Andrew caught himself before he nodded. John didn't need Andrew to approve. But since they couldn't follow Sacramento immediately, John was right. If they wasted time casting around to find his truck to make sure he made it over the territory line, he could circle around to attack the house.

Everyone relaxed as they turned back to the van: Silver allowed Andrew to pull her against his side, Susan sniffed, and John limped over to her. To Andrew's surprise, Susan noticed the limp, even after the upset and in poor lighting for human eyes. "Were you attacked too?" Her tone wavered, but no tears materialized.

Andrew kept his mouth shut. He didn't know what story John would choose to tell her. Silver speared him with a look. Even not having been out on the hunt, she could probably guess what had happened. It was common enough.

After a tired sigh, John went with the truth. "We strayed off the land we actually own. Some codger on his back porch with a twenty-two decided to shoot at the coyote or stray dog. Or maybe even Bigfoot, Lady only knows. It's nothing, I just didn't have time to dig out the bullet before it healed in. I'll do it when I get home."

"Not silver, huh?" Susan said with a weak laugh, then looked back at Silver. "Metal, I mean."

"Yes, though it's not so simple." Silver turned her look on Andrew this time, and it took him a long moment to realize he was supposed to fill in the rest for the human. He frowned and shook his head, but Silver started to pull away, so he gave in as he opened the minivan's side door and handed her up inside.

"It doesn't have to be a silver bullet to kill a werewolf," he explained. "Head shots are generally lethal." As he knew from experience, but he wasn't going to mention that. He'd executed Sacramento's son that way. The Were stigma against guns aside, it had been the cleanest death he could offer the man. European claims about their favored beheading with a silver sword being quick and clean were so much bullshit. The guillotine had been necessary for a reason. "Or enough shots in a row can soak through our ability to heal another injury without rest and food."

Andrew scooted into the first row of seats beside Silver. The cut on her temple had stopped bleeding so he lifted her arm first to run his hand along it. She winced when he neared purpling finger marks at her wrist, but otherwise she showed no pain.

Silver made a token effort to fend him off. "I'm fine." She submitted to his touch after that, letting it calm them both down. He could feel her heartbeat pounding under her skin.

The sound of Susan talking to John carried into the minivan. "No, Silver's the one who got hurt. I was just stunned. I'll have a goose egg there later, I guess." The passenger door opened and slammed, though John stayed outside, probably to wait for the patrol. Susan knelt up on the seat to look back at them. "Is she okay?"

Andrew shook his head. "She heals like a human." Silver braced when he started to slide a hand down her back. He rolled up her top and growled at the ugly spread of the bruise he found low on her back. It was huge. Silver snapped her teeth at him when his fingers just brushed it. He took his hands away immediately and kissed the back of her neck in apology.

Silver's injuries cataloged, Andrew returned to the cut. He started by licking his thumb to clean away the blood, but that was inefficient and he switched to licking it directly. Silver's heart slowed.

Then the stupid human made some noise, maybe shock, maybe disgust, and Andrew realized that he'd let his exhaustion in the wake of fear for Silver make him slip into behavior unacceptable to humans. He raised his eyebrows at Susan, daring her to make a comment. She shrank back.

Silver hit him. "Leave her alone. She called you all here quickly, didn't she? She did well. Otherwise Sacramento might have had much more time alone with me to craft his 'message.'"

"If one of us had been with you instead, you wouldn't have been in that situation at all." Andrew smoothed Silver's hair away from the cut again, even though it hadn't fallen forward in the last few seconds. "Silver—" Words deserted him as the fear surged up again in a dozen mental pictures of what could have happened. "I'm sorry . . ."

"You bear the marks of my enemies," Silver murmured, and rested a hand on his chest for a moment. "You don't control your enemies either."

The rest of the pack returned from their sweep of the area. One peeled off to drive Susan's car home, and the rest piled into the van, except for the beta, who hesitated at the side door. Pierce cultivated a very pretty image to go with his slimness, one lock of dark, wavy hair dangling over his eyes, but his face was clouded now with annoyance. He added another couple finger marks to the crushed padding at the side of the first row of seats as he hoisted himself into the back. In the normal course of things, he should have been riding shotgun unless John specifically invited Andrew or Silver to join him. Susan had nowhere near the rank necessary for that position in the vehicle.

There must be a standing order that the pack wasn't supposed to call Susan on that kind of thing—Andrew couldn't imagine that Pierce would have swallowed it otherwise.

As John climbed in and started up the van, Susan punched the passenger light, flipped down the visor, and explored the skin along her hairline with cautious fingers. "I've decided, Silver. If I'm going to be that fucking scared anyway, I think I'd rather know why."

Silver laughed. "Good."

John swallowed a growl. "Dare? What has your mate been telling my girlfriend?"

Andrew suspected that John knew Silver well enough by now that he'd bypassed her not out of stupidity but to needle her. Silver's growl in response was instant. Andrew edged away from her and thumped the back of John's seat. "Talk to Silver. Leave me out of this."

"She's been showing me just how much ignorance you've been keeping me in." Susan rounded on John, lingering upset showing now in the shrillness of her voice. "It's bullshit, John."

If they'd been in wolf, every pair of ears in the vehicle would have locked on to the human. That was not a tone to use with any alpha without being aware of exactly what you were doing.

Silver closed her eyes for a moment as if pained, then sat forward. Reminded, Andrew buckled first her then himself in. Silver waited for him to finish, then turned to Susan. "I'm not saying you shouldn't stand up for yourself, but if you're going to question an alpha's authority like that, it's better to do it in private."

Hearing Silver say it like that snapped things into place in Andrew's mind. For good or ill, Susan was interacting with Were every day, and he didn't think any of them besides Silver had stopped to consider how little a human might know about things they took for granted. Of course she'd seem clueless or rude most of the time.

Susan angled the visor mirror to see Silver rather than craning around. "No one's ever allowed to question the alpha?" Now Andrew was looking for it, the confusion was even clearer in her voice, though stale adrenaline clouded her scent.

"It's a question of tactics," Andrew broke in when Silver hesitated. He leaned back with his arm resting along the top of the seat in an attitude of forced relaxation. John wasn't going to like this at all. Andrew still wished the timing on all of this was better, but Silver was right. The human did need help. "If you ask for something in public, getting your way will always be balanced against his need to appear strong before the pack. Ask in private, that's out of the equation." He paused, but his dominant instincts, cooped up with another alpha, wouldn't let him stop there. "Or you can say whatever you want, to be an asshole." He leaned forward to throw a flash of teeth in a smile to John.

John snorted and took a turn with more speed than necessary, jerking them all sideways. "How many of his pack do you think Sacramento brought with him? He'd have to have left some at home to guard the lower-rankers."

Andrew unclenched his fingers from the back of the seat when they pulled into the pack house driveway and he didn't have to worry about any more sharp turns. Clearly John wanted a subject change. Fair enough. Figuring out how to deal with Sacramento was important. "More than the one we saw. I doubt he could spare more than three."

Andrew climbed out of the minivan first and helped Silver with a hand down. John gave him a curt nod of agreement with his estimate and ignored Susan. He strode for the house without looking back.

"His numbers don't matter, anyway. I'll settle this with Nate directly tomorrow morning," Andrew said. It was past time he and Sacramento had a talk face-to-face. The politics of challenging for Roanoke didn't matter if Silver was going to be hurt. He needed to take care of Sacramento himself.

John paused in the front doorway. "No." Then he pushed inside.

Andrew jogged to catch up. "What in the Lady's name does that mean, 'no'? He's my problem, and I'm going to take care of him." John's back was to him as the man bent to take a beer out of the fridge, so Andrew grabbed his shoulder and spun him to face him. Maybe the dig earlier had been a bad idea, but John dodging Andrew's gaze in this argument was an uncalled-for slight.

"He hurt Susan," John growled low. Then he raised his voice. "He was in *my* territory, hurting people under *my* protection. If someone else deals with him, I look weak. If he steps back onto my territory, I'll punish him. If he doesn't, I will be the one to take the matter up at the Convocation. You'll do nothing to him until then." So that was it, Andrew realized. He didn't want his pack to know how much he was motivated by what had happened to a human.

"He hurt Silver worse. Your human was incidental." Andrew lowered his voice too.

The strength of John's reaction caught Andrew off guard. He hadn't meant to stab the man in a sore spot, just prod him. John's face twisted with rage and he shoved Andrew.

Normally, Andrew would hardly have noticed in the midst of

such a charged argument, but this time there was a counter behind him. The edge hit him square in the small of his back with
all the force of John's considerable shove. Pain exploded across
his muscles as the old injury reopened. He would have collapsed
if the counter hadn't propped him up long enough for him to get
his hands on it. His legs didn't work anymore.

"Lady!" The tears in Andrew's eyes were only from the pain,
but they still increased the burn of the humiliation. Silver
reached him a second later and helped him make it to the slightly
claw-scarred hardwood floor without falling. Even with werewolf strength, he couldn't hold himself up on something behind
him.

"Lady's light, man, I didn't mean— I thought you were
healed!" To his credit, John's shock smelled sincere.

"Not enough to withstand that, apparently. Congratulations.
I guess you get to deal with Sacramento your own way." It came
out more acid than Andrew had intended, and John's lips
thinned. Andrew tried to flex his foot and gasped at the knifing
pain. That had been much easier to bear when it had come as
small bursts of pins and needles in the original healing process.
But at least his back was healing at something like normal speed
this time.

Silver placed her good hand on her hip, radiating anger. "Are
you two *completely* prey-stupid? Stop whimpering about revenge for injuries to people who can take care of themselves,
and think for a minute. This is what Sacramento was trying to
provoke you into, Dare."

Andrew pinched the bridge of his nose and closed his eyes to
shut out the feeling of John and probably half the pack watching
him sit on the floor like a cripple. Silver was right, this was

clearly what Sacramento intended, but why? "I suppose it wouldn't look good to the other alphas if Sacramento starts spreading rumors and then I go running to pound him for it. Lends them weight." He opened his eyes and looked up at John. "You have a much stronger case for his territory trespass." He gritted his teeth. The words didn't come easy, but he got them out. "You're right. You should be the one to deal with Sacramento."

Silver knelt beside him and pressed a kiss into his hair. "Death says, 'Took him long enough,' which means he's impressed you got it right."

Andrew snorted. That was kind of Death.

If it had been him and Silver alone, Andrew would have waited on the floor a little longer, but everyone was watching. He used Silver's shoulder to lever himself upright, standing as tall as he could manage while little rivers of agony flowed down his legs. He locked his jaw so he didn't make any noise.

John faced Andrew with his expression schooled to something neutral. "It's only been a few months, Dare. It's no reflection on you if you're not healed up to full strength yet."

"Unfortunately, I don't think circumstances are going to give me any more time. The longer I wait, the more people are going to believe what Rory and Sacramento feed them. If I want Roanoke, I have to challenge soon." Hand on Silver's shoulder, Andrew limped for the basement. At least there would be a semblance of privacy down there.

Susan watched them from the foot of the stairs as they crossed out of the kitchen, hand tight around the bottom banister post. "Do I even *want* to know what all of that meant?"

Silver gave her a thin smile. "I'll get back to you on that."

8

Silver woke when Death returned the next morning. He left them most nights, whether they were doing more than sleeping or not. He had hunting to do and business of his own to be about, Silver figured.

Dare's tame self was dominant for the moment, his arm flung over her stomach. His wild self curled over their feet, keeping her toes warm with its fur.

Dare groaned and brought up his arm to shield his eyes. She sat up and smoothed the fur on the flank of his wild self. "I'm going to wash. Go back to sleep." He mumbled something else, but he was tired from rehealing his old injury. His breathing evened out again as she stood up.

Death paced to join her. "Do you think your campaign for the human has distracted him enough that he hasn't noticed your heart's not in the fight for the alphaship?" Death used her brother's voice, though the smugness was his own.

Silver snapped her head to look down at Death. He looked up in turn, ears turned tight on her, grinning at her discomfort. She should have known he'd notice.

She started to answer automatically, but pressed her lips shut on the words. Better to first find an out-of-the-way corner of the den where people couldn't hear her. It made Dare uncomfortable when he noticed her speaking to Death, and it probably made the others think her even more insane.

Once there, she glared at Death. "I'm helping Dare!"

"Of course you're helping. And he needs it. But are you really doing all you could, if you threw yourself into it?"

Silver swallowed. She didn't have much hope she'd convince Death, but maybe laying out her reasoning would help her be a bit more easy. "Dare needs this. He needs a purpose, needs to lead and protect. I don't feel strongly enough to deny him what he so clearly needs." The scorn in Death's snort was so withering, she had to continue. "All right. No, I don't want to lead a pack, with everyone watching, everyone judging. With the painful silences when Dare invites me on a hunt. Can you imagine how much worse that would be, if we were alphas, and no one wanted to speak up to gainsay us because of our positions? I'd be an embarrassment to him, unable to shift, seeing things that aren't there."

Silver dropped her hand to Death's fur. One of her own hairs, shimmery white as the Lady's face, had tangled in her fingers, and it glinted against the rich blackness of Death's fur. He felt real enough. Better to say she saw things that existed, but usually invisibly, intangibly.

"Humans have carved this world into their image without ever shifting. Perhaps you can learn from that woman as she learns from you." Death used what Silver thought of as his own voice, some ephemeral weight to the words that she couldn't quite place. But Susan was so confused and useless. What kind of model would she ever be?

She started to answer, but—

Silver wants Death to find just as she tries to get clearer on these points. Couldn't hang like it needs. Can't think fully while watching the speaker . . . to Death, and a revelation.

Andrew reawakened from his doze to the sound of Silver showering in the basement's bathroom. There was a guest bedroom upstairs they could have used, but he preferred the privacy down here, without ears in the rooms to either side. Even though that privacy meant sleeping on an air mattress in the middle of the floor with the couch pulled aside, it was worth it. He considered getting up to join her in the water, but his back ached with a dull throb, so he put off moving for a while longer. Really, he should be considering his pitch, who he should talk to next. One of the other Western alphas? Should he start calling people in Roanoke?

Silver returned wrapped in a towel. She flopped down on the edge of the bed, making the mattress buck from the displaced air. She handed him her brush and he started brushing out her hair as he usually did. The borrowed bathroom's shampoo must have included conditioner, as the knots gave up without a struggle. But that wasn't the point of the process anyway. Being brushed felt even better in wolf, but was still enjoyable in human.

He settled himself so he sat with the length of one shin tucked against her ass. While he worked, she cradled her bad hand in her lap and did her usual exercises, twitching the fingers as much as she could. She'd worked up to perhaps half an inch of movement since she'd started, but had plateaued there.

He kept working in silence until she smelled a little more relaxed. "I agree with what you're doing for Susan, but is there any way it could wait? Two weeks isn't going to change her situation substantially, but it really could for us."

Any relaxation in Silver's muscles disappeared. "So she should just suffer as an outsider until then?"

Andrew opened his mouth to reply, but there was more to Silver's tone than anger on the woman's behalf. He moved his legs to either side of her so he could pull her back against his chest. He rested his cheek against her hair. "Who are we talking about, you or her?"

Rather than answer, Silver grumbled something about prickles and pushed his chin away. Andrew rubbed a hand against his jaw. He supposed he did need a shave. "I know it sucks, being around this pack without real status, but if we win Roanoke, that will change. We'll belong." Andrew drew in a slow breath. It had been a long time since he'd belonged anywhere.

"It's not just that," Silver snapped. "I don't want to live down to what they're expecting of me, crazy and crippled. But the more they sit there being so pitying, the harder it is not to."

"You can't expect them to take you on your own terms just like that, though. It's not fair to you, but couldn't you give them at least a little time to change their assumptions? Besides, Seattle and several of the pack members knew you before— Before. There's that change for them to struggle with too." Andrew trailed off to a sense of impending doom. That had been the wrong thing to say, he'd known it even as his lips finished moving, but there was no way to call it back now.

Silver jerked away from him. "I'd thank you not to remind them of who I was before. I don't need them trying to draw her out of me." She used her good hand to hold up her towel as she pushed to her feet and rounded on him. "Maybe I'm helping Susan because I recognize what they're doing to her. No one *sees* her. Not really. She's there, she has to be soothed or nudged out of the way, but she's not a person. Like they think I'm not. I need to be managed, kept happy, but it's not like I have a mind of my own."

It took Andrew a moment to get to the edge of the stupid mattress so he could stand too. "Silver, no . . ." He tried to think of what to say, but the problem was that she was right about many of the pack members' attitudes right now. She needed to give them time to change, but he was certain she didn't want to hear that at the moment.

Silver took several steps back and lifted her bad arm across her chest with her good, her version of crossing her arms. "I don't care if you help with Susan or not, but that's what I'm going to do. Don't get in my way."

She rummaged in the suitcase and Andrew left her to it. He'd learned early that you could push Silver all you wanted, and she might even verbally agree with you, but once your back was turned she'd do what she felt was important anyway. Better to win her over slowly once she'd cooled down.

When he came out of the bathroom, showered and shaved, she was gone. Andrew stopped on the foot of the stairs out of the basement as his back flared with a stabbing pain. Dammit, the last thing he wanted to do was use his cane in front of John. But he knew what agony he'd be in by the end of the day if he didn't, so he retrieved it from the pile of stuff they'd brought in from the car. He thumped up the stairs. He needed coffee before he dealt with anything else this morning.

Pierce was cooking eggs at the stove while John read the paper, coffee mug already almost empty. John leaned against the counter with his weight distributed evenly, any trace of the bullet or the wound from digging it out last night long gone.

Andrew eyed the coffeepot, but lingered in the entrance to the kitchen, waiting for an invitation. Pierce must have caught some signal from his alpha or read the atmosphere, because he loaded up a platter with the eggs to serve in the dining room and left.

"I know you can't stop her—or at least you won't try—but I assume you at least know what in the Lady's name Silver thinks she's doing with Susan?" John didn't look up from his paper.

Andrew growled. He wanted coffee before this conversation. John had reopened his back injury, and now he expected Andrew to put up with his whining about the situation he'd gotten himself into with the human? "I gather she sees parallels between her own situation and that of your mate." He chose the word to see how John would react. It didn't really sound right when applied to a human.

John didn't disappoint. He closed his newspaper and crossed to slam his mug with the coffee dregs into the sink. "I wouldn't call her my mate."

"Oh, so the kid's not yours?" Andrew took another step back, pairing the challenging words with the nonthreatening movement. Now was not the time for a shoving rematch. "You're right, though. Silver's not going to leave this alone until she's satisfied."

"What would you have me do?" John turned to face Andrew.

For all that his words were angry, there seemed to be a real question hidden in there. Andrew was struck by how solid the other alpha looked. Plain, straightforward, and . . . solid. Not twisty, to be able to deal with all the moral gray areas and complexities of emotion. In most situations, being so solid would be a good thing in an alpha.

"Honestly? Pick one or the other." Andrew grabbed one of the mugs from the drainboard and helped himself to the coffee. He'd earned it with this conversation, invitation or no. "Either cut her off, or make up your mind and *sell* your pack on her." He gave John a steady glance, centered to the side to avoid direct eye contact. "Sometimes people give up questioning your choices if you lock your teeth and wait long enough. As I have cause to know." He didn't plan to let John forget the grief he'd given him when he and Silver first got together, claiming Silver couldn't give consent.

"That's different and you know it," John snapped, scowling at the floor. Silence fell and stretched. John sounded to Andrew like he wasn't sure about it.

Andrew grimaced over his first sip of coffee and rummaged in the fridge until he found some creamer.

"Pierce likes to make it strong," John said, and started putting away clean dishes from the other side of the sink, maybe just to have something to do with his hands. "Getting rid of her isn't an option at this point. She'd never leave Edmond, and if we make it into a custody battle, she has a lot to hurt us with."

"Whose fault is that?" Andrew let a snap into his tone. Enough. No one ever tripped and fell into someone's bed, and no Were accidentally shifted—oops, sorry—in front of a human.

Somewhere, buried however deep, they had to want to make a mistake like that.

"All I could think was—" John's shoulders drew in, and even his solidity seemed to collapse. "She needed to know what her own son was going to be."

Andrew growled. He couldn't think of anything more stupid, but at the same time he understood the man's motives. Almost. "Do you love her?"

"Does it matter?" John shoved a stack of plates into the cupboard with an emphatic crash.

"Yes." Andrew gulped his coffee. Better at this point to toss it past the taste buds. "If you don't, you're the dumbest fucking Were I've had the misfortune to meet in a long time. If you do . . ." What could he say? Still stupid, but at least comprehensible? Andrew had a sudden memory of Silver's laughing voice, soon after they'd first met. *Dirty hypocrite,* she'd said. He'd fought against a lot of resistance, for love of Silver. "Make it worth it," he finished instead.

"Ah, he learns. Slowly," Death said.

Andrew choked as some coffee went down the wrong way in his surprise. Death was using his dead wife's voice this morning, Spanish accent smoky around the vowels. Andrew knew if he ignored the figment of his imagination, the feeling of being watched would get worse as Death hulked big and black at the edge of his vision. If he looked straight at Death, he'd disappear, but Andrew would look as crazy as Silver for glaring at nothing.

Today, Andrew kept his eyes on John, and Death prowled around to stand behind John's legs. The dark wolf flicked his tail once. "He can't tell you if he's in love, of course. He doesn't know himself. But I'd keep asking the question until he decides."

Andrew continued to ignore Death. If you didn't react to whatever he was saying long enough, Death wandered off to more interesting pastimes. Usually.

John cast a look around the kitchen, then picked up his newspaper in a last tidying motion. "I can't get out of going in to work today, at least for a few hours. Would you keep an eye on Susan? She called in sick and I suspect she's still going to hang around Silver as much as possible."

Andrew wrestled down a growl. Who did John think he was, a member of his pack to be ordered around? It had been phrased as a request, but that didn't matter. Andrew could hear John's unthinking assumption that Andrew would agree. He clenched his hands around the head of his cane. "No, I think I'll just protect Silver and ignore her." He wrestled his sarcasm down. "Don't be a purse dog. Of course I'll watch out for her."

John dipped his head, grudgingly apologetic. "Even with . . ." He made a minimal gesture to the cane. "You're the one I trust the most to keep her safe."

Andrew didn't believe that for a minute—he was the most handy, and probably the one Susan would accept most easily—but he decided to accept the fact that John had bothered with the lie. John smelled sincere about something, anyway.

9

It had seemed like a good idea at the time for Susan to call in sick to give herself time to recover from the attack, but that left her hanging around the pack house. Sometimes she enjoyed the warm feeling of always having someone else around. It was easier to relax there, because the pack didn't have any of the show rooms, decorated for company and not to be disturbed, that she had grown up with. It would be hard to have any when every hardwood floor had claw scratches and every fabric surface a film of hair. But now every werewolf reminded her of danger and things she was trying not to think about, like getting attacked by enemies, or killed by friends for what she knew.

By midmorning, she gave up and suited Edmond up in his jacket and collected his diaper bag. She searched out Silver where she was dozing on the couch in the basement. Someone had folded the guest air mattress and bedding neatly at the side for the day. "Do you want to come over to my place? I have to go back there anyway to get my work laptop, and I figured we'd have privacy to talk again . . . ?"

Silver stretched and smoothed her hair back into order. "I'd be happy to." She smiled, knowing but sympathetic. "A lot of ears swivel to follow one around here." She came to pet Edmond's hair and then led the way upstairs.

Dare met them at the front door, hands light on his cane. Combined with the white streaks at his temples, it made him look even more distinguished, like some of the higher-ups at the bank Susan had met at receptions. He conveyed the same sense of distracted kindness, like he was willing to help, but he balanced always on the edge of anger about much weightier matters.

"Mind if I join you both?" he said with a tight smile and a gesture toward the door. His voice lifted, but it was clearly not actually a question.

Susan stopped, set the diaper bag down for the moment, and adjusted Edmond to a more stable position on her hip. "Why?" She was going to her place to get away from werewolves, not drag a bunch of them with her. Dare was intimidating enough that she didn't want him around while she asked Silver questions, either.

Edmond squirmed. "Woof," he commented, eyes bright with interest at getting to go out.

The baby seemed to short-circuit some annoyance in Dare's expression. He stumped forward a step to touch Edmond's cheek. "I'm protecting Silver. And John was worried about you."

Susan snorted and slipped on her shoes, juggling Edmond. "Won't I be in more danger with you around? You're the one he's after, aren't you?" The trouble was, the easiest solution would be to leave Silver here and go to her house alone. Susan didn't really like the idea of being alone, either.

"I am." Dare sighed. "But I sincerely doubt either of you are in danger now. He's made his point, and he'll wait for me to come to him."

"And he won't catch either of us off guard." Silver patted the pocket that held her chain.

Susan hesitated until Edmond, almost lunging out of her arms in impatience, decided her. Better Silver and Dare than staying here at the moment. "Fair enough."

Susan led the way outside to the car and buckled Edmond into his car seat. She dumped off the diaper bag next and left the door open for Silver. She moved up and opened the passenger door for Dare. He was the one with the cane, after all. "Do you all think I'm weak enough to need special protection even though I'm not the target of all of this?"

Dare ignored the car door Susan had opened until he put his hand on it, as if pretending he'd opened it himself. Silver slid into the car without the pretense. "I don't think you are. And John's treating you like you're one of the pack," Dare said as he buckled up.

Susan chewed over his phrasing as she started the engine. "Treating me *like*. Is there any way for me to *be* part of the pack?" Part of her shouted she was suicidal for even considering wanting to be part of something so dangerous. But something else in her ached to belong, to be part of that large, close-knit family, and not have her son's and John's life fenced off from her.

Dare looked over at her, and then past her out the window. "I honestly don't know. You have my sympathy, of course. Silver and I are in the same situation at the moment, forced into close proximity with a pack but not part of it. At least you don't have the genetic imperative to deal with."

Susan was grateful for the city traffic that forced her to keep her eyes on the road. She knew enough at least to suspect there would be pitfalls with eye contact, and this way she had an excuse to avoid it altogether. "Is it? Genetic, I mean? I can never tell what is and isn't with you guys. For all I can tell, when you're not—changed? Shifted . . . ?"

"In wolf form," Dare supplied. " 'In wolf.' "

Susan nodded. "In wolf—" She stumbled over the slang. Maybe she'd be better off thinking of it as a whole new language. "When you're not in wolf, it could all be cultural, from what I've seen. Certainly not outside of human norms, except for the physical stuff."

Dare shook his head. "You can't see the emotional underpinnings. You think we're doing it for the same reasons humans do, but it's stronger and deeper than that. Impossible to ignore."

He watched the road with focused attention the way her mother always did, like he had to be as aware of every hazard as the driver. It always annoyed Susan, like a vote of no confidence in her own observational skills.

"Is it really like you have a wolf inside you? That, you know, wants things your human self wouldn't?" Susan winced. She hadn't meant to ask that. But that's what it was like in a good portion of the books and movies she'd found. She imagined that side of Edmond, lurking in him even when he was a baby.

Dare snorted. "You've been reading human fiction, haven't you? Don't. We don't have some separate wolf mind any more than you have some autonomous self that's the mother, and the rest of you isn't. You *are* a mother. It shapes your whole self, even if it's not everything you are."

Muscles relaxed in Susan's shoulders. She hadn't even realized they were tense. That seemed much more comprehensible. Just people, even if they were people with strange instincts and customs. "I asked John what it felt like a couple times, but he said it wasn't something he could put into words."

Edmond started to fuss and Susan flipped the rearview mirror down to see his little face screwed up with frustration. "His toy's in the bag," she directed Silver, and then had to look away again, though she heard rummaging sounds. When she next stopped at a red light, Silver had the yellow plush rabbit, but she was holding it between two fingers like it stank. Edmond grunted in frustration as he grabbed impotently for it.

"What? What's wrong with it?" Susan twisted a hand back and Silver dropped it in. She sniffed the toy, but it just smelled like clean plush.

"It's food," Silver said. "Didn't Seattle get him a proper puppy?"

"At least a bear would be better. Isn't that what humans usually give their children?" Dare's voice held a rumble of amusement at Silver's phrasing, but he seemed relatively serious about the subject.

Susan dropped the rabbit into her lap. "You guys are freaking kidding me. You mean there was a reason they kept giving me stuffed dogs all the time? I thought they were like baby shower gifts."

"Not dogs." Dare snorted. "Human children have bears and blankets. We have wolf pups. Puppies."

"Well, I have half a dozen. There should be one all the way at the bottom of the bag."

Silver rummaged deeper and pulled one out, a dark, steely gray. She wiggled it in front of Edmond, and he grabbed hold. Susan flicked a glance at Dare. "They didn't say anything, they just kept pushing them on me. I didn't know what they wanted."

"That one I don't think they were keeping from you on purpose. They probably didn't realize there was anything to explain." Dare gave a short laugh, ironic for no reason Susan could figure out. "Not spending much time with a pack over the past few years threw me in more with humans. I think I probably know more about them than many Were."

Susan wasn't quite sure what to say to that. Was knowing about humans a good thing or a bad thing? Silence settled over them as she turned into her neighborhood.

"There," Dare said as they pulled away from a light. He pointed. The park she and John liked to take Edmond to showed as flashes of primary-colored metal among mature evergreens. "The seesaws. If you want to understand shifting for a Were, imagine one of those."

Susan glanced over before returning her attention to the road. She'd seen the seesaws at that park plenty of other times anyway. She murmured a noise prompting Dare to continue.

"In the new—the new moon—it's like all the weight's on your side. You have to really push to get anywhere, and then the weight switches and it's *still* all on the wrong side when you try to get back. In the full, it's like you're evenly balanced. You can swing back and forth with hardly any effort." He exhaled with a note of dry humor. "And it's especially easy for your temper to knock you one way or the other."

Susan snorted as she pulled into her driveway. Her two-bedroom unit was one of a new townhouse row with the garage hidden at the back, so she had to drive around to pull in. No wonder the pack seemed more emotional around the full moon. Dare's metaphor did make a certain visceral sort of sense.

"Have you seen Seattle shift?" Silver asked.

Susan laughed raggedly and shut off the car. "It sounds sort of dirty when you say it like that."

"Not particularly." Dare opened his door and wrangled his cane out first to take the weight as he pushed himself up. "Seeing the exact moment of shifting is somewhat intimate, but no worse than being nude is for humans."

"I've only seen him shift once." Susan hardly remembered what it looked like, either. She'd been too shocked to process any of it at the time. He'd hidden it from her since then.

Susan started extracting Edmond from his car seat before she remembered she should have unlocked the house door for her guests first. She threw them an apologetic glance. They seemed unbothered, waiting on the step. Silver had her hand tucked into the crook of Dare's elbow. They looked fantastical with their touches of white, an ice princess and a mortal king. "You should show her a shift." Silver smiled when Dare started.

"No." Dare caught Silver's eyes in some sort of staring contest. The denial in his expression softened a second later. "What good would that do?"

"You don't need to—" Susan started, but Silver forestalled her without breaking her stare, lifting a finger from Dare's arm to point at her.

"Don't be so low-ranked, Susan. We're just off the full, it won't be much work. Shifting will be good for his back. It helps healing. And I don't mind if he shows you."

Susan sensed more communication between them in the

shorthand that long-term couples developed. Dare snorted finally and Silver looked triumphant, though nothing more had been said. They stepped out of the way to allow Susan and Edmond up to unlock the door.

Not really living there anymore was a two-edged sword, Susan decided as she surveyed the house with eyes critical in the face of company she wanted to impress. Not much time to accumulate clutter, but since it was out of sight and out of mind, not much motivation to pick up what there was, either. Her mother would have gone into silent disapproval mode immediately, seeing the mountain of opened but not recycled mail on the kitchen table and the clean glasses still in the dishrack.

Susan pulled off Edmond's coat, set him in front of his toys in the living room, and started a quick clutter triage. She swept the mail into stacks and gathered jackets from the furniture to hang up. The sound of happy button smashing came from Edmond's direction. No matter how many expensive, impeccably-researched electronic development toys her parents tried to press on her, Edmond always ended up back at the board of bright plastic buttons and pictures Tracy had given him as a present to take home. It was clearly a werewolf hand-me-down, as it had teeth marks on several edges.

Dare adjusted the blinds even more tightly shut, then gave Silver a look. Susan had dated enough guys to interpret it as "Do I have to?" Silver laughed and took his cane. Susan looked away quickly as he shrugged off his shirt. He was definitely eye candy. Time in John's house had taught her Were walked around in the nude all the time, but it felt wrong to appreciate another woman's man too obviously. Were all Were men this hot? Susan peeked again, catching sight of a line of hipbone as Dare pulled down his jeans. He was a lot leaner than John, muscles not so defined, but there still didn't seem to be an ounce of fat on him.

Dare folded his clothes and turned to set them on the nearest chair. Susan caught a quick glimpse of his back that made her forget about the ogling. The skin was ridged and rutted with ugly scar tissue nodules, too shiny where they weren't white. He turned back quickly.

Then he shifted.

It wasn't anything like the movies, and yet it was. The idea of pulling, stretching, that was the same, but Susan had always thought in the movies it looked jerky and painful: clay squeezed and pummeled by an inexpert sculptor. This was like watching someone very skilled at yoga stretching, stretching, until his body gracefully achieved a position you would have sworn was impossible. That was the difference, Susan realized. This didn't look unnatural. It looked right. Impressive, and clearly an effort, but still right. She didn't even notice bare skin turn to fur until it was already over, and she wondered how she could have missed something so obvious.

Dare gave a canine snort when he was done and shook himself all over. He looked like a typical gray wolf on a *National Geographic* special, only larger. His scars showed as a white band across his back, the fur coarser than that surrounding it.

Susan let out the breath she'd been holding. That had been amazing. Magical, in a way. Though they were some kind of supernatural creature, so that did make sense. She'd have to ask John to do it for her so she could watch again.

She held out a hand. "Can I pet—is that rude?"

"If you'd hug someone in human, petting's fine in wolf." Silver knelt in front of Dare and scratched behind his ears and into his ruff. He stayed aloof for a moment, but then he got into it, shaking his head back and forth like Silver was roughhousing with a regular dog. Susan let her hand drop. She certainly wouldn't hug Dare as a human.

Dare licked Silver's face. She sputtered and covered it with her arm, freeing him. He came to stand more solemnly before Susan. He turned in a wide circle, showing her all angles. He ended with his head by her hand, and bumped it up so her hand was on his ears. He looked resigned, if a canine could look resigned, so Susan didn't so much pet as assure herself he was real. The guard hairs were coarser than those of some dog breeds, but his ears were warm and soft. Silver made a grumbling noise under her breath, and Susan removed her hand again. Fair enough.

"Woof!" Edmond fell onto his hands and crawled for Dare. When he reached the Were, he used Dare's flank as he would a piece of furniture and pulled himself up, tiny fingers clenched around handfuls of fur. Dare yipped. Susan stepped around to pull Edmond away, but he had such a tight grip, picking him up seemed likely to end with Dare missing two patches of fur.

Dare woofed at Susan and she let go of Edmond. The boy burbled with satisfaction at the game. When she reached again, Dare shook his head, a motion that looked strange performed by a canine, but unmistakable nonetheless. Dare let Edmond cruise along his side until he got within range of Dare's muzzle, which Dare used to gently knock the boy over. Edmond shrieked with delight and Dare nosed him, rolling him around.

Susan twisted her fingers together. Intellectually, she knew that since this wolf was a thinking person, there was even less chance he would hurt Edmond than a friendly, socialized dog would, but it was still hard to watch her son with a predator.

Silver placed her hand on Susan's arm and Susan jumped. She'd forgotten about the other woman. "Please, let him," Silver said in a low voice.

Susan gave Silver an incredulous look. Would Dare's self-esteem be hurt if Susan thought him too scary to play with her child? He seemed like a big boy. Susan figured Dare could deal with it, but she did follow Silver when she tilted her head away.

Silver pulled Susan into the kitchen and out the side door into her fenced patch of yard. The careful landscaping that had come with the house was in the same state as indoors, the shapes and colors of the bushes disguised by the green legginess of the weeds springing up between. She never seemed to find time to garden, but she didn't make enough to hire a service as her parents did for their impeccable yard.

Susan left the door open to make sure she still had a view of her son and Dare, then crossed her arms, partially for warmth. The temperature hovered on the edge of too cold to be out without a coat, but she didn't want to bother going back in. "What was that about?" she asked with a bit of a snap. "I know Dare's not going to hurt him, but you have to admit I don't actually know you two that well, less than I do the rest of the pack."

Silver ducked her head in apology, escaping white hairs puffing over her face and catching light in the cloudy brightness. "I know. It's just— I've been trying to help Dare heal that too, but I haven't been making much progress. He needs to be able to see a cub without flinching from him or her."

"Heal what?" Susan checked through the door again. Dare

had collapsed, and was letting Edmond ruffle his fur every which way. "He has a problem with kids?" He didn't seem to at the moment. His behavior was practically paternal, if one could say that about a canine.

Silver followed Susan's gaze for a moment and then looked away. "He misses his daughter so much sometimes, it makes me bleed inside to watch him."

Susan froze, not quite sure what to say. Dare had a daughter? Had she died? What did you say to that? I'm sorry?

Silver saved her by continuing a second later. "I'm telling you this because I think you're more likely to hurt him by accident, not knowing it's there, than to use it against him. But if you do, you'll answer to me."

The savage way Silver said it reminded Susan all over again that these people weren't as human as they usually looked. And Silver was one of the nice ones. Susan held up her hands. She had no wish to hurt Dare or piss off Silver.

"His wife was accidentally killed in a territorial dispute. His wife's pack disagreed with how he chose to deal with the situation, and so they forced him out, and barred him from his daughter. He hasn't seen her in over a decade."

"How he chose to deal with the situation?" Susan winced. That sounded like code for something that was much more what she would have expected for a werewolf, rather than this romping with children stuff.

"We all make mistakes." Anger grew in Silver's expression, and Susan took a step back. "How would you like it? Knowing your son was alive and whole but you could never see him again? Ever?"

Susan threw a guilty look back to the house. She honestly

didn't know. Go mad, maybe. Even thinking about the hypothetical made her whole body tighten with fierce rage.

Silver took a deep breath and rubbed her palm down her thigh, calming herself. "But there's nothing to be done about it. Lady knows we all wish it was different. He needs to learn to deal with cubs and heal that catch in his voice."

Susan stuffed her hands into her pockets. Now she especially didn't know what to say. Everyone's voice broke from emotion sometimes. She didn't understand the significance Silver's tone had given the phrase. "He sounded okay to me," she said tentatively. It was probably a Were thing. She had caught hints that their senses were better, so maybe a subtle break in his voice was clear as day to them.

"Not literally." Silver crouched, hand out like it was resting on something. It seemed strange, but Susan found that if she turned so she could see no farther than Silver in her peripheral vision, it looked natural enough. "Humans might call it a soul. When we die, Death takes our voices back to the Lady. That was his punishment: he has no voice of his own, so he must collect them for the Lady, and borrow them for a while. Our voice, it's . . . us." She made a fist and held it against her core.

Something about Silver's words in that moment, air chill and clear, clouds blanketing the sky, and background shush of traffic surrounding them, resounded with a simple spirituality equal to any she'd ever heard in a church. Susan shivered. She didn't think much about the God of her childhood, but she knew she didn't believe in any other. But something deep in her believed in Silver's belief. She felt slightly shaken. She'd seen the edges of how different the Were really were, but some part of her must not have quite understood it until now.

Susan wanted to stretch the moment—there was so much still to understand—but it was almost like recognizing it started its death. The insistent sound of Dare's ringtone from inside finished it off.

10

Andrew moved out of sight of the doorway to shift back before the call went to voice mail. When he saw JOHN on the screen, he had a momentary impulse to let it anyway. Was he checking on his girlfriend already? But it could as easily be something important about Sacramento. Andrew clamped the phone against his shoulder as he pulled on his underwear. He could hear Susan returning and he knew humans and their nudity taboos. "Hello?"

"Dare." John's tone was curt. "I found Sacramento's trail down in Fife."

"What—"

"That's south of Seattle, just before you hit Tacoma."

Andrew tried unsuccessfully to break in to explain that he was trying to ask why John was telling him this, not where Fife was. Though he didn't know that either. Seattle had far too many associated cities he'd never heard of when he lived back East.

"It should take you about an hour to get down here, then you can help me track him." John finally paused, but Andrew was too taken aback to jump in immediately.

"Help you? What changed your mind?"

John made a frustrated noise. "You were desperate for a shot at him, weren't you? You're right, this is your trouble, so you might as well be here to help deal with it."

Andrew looked over at Silver, who raised her eyebrows and looked as confused by the reversal as he felt. Susan sat her son in front of his toys and knelt with him. She frowned at the phone, probably frustrated by hearing only half the conversation.

Andrew scrubbed at his face. "I'm sorry to have brought the trouble on you, Seattle, it wasn't what I intended."

"Just leave me *out* of it in the future," John snapped, and ended the call.

His back was starting to protest, so Andrew stepped over to Susan's couch to brace himself while pulling on his jeans. John must have reconsidered once his initial protectiveness of Susan had worn off. It really was the best thing for his pack to keep the trouble localized to Andrew. Understandable, but a lot to mentally adjust to so suddenly.

Silver set a palm against his back. "You're not healed."

"I'm tracking him, not fighting. Besides, John is helping." Andrew stepped away from Silver's touch and unclenched his fingers from the couch. It had a slipcover to protect against baby messes, but that wouldn't prevent a Were from gouging finger marks in the foam. They both knew the fighting would come when he caught up to Sacramento. The political fallout wouldn't be good, but now John was stepping back, it would be worse to run like a coward from the fight Sacramento was picking.

"So John suddenly asked you to take care of Sacramento instead of him?" Susan pushed to her feet, careful to avoid tripping over Edmond's scattered toys, plush and plastic alike. "Why?"

"With him. Because it's my responsibility." Andrew lifted his shirt and held it for a while. "He sees that now he's thinking clearly." John's last comment kept intruding on his thoughts. Leave him out of it in the future. Was that a withdrawal of his support in Andrew's bid to challenge for Roanoke? Worse, a withdrawal of his invitation to stay on Seattle territory until then?

He looked over at Silver. Maybe he'd interpreted John's last comment wrong. But he saw the same sinking feeling in her face that lurked in his stomach. Leaving him out of it was a clear enough request.

If John wanted to disinvite them and the trouble they attracted from his territory, they had nowhere to go. They'd have to stay on the move, maybe go out to Arizona ahead of the Convocation and find a hotel in the somewhat neutral territory. But even that would be politically difficult, because it would smack of trying to mark the territory as theirs before anyone else arrived.

But at the end of the hunt, John didn't owe him anything. Anything he'd done had been out of kindness and deference to Silver's former place in his pack. That didn't make the possibility of being forced to leave any easier, though. Dammit.

One problem at a time, he reminded himself. First, tracking Sacramento. "I'll most likely have to track in wolf," he told

Silver. Her expression tightened with frustration, but she didn't disagree. "My car's back at the pack house, so if Susan would drop us off, you can stay with them."

"Of course," Susan said. "I'll stay at the house too." She picked up her son's coat and hesitated with a quick glance at Andrew's back. "Good luck."

11

Silver held off her own reaction to her cousin's change of voice until they were traveling again. Back to Seattle's home so Dare could track and deal with his enemy, and then Seattle might ask them to leave his territory. Had Silver given Susan enough knowledge to work with once they were gone?

Death stretched himself deliciously, black fur ruffling up and falling flat again. "Forget her, what about you? Where will you go?" He used the voice of the monster that had chased Silver for so long, the monster she and Dare had finally killed together. She heard herself make a small hurt noise, the fear rising easily to the surface, even now. Dare squeezed her knee and she summoned a smile to reassure him. They wouldn't run forever. Soon, things would be resolved, one way or the other.

"And yet both of you give up so easily in this battle." Death snapped his teeth at a fly, returning to his more habitual voice. "You have another option, one you've already thought of."

"If it comes to it, why not hold Susan with us?" Silver asked out loud. She had thought of it almost immediately. She didn't like it—Susan was a friend, and that kind of thing worked only if you didn't consider the feelings of the person being used for leverage. But better she voice it than leave it hanging over them both.

Dare growled. "No." His wild self bristled.

Susan looked away from her concentration on their path ahead. "What?" Clearly she couldn't guess, as Dare had, the next step Silver had left unspoken.

"I spent so long on the move before, and now we'll have no-where to stay if Seattle asks us to leave." Silver frowned at her knees, smoothing her palms over them. "Why not stand and fight this time?" Yes, she'd wanted to leave the pack's pity behind. But remembering her time spent always on the run after the monster took her pack, the choice seemed less clear.

The fur on Dare's wild self's ruff smoothed out, and his expression tightened with concern. "Ah, love. I'm sorry. But we were lucky Seattle helped us as much as he did."

"Where do I come into this?" Susan glanced back for a longer moment this time, scent gaining a layer of frustration.

"Silver was pointing out that we could force John's hand if we kept you with us. But forced support is hardly support at all. It's not worth it."

"As a hostage, you mean. Your reasons against it are so logical," Susan said, annoyance sliding into her voice, twisted around fear.

Dare smacked his palm against his thigh to emphasize his

point. "And I don't do that to a member of an ally's pack. Or another man's mate, all right?"

Silver nodded. Yes. That was the right answer, but she felt less burdened by the weight of the choice now the reasons against it had been said out loud.

"If only John felt the same way," Susan said. Dare started to speak, but Susan hurried on before he could. "No, I know. It's not the same situation. One is against your social rules, one isn't. John's supposed to put his pack first and all that, but you've been doing more than that, haven't you?"

Silver and Dare exchanged a glance. He looked surprised, but Silver smiled. It was a rare Were that truly understood you couldn't just look to your own pack. Maybe it was different for humans, with their mishmash of loyalties to many different groups. They'd have more practice stretching their minds around such complexity.

"Out of the mouths of humans . . ." Death said in an echo of her thoughts, his tongue hanging out in a pleased canine grin.

"It depends on your definition of your pack," Silver told Susan. "Some might say that the trouble you abandon your neighbor to will arrive for your pack next. Others might say you should think bigger. We're all Were. Or people, if you like."

"Idealism," Dare muttered on a note of amusement, but Silver could smell agreement buried somewhere, even if he didn't realize it himself. Susan was more doubtful, but Silver didn't blame her, given their current situation.

They didn't say much when they arrived at the den. Verbalizing her worry once more wouldn't help him with Sacramento, so Silver only embraced Dare and pressed a kiss to his forehead. "Lady's luck," she murmured, and he snorted. She knew he didn't believe, but that wouldn't bother the Lady. She watched until he had disappeared down the path.

Susan headed for the den with the baby and Silver followed. A scent made her stop. It was hard to pinpoint, but one breath held a faint taint of fear, gone again as she inhaled deeply. She glanced at Death, but he looked merely intent. That could be for many reasons, not just his love of trouble.

Silver ran to catch up to Susan. "Something's wrong. It could be nothing serious, but you should still take the cub and go back to your home." She stroked the soft hair on the sleeping cub's head, then pushed Susan's shoulder to turn her back.

"I can't just leave you alone," Susan said, sounding unsure as she cradled the child closer to her chest. She swallowed. "Not after what happened last time."

The wind shifted. "Lady!" Silver spat, and caught Susan's arm again. The underling that had herded them into Sacramento's arms before was herding them now, circling around from their back trail. He'd clearly waited to reveal himself until Dare was too far gone to be called back. How was he here, when Seattle had said Sacramento's trail was far off? Had her cousin lied?

Susan resisted Silver's pull, trying to find the threat for herself. Silver felt the moment when her human eyes caught up with Silver's nose in the tightening of her muscles. She clutched the baby against her chest. "Shit."

"Look weak with me for now," Silver said, huddling with her bad side against the woman to leave her working hand free. It frustrated her to allow herself to be herded, but she needed to know the situation inside. It was safer for Susan and the cub to be with her than it was for them to face the underling alone.

Inside, Sacramento waited with Seattle and another man.

This new underling was darker in his skin, the fur of his wild self shading from light brown to reddish on its underbelly. Sacramento patted Seattle's shoulder and smirked like someone watching a doe bound into the ambush set by his pack. The expression pulled at the angry red line of his scar, but he showed no sign of pain. "Welcome, Silver."

Seattle jerked away from Sacramento's hold, or tried to. Sacramento held something to his head, something Silver couldn't quite understand, though her heart sped and her throat closed. Something in her remembered what it was and knew to fear it.

Seattle rocked back to his heels and gritted his teeth. "I did what you asked, Sacramento. Leave."

Sacramento laughed. "Why would I leave when such lovely company just arrived? Take her silver," he directed his sandy-haired underling. The underling nodded, blocked the den's entrance with a slam, and pulled on a glove. His face showed only willingness to follow the order, but his scent soured with an undercurrent of fear.

He held out his hand nonetheless and Silver hesitated. She wished she remembered more about the weapon that kept Seattle still. Without him, she and Susan had little chance of taking on the underlings with their physical strength. She had only one working arm and Susan was burdened by the baby. That was also the way of fools, to rush forward into danger when the way out lay in sneaking around.

The underling made her decision for her by catching her good wrist and squeezing until the pain was so great she had to whimper. He pulled the chain from her pocket with his gloved hand and held it at the length of his arm, fear smell fading when it didn't burn him.

The fair underling turned to Susan next. "And your—" The word twisted away from Silver, but Susan clearly understood it. She reached around the baby to hand something over. He strode away to dispose of that and the chain.

"Now." Sacramento relaxed fractionally. "Let's go join the others, hm?" He prodded Seattle forward. The darker underling gripped Silver's bad arm and jerked her along. Susan followed without having to be touched, her whole body hunched protectively around the child.

"At what point do you stop pretending to be weak and actually do something?" Death asked, waiting for them at the bottom.

Silver couldn't answer him out loud, so she tried to frown him into silence. Not yet. Soon. She'd know when. She hoped.

Susan couldn't take her eyes away from the silenced gun in Sacramento's hands. She'd thought the couple of sessions she'd had with her brother at the range had made guns more familiar, but she found now that they'd just made the fear that much more visceral. She'd seen what a gun could do. Maybe all these werewolves could absorb bullets without a second thought, but she couldn't, and what about Edmond? What could he heal?

John looked as scared as her, though. What had Dare said about head shots? Susan tried to swallow, though her throat was almost too constricted to allow it. Silver had used her chain to hold them back last time, but judging from the grinding racket that had come from the kitchen, the blond thug had fed that down the garbage disposal. Edmond whined and tried to twist around in his sling. She readjusted him on autopilot.

They filed into the basement while Sacramento kept the gun trained on John's head. The new Hispanic man shut the door with a firm click. The battered couch and floor pillows usually kept down here in a pile had joined the folded air mattress against the wall. The pack huddled in the clear space.

A muscle jumped in John's jaw as he came to a stop beside the couch. "So now what? I got Dare to go where you said, aren't you going after him?"

"I told you, I have what I want right here." Sacramento gestured Silver forward with his free hand. Silver planted her feet and didn't move.

"Dare only needed to be sent far enough away to give me some quality time with his mate before he comes running back." Sacramento smirked. "It's important he see the end of it, of course, but things end too soon if he gets to try to foolishly rush me from the start."

"You cat's bastard." John's face twisted, rage trumping the earlier fear. Susan didn't understand werewolf rules about fights, but even she could tell John had just realized how far Sacramento planned to step over the line, even if he hadn't used the word "torture." "*Dishonorable—*"

John went for the gun, faster than Susan could quite process. One minute he was standing one place, the next he was in another, wrestling for the gun.

Susan dropped to her knees instantly, concrete beneath the carpet jarring them painfully. She leaned down, keeping Edmond shielded under her body, so she didn't see what happened.

But she heard the shot just fine.

Every muscle in her body clenched at once, keeping air from her lungs. John! She looked up, even as part of her screamed that she shouldn't, that it might be bad. She had to know. Either way.

John fell to his knees, bringing the hole in his chest to her eye level. It seemed so small and neat, even as the blood spread and spread. His eyes were glassy, and his chest didn't move. He toppled forward, revealing the matching hole on the other side.

Had the hole been on the left? Susan couldn't remember, couldn't figure it out from the hole in his back, seen from her angle. Her right, his—what? Did a shot through the heart kill a werewolf? Dare had only talked about head shots. Let John not be dead. Please.

Susan crawled toward him, but Sacramento reached him first and leaned down. "Lady damn it, look what you made me do." He jammed the gun into his waistband at his back, turned John over, and felt his throat for a pulse. John jerked, shuddered, and drew in a ragged breath.

Sacramento straightened with a snarl. "No more of that, right? You all follow my orders now." He crossed back to the center of the room and stared down anyone who would meet his eyes.

Susan ignored him once he got far enough from John. She crawled the rest of the way and knelt over him. He looked so pale. Did werewolves suffer from shock? Should she be putting pressure on his wound? The uncertainty and worry made her stomach clench. Edmond started crying with a long-term, grating note. She pulled up John's shirt until it bunched under his armpits and wiped away the worst of the blood with her fingertips. Already, the bullet hole looked shallow. As she watched, flesh knitted all the way to the surface, leaving clean skin under the blood smears.

Susan started as Silver knelt beside her, appearing out of nowhere as far as her pounding heart was concerned. The man with the gun was still around. She couldn't afford to be this distracted. Then John murmured her name, and Susan ignored even Silver again for a few moments. "John?"

John's eyes went to her, then flickered closed. She cupped his cheek and shook his shoulder more urgently, but he didn't open them again. "John?"

"He used all his energy in healing. He needs to sleep. And eat later, but for now, sleep." Silver tugged John's shirt down. She touched Susan's shoulder, petted Edmond's head. The baby's crying faded into sniffles.

"Silver." Sacramento's voice cut off further explanations. He set the gun on a bookshelf and rolled his shoulders. Time to get down to business, his body language and grin said.

Silver sat back on her heels and regarded him as blankly as before. She didn't go anywhere.

"If you're our alpha now, you have another challenge to answer," Pierce snarled, and started unbuttoning his shirt.

"Don't make me laugh." Sacramento didn't touch his clothes.

Susan wanted to shout at them to stop, freeze until she'd forced someone to explain what was going on. Challenge? For alpha? Which Sacramento had won by half-killing John? Did they fight as wolves or humans?

Sacramento slammed a fist into Pierce's nose while the man still had his head tilted down over his buttons. Pierce staggered back, unable to regain his balance before Sacramento rained a dozen other blows to his face, his jaw, his stomach. He got in a few blows in return, but none sounded like they carried as much force as Sacramento's. "Come back to me when you're a real alpha, little beta, and I'll give you a proper challenge."

Pierce half-collapsed and caught himself with one hand against the wall. Sacramento gave him time for a couple breaths, then grabbed a handful of fabric at his collar and dragged him farther along the wall. "Stay out of the way, hm, little beta?" A collar hung from a chain on the wall, and Sacramento picked it up and snapped it around Pierce's neck. Susan had made John explain it once, so she knew it was something to do with controlling people who acted up in wolf form, not sex, but she still hated the look of it.

The chain had enough length to allow Pierce to sink to a sitting position. He tried to let his head sag forward, jerked against the collar, and brought up his knees to hide his face instead.

Sacramento dusted his hands together melodramatically. "Anyone *else* of low rank want to pick up a few bruises?" He stared around the room, and this time everyone sank back. Sank back with burning frustration in their eyes, in the case of some of the pack members, but sink they did.

Susan didn't have to decide whether to sink or not, because Sacramento's eyes passed over her head. She took one painfully tight breath, then another, and when the stalemate seemed to hold, she bent over John again. He was just sleeping, Silver had told her that. Susan watched to make sure he kept breathing anyway.

12

Silver had trouble pinpointing her cousin's smell over the blood and Susan and the baby, but she could see from the steady rise and fall of his chest that his heart was laboring on despite his earlier wound.

Sacramento stepped to the side with his underlings, talking with them in low voices. He glanced once at the weapon that had started this all but didn't pick it back up. Perhaps he thought he had no need of it now the pack was so cowed.

A thought nagged at Silver, however. Why wait to use the weapon on her cousin? Were were difficult to kill, but this weapon could do so even if that was not one's intention. If he didn't fear the risk of killing by mistake and bringing the wrath of all the Western packs down on himself, why not use it sooner? And if he was intelligent enough to realize that while lones such as herself and Dare might provoke only limited outcry, a dead alpha was a different matter entirely, why use it at all? Sacramento had held the weapon confidently enough, but Silver began to wonder if he'd really thought things through before her cousin forced his hand.

"And will you use his weapon against him?" Death paced a circle around her cousin's prostrate wild self, as if assessing it for weakness. It looked hurt too, but not fatally. Death made no move to its throat for its voice.

Silver couldn't talk here, not with Sacramento listening as well as Susan, but she glared at Death. She knew better than to make the same mistake as Sacramento. She was even less familiar with the weapon than him.

Death sat at her cousin's head and thumped his tail once in impatience. "What will you do, then? Sacramento has won his challenge. You are the only one of high rank left, if you choose to admit to it."

Silver looked down at her hand on her cousin's bloody chest. Lady, it stank in this room. Blood mixed with everyone's fear, with nowhere to go, no source of fresh air. Easier to think about that than Death's question. What did he expect her to do? Her challenging Sacramento head on was laughable. And even if she did, why would anyone here listen to her? They all thought she was crazy. They wouldn't want a madwoman as their alpha.

Silver swallowed around a twisting, knotted lump of frustration. A challenge wasn't the only way. She had to wait, keep Susan calm, and seize any opportunity to distract or trick Sacramento that presented itself. Her cousin couldn't hear her, but she began a song to him anyway, words soft under her breath. The song would do Susan as much good, especially if she thought it was for her lover's sake.

"—Lady's light over forests and the sea."

It took Susan three or four lines, but then the niggling familiarity of Silver's tune crystallized into recognition. *When true simplicity is gained . . .* She matched the snippet of words remembered from some elementary school concert with the line Silver had just sung, and so lost the thread of the next. "That's 'Simple Gifts,'" she said when Silver let the song trail off. "That's a human song."

Silver threw her a small smile. "And no human ever reused a tune? There are those that were ours in the first place, too."

A young man flopped down at John's feet. The puppyish bounce had gone out of his movements, and he let his dishwater-blond-haired head hang a little. Tom, the name floated to the surface of Susan's mind. She'd met him at breakfast.

He seemed to have started a general movement, because the rest of the pack followed him, surrounding them in a huddled mass, children at the center. She could feel the people around her practically vibrating with anger, but none of them *did* anything. There were only three bad guys, and a dozen adults in the pack.

Edmond must have felt the tension too, because he started to wail. She bounced him, desperately, but he was unhappy and determined to let everyone know it. The Hispanic man glanced over on his way past to stand at the foot of the basement stairs, then away again, dismissing them. With him looming in front of the stairs there was nowhere else for anyone to escape. There were windows high on one side of the room, but they were so narrow only Edmond might have fit through.

Maybe Edmond's upset would be good for something, though.

Under cover of the noise, Susan leaned over to Silver. "Why doesn't everyone rush them at once?"

"It keeps low-ranked Were safe, if they don't fight whoever defeats their leader. Leaders come and go, but if you keep your head down, you can endure. If you don't fight, you don't get hurt." Silver said it without emotion: not judging, but not agreeing either.

"And when the new leader is batshit? You're just screwed?" Susan waited, but Silver only made a frustrated noise.

Sacramento retrieved his gun and smirked when everyone flinched. Susan held Edmond closer, shushing him desperately. If Sacramento would just allow them a quiet moment, she'd feed him. Sacramento snapped his fingers at his blond thug, and the man waded between everyone to jerk Silver up with one hand under her bad shoulder. He dragged her over to Sacramento and stepped back.

"Now." Sacramento backed Silver up until she was pressed against the wall. He dragged a thumb along his scar and then mirrored it by caressing the silencer down her cheek. She kept her eyes steady on his face, but he pretended like she'd looked at the gun. "What, this? I like to call it poetic justice. I could kill you and ship him the body with a self-satisfied phone call about how you'd gotten what you deserved for your crimes—if my son had crimes, I'm sure you do—but I think Dare deserves something a little more personal. Something that takes a little more time." He lifted the gun away, holding it and his other hand up in a parody of surrender. He set it on top of the bookshelf again. "Guns make everything too quick."

Sacramento took out his phone and slid his finger across the screen to find the number he wanted. He smirked as he lifted it to his ear. "You're missing playtime at the Seattle house, Dare," he said after a pause for Dare to answer, and hung up.

He slipped his phone away and pressed his palms together. "So. We have perhaps half an hour while he turns around and speeds back here. What do you think we can do with that time?" He turned to Silver to ask the question. She stayed pressed against the wall, though her chin lifted a few degrees, maybe from defiance she couldn't suppress.

Sacramento lifted Silver's good hand, settling it over his in a parody of a courtly dance hold. Then with great deliberation he took her pinkie and started to bend it back.

A growl began in Silver's throat, but Susan was already pushing herself to her feet. She couldn't just stand here, like the others. She couldn't. "Don't! She heals like a human!" That was what Dare had said, wasn't it? If Were weren't used to real injuries, maybe she could stretch the truth to exaggerate the danger. "You hurt her too much, she'll go into shock. Humans die from shock. Too much trauma and the body shuts down."

Sacramento turned to her. Susan felt his gaze like a tangible weight, as if she'd interrupted the CEO in full flood to defend another, only to get herself fired. "And you *are* a human. One who keeps turning up in the oddest places. Places she shouldn't be, listening to things she shouldn't hear."

He stepped up to her, reaching like he would take her chin as he had Silver's. Susan hugged Edmond tightly, determined that whatever else he did, he would not hurt her child. Not while she was still breathing.

And he stopped. His eyes went to the top of Edmond's head and his nostrils flared. He turned the reach into a mocking gesture to indicate her, but the hesitation had been there. "Has he told you all his secrets, then? Is it true love that transcends the bounds of species?"

"Twoo wuv . . ." Tom muttered into his hand and tittered like someone whose involuntary response to fear or upset was dumb humor. He grunted at a smack from behind, someone probably putting their own panicked fear into the strength of the blow.

Sacramento ignored the young man. He pushed into Susan's personal space rather than touch her, an extra edge to his suppressed violence now. More and more of Susan's instincts joined the chorus screaming at her to cower as Silver had pretended to. He'd already shot John. Neither she nor Silver could survive it if he shot them the same way. Sacramento chuckled. "Maybe I should take care of John's dirty little problem while I'm here, don't you think?"

"Why not?" Pierce threw himself to the extent of the chain, jerking a strangled noise from his throat. "You've already assured he'll beat you into a whimpering pulp when he recovers. Why stop halfway?"

Sacramento growled. Between one blink and the next, he was gone from in front of Susan and had Pierce by one wrist. He began with Pierce's forefinger. There was no slow bend back this time, just a quick snap. Pierce whimpered, but that wasn't the worst part. The worst part was Sacramento's grin as he held the finger back. When he let go half a minute later, the finger stayed, healed in that position. Then the middle finger, then the ring. "If you'd accept my authority as your alpha, I wouldn't need to hurt you. An alpha doesn't hurt his pack. But if you keep challenging me . . ."

Susan wanted to vomit. She wanted to scream at the others to do something. But wasn't she herself standing idly by? But they didn't have a baby to consider, they all healed quickly. Maybe they were keeping themselves safe, but what about Silver? What about Pierce?

"No!"

The tone of the word so matched Susan's own feelings it took her half a second to figure out who'd actually said it. Silver's voice vibrated with rage and she threw herself at Sacramento as the man moved on to Pierce's pinkie. He casually backhanded Silver into the wall. She landed bad shoulder first with a dull thud that suggested concrete behind the paneling.

Susan drew in a sobbing breath. Edmond hiccupped from his recent tears and started to squirm. Sacramento had stopped when he noticed the baby in the way. Was that a Were thing? Would even a guy like Sacramento refuse to hurt a child? If that was true, Susan was safer than most people here while holding him.

The thought gave her enough courage to speak up again. "Silver never challenged you. Why are you hurting her?" When Sacramento transferred his attention to her she held Edmond high to make sure he noticed the baby.

"Sorry, sweetheart. She's not part of the Seattle pack." Sacramento grinned. "Fair game."

Susan overfilled her lungs and held it, trying to use the tight feeling to still her shaking. "What about me? I was the alpha's mate. What status does that give me? High enough? I can't fight, not with the baby to take care of, but can't I name a champion or something?" Susan had no idea if any of that was true for Were, but the longer Sacramento was listening to her babble, the longer he wasn't hurting anyone. Dare would be here eventually.

"I'd fight for you!" Tom stood and ducked his head to her, almost a bow. He needed a haircut, and the motion made his bangs fall into his eyes. Susan tried to read him. Did he understand what he was getting into, or had he accepted her pretensions to authority and was following orders instinctively? Scary thought. He'd be more ready for it than Pierce had been, but he'd be letting himself in for a world of hurt. Could she really in good conscience ask him to do that?

"It's not a true challenge, but if the young man asserts that you've been his alpha all along since your mate was incapacitated, never Sacramento, you may ask him to deal with the Were threatening your pack," Silver said. She pushed herself standing, bracing with her good hand all the way. Her face was white, but she met Susan's gaze, then flicked her eyes to Tom. Susan wondered if she had the same thought. They needed this, needed someone who could heal the damage to stall Sacramento, but did any teen really understand when they decided to fight for some greater cause?

Sacramento raised his eyes to the ceiling and spread his hands in a clear "Oh, *please*" gesture. Tom cracked his knuckles and rolled his neck. His grin reminded Susan of every male, age fifteen to thirty, who had ever invited their friends to watch them do something stupid on a reality TV show.

Tom threw the first punch and Sacramento blocked it easily. Susan checked that John still looked stable, then worked her way around the outside of the room to Silver. The way she held her shoulder didn't look good. Susan's brother had looked like that when he'd broken his collarbone playing football with older neighborhood boys.

Sacramento blocked another of Tom's blows, and another, then grinned. Clearly, he was playing with the young man, as he hadn't bothered to with Pierce. Susan tried not to imagine what he would do to Tom when he was in earnest. Maybe Dare would get here before Sacramento tired of the game. She doubted it, but it was a nice thought.

Then Sacramento went on the offensive. Each time Tom made it to his feet, cocky grin still hanging on, Sacramento hammered him right back to his knees again. Blow after blow landed, and the bruises began to linger. Tom's split lip seeped blood. Susan pressed fingertips to her lips to hold in any sounds. Tom didn't need her squealing each time a blow landed.

Tom finally curled into a ball and didn't get up. Susan swallowed convulsively and bounced Edmond as he began to sob. Sacramento growled under his breath as he stood over Tom. He kicked Tom a last time in the kidneys. Tom yelped. "Enough! Enough throwing infants at me." Sacramento left Tom curled up and moaning and strode for the stairs. His stomach growled, suggesting his reason. The blond and Hispanic thugs positioned themselves again at the bottom of the stairs after their alpha passed between them.

The pack surrounded Tom to help him up. They supported him, of course. Susan's frustration boiled over. Tom had listened to her like a dominant Were, so maybe she could use that. "*I think Silver's enough part of the pack that she doesn't have to have her f—*" Susan flicked her eyes down to her son. "*—freaking fingers broken. And clearly Tom agrees. What about the rest of you?*" She tried to channel a tone of her boss's that told you there was only one correct answer, and he was waiting to hear it.

A few nods and mumbled words of assent formed enough of an aggregate positive answer for Susan's purposes. She drew in a deep breath. She hadn't been sure that tone would work. Maybe they *could* work together to keep anyone else from being hurt until Dare got here.

13

The Lady's light that marked the center of any healthy pack's territory was dim around Silver. So many pack members gathered all together should have coaxed it ablaze. Though perhaps it was the tears of pain she viewed it through. This was a duller ache than the snakes biting at her arm had been, but it still made it hard to think. "It's a shame you break so easily now," Death commented.

He nudged his nose under her bad arm so she could settle it so it would not move. She gritted her teeth as hard as she could and the pain receded. The sour scent of the beta's smothered pain seeped in as her mind cleared. Silver started toward him, need to soothe instinctive. Maybe the pack hadn't trusted her before, maybe they would dismiss her again once this was over, but for the moment she was the only alpha dominant they had.

Susan had proven herself very close to one, however. Silver

turned the how of it over in her mind. Susan had spoken like she already had the authority, rather than trying to coax the others into giving it to her. Perhaps it had only partially worked, but it was more than Silver had accomplished, waiting, trying to coax this pack into accepting her as someone who could think for herself.

But in this situation, Susan could only do so much. Now it was Silver's turn. "Dare will be here soon," she told the others, putting confidence into her voice. "But we can't allow Sacramento to hurt anyone else while we wait. I won't ask you to fight him, but you know his challenge was not valid." She gestured to where her cousin slept, wounded by Sacramento's weapon. Most of the pack's heads turned, following her words. The underlings just snorted. Good. Let them underestimate what she was doing. "Don't fight, but protect." She poured intensity into the word, and released a breath of relief when Death whuffed in approval.

Now, then. The beta needed his fingers fixed. Silver went to her knees in a controlled fall beside the beta. "Help me with the name?" Silver asked Death, pressing fingertips to her eyes for a moment.

"Pierce," the beta himself said. "Silver. Is Dare going to be able to beat him, when he comes?" He sounded so lost, shadows congealing around his damaged hand. Silver knew there shouldn't actually be shadows there, knew they shouldn't writhe maliciously, but her own pain had scoured away some of her mind's ability to control her eyes.

Silver pulled her mind back to the task at hand. She imagined every beta sounded so, when they first picked up an alpha's burden and found it too much. It was part of growing up. When he shouldered that burden again, after truly knowing it, then he would be a real alpha.

"I don't know." Silver looked at Death for the answer, but he just returned the look and smirked. "But he'll have my help." Silver let her head dip, thinking she didn't want to see if he still dismissed her for not being able to see his world. But then she couldn't stand it, so she looked anyway.

She didn't find it. Pierce's gaze was level. Trusting. Foolish boy. Silver leaned forward to kiss his forehead and braced his wrist as he snapped the first finger back. Death laughed, and Pierce whined deep in his throat. Silver squeezed his wrist until he did the others. She sat back on her heels. Pierce leaned forward to follow. He left his injured hand cradled in his lap, but he brought the other up to her cheek, the Lady's light seeping back into him. He rested his forehead against hers. "I don't know what I should be doing . . ." It was the barest whisper, trying to keep it from the others.

"I know." Silver exhaled slowly. Shadow tendrils pierced her shoulder too, and they twined and slithered as once the snakes had. They had no teeth, at least, no poison. That did not make them comfortable. "I know." Her own plan did not go much further—keep everyone from being hurt until Dare arrived, that was as far as she'd gotten. She could only pray to the Lady new possibilities would show themselves as the situation changed.

Andrew had plenty of time on the drive back to blame himself. He should have gone inside with Silver and Susan, should have known Sacramento would try a trick like this. Had John been overpowered or threatened into making the call? He wasn't answering his phone, so Andrew doubted he was sitting around in Fife at the start of a trail.

Pictures kept flashing through his mind of what could be happening at the house. Silver bleeding out her life with human inexorability, or screaming her throat raw. He tried to wrestle his imagination down but he wasn't even strong enough for that. What about Susan? Would Sacramento ignore her as incidental once more? And what would he do to Silver . . . ?

Action finally enabled Andrew to shove the thoughts aside as he screeched into the pack house driveway and turned off the car. He slammed the car door, leaving the key, and ran for the front door. Imagining did no good. He'd see what Sacramento had done, and then make him pay for it.

The scent of fear came and went in patches, like the source was behind some barrier. Shut up somewhere. Must be the basement, since it was easy to keep the whole pack from escaping down there. When he yanked open the door a blast hit him, the stink of terrified Were marinated with a generous splash of pain and blood. Andrew switched desperately to breathing through his mouth.

He turned a corner and saw that the door at the top of the basement stairs stood open. His feet took him toward it without conscious thought but he jerked himself to a stop. Sacramento would have heard him arrive, but Andrew had a beat or two to plan. Essential to take advantage of it. This was part of Sacramento's trap. He knew that. Sacramento had called him here, baited it with the suffering down below. But what else could he do? The only help he could call was down there in that room.

He didn't know how Sacramento had subdued the pack, but if

Andrew could undo that, that would swing the odds in his favor. He'd been their alpha before, however briefly. That and the fact that he wouldn't hurt them, maybe that would count for something. Andrew ran again, into the basement and down the stairs.

Sacramento stood behind Silver in the center of the basement, couch moved up against the wall to create more space. His hand rested on her shoulder, deceptively gentle. She held herself straight and confident, and like something was broken. Andrew couldn't breathe for a moment, but at least she was standing. It wasn't her blood he smelled.

Sacramento's gelled hair was as impeccable as it had been the last time Andrew saw him, though his shirt was crumpled and sweat-stained. The just-groomed-after-a-fight look was somehow even more of a slap in the face because of the pain all around him.

Sacramento smirked, enjoying his moment, so Andrew forced himself to look away from Silver to see who else was hurt. Who else could help him. Susan stood off to the side with the baby in his sling, unhurt probably because of the child. John was laid out on the floor, surrounded by most of his pack. His shirt had a small bloodstained hole. A bullet hole. Andrew drew in a deep breath, trying to find the gun by scent, but the basement stank too much for that. He found it by eye instead, up out of the way on a shelf for now. With that marked, Andrew moved on.

Tom was curled into a ball among the huddled pack, looking like he'd been beaten nearly unconscious. He was the other source of the blood, though at least none still flowed. Pierce was chained up, huddled around his hand like it was another injury healing slowly after too much other abuse.

"Congratulations. You've given me the justification I needed to take you down without political repercussions." Andrew pushed the words out around a snarl. Fights weren't supposed to end in death, and he shouldn't kill Sacramento—couldn't, without shooting his plans for challenging for Roanoke in the head, even with what Sacramento had done. No one in the pack was dead. In the Convocation's eyes, they'd all heal.

But that didn't matter anymore. Someone needed to take Sacramento down. Andrew sought Sacramento's eyes to force a dominance struggle in the eye contact as he untucked his shirt, ready to shift.

To his shock, Sacramento turned his head, breaking the contact. He laughed. "No, Dare. Not yet." He tightened his hold on Silver's shoulder and twisted it.

Bones creaked and Silver's expression grew glazed with agony. She whimpered, a gasped, panting sound that hardly left her time to breathe. Andrew could barely see with the pounding beat of rage in his head. Sacramento just smiled and twisted harder when Andrew jerked another step forward. "Just getting started, Dare. Nice and slow so there's no shock and this doesn't end too soon, hm? Death takes her when I say."

"Sacramento—" The second of Sacramento's men, the one Andrew hadn't met before, started forward, disgust settling into his scent.

Sacramento spared a snarl for him. "Go guard the front door." When he didn't move, Sacramento raised his voice. "Both of you! Now!" His tone threatened that whoever heard the order and ignored it would soon find himself without a pack. Neither of Sacramento's goons disobeyed.

Andrew stepped aside to allow the goons to reach the stairs. Sacramento watched and dug fingers into Silver's shoulder when Andrew would have come closer.

Andrew reached down into the calm of a fight, used it to force out words as he locked his muscles down. "Your business is with me, Nate."

Calm more or less achieved, it urged him to wade in anyway. It whispered that Silver couldn't get hurt any worse than she already was before he took Sacramento down. Only Andrew knew she could, so he stayed where he was. His heart bled to not be able to stop her pain.

"Oh, but you killed my son, Andrew. I think it's only fair I kill your mate. After I make her suffer a little."

"He never suffered. He died for his crimes, but he never suffered. He enjoyed *causing* suffering. Looks like he got that from you." Andrew's mouth kept going, but it felt like it was almost divorced from the rest of him. Keep tossing out insults, while the rest of him screamed. Kill Silver? He'd have to kill Andrew first.

Shadows slipped into Silver's veins and then slashed their way out again. Distantly, she recalled the pain of the snakes in her arm before they'd died, when they had called the Lady's light to burn her up. That had been pain. This was just a distraction. And Death was with her. It was ironic, that she should find that comforting. But he kept her anchored, so mist did not cover her eyes and make her lose track of Dare.

"You are the one who brought torture into this," Silver said. Her words were weak and dissipated into the air with her panting, but she felt the shadows congeal around her captor once more. Death stood before them, poised to attack at a moment's notice, but he did not interfere. This was Silver's task, and she knew it. If she was to make this pack believe she wasn't useless, she needed to *be* not useless. She couldn't wait for Dare, or Seattle, or anyone else to save her.

Sacramento shook her to make her words stop and Silver stayed limp so the shadows didn't cut so badly. Even so, she still bled drips of liquid pain like acid from her shoulder. So hard to think when it hurt so much. Lady, what was she supposed to do? She didn't have the strength to fight Dare's enemy any longer.

Sacramento hadn't used his own strength to defeat her cousin, though. He'd used a weapon. Silver searched out where he'd put it aside for later. She tried to see the weapon for what it really was, tried to see it properly. It glinted with shadow, something that wasn't possible, and she could hear it hissing of her death even from the other side of the room. The snakes had hissed so. Someone needed to reach the weapon and kill it before Sacramento could use it.

"An adequate leader knows how to do what must be done herself," Death said. "A good leader knows how to get things done, whoever does them." His tail flicked.

"Susan!" Silver put all her remaining command into her voice and looked straight at the weapon for as long as she could. Then Dare's enemy made the shadows cut her until tears flowed and her eyes wouldn't focus. She could only hope Susan understood what Silver needed her to do.

Susan felt as frozen as Dare seemed to be as they listened to Silver whimper. Silver calling her name brought her back to herself. She saw Silver look at the gun, request clear enough. She should have thought of it herself. But she'd only ever fired a gun at the range with her brother, and she didn't think Sacramento would believe any bluff she attempted.

Silver sobbed and something in Susan snapped. No. No more. *She* had to do something. Not "someone." Her. Right now. She shrugged out of the sling. If the thugs wouldn't touch her when the baby was in the way, then Tom needed that protection more than she did at the moment. Tom was sitting up now and though his expression creased with confusion, he cradled Edmond instinctively when Susan handed him over. Susan pushed up and walked at the edge of the pack until the last minute, like she was just moving within it. She reached the shelf and carefully lifted the gun from the top. She had to stop Sacramento from hurting everyone. Stop him hurting everyone so that it *stuck,* this time.

Andrew and Sacramento were locked in a staring contest now, Sacramento laughing as he squeezed Silver's shoulder and she whimpered brokenly. He didn't notice Susan. Because she was human, perhaps.

Susan was glad to be human, then. He didn't notice her as she circled around to stand so she had a straight line to his head without endangering Silver. Susan's hands shook, but it was point-blank range, and she remembered the grip at least from when her brother had dragged her to the range. She remembered to take off the safety, only to discover Sacramento had never even put it back on.

She pulled the trigger.

It was louder than she'd expected, even with the silencer. Good thing they were down in the basement. One. She focused on the hole, to be sure it had appeared on his head, not anywhere near Silver. Everything else, she ignored.

Two. He slumped sideways from Silver. Susan stepped closer to shoot down at his heart. How many had Dare said would kill one of them? She couldn't remember.

Three. Four. Susan fired until she emptied the clip.

Then she put the safety back on and dropped the gun because her hands were shaking so hard—her whole body was shaking so hard—her guts clenched into a knot that was too tight to bear, and she doubled over, vomiting. She didn't want to see the blood, but she couldn't not see the blood. Stomach empty, she kept retching. "You wouldn't stop hurting people!" She meant it to come out screamed, defiant, but it came out as a sob, more sobs following it. She collapsed to her hands and knees.

14

Andrew saw the light go out of Sacramento's eyes after the first shot barked. Fresh blood scent flooded his next breath. The shock that had begun when he saw Susan lift the gun kept him frozen as she fired again and again. Tears streamed down Susan's cheeks as she fired, but she remained silent until she'd emptied the clip and dropped the gun.

Andrew sprinted to Silver when Susan stopped firing. He caught her around the waist as she swayed, almost following Sacramento to the floor. The smell of the gunpowder poisoned the air, layering over the blood and the stink of death.

"I didn't mean she should actually kill him." Silver's eyes were too wide, shocky. "Just remove his weapon. Dare, they'll kill her . . ."

Andrew folded Silver into his arms. She gasped and he adjusted his grip. He hadn't even touched her shoulder, but her whole side must be on fire. "It's all right, we'll figure it out." He pressed his cheek against her hair and inhaled her scent. She was alive. Thank the Lady, she was alive. And Susan, and all of Seattle.

Susan had stopped retching now and hugged herself. Stupid human woman. Stupid, moronic, idiotic, brave human woman. She'd done what none of the rest of them could—or was it, none of them could bring themselves to do?

Andrew's stomach twisted with an instinct to comfort her. The pack had all drawn back, whether from her, the gun, or the dead body, he couldn't tell in the layered scents. But unfortunately there were others in need of more immediate attention. Susan would have to hang on for a few more minutes. He nodded in thanks to the pack member unlocking Pierce's collar and helped Silver move with him as he went to Tom. He put a hand on the young man's shoulder and Tom lifted Edmond off his lap so Andrew could see none of his wounds still bled. No way to tell that by smell in the atmosphere down here.

The blond goon stuck his head around the door. Whether he anticipated helping his alpha clean up, or if the number of shots had worried him, Andrew didn't know, but his face twisted to shock at seeing his alpha down.

He shouted for his compatriot and thundered down the stairs. The second goon arrived as the blond knelt to verify his alpha's lack of pulse. He shook his head at the darker man, and their heads turned as one to Susan and the gun tumbled beside her. She still knelt hunched and didn't seem to notice the danger coming for her.

"Stop!" It was a wrench to make himself let go of Silver, but Andrew could feel from her muscles she could stand on her own.

He strode over and yanked on the goons' shoulders, stopping the men long enough to get between them and Susan.

"You've seen how a cornered mother will fight for her young. Your alpha pushed her. You saw it. He should have known better than to play with his prey, threaten her young." He kept his head high, but didn't meet either of the goons' eyes for a challenge. He had to make them believe he wasn't protecting a member of the pack. He was telling them that their alpha should take the blame for taunting a weak, brainless creature into killing him. He stayed silent, willing the men to accept what he was trying to feed them. When one Were killed another outside of a challenge, it required talking. Negotiation, possible punishment or retribution. A mad, dangerous animal that killed someone needed simple disposal. And if he could play this right— "We'll take care of her."

It almost worked. Andrew could see the blond man waver. But the darker man recovered his wits first. "Of course you will. Seattle's fuck-toy? Of course she'll get the punishment she deserves if you let Seattle do it." He shoved Andrew aside and grabbed Susan's wrist. He dragged her halfway to her feet before Andrew broke his hold by smashing a fist down on his wrist.

Andrew took up another stance in front of Susan, better balanced this time. "Would you like to stick around? See what Seattle has to say to you after he wakes up? Or maybe you'd like to make your case before the Convocation. You could explain why either of you should live when you have so little honor as to defeat an alpha with a gun and then *torture his pack*. Plenty of punishment to go around."

The blond man snarled. "They weren't real pack members."

The darker man put his hand on the other man's shoulder,

forestalling any other outburst. Andrew tried to read his expression. Did he realize how bad what Sacramento had done would look to the other packs, no matter the technicalities they tried to argue? Andrew took a few steps forward, pushing them back from Susan. "I'd suggest you take your former alpha and get out while the Lady's light is still dim."

"This won't be the end of it," the darker man said, low. "We all know it." He tossed keys to his companion. "Bring the car around and back it into the garage." The blond man hurried away while the other knelt beside Sacramento's body and closed his eyes, lips moving in a prayer.

Death slid in from the corner of Andrew's vision and circled the body, smirking. "You speak of making cases: he may have tortured, but she killed," he said, Sacramento's voice tainted with Death's sardonic humor. "You know she wasn't protecting her cub. Look how she gave him to the boy, to keep him safe. She knew the children were the only truly safe ones here."

Andrew tried to help Susan up, but she fought his hands. He couldn't really blame her, so he let her be. He remembered that feeling all too well. Like you had to hold yourself together or you'd explode from the pressure of what you'd done. Any touch was a point of weakness that might make you fly apart.

The remaining goon roused from his prayer and flicked open a pocket knife. Andrew tensed, but nodded in approval when he started cutting a large square of carpet around where Sacramento lay. They could roll him up and carry him out to the car that way. The two Were looked muscular enough to be renovators. The garage would hide them from prying eyes, but it never hurt to be careful.

Andrew let the goons cut, roll, and carry without interference.

He escorted Silver to the couch and tilted her head to check her shoulder. The bone looked straight at least, for all Sacramento's manhandling of her.

"I'm sorry," he said, and stroked her hair. She shook her head, perhaps denying the need for it, though it might have been at something Death said. Silver had the glazed look that meant she was having more trouble tracking the real world than usual. After a moment digging around in his memories of human treatments, he shrugged out of his shirt. He slid it under her arm and tied the arms around her neck to make an improvised sling. Since it was her bad arm, her muscles couldn't pull at her shoulder, but he suspected the position would help keep the weight of the arm from pulling on the injury.

Silver blinked and sense seeped back into her eyes. She put her good hand on his cheek and kissed him. "Death says Seattle's rousing," she said.

John groaned, as if he'd been listening to Death too. His hand groped to his chest, fell back after he found healthy skin where he'd been shot. His eyes popped open and he jerked upright. "Lady!"

Andrew strode over and offered John a hand up. He must not have been able to keep the sardonic note he was feeling from his expression, because John glowered at him and got up on his own. "You're a little late to the division of the kill," Andrew said, and went back to Silver.

They must have made quite a tableau as John stared around the basement—Tom black and blue and holding John's crying son, Silver Lady-white with residual pain, and Susan beside a hole in the carpet and smelling of gunpowder. The rest of the pack seemed still to be trying to come to terms with it all, staying together for strength.

"What happened?" John asked, voice husky from trying to take it in all at once.

"I was wondering that myself. What did he threaten you with?" Andrew nodded to John's chest. "The gun?"

John bristled like Andrew had called him a coward. "You may be comfortable with them, but I've never had call to stare down the barrel of a gun before. Susan?" He went to the woman, putting his hands to her shoulders. Andrew didn't bother to correct that he'd never been directly threatened with a gun before, either.

Susan shoved John's hands away and wobbled to her feet. She stooped over her son, cupped his head, and murmured something probably intended to be thanks or apology to Tom. "I need . . . space . . ." She ran, stumbling up the stairs. The front door banged. John followed.

"John!" Andrew's voice stopped the man in the doorway to the basement, but he didn't come back in. "Your pack needs you. Send me after your mate. Send any of your pack after your mate—" Andrew's tone grew a little desperate at the end as nothing changed on John's face. He shouldn't have to tell the man this. It should be sheer instinct. He needed to recapture his authority after what Sacramento had done, but more than that, his pack needed him. For comfort, reassurance.

"I can't . . ." John wavered for a moment and then disappeared, chasing after Susan.

15

Silver wanted nothing more than to curl up against Dare and never let go, but Seattle had cracked under the strain, and now Dare was left with his duties. Someone helped her settle her arm better so that movement did not twist up the shadows and cut her, and made her swallow something that dulled the ache that remained. She ate, and assigned herself to make sure the brave boy who had helped them ate too. Several blows to the throat had made him reluctant to swallow even though he needed the nourishment.

He looked at her like she was a hero, which was strange. Hers hadn't been the warrior's part in this fight. That had been Susan's. Brave woman. Silver wished she could comfort her, but she was still running. Silver knew about running. She'd run for a long time herself.

Dare's part was to clean up, it seemed. Calm everyone down,

make sure everyone ate. Silver did her best to help, putting each piece of food into the brave boy's hands so he would remember to keep going.

"I wish I could have taken him down," the boy said, catching her hand and smoothing it when she handed him something. His voice was still rough and he couldn't find a position to lie down that didn't hurt him. "Saved everyone some hurt."

Death returned then, slipping between those gathered to eat and recover. He carried a whiff of blood like he'd been watching down below where the pack were still scrubbing away blood-stains so everyone could relax without the stench in every breath. "The boy's time will come," he said in Sacramento's voice, though with more weight than the man had probably ever given it in life. "He has growing to do, but he'll have his own battles to fight. Those with hearts that seek to protect always do."

Silver repeated the words for the boy, and he gave her such a grin that the shadows hid deep inside her shoulder for a few moments. "Someday I'll save everyone," he declared, and Silver smiled back.

Dare brought the beta—Pierce. Cemented by the pain, the name came more easily to her now. She took to handing Pierce food as well. He bristled under the attention. She could see from his movements that he was superficially healed, but he had not the Lady's light about him of a healthy Were. He needed food and rest yet.

"Someone needs to make sure there's no blood left," he whined at Dare, who pushed him back down again.

"That's being taken care of." Dare threaded his fingers into Silver's hair, and she touched his wrist. No rest for either of them, though she could feel how much he ached for it. He'd sustained no injury in this battle, but he had not his full light, either, a ghostly trace of shadows in his back. "Stay with Silver for now."

Pierce turned his sullen look on her as Dare disappeared off on another task. Silver held his eyes, and she could see the memory return of what they'd shared below, when she'd helped him re-break his fingers. He let his head hang, finally resting, leaving things to her and Dare. Trusting.

For all that such trust worried her a little, something in Silver curled up, warm and content.

Andrew cursed John under his breath as he helped everyone clean up. They'd pulled up the carpet pad to throw out and scrubbed the bare concrete beneath just in case. Later they could pull up the rest of the carpet in the room, to present to installers as someone's weekend do-it-yourself project run out of steam. He'd have to call some installers—*John* would have to call some installers. Andrew had to remember that however much of an idiot Seattle was being, this was still his pack. Once the man pulled his muzzle out of his ass, Andrew would hand over the arrangements. For now, it was nice to have something to concentrate on when his thoughts turned to how easily Silver could be dead instead. The pack seemed calmer for having a direction for their efforts too.

He checked back in on Pierce and Tom. They sat on the living room floor with Silver, who had an industrial-sized jerky package beside her. Those of the pack not cleaning up downstairs were starting a meal—late for lunch now, early for dinner, but the injured couldn't wait that long.

Tom had shifted and lay curled up with his head in Silver's lap, taking puppylike pleasure in the feminine attention he'd earned. Pierce ate with a single-minded intensity, marking time until he'd be released to do something useful.

Andrew let himself down to the floor behind Silver. Tom gave up his place without complaint so Silver could scoot back into Andrew's arms. Andrew leaned over to grab the jerky. She snorted, but took pieces when he handed them to her. Where the hell was Seattle? He wanted to slip off somewhere private where he could hold Silver tight forever and breathe her scent and remember she was alive. Reaction made him feel shaky.

But there was the front door and John's voice, low and trying to soothe, Susan's scent of gunpowder and fear and tears. Andrew pushed himself up to go meet them, tearing himself away from Silver's touch.

Susan's expression was blank and dead, tears stopped for the moment, though her face was crusty with salt. John had his arm around her waist, guiding her inside. In the hall she stopped and blinked, then flinched away from John. "Edmond," she said, looking past him. "I have to take care of Edmond."

"He's upstairs," Andrew said gently. "The pack's been switching off so someone's always in the nursery with the children. He's been well taken care of." Susan stared at him, so he repeated himself. This time, she seemed to get it. She jogged for the stairs. Andrew wanted to call after her and tell her to make sure she never let Edmond go, whatever happened now. But things were different for Susan than they had been for him. No one was going to try to take away her son.

John started to follow her up the stairs, but Andrew blocked him. "We need to talk."

John tried to push him aside. "Not now. I have to—"

Andrew gathered up a handful of John's shirt. "We're going to talk. In front of your pack, or outside where they can't hear. It's your choice."

Through sheer stubbornness, Andrew got John out the back door. They crossed the pack house's spacious backyard nearly to the fence line, where trees loomed high all around them. Andrew felt better already, just breathing in the scent of needles and sap rather than gunpowder.

Andrew didn't want to have this talk, but clearly someone needed to remind John of what being an alpha meant. John was probably wrung out from healing the bullet wound, but as an alpha he didn't have the luxury of falling apart. His pack needed a strong alpha presence to provide a foundation for their calm. Why couldn't John see that? Why had it fallen to Andrew to make John understand?

"Now you know how I feel." Sacramento's voice made Andrew jerk his head to look, but it was only Death lounging on the bench of a much-gnawed picnic table. Death laughed at him silently, jaws parted.

John followed Andrew's gaze, then looked inquiringly at Andrew when he presumably found nothing there. "Jumping at shadows," Andrew excused himself. "Now. If you will allow me to teach you your job, Seattle, you need to be where people can see you, looking in control, even if you don't feel it."

He waited for John to respond, but the man just shook his head. Perhaps he meant that he didn't know how to even pretend control at the moment. Andrew sighed. Maybe the minutiae of cleaning would help focus John, as it had him. "Tomorrow, you can pull up the rest of the carpet in the basement, and call some installers. Get Tom to laze around in wolf. That'll explain all the layers of hair and you can tell them it was ruined from the dog peeing on it."

John nodded, but he still looked glazed. "I can't— If only I'd fought him for the gun when he first arrived—"

Andrew hauled back and slapped him. "Seattle! If you don't start taking care of your pack, you. Will. Lose. Them." He knew he sounded angry, and he played that up to get the man moving. John growled and jerked out of reach, hands coming up in fists, but automatically, like his mind was still elsewhere.

Underneath the show of anger, Andrew felt wrung out. He hurt with the weight of the what-ifs for Silver, hurt with sympathy for the pack and their distress. He was the one who'd brought Sacramento here, but he couldn't truly help them. That had to be their alpha. "They're hurt, they're scared. They need their alpha with them, helping each of them, not just his mate. Susan is stronger than I ever expected, stronger probably than you realize. She'll survive."

That, finally, brought John's eyes to his face. He stared at Andrew for the space of a breath, then another, before he turned and headed back inside. Andrew could only hope it was to talk to his pack and not to follow Susan again. He stayed outside for about a minute before he couldn't stand it and went back in to check that Seattle was doing his job.

16

Things were relatively simple for Susan for a few hours. She nursed Edmond, checked his diaper, put him down to sleep, and locked herself in John's bedroom. As evening dragged into night, she gave in and took several allergy pills to knock herself out until Edmond needed feeding again. She didn't remember any dreams, but then again it felt like she never got deep enough into sleep to have them. After she got up the first time she only dozed until morning was far enough advanced that she could check on Edmond again.

A plate of breakfast waited beside John's door when she got back from the nursery, and Susan took it in with her. After some consideration, she called in sick to work again. Unfortunately, she soon found that, alone with her thoughts, they overwhelmed her.

She'd killed someone. She'd pulled the trigger, she'd seen the blood well up on Sacramento's temple. She'd seen the body fall.

How could she have killed another person? Not human, but still a person. But hadn't she stopped him from killing Silver, maybe Dare? She'd grown up taught that capital punishment was wrong, but what about self-defense? Or defense of people she cared about, anyway. Could she have stopped him without killing him? Would a bluff with the gun have been enough? She had no idea.

It all circled back. She'd killed someone. She'd had to. Hadn't she? But what would the Were think? John's pack, or the others? She had the vague sense that Dare had defended her from Sacramento's thugs. She presumed they would tell people about her. Susan supposed she should be worried that they'd show up to kill her, but she couldn't get past the crisis of what she thought of herself.

She'd killed someone.

She was on the floor, curled with her back pressed against the end of the bed, when someone finally knocked. She didn't choose to answer, so the knock came again. John's voice followed. "Susan?"

"I know perfectly well you can break that lock. Do it if you're going to, or go away." Susan hadn't meant it to come out that acid, but wasn't it all John's fault? It was his world that had forced her to kill, one of his kind that had been hurting them. If he'd fought Sacramento earlier, then Silver wouldn't have come, and his pack would have been safe.

She just didn't want to deal with any of it right now. John, or Were, or anyone until she could breathe again without the pressure of the thought that she'd killed someone.

John did go away, after a while. She could hear his voice as he talked to the others, a little more commanding now. When he knocked again, she shouted, "Go away!"

Edmond crying outside the door startled her out of her thoughts next. She pushed to her feet immediately. She opened the door to find Dare there, the squalling baby in his arms. Susan reached for the baby and hooked her toe around the bottom of the door, ready to close it on Dare the moment she had Edmond.

He didn't let Edmond go. "You don't have to say anything, I just hope you'll listen," Andrew said, low. He relinquished Edmond once he was inside and shut the door before Susan could ask him to. She didn't want to face John yet. She didn't know if she'd scream at him for being a Were or fall sobbing into his arms. Dare was enough of a stranger she could keep better control.

Edmond quieted when she nursed him, sitting on the edge of the bed. She didn't bother trying to cover up. Were didn't care about nudity, and she didn't have the energy to care on her own account.

"Well?" she said when Dare settled on the room's chair, leaning forward with his wrists resting on his knees. "Get it over with." Even considering what he might say made the emotions swirl in closer. Susan's heart pounded as her eyes teared up. Was he here to say the Were wanted her executed? Did he pity her?

"How much did Silver tell you about what happened to my wife?" After a moment, Dare exhaled on an amused note, probably at the surprise on Susan's face. She hadn't expected him to say that.

"That she was killed. And your in-laws kept your daughter." She had to climb out from under the morass of her own situation, but Susan did remember her politeness after a moment of looking down at her own son. "I'm sorry."

"Mm." Dare rubbed a thumb over his opposite palm for a few moments, maybe choosing his words. "A rival pack killed her, and then I killed them. Seven of them, the majority of the pack's fighters, including the beta. After the first couple, the rest probably surrendered, but I didn't pay any attention. I killed them all and tore out their throats." He paused, repeating the measured movements with his hands. "Were believe that when we die, Death takes our voices back to the Lady. To tear out the throat is to deny what you'd call the soul that rest. Symbolically, of course. I don't believe in Her literally."

Andrew—having been trusted with what he'd told her, she couldn't think of him as Dare anymore—paused again as if for some reaction. Susan had no clue what to say. It must have been much worse for him, but that was Andrew. He was better at all of this stuff than she was.

"So I fled home. Boston took me in. Kept me from killing myself." Andrew's rubbing thumb stilled and then he let his hands fall, tone giving the admission no more weight than the sentence before it. "Gave me some advice. My daughter was three years old at the time. Benjamin told me that I was probably thinking I had done something so wrong, so evil, that I needed to remove myself and the possibility of further evil from the world."

He paused and Susan wondered what he expected her to say. She didn't want to end it, she realized, confronted with that thought. She wanted to run and run until she'd outrun all of this and didn't have to think about it anymore. Run until she wasn't someone who'd killed anymore.

"And he told me that there was no evil I'd prevent by removing myself that could ever outweigh the evil I'd do by depriving my daughter of a father. The kind of father I would be, if only I always remembered to live as the father I'd want her to have. Live like that, and it's hard to do evil at all."

"I don't want to kill myself." Susan exhaled on a note of breathy hysterical humor and Andrew smiled in reciprocal punchiness. But there was more to it than that. She wasn't sure how Andrew did it, made the words ring with something that had nothing to do with the actual physical sound of them. Maybe he hadn't reacted in the same way, but Andrew had *been* where she sat now. He'd picked himself up. He was proof it could be done. He'd done it for his daughter. She had a son. A son, and a lover, and friends in this pack. "But thank you."

Andrew pushed himself to his feet after a last pat to her knee and opened the door. Silver peeked inside and the two of them exchanged a look, communicating Susan wasn't sure what. "Are you next?" she asked Silver.

Silver shook her head. "My dark hours had different sources than yours and Dare's." She looked at the floor. "Death offers 'This too shall pass.' Which is the sort of thing only he can get away with saying, because it's completely true but also such bullshit."

Susan looked down at Edmond. Full, he squirmed around to try to stand up on her thighs. She did have a son. And she was luckier than Andrew had been, since no one was trying to take him away from her. All in a rush, Susan wanted to get it over with. Maybe John would be angry at her for doing it, maybe he'd be disgusted or pitying, but she wanted to know. Better to rip the Band-Aid off. She stood and held Edmond out. "Would you guys put him down for me? I'm going to go find John."

Silver nodded, and held out her good arm for the baby. Susan eyed her sling. Silver was practiced in using one arm, but what about with a broken collarbone? Andrew must have had the same thought, because he took Edmond before Susan had to say anything to Silver. "You won't have to look far," Andrew said, tipping his head to John coming up the stairs. Andrew and Silver slipped off toward the nursery.

"John?" Her voice came out wavery.

John's head was down, so Susan couldn't read his face, but his body slumped like the very definition of hangdog as he came into the bedroom with her. She sat down on the side of the bed with a thump. Not angry at least, then. She swallowed the phrases that crowded into her mind. She'd had to. She hadn't wanted to. Sacramento could have killed John too, if the bullet had gone somewhere else in the struggle.

"Susan," he began, and her stomach twisted with nausea as she waited for him to come out with it. "I love you."

Susan's laugh at the unexpected words came out half as a sob. When he lifted his head, John's expression held only guilt and worry. She held out an arm and he sat beside her and drew her into a tight side hug. She'd really needed to hear that. It seemed out of character for John, though. Like he avoided physical affection in front of other Were, he'd never been one for stating that out loud. The handful of times he had stood out in her mind. When she'd told him she was pregnant. When he'd first held their son.

"Who told you to say that, Silver or Andrew?" Susan twisted to see his answer in his face, but she didn't even need that. His muscles told her everything when he froze. The urge to scream came back. Dammit. Why was affection so *difficult* with John?

John turned so he could get both of his arms around her, tone a little panicked. "He didn't say to—say it. Well, he did, but he said to say whatever was true, not that specifically . . ." He trailed off, perhaps in hopes she'd say something and rescue him from further flailing. Susan stayed silent. She needed so badly to hear this, and maybe John needed badly to be forced to say it too.

After a stretching pause, John drew in a deep breath. "I love you."

He sounded so earnest that this time Susan leaned her head against his chest to release him from further verbal efforts. "I'm sorry I killed him."

"No, don't be sorry for anything." His voice was emphatic. "*I'm* sorry. If I'd fought earlier, Sacramento wouldn't have been able to draw any of you into danger. You did what you had to do."

She drew in a deep breath. "Andrew thought you might kick him out, once all this was over. Thought of it immediately, like he was expecting it all along. Would you really have tossed him and Silver out, or was it all an act because he had a gun to your head?"

"I had to say something to end the call quickly, but . . ." John trailed off like he was considering lying. That would be the easy answer, Susan supposed. After all, if he said he wouldn't have done it without being threatened, she could never prove otherwise. She punched him in the side, letting him see from her glare that she'd heard the pause. She wanted the *truth,* dammit.

"He's not part of my pack," John finally mumbled. He looked as sheepish as he sounded.

Susan tugged away from him, not breaking the hug, but putting a sliver of distance between them. "That didn't matter to *him*. He and Silver have been nothing but kind to me, when many of your own pack barely tolerate me."

"I know."

Susan blinked at him. She didn't quite know what she'd been expecting, but it hadn't been such easy agreement.

John spoke into her silence. "You have to understand, Dare doesn't just have a decade on me in age, he's got much more experience. He lived in Europe, and let me tell you, their inter-pack politics aren't just metaphorically bloody like they are here. And it sounds like he was the glue holding Roanoke together, and they're hardly simple, either. Not like out here where it's one alpha, one pack, one territory. That's what I took over from my uncle. Simple." John let out a long sigh. "Or that's what I thought I took on, at least. Life is never that simple. I've been realizing that for a while now."

Susan stared at the carpet in front of them. Someone had lost a big puff of fur, not just individual hairs. "I'm especially not simple, aren't I? What I am, I mean. And now what I've done." As admitting to herself what she'd done grew easier, the looming thoughts of her future pressed down to fill that space. Her throat grew almost too tight to get the words out. "What are they going to do to me?"

John pulled her against him. "I don't think anything of value in life is simple. You're my fresh air, the place I can be myself and not think about the responsibility of my rank or how I might fail it. But now I have failed it." He let a long breath trickle out. Susan didn't say anything. Her heart rose a little to hear him say that it had been the real John she'd been seeing when they were alone, but he was right. He *had* failed them in some ways.

"I don't think I'm built to be like Dare. He takes responsibility for . . ." John laughed, low. "The world, really, as he meets it, person by person. He wants to protect them all. But I know I can protect *you*. They're not going to do anything to you. I won't let them."

"Do you get to 'let' them?" Susan let her anger at John rise and cupped it in metaphorical hands for a moment to warm her.

It was all very well for John to say "there, there" and tell her it would be all right. She was smarter than that. But then, what else could he say when the situation was out of his control?

"I'll do anything I have to." That came out in an emphatic burst and then John was silent a moment, perhaps thinking of how to support it with something concrete. "For an alpha's death, we'll have to take the matter before the Convocation of North American alphas. It's in a couple weeks. That's why Dare showed up in the first place. I know it doesn't—" he hesitated, "sound good, but being human might help you. They'll be more likely to believe you were simply a mother defending her young."

Susan pressed her lips together hard, and tried to look at that from a Were perspective. What wasn't John saying? "Humans don't put animals on trial when they kill someone, we put them down." She could feel shaking beginning in her muscles, trying to take her over. John and Dare and Silver, they wouldn't let anyone put her down, she reminded herself. *She* wouldn't let anyone put her down, even if she had to pick up a gun again.

"We don't see you like that!" Beyond the denial, John seemed to be having trouble finding words. Susan suspected that meant a lot of Were saw her exactly like that. "It's more complicated than that. But even if it had been a Were. If Silver had been the one to pull the trigger, that still wouldn't necessarily mean she'd be . . ."

"Killed," Susan filled in, since John apparently was too cowardly to say it. Someone had to.

"If it comes to that, I'll say I did it, and that my pack's just trying to push responsibility onto the human to save me. I told you, I'll do *anything* necessary. But I don't think it will come to that. I've given it a lot of thought." John let her go and turned so he sat sideways, facing her. "I have an idea for something I can do to at least help this."

Susan listened to John's plan, and nodded slowly at the end. She'd been wrong. He did have something more to offer than just platitudes.

17

When they left John and Susan, Silver passed the nursery and gestured Andrew downstairs. Edmond squirmed and Andrew adjusted his grip. He assumed she wanted to take the baby downstairs with them so she could hold him. It seemed like a reasonable idea to him. He'd seen the longing way she looked at all of the children.

Many of the pack had called in sick today, so there were several of them clustered around the TV in the living room for the communal experience of mocking a team of humans trying to complete challenges together in the jungle.

Andrew sat beside Silver after settling Edmond on her lap. Andrew had the side of the couch, with two teen Were beyond Silver, one cross-legged and the other straddling the couch arm. Pierce joined them, folding to the floor in front of Silver's feet. His hair was still a little damp from the shower and free of product for once. He offered Silver a brush hopefully. Before Andrew quite knew what had happened, Edmond ended up back on his lap so Silver could brush.

Pierce had apparently grabbed one of the brushes used on wolf forms by mistake, so every so often she stopped to pluck out a light-colored hair from among the dark. Pierce didn't seem to mind, since it extended the brushing process. It was harder to make a massage out of it like you could for a wolf form, since there was less to brush.

Edmond remarked "Woof!" to no one in particular and tried to climb up on the arm of the couch. Andrew prevented him from getting all the way up, but helped him stand on his thighs. Edmond looked around the whole room with interest from this new angle. Andrew remembered this stage with his daughter, the calm before the storm of her getting into absolutely everything she could reach as she cruised around the house.

Andrew's throat constricted at the thought of his daughter, but Edmond was clinging to his thumb with one tiny hand, and he couldn't just dump him off his lap. He took a deep breath to clear the constriction and reminded himself how different Edmond smelled.

John entered, Susan lagging a little behind as he increased the length of his stride. He smelled like he wanted to get something over with. Andrew winced internally. Here he was playing with the man's son while Silver brushed his beta.

"Dare? Silver?" John came to a stop and stood braced, hands loose at his sides.

Andrew sat Edmond down on the floor where he promptly pulled himself up again using the couch. Andrew caught Pierce's eye, and he nodded acceptance of the responsibility of watching the child. Andrew stepped around the baby and couch to face John. This was undoubtedly his warning to leave John's territory. He should have anticipated this, instead of letting himself get comfortable playing with children.

Silver took a moment longer to disentangle herself from the couch without jostling her shoulder. He exchanged a glance with her as she joined him, and found her expression also controlled against whatever unpleasantness was to come. Andrew inclined his head. "Seattle."

John shook his head and went to one knee, head bowed. "Seattle."

Andrew's next breath caught on the way in. He finished it in a ragged gasp. John couldn't be ceding him the pack, just like that. Could he? It made no sense. "Get up," he said sharply, and reached under John's arm to drag him up. Did John think that was what Andrew had been aiming for? To take over the pack by undermining his self-confidence? John should have known that if Andrew wanted the pack, he would have challenged honorably.

"No." John threw Andrew's hand off. "You—you and Silver—could use the status of being alphas going into the Convocation, couldn't you? I'll make it clear I abdicated by choice. It's the most concrete sign of endorsement I can think of. I just need—" He swallowed. "Need you to promise to defend Susan against any charges, the same as you would any member of your pack. I can't do it myself, not when Sacramento's men will make sure everyone knows she's my lover and I have a conflict of interest."

Andrew looked over at Susan. She was white-lipped but composed, so John had apparently explained his plan to her ahead of time. Maybe there was hope for the man yet.

That pause seemed to worry John, because he set his shoulders and stumbled into explanations again. "I made mistakes, dealing with Sacramento and after. I let my pack down. I have a lot left to learn, clearly. If you'll accept me as your beta, maybe I can start learning it, before you move on to Roanoke."

Andrew drew a deep breath as he scanned all the Seattle pack members gathered in the room. "Gathered" was the operative word, he realized. They'd already been gathered around him and Silver before John walked in, some sign of subconscious acceptance. No one growled or snarled. He saw expressions of awkwardness and resignation, but no anger.

Then Andrew looked at Silver. Something instinctive shouted at him to accept before the offer was withdrawn or the pack changed their minds. Having an alpha's status in the Convocation would go a long way toward getting him the time to win people over. And if he admitted it to himself, something in him itched to lead. But this was not just his decision.

Silver met his eyes at the same moment. She smiled, a smile of the same kind of rightness he was feeling. He drew her to him, meaning to whisper against her ear, check for sure, but a deep breath of her scent, eager with anticipation, told him all he needed to know.

"Yes," Silver said, for the both of them. "We won't have to defend Susan *like* a member of the pack when she *is* one." She stepped away from Andrew and spread her arm to invite John to stand for a hug. "And of course you're beta." They embraced, John chuckling roughly in relief. He probably laughed at feeling the weight of responsibility lift from his shoulders, even as it settled on Andrew's. But Andrew might as well get credit for the responsibility he seemed to always end up taking on anyway.

He heard the Were behind him go to their knees, acknowledging the new alpha pair. He turned his head to catch Pierce out of the corner of his eye, to see if he would object to being demoted. Pierce didn't kneel, as he was already sitting, but he did incline his head. Not too grudging.

Andrew checked on Susan next. She caught him at it and with a wry smile, she went to her knees too. Her look was as clear as words: see, I'm learning. Andrew gave her a thin smile of encouragement. She'd have a lot more to learn yet if he was going to keep her safe at the Convocation.

18

Andrew paused after stepping out of the rental minivan to let the sunlight seep into his skin. The Convocation had been held at this ranch south of Flagstaff the last few years, and the drive from the airport had been comforting in its familiarity. Pines topped the scree-slopes flanking the highway and spread out beyond, as abundant as other species of evergreen in Seattle, but giving the impression of sparseness with little else but grass and rocky soil beneath. He wouldn't have chosen it for a permanent home, but there was beauty in the wild spaces and easier running beneath the pines. The smells were dustier with less underbrush, but the trail of a cottontail rabbit or coyote carried more easily.

Tom jumped out of the minivan next and drew in deep breaths like he could inhale the whole place. Andrew had tried to talk him out of coming. Officially, alphas were only allowed their betas and mates. Unofficially, everyone looked the other way when teens tagged along and treated the gathering as a kind of singles mixer. At least if Tom ran around with the teens the other alphas would be bringing, it should keep him safe and out of whatever might go down. People wouldn't bother a group of young people that contained members of their own pack too.

Andrew opened the passenger door for Silver. Her expression had a pleased intensity as she absorbed all the scents. He supposed even if she'd visited Arizona before, she wouldn't remember it, so he stayed silent, letting her take it in. She caught on after a moment and smiled, dry. She leaned up to his side, to whisper on a bare breath for some semblance of privacy. "How's Death going to find shadows to lurk in with all this sun?"

Andrew laughed and pressed a kiss into her hair before releasing her to range farther off the parking area gravel in her exploration.

"So does one of the packs own this place?" Susan got out after Tom, even though he had been in the row of seats behind her. She shut the door but didn't circle around to the side with the car seat yet. She stood with her eyes shaded against the late afternoon sunlight, looking off to the rocky line of the mountains.

Andrew shook his head. "This is neutral territory. Salt Lake City used to claim it—or maybe it was Reno, I don't remember—but when the Mexican border started being so heavily patrolled for illegal immigrants, everyone pulled their boundaries north to avoid getting seen in wolf. In Arizona, they went the rest of the way and turned the whole state neutral so we can have a place to meet without fighting either the heat or the tourists farther south. It's also helpful that the ranchers around here are very much in favor of 'Shoot, shovel, and shut up' when encountering 'varmints.' It provides a little bonus motivation to stay in human. Even though it's the new, there's always someone . . ."

Thinking of all the people who might be itching for a fight enough to struggle through a shift in the new made Andrew shade his own eyes and frown ahead at the ranch. They shared the gravel parking area with a variety of mostly rental vehicles. A double row of cabins extended outward from the converted barn that served as the main hall. About three-quarters had windows open, suggesting they'd been claimed and the occupants were airing them out. The cabins on the Western packs' side of the road had the bulk of the open windows. On the other side, the cabin Rory always claimed was still shuttered and silent. This would be Andrew's first year not on the Roanoke side, attending as Rory's enforcer.

John came up and settled a step behind Andrew to conduct a similar survey. Andrew caught himself bracing for John to be pushy with his stance, but his body language suited a beta, as it had since his abdication. He waited in patient silence now. Andrew flicked a glance back over his shoulder. "You guys do first-come, first-served with cabin choice like the Roanoke sub-packs do, or do you have a usual one I should know about?"

"Nah. Pick one with the prettiest curtains," John said. He waited a beat, maybe to see if Andrew had any other questions, then returned to the van. He clapped Tom on the shoulder to stop him bouncing around and made him help pull the luggage out of the back. Silver drifted back to sling her own light bag over her shoulder.

By the time they reached the cabin row, Andrew had decided on the cabin at the far end. The one closest to the meeting hall on the Western side was inevitably already taken. Since the first cabin on the Roanoke side was Rory's, the symbolism of distancing himself from Roanoke as much as possible suited Andrew. He pushed away circling thoughts of whether he would appear scared of Rory, or appear confident for being willing to appear scared, or—

The interior matched Andrew's memories of the Roanoke cabin. The owners must have bought furnishings in bulk. Layered scents of strange humans had faded to musty dust with lack of use in the off-season. The cabin had two bedrooms, one bathroom, and a tiny kitchen. The rest of the space formed a living area, one wall filled with a rock-covered fireplace raised above a step that provided extra seating. Andrew dumped his shoulder bag beside the bed in the back bedroom. Silver sat and bounced on the bed as if judging the quality of the springs, then flopped backwards.

John hauled the baby's stuff into the other bedroom. Tom paced the living room from where the carpet ended at the kitchen area to the fireplace step, then tugged aside the couch, presumably to give himself more room to stretch out in his sleeping bag. Andrew remembered the particular brown shade of the couch too, only saved from being ugly by how faded it was.

Andrew wandered to John and Susan's room, leaned a shoulder against the doorframe, and watched them unpack the portable playpen for Edmond to sleep in. "It'll be best if I start talking to the Roanoke sub-alphas personally before the official start tonight, but I want to wait on Boston first. He can let me know where I stand with them."

A knock sounded on the door. Andrew frowned. Was that Benjamin now? Or someone else here to cause trouble? He drew a deep breath in front of the door, but the scents were too diffuse with the visitor just arrived and the door in the way. He settled his expression into an alpha's confident mask and opened the door.

"I'm here to speak to Seattle." The woman on the step was blond and leggy with her hair back in a severe ponytail. She wore dark jeans and a long-sleeved top with a high neckline. Behind her, another woman had her head tipped down so her long dark hair obscured her face, her stillness a pressuring weight that didn't quite tip over into challenge. It seemed more than just support for the other woman as spokesman, but Andrew couldn't tell what.

"Yes?" Andrew said. If the women's business was serious, he'd have to make them wait and get Silver. He assumed the two Sacramento pack goons had begun spreading rumors about the murdering human and Andrew's part in the incident as soon as they returned home. Everyone would know by now. He could only hope that people would wait for the matter to be addressed formally when the Convocation opened.

The blond woman's gaze remained behind him, not on him, for another few beats. Andrew finally realized that she must know John and was waiting for the Seattle she expected to arrive. Andrew assumed she was a Western beta, or maybe a mate. Michelle was the only female alpha.

Understanding dawned in the blond woman's face, and her eyebrows rose. "Another change of leadership. Fair enough." She backed up onto the gravel track and braced with hands clasped behind her back, feet apart. It was a very masculine gesture, and dominance-related. At Convocation, each cabin became something like sovereign territory, so the woman was inviting Andrew out to speak on neutral ground.

Then he got it, in turn. This woman was acting like an alpha.

And while Portland *had been* the only female alpha, he knew one alphaship that had recently come open. "Sacramento?" He stepped onto the gravel too. He hadn't expected to have to deal with this the moment he arrived, dammit. At least she didn't smell aggressive.

Sacramento nodded, and extended a hand. Andrew shook it and politely avoided her eyes. Her grip was firm without any of the squeezing games some of the alphas played. The dark-haired woman remained where she was and didn't look up.

Andrew heard Silver's tread on the cabin's threshold, and she came even with him a moment later. He glanced at her out of the corner of his eye. She showed her dominance with centered grace in contrast to Sacramento's rigid stance. She looked powerful and beautiful, sun shining off her hair.

"If you want Seattle, it's not just me you need," he told Sacramento. "My mate, Silver."

Silver stepped forward and offered her good hand. Sacramento ignored it, and stared at her injured arm in the sling. "You've heard of me," Silver said, ostensibly a joke but edged enough that Sacramento's attention jerked back to her face. "Before you decide what to think, remember not that I was hurt, but that I *survived*."

Sacramento finally shook Silver's hand as befitted an equal, face a little blank with her surprise. "Seattle," she murmured.

Andrew searched Silver's back and what the breeze allowed him of her scent for any sign of hesitation. She could do dominant damn well when it pleased her, but he was more worried about whether now pleased her. Dealing with the pack in the wake of Nate's death had centered her somehow, and he could see nothing put power in her stance. Good.

John stepped into the cabin doorway. He frowned at Sacramento and then laughed in dawning recognition. "You're the one who took over?" He glanced at Andrew, who nodded. With official greetings between the alphas over, John had his permission to greet a friend.

John strode over to Sacramento, grinning. "Congratulations, Allie!"

Sacramento froze, the dark-haired woman growled, and Andrew winced. Personal friends could use an alpha's name without disrespect, but he would have thought John could read this situation better than that. Sacramento was new to her power and probably feeling threatened as a female alpha. This was no time to use anything that even hinted at disrespect, especially a diminutive.

John backed up, hands open and apologetic. He glanced at Andrew and Silver for help.

"Kick him in the balls if he does it again," Silver told Sacramento. "I believe Portland said she threatened to before, so he should have learned his lesson by now." John flinched protectively, which was probably a good idea. Sacramento looked like she was considering the idea.

"Allison," Sacramento said firmly. She feinted a knee toward John and flashed Silver an edged smile. "John knew me in something of a persona. Power behind the throne is much easier when everyone dismisses you as an empty-headed beach bum."

She addressed that to Silver, but she caught Andrew's eyes afterward and snapped the elastic off her hair. She shook it free with her best prim librarian neck-twirl and fluffed it. She smiled vapidly, but Andrew was too used to looking underneath now. He gave her a solemn nod of respect. He wasn't going to judge her for not challenging Nate. He knew what it was like challenging when you didn't have your opponent's sheer physical strength.

Sacramento's lips thinned like she didn't quite trust Andrew's respect, but she returned the nod and recaptured her hair. She returned to her braced stance. "You've done me a service," she said with heavy formality. The "but" hovered like a raptor in the sky, ready to swoop.

"Wasn't me," Andrew said. He shouldn't have been surprised that someone was happy to have been saved the trouble of deposing Nate. As Sacramento implied, however, it all came down to the "but."

"Lady." The dark-haired woman shook her hair back and strode forward in impatience. "Screw 'service,' Alli— Sacramento. You said you were coming to warn him, and you're giving him a chance to spin his bullshit story? A human did it? That's convenient for him. Everyone knows about the bad blood between him and my father." She stopped just behind Sacramento's shoulder, a beta's position.

With the woman's face finally exposed, Andrew could see the resemblance. It was there in her scent too, now he knew to look for it. Perhaps that was why she'd been hiding her face. His heart sped, ready for action, and it was almost a relief to have the hunter's cocked shotgun finally fired. Here was the reaction he'd expected. Perhaps Sacramento agreed and the heavy formality was simply her being cautious in her new position.

"That human's a friend of mine." Silver stepped forward to face Nate's daughter squarely. "And of several in the pack. Some of us have those, you know. Human friends. Your father," Silver's lips twisted like the word was bitter, "tortured us. Can you blame her for snatching up a weapon and doing what none of her friends could do? She saved my life. And instead of being thanked, she's going to stand trial for it."

"Tortured—!" Nate's daughter bit off the word. "We have only your word for that." She jerked forward and Sacramento caught her arm. "After he killed my brother, too."

"He was raping human women." Andrew had used that sentence so often, it had blended into an inseparable unit in his mind. Why did that need so much justifying? He spoke to Sacramento, ignoring Nate's daughter. He could see in her face he wouldn't reach her. "It doesn't matter they were human—"

"He wouldn't have stopped with them." Sacramento's tone made Andrew want to shiver. He'd wondered if he'd have to convince her, but he had no doubt now; she knew.

"We could all defend ourselves, but most of the women in the pack knew that. Even his half sister can be forced to admit it." Sacramento shook her beta's shoulder, and the woman ducked her head, acknowledging Sacramento's words even if the rage didn't fade from her face. "Nate wasn't like that, but then again there was always—" Sacramento drew in a tight breath. "Something. And he raised his son personally."

The way Nate's daughter flinched made Andrew wonder— did that mean he hadn't raised *her* "personally"? Lucky for her, so far as he could tell. Maybe it was easier to defend a man she'd seen mostly from afar.

Sacramento drew in a quick breath. "That's neither prey nor hunter. I may think you did us all a service in turning your human on Nate, but you did kill him, and you'll answer before Convocation. I've entered the matter myself." She hesitated a beat. "I wish I hadn't had to."

Nate's daughter gave a growl of disgust and jerked out of

Sacramento's grasp. She stilled just out of reach, drawing into herself. "Some justice *you're* offering him." A breeze twisted around them and brought her scent more clearly—grief more than anger.

Silver reacted to the grief by extending her hand in an unconscious impulse to comfort. "His case will be heard, not forgotten, as the Lady will not let his voice disappear into emptiness. We're offering him the Lady's justice." Silver stopped well short of anything so foolish as touching the woman, but offered her a thin smile of sympathy.

Nate's daughter's stillness transformed into unexpected movement as she shoved Silver aside, hand on her bad arm. Silver whimpered and tears welled up. Andrew's throat squeezed. Silver was perfectly capable of playing up her reactions when she needed to, but this didn't seem like that. It seemed more like she'd stopped hiding the reaction this time. Dammit. Andrew strode to her and hovered his hand over the sling, trying to see if he could readjust it to help. Silver pushed him away.

"Stop," Sacramento snapped. She took her beta's chin in a tight grip. "Something tells me that's your proof of what Nate did." She nodded to Silver's arm. "If you're so determined to argue your father's case, don't harm it this way."

Silver drew in a ragged breath and then addressed Nate's daughter in an even tone. "He fought for revenge in the name of one—your brother—at the expense of every other Were. Real alphas try to protect anyone lower-ranked." She made a fist and held it to her core. "Real alphas, all their instincts, in here," she thumped her fist, "won't let them do otherwise. A real alpha isn't the wish for power, it's the wish to protect."

"Spare me." Nate's daughter kept most of the edge from her

tone while held so tightly by her alpha. When no more argument seemed forthcoming, Sacramento let her go and she strode away.

Sacramento watched her go, then turned back to Andrew. "I do say so myself, but I think the Sacramento pack gained by the change of alpha," she told him. "I won't argue loudly."

Andrew dipped his head deeply in acknowledgement. That was better than he could have hoped for, even if it wasn't much. He should at least have gained Michelle's support with the change in Sacramento leadership. Even if Sacramento didn't support him, he wasn't going to turn away her gift of not fighting too hard.

"And my voice will be twice as loud," Nate's daughter threw back over her shoulder.

Andrew watched, Silver beside him, until the women were out of sight inside another cabin. "Death says 'and your real opponent isn't even here yet,'" Silver murmured. Andrew snorted. As if he could forget Rory.

19

When Silver and Andrew returned from whatever business they had with the female Were at the door, Susan checked if Edmond was still sleeping and pulled Silver into the other bedroom to go over her lines again. Not that Susan had real lines, but she found thinking of this trip that way helped her stay calm. Like if she memorized Silver's directions and said the right thing at the right time, it would make everything magically turn out all right.

Silver came complete with ham sandwich, as Tom was making a huge pile of them in the kitchen. Susan sat on the edge of the bed and smoothed the coverlet, a Southwest Native-inspired design of black diamonds over deep reds and oranges. Silver joined her and offered the sandwich. "Want half?"

Since Silver couldn't do it one-handed, Susan tore the sandwich for her, taking only about a quarter. She wasn't that hungry. "I know we talked about how to act if I get called in front of the Convocation, but what about situations like just now? If someone comes to the door socially? I'll go crazy if I have to hide in the bedroom this whole trip." Not that anyone had made her hide just now. It had just seemed easier than dealing with the pitfalls of social etiquette so soon after arrival.

"That wasn't social," Silver said with a thin smile to soften the correction. Her sandwich didn't look like it had a life expectancy of more than another half minute or so. Werewolves always ate so much. "That was the new Sacramento and the daughter of the old. One with no particular love of her old alpha, the other with too much of the blind variety."

Susan pulled a section of bread from her uneaten sandwich quarter and rolled it into a little ball. "Can't see why anyone wouldn't love him," she said weakly. Silver's laugh helped her relax a little.

"Dare does have a friend who will be visiting soon. I haven't met him, but with any of these alphas, it's best to act like you're high-ranked without challenging them. Stand straight, don't drop your head, but don't meet their eyes." Silver finished off her sandwich and licked her fingers. "Most Were don't bother to learn to appear other than they are. I had to be—what does Dare call it—" Silver looked down at the floor like someone had said something to her. "A switch."

Susan laughed awkwardly. Was that supposed to be dirty, or not? She wondered that about a lot of Were stuff, with all the domination talk. Now was definitely not the time to ask, though.

"Speaking of," Silver said, her head coming up. She must have heard footsteps Susan had missed, because a knock sounded on the door moments later. She pushed to her feet and Susan followed her out to the living room. Susan finished off her sandwich as Andrew opened the door.

The man there was tall and handsomely black. He had a sheer presence that made Susan think of Morgan Freeman, though this man was much younger. Andrew started forward, a grin beginning, but the other man folded his arms and looked gently disappointed.

"Benjamin?" Andrew asked, rocking back a step. He pulled up a sober and neutral expression. "Boston?"

"I thought you were smarter than that, Dare," Benjamin said, accepting Andrew's invitation to step inside. He turned as Andrew shut the door. "And then I hear you've gone and killed Sacramento—"

"It wasn't me." Andrew preceded Benjamin into the kitchen area, and offered him the now nearly empty plate of sandwiches. Benjamin lifted a hand in polite refusal.

Susan stayed in the living room and gritted her teeth. It was insane, to want the credit, she reminded herself. But she still somehow felt that if she'd done something like that, it should mean something, not just become one more notch on Andrew's weapon. She tilted her chin even higher. Avoid eye contact. Stand straight.

"I know that. It doesn't matter if you pulled the trigger or influenced someone else to do it for you. It amounts to the same thing." Benjamin gestured in frustration, while Andrew locked his body language down. He leaned slightly over a chair, hands tight on the back.

Silver, in contrast, grew animated. She strode to stand in front of Benjamin and gestured to Susan. "Is it that she's a woman, or a human, that makes you think she's incapable of thinking for herself?"

Susan swallowed as Benjamin's gaze flicked to her, bracing herself. He looked at her—and then away again a split second later, dismissing her. Susan gritted her teeth harder. She hadn't felt that invisible since the time she'd had to duck into one of the high-level bank executives' meetings to hand some hard copy to the manager of her branch.

"You must be Silver." Benjamin's expression softened into interest.

Silver dismissed the pleasantry with a chop of her hand. "Dare was hardly in a position to do any influencing. Susan killed Sacramento because it was necessary. Don't take that from her."

Benjamin's eyes lingered on Susan for longer this time, but she still didn't feel he really saw her. He drew in a deep breath, smelling. "Nursing." He gave Andrew a dry smile. "Not yours." His gaze found John next, where he leaned uncomfortably against the kitchen counter. "Yours, I presume. Mothers will go to unexpected lengths to protect their young, I suppose."

"I'm not *stupid*." Susan found herself speaking. Having started, she couldn't stop. All the frustration of dealing with what she'd done and then having that dismissed boiled up. "I could tell they wouldn't touch me when it might hurt the baby. I could have hidden behind him in the corner, and not only would he have been okay, so would I, but then Silver would be dead, or maybe Andrew trying to save her, and they've been so kind to me . . ." She stumbled to a halt in silence that had gotten somehow even quieter.

"Your pardon, ma'am," Benjamin said, and bowed to her. "I see I was mistaken."

Susan found she was shaking. John crossed over to her in a couple strides and drew her into his arms. She felt the tension of doing it in front of a new Were in his muscles, but she didn't point it out. At least he was trying.

"Others will assume the same thing," Benjamin continued when she'd had time to take a calming breath. His tone held gentle warning, rather than justification of himself. "I'm not saying you shouldn't defend yourself, but you might want to accustom yourself to the idea so it's not such a heated defense."

Susan squirmed away from John so she could press her hands along the sides of her face. "I know." That didn't make it any easier to meet it squarely, though. "I need time to wrap my head around it." She paused in the bedroom doorway on her way to the front door. Edmond was still sleeping. Good. "I'm going for a walk."

"Not alone," Andrew said. "We don't know how someone like Nate's daughter might react if she finds the human who pulled the trigger wandering around alone." He turned to the kitchen, where Tom was making the most conspicuous effort to be inconspicuous Susan had seen in a long time. "Go on, eavesdropper. Show Susan the sights." He ruffled Tom's hair as the young man crossed to the door, and pushed him forward off-balance. The teasing quality of the roughhousing seemed a little forced on Andrew's side, but not on Tom's. He escaped and opened the door for Susan with a gallant gesture.

Susan crunched along a gravel path into the trees, leaving the cabins behind as soon as possible. Tom bounded along behind, beside, ahead, and generally around. All the boyish energy was misleading, though. When he matched her pace for a while and scraped his shaggy hair out of his eyes to look at her better, his question surprised her. "You weren't just taking credit to help Dare, were you?"

Susan took a while to straighten out her answer in her own mind. The heat of the sunlight felt almost like pressure against her skin, concentrating her thoughts. "It's a hard thing to do—to have done. Having done it for the right reasons only helps a little, but it still helps. I'd rather people knew that."

"You looked like an alpha dominant to *me*," Tom said. Some small animal rustled at the base of the nearest pine. Tom strode to look and the moment was broken. Just a bouncy young man again.

"Is that different from an alpha?" It was still a strange feeling, encountering something she didn't understand and just asking about it, rather than trying to ignore it and stay in her human sphere.

Tom snapped off a twig and stripped the needles as he returned to the path. He didn't seem to mind being questioned. "Alpha's the job. If you're an alpha dominant, you have the right personality, whether you currently have the job or not. Silver and Dare are the kind who have 'alpha dominant' going on so bad they get itchy when they can't lead things." He grinned. "I'm surprised he doesn't go to the mall to herd people or something, sometimes."

Susan squinted up ahead at where the trees were cleared around a building. She'd never considered herself the leading personality type. Tom's opinion was flattering, though. As they approached, the building resolved into stables with faux-distressed wood siding and corrugated metal roofing that looked shiny and unweathered, a match to the main hall. Where the bones of the hall had looked like a legitimately old barn, the stables' frame looked as new as its covering. It was built low with two walls partially open. It was clearly empty, but the smell lingered faintly. Susan didn't know if it was specifically horse-related, but it spoke to her strongly of the animal barns at county fairs when she was a small child.

The lack of horses also reminded Susan she hadn't seen any employees around the place. She jogged a few steps to catch up with Tom, who was peering into corners inside the stalls. "So does one of the packs own this place? Andrew said it wasn't on anyone's territory."

"Yeah, it's not Were-owned. We rent. In the off-season, you throw enough money at a resort ranch owner, they can be talked into letting you have it without staff for a super-isolated business-jargon retreat thing. If we come late enough in the spring, it usually doesn't snow. I think they board the horses elsewhere for the winter whether we're here or not." Tom patted one of the stall's posts. "All the packs chip in for the cost." He pulled a face of dramatic woe. "And if you want to come along as a single teen, you have to help with all the cooking and cleaning and running the nursery for the alphas' kids stuff that there's no staff around to do."

Susan frowned further into the stables, but the stark contrast between sunlight and shadow made it hard to see anything. "So you can be yourselves without any humans to walk in at the wrong moment." The thought gave her a certain perverse impulse to catalog every single detail she could about the proceedings.

Susan turned and strode away from the stables, back along the path. She had a lot of restlessness to walk out yet.

20

In the wake of Susan's departure from the den, Silver scrambled to think of something to say. She found herself wanting to like Boston. His wild self had red tints to its brown fur she hadn't seen before, making him attractive in that form as well. He apologized with a grace that made it to his scent, completely honest. That was rare.

"Yes, I'm Silver," she said, inclining her head. "I'm sorry for that, but I know a little about people assuming I must have been influenced."

"Show him your wounded prey face," Death said, tone mocking. "Then maybe he'll understand how easy that is to manipulate." He came to stand beside Silver's legs the way Boston's wild self stood by his. It made her feel like she had support for her alpha status as she faced Boston, both wild selves equal.

Death had a point. Silver did want to shake Boston's certainty about what he saw. He had the manner of someone with enough years of experience processed by a keen mind to make his judgment usually very wise, but he'd never encountered someone like her before. Silver supposed there had never *been* someone like her before. She reached down into herself for the feeling she'd clutched to her when she'd run after first losing her wild self. Don't look at me, don't see me, don't stop me, don't remember me. I'm weak, too weak to bother with. She felt it slide into her muscles, making them tight as she tried to look smaller, but all the body language came from the first fear. Don't hurt me.

Boston drew in a sharp breath. "That's impressive." He took a step forward and tried to catch her eyes.

Silver made her next breath deeper, using Dare's scent to calm the fear. It helped that here the drier, sharper scents of pines filled her nose, rather than the lush evergreens of home and where she'd been attacked. She met Boston's gaze squarely. She felt his wisdom even more deeply now. Maybe he'd never met one such as her before, but the weight of his knowledge was clear. She wondered what wounds might lie deep in his past, worn away by the years like the wind and water over stone, until it smoothed to a strong and dependable foundation like the mountains that surrounded them.

She broke the gaze first, ducking her head. Wisdom like that was truly worthy of the Lady.

Boston pulled her into an embrace, laughing a laugh so warm and rich it almost made her forget what she'd seen of his foundation. He sounded like a favorite uncle. "You're a lucky man, Dare."

Silver wiggled away, laughing herself. They were equally lucky, perhaps, to have found each other, but she'd hardly have rated herself so highly. She stuck out her tongue at Dare when it looked like he was going to agree with Boston, and he stuck his out in return rather than answer.

When Silver stood back, Andrew embraced Benjamin himself. He almost didn't want to admit to himself how steadying it was to see Benjamin. He looked the same as when Dare saw him last, misleadingly changeless in the way of many werewolves over a century. Seeing the frustration on his face when he first arrived had been a sock to the gut. Benjamin must have smelled something of that on him, because he clasped the back of Dare's neck, comforting, as he grimaced in apology.

A cry from Edmond interrupted them all. John ducked into the bedroom and returned with his son and the baby's bag over his shoulder. "I'll go drop him off at the nursery. They should have it set up by now."

"Hurry back for the strategy session, Seattle," Benjamin said after clapping Dare's back and turning away.

Andrew couldn't contain a shaky laugh. He'd forgotten that the rumor mill hadn't gotten hold of that piece of information yet. He hesitated before explaining. It would sound better coming from John, and if the man's pride was smarting, better he practice here before saying it in front of the assembled alphas.

"I abdicated." John took a better grip on the squirming baby to stand tall, chin high. "Dare can use the status, and I can use someone with more skill, defending my . . ." He hesitated and licked his lips.

"Mate," Silver finished for him, not unkindly.

John jerked a nod of agreement and took his son outside.

"I see I missed a lot." Benjamin drifted back to the kitchen area and selected a sandwich.

Andrew sat on the step in front of the fireplace while Benjamin took the couch. Andrew and Silver summarized the events with Nate as Benjamin ate.

At the end, Andrew sighed. "If I had it to do over, I still wouldn't stop Susan. Sacramento would have killed Silver, I have no doubt of that. Political ramifications don't rate, balanced against that." He took Silver's hand awkwardly across her body, since the side nearest him was her bad side, and she squeezed back.

Benjamin sat forward to brush crumbs off his slacks. "I would have done no different. At least if the human's willing to continue to present herself as dominant, we might be able to get them to think about Sacramento's behavior, and how reprehensible it was."

"I'm not using her trial for political leverage. Even without my promise to John, her life isn't worth any amount of power I might gain if I throw her to the hunters," Andrew said, trying to keep the frustration out of his voice. Benjamin didn't deserve to be snapped at.

Andrew had rolled his choices over and over in his thoughts on the way out here. Pretending Susan hadn't known what she was doing seemed most likely to save her from punishment; admitting she had known seemed most likely to keep his goals of challenging from dying unborn. Andrew couldn't see a way around that choice.

Benjamin made a calming gesture, palm down. "Small steps. First we deal with making sure the human stays safe. Then we link Sacramento's actions to Rory. I'm sure Rory's beta was fully aware that his alpha was talking to Sacramento. The beta supports you."

"Laurence?" Andrew thought back to the last time he'd seen Rory's beta. The man had come West to beg him to take over the pack, still suffering from the beating Rory had given him out of frustration with his own eroding control. Yet another reason Rory should be deposed, as if they needed more. A good alpha never took his emotions out on his pack. "He certainly doesn't support Rory. I thought of him, I just wasn't sure how to approach him without it looking underhanded."

"You're right, we can't ask him for visible support, but there's no reason he can't give us information. And if we ask the right questions in front of the Convocation, no one can fault him for answering them truthfully, can they?" Benjamin spread his hands, the picture of sober innocence.

Andrew nodded. If they asked Laurence if he'd heard his alpha talking to Sacramento, the Convocation would be able to smell the truth in the answer, where Rory's status would probably let him dodge any such direct question.

"Then, from there, we lay out the other reasons Rory's unfit." Benjamin sat back. "A full quarter of the sub-alphas are with you. Another quarter are for anyone but Rory."

Andrew snorted. "But the rest vehemently want to be independent again, I assume. Sure, nothing easier." He scrubbed a hand over his face. How was he ever going to pull this off? It sounded so simple when Benjamin laid it out, but Andrew knew things would never go that smoothly.

Silver let a bark of exasperated laughter slip out. When Andrew looked at her inquiringly, she nodded to a patch of the floor. "Death wants to know why we're bothering with a plan at all, when it won't even last past the first conversation with these people."

Andrew rolled his eyes. Death had a talent for not only stating the obvious, but giving it an extra obnoxious flare. It was only a full second later, when he caught Benjamin's expression, that he realized that Silver had slipped up. And he hadn't noticed. They couldn't afford that during the Convocation. Silver knew she shouldn't talk to Death in front of people, but he couldn't blame her for the mistake when he hadn't noticed it himself.

"Death?" Benjamin asked after a moment of silence, perhaps while he watched those realizations cross Andrew's face.

Silver winced and bent over her knees, pressing her hand to her face. After a moment, she drew a deep breath and straightened. "Sorry. I won't let him trick me into that again."

Andrew rubbed a hand on her back. "Don't stress about it now. We don't have to worry about Benjamin." He shot a hopeful look at the older man. Could Benjamin pretend he hadn't seen that?

"Dare never said you were dying." Benjamin's face creased with concern, and he invoked the Lady by pressing his thumb to his forehead. "You see Death coming for you?" He left the couch and knelt in front of Silver, setting a hand on her knee.

Silver put her hand on his and shook her head. She seemed too surprised and touched by his concern to laugh, though Andrew imagined that Death was chuckling at the confusion.

"Death stalked me once, but we were both so lonely. He without the Lady, I with my wild self burned away by the fire poured into my veins." She patted her bad arm. Her voice had fallen into the pattern she used when telling a story, or speaking of the aspects of her world most divorced from reality. "So now we walk together." Her tone lost the story weight, and resumed her usual humor. "And he seems to think that the world is dying for his opinions."

A black canine silhouette slipped out of the far bedroom and loped into Andrew's peripheral vision. "It's easy enough to explain away Silver, but what would he think if you told him what *you* see? I dare you to admit to it." The hallucination of Death chuckled at his pun and ghosted through the front door.

Andrew gritted his teeth. Of course Death would show up at the worst possible moments. That's when his unconscious would be dwelling on Death, hoping he wouldn't appear. Andrew should view this as getting it out of the way, before he had to keep his cool in front of all the other alphas.

Benjamin pushed to his feet, smell of his concern fading as he smiled. "Having the gods speak to you is not something to apologize for. At least to me. There are enough alphas of Dare's mind on this continent that it is perhaps something to keep quiet, however."

Andrew shook his head, and refused to rise to the bait. Benjamin knew he was an atheist, and after one abortive attempt to push Andrew into finding solace in the Lady after his wife's death, Benjamin had left him alone. He didn't begrudge Benjamin his personal faith, any more than he did Silver. "Real or not, Death's probably right. We may be at the point of waiting to see what people say before we can plan further."

21

Half an hour into her walk, Susan started to feel flushed. She winced when she checked her arms. If her skin was this red already, she'd be a lobster when the sunburn finished ripening. The altitude must have made the sunlight worse. The sun was getting low in the sky, but it would still probably be a good idea to get inside. She glanced over at Tom, but he was only tanned. Noticeably more so than when they'd left the cabin. Was that part of the werewolf accelerated healing process? They burned, it healed, and turned into a tan?

She didn't feel like going back to the cabin full of strange Were, so she angled her path toward the main hall they'd passed on the way in. She heard the low rumble of voices inside as she approached a back door, open presumably for air flow. Damn. If it was full of Were, she didn't want to go in there either. She checked her watch. It was getting on for dinnertime.

"Want to spy on them?" Tom tipped his head to the open door. "I know the secret spot."

Susan glanced back to the building. Did converted barns have secret spots? She'd have imagined them as pretty open inside. "How are we going to spy when everyone will just hear or smell us or something?"

"We'll be upstairs. No one on the main level will smell a thing with the scent clusterfuck you get down there." Tom illustrated the two levels with his hands.

Susan stepped into the doorway without even token hesitation. Not only was she curious, but getting more information about the Convocation by seeing it in action seemed like a good idea. If Tom thought they would be safe from Were notice, she presumed they would be.

The back door led into an industrial kitchen, all stainless steel with stacks of boxed produce and other food on a central table. The fridges were undoubtedly packed full too. Susan didn't even want to think about how much food a whole hall full of Were could eat. Farther in, double doors led into the main room. Susan got a glimpse through their windows of crowded movement set against more dark, weathered boards.

Tom interposed himself before she could cross the threshold. "The teens will be around cooking dinner," he said in a low voice. "I'll cut through to open the other door, but you'll have to meet me there." He leaned around the doorframe and pointed along the wall. Susan assumed he meant around the corner, because there were no other doors to be seen on this wall.

Susan crunched slowly around the building to give Tom time to converse with anyone he met inside. She saw the door as soon as she turned the corner, and it opened a few seconds later. Tom gestured her enthusiastically into a room stuffed with lights, wires, and other AV equipment. Stairs disappeared up into dimness. Tom put a finger to his lips and led the way up, walking on the balls of his feet so the metal stairs didn't clang.

At the top they emerged onto a balcony of sorts. It looked like it had once been a hayloft, but now it extended only about ten feet into the room. Wires snaked everywhere, linking speakers and lights into a complicated snarl. Susan wondered if they held concerts down below. A girl had found a few feet of railing without a light clamped to it, and was peering over.

"Ginnie-gin!" Tom said in a low, laughing voice, and held out his arms for a hug. The girl whirled and ran for him. She looked about ten, with delicate features and brown hair fastened into a ponytail with parental tightness. She threw her arms around Tom's neck and her legs around his waist. He made a production of staggering around like she was terribly heavy. "When did you get so huge? You're like a sea wolf. What if you keep on growing forever without stopping?"

"Nuh-uh. Sea wolves are only in stories. Humans would see 'em on satellites." Ginnie seemed quite proud to be able to correct Tom's woeful ignorance. She smiled at Susan, perhaps hoping for an appreciative audience.

Then the smile slipped and disappeared. "She's a human!" Ginnie whispered into Tom's ear, giving it the stentorian quality that would be called stage-whispering in an adult. "She's not supposed to be here."

Tom hesitated and Susan stepped into the silence. Not only would she have to explain to the Were below, she'd have to tell Edmond someday too. Better to practice now. "My mate and my son are Were. And I'm at the Convocation for some business I'm involved in."

"Oh." Ginnie's expression suggested she was only accepting that provisionally.

Tom took her over to the railing and pointed down. "Isn't it fun to spy on everyone? Do you know all the alphas?" Tom's covert glance at Susan suggested that this was for her benefit, but Susan couldn't distinguish any of the Were the girl pointed to from the rest of the mass of people milling below.

She came right to the railing to get a better look anyway. The gathering looked like some kind of athletic event. The Were were so fit and well-muscled, and they all looked pretty young. Their voices created a constant rumble of conversation.

"And Billings, and Philadelphia." Ginnie looked at Susan for a reaction again, and she nodded like she had any idea if that was correct.

"Every alpha can bring his mate and his beta." With Dare and Silver doing it so much, Tom had started to pick up their habit of lecturing her at random too. Though maybe Susan should give him the benefit of the doubt and assume he was talking to the girl. "Except for Roanoke when he brought Dare as his enforcer too. No one wanted to argue with him. The rule keeps the numbers limited, so nobody feels strong enough to start fights. And then roamers, like me, who want to find a girlfriend or boyfriend or a new pack or whatever. We're not allowed to attend the meetings."

"And I can come because both Mommy and Daddy are here and Daddy doesn't want to leave me at home anymore." Ginnie looked a little put out by the idea of such smothering, but her excitement at being there overshadowed it a second later.

"Look, there's Mr. Dare too!" Ginnie leaned over the railing to point at the full extent of her arm. Susan leaned too. Andrew sat down at one of the tables below, Silver beside him. John seated himself on Silver's other side a beat later. Susan's heart sped seeing him without the baby, but then she remembered the nursery. They must have decided it was getting too late, and left for the meeting without waiting for her to return to the cabin.

Seeing Were she already knew in this context, their positions undoubtedly so carefully calculated, made Susan's perceptions twist again. She supposed every decision on how to sit or stand down there reflected dominance in one way or another.

Footsteps on the stairs up to the balcony distracted her. Another girl arrived from the stairwell, expression haughty. "No wonder it stinks up here. What's a human doing here?"

The girl looked momentarily like a young woman in the uncertain light, but Susan was familiar enough with teens to subtract two or three years' worth of makeup and plunging neckline. That yielded an age of roughly fifteen or sixteen. She would be a knockout in a few years if she stopped trying so hard. She had deep black hair and a smoky quality to her skin and eyes. A faint flavor of accent to her words completed the exotic picture.

Ginnie pushed past Tom to face the older girl. Tom seemed to hardly notice, he was staring so hard at her. "Don't be a cat," Ginnie told her sternly. "Just because she's a human doesn't mean you don't have to be polite."

Susan rubbed at her temple. Sea wolves, cats . . . Maybe that was the girl's translation of catty? Then she got it. Were would hardly call someone a bitch, would they?

"What's your name?" Tom asked, still staring.

Ginnie finally seemed to notice that his attention had wandered away from her. She tugged on his hand. "Her name's Felicia. She's from Spain. Her and her family's staying with Daddy right now."

"Hi, Felicia." Tom scraped Ginnie off his hand so he could offer it to shake. Felicia considered it suspiciously for a moment before accepting it. She dropped it almost immediately to glance over her shoulder at the room below. She seemed nervous, perhaps about someone down there.

"I have an appointment," she said abruptly. She encountered Ginnie's stern look once more and snorted. "See you later," she added with precise politeness, then disappeared down the stairs. Tom followed her with his gaze until she was completely out of sight.

Susan turned her head so Tom wouldn't be able to see how much she wanted to roll her eyes. She could practically see his metaphorical tongue hanging out. Ginnie looked so unhappy, Susan bent to put herself on the girl's level. She pointed into the room. "Which alpha is your daddy?"

"My daddy's Roanoke. He's really important."

Tom finally snapped out of it. "Staying with your daddy, Ginnie?" When the girl nodded, he grabbed Susan's wrist and dragged her toward the stairs. Susan jerked out of the hold on principle, but then decided to follow anyway. What was wrong? What did he know that she didn't?

"See you later, sweetie," she told Ginnie as she jogged after Tom. She caught up to him at the foot of the stairs, where he hesitated, staring through the kitchen to the doors into the main room.

"What was that about?" Susan asked in a low voice.

Tom rocked on the balls of his feet, full of thwarted urgency. "Ginnie's father is the one Dare wants to challenge. But Dare's in-laws are from Spain. Rumor says they wanted to kill him, before he came back here. If Roanoke's working with them, that's really bad." He listened, head tilted. "Lady damn it, they're starting already. They'll notice an interruption, but someone should warn him. I don't want to leave you alone either, though."

Susan drew in a deep breath. The family showing up for revenge fit with what Silver had told her about what happened with Dare and his wife. "Go," she urged Tom, putting a hand on his shoulder. "I'll walk straight back to the cabin from here, no detours. Cross my heart. And you're just a good-for-nothing roamer sneaking around, right? No one will think anything of it."

Tom nodded and strode through the kitchen. Susan hung back, sending silent good luck wishes after him. Just when it seemed like the politics of the situation were impossibly complicated, something else sprang up.

22

Silver watched Dare sideways during the opening prayer. While he bowed his head and pressed his thumb to his forehead with the rest, his lips didn't move with the words. Death snickered, and she tried to kick him under the table. Things would be very serious from here on out. She needed her attention on what the alphas were saying, not on Death's remarks.

Roanoke rose. Silver had met him once, but the snakes in her arm had been alive then. Her memories were full of holes. He gave the same impression of muscle-bound strength, but she saw less confidence in him than she remembered. More bluster. "We are met in Convocation. I stand for Roanoke. Who else stands?"

"I stand for Boston." Boston rose next.

Silver tried to keep track of the names at first, as the Roanoke sub-alphas and then the Western packs introduced themselves in order of the length of time that each alpha had held that rank.

But names were slippery. She found more value in watching everyone's wild selves. Wild selves couldn't hide emotions the way tame could. More than just Roanoke seemed ill at ease. Several wild selves snapped defensively at the air while their tame selves smiled blandly.

The wild self of Roanoke's beta was the worst. Where the other wild selves stood beside the tame's legs, his hid behind them. A bad sign, that the man who they'd hoped would have information seemed so afraid, crouched low with ears flat and tail tucked in. But they couldn't ask him anything until this ceremony was over.

They came to the point that her cousin—she needed to learn a new name for him now he was no longer Seattle, she supposed—should have stood. Silver schooled her face to neutrality and kept her breathing slow. Her heartbeat should follow, and hopefully her excitement would not be too much of a stink in the air. They had far more controversial things to convince these alphas of later. Her becoming Seattle with Dare should be the least of her worries, but it was the first obstacle to jump, so it loomed largest at the moment.

A few people murmured, but Denver seized the opportunity to jump in precedence and stood. It was hard to pick out words with so many overlapping comments, but Silver gathered the sense that people thought her cousin was stupid for having missed his moment. Now he'd have to wait until last. Silver let her held breath trickle out. Good.

"I stand for Sacramento." The new Sacramento stood a few moments longer than the other Western alphas had, giving people time to murmur about the new alpha being a woman.

Not loudly; that gossip had carried around like a dry wind over a desert already, Silver guessed. Portland, who had stood already, cleared her throat, not quite a growl. The murmurs subsided. Sacramento nodded once in thanks to Portland and sat.

Dare squeezed her hand. Their turn. Silver drew a deep breath. She rose with him. "We stand for Seattle," they said, overlapping. What had been listening silence became stunned, and every pair of wild-self ears in the room focused on the two of them. This time, the voices were loud, like a slap of sand against the face, carried on the dry gossip wind.

Silver didn't allow herself to wince. For all they might be scandalized, no one else had any say in this. Dare might have his reputation and she might have her appearance of weakness, but she knew now that Were would follow her, trust her, when she proved her strength, same as anyone else. She could stand tall and unafraid, knowing that.

"This was not a dishonorable challenge." Silver's cousin repeated it, louder, when no one listened. He started to stand to draw people's attention, but he was beta, and that wasn't right. He subsided when he remembered. "Dare has always had honor in his dealings with me, and I abdicated to him."

Silence settled, like wind suddenly falling away so you staggered in the direction it had come from. Abdications happened, but not often. By the time an alpha was old or tired, usually one of his pack had already sensed that his voice no longer rang with authority, and challenged him.

Silver let the silence stretch a little longer, listening and smelling with every breath to judge Dare's breaking point. When frustration overcame his good sense, he might snap at them. She stepped in before he could. "Are we going to stare at each other all day, or are we going to get on with dinner? Lady knows he's nice to look at, but I'm hungry."

Dare choked at the inappropriate joke, but that was a trick she'd stolen from Death, and it worked as well as she'd hoped. The laugh was low, under people's breaths, but the moment ended. Everyone broke into talk at once.

"Silver! Dare!" The urgent whisper behind her made her turn. Tom must have been there for some time. Silver had been too focused on the alphas to notice him. Dare gave a look that said clearly "You or me?" Silver kissed his hand before dropping it and turning back to talk to the young man. She'd shaken things up, better Dare be the one to now begin the process of quieter politicking.

Tom pulled her back as far as he could. There was really no way to avoid being overheard without going outside, but there was always some privacy in the fact that people often didn't bother to listen.

Dare nodded to her once before turning back to the gathering. At least the worst part of the evening was over for now, and they could eat dinner in peace.

Andrew didn't spend too much time wondering what Tom wanted. Something Susan-related, perhaps, but with all the Were except the teens in the main hall at the moment, Andrew doubted she could have put herself in the way of serious harm. He could only chase one rabbit at a time, and he trusted Silver to handle it.

"Before we eat, I have a point of business, if no one objects."

Rory stood and rapped a knuckle on the table for attention. Andrew had worked with the man long enough to see that he was practically vibrating with excitement under his calm act. What now? What was he up to?

Whatever it was, Andrew didn't intend to let him put his plan into effect unopposed. Convocation tradition said no business on the first day, just prayers, introductions, and dinner. Anyone else, Andrew wouldn't have objected, but Rory was probably trying to assert control of the whole meeting from the beginning. He stood.

Silver gasped, left Tom, and crossed to clutch at his shoulder. "Dare!" Andrew lost the thread of what he'd been about to say. What had made Silver smell so fearful?

Rory didn't delay in seizing the opportunity Andrew's distraction had given him. "Everyone agrees, then? Good. There's someone else who needs an introduction. I know there's been bad blood in the past, but when I received a request to host a delegation for the Convocation, in the interests of developing a closer relationship among all our packs, I judged that it was worth changing the way things have always been done."

The front door opened with the bang of a visitor who wanted every eye to be on his entrance. His wife's younger brother Arturo entered first and Andrew felt like he was suddenly drowning. How could the Madrid pack be here? It was like a nightmare, too nearly his deepest, blackest fear to be real. It was impossible. They shouldn't be here. Each breath was an effort to fight it past the constriction in his chest. The Madrid pack. Here.

But he couldn't break down, or run, or launch himself at the man. Andrew fought his face into impassivity, though he knew he probably stank of fear and rage. He had to hang on to control.

Someone who wanted to be Roanoke didn't have the luxury of giving in to his emotions in public. Andrew took a metaphorical white-knuckled grip on his emotions and started cataloging the little details of Arturo's appearance to distract himself.

Arturo had grown into himself a little since Andrew had seen him last, cut his hair shorter to tame the curls and trimmed his beard down to black lines along his jaw. That jaw was clenched in an expression that was much more familiar: aggression hiding discomfort. He still lacked some indefinable measure of confidence.

Since Arturo had entered first, that meant whoever followed would be the high-ranked one. When North Americans even bothered with precedence, they put the highest-ranked first. In Europe, the highest-ranked always entered last, as if sending their vassals to scurry forward and prepare the way for them.

Raul followed. He must have moved up in the ranks of the pack, if Madrid was sending him out on errands like this. Andrew clenched his teeth on curses. He remembered Raul well, for all the man liked to fade into the background. Raul waited and listened. When he'd been quiet for so long everyone had let something slip around him from pure inattention, he struck. One key piece of information in the right ear, and suddenly everything was going Raul's way. Andrew had learned that the only way to deal with him was to be just as quiet in return, so he had nothing on you. And that was hard, because he played a long, long game.

Andrew tried to catalog appearance details again, to hold down the stomach-churning thought: what key piece of information did Raul have now? Raul still carried an air of cockiness that combined with his impeccably styled hair, manicured nails, and defined muscles to suggest he had stepped out of the bull-fighting ring for a night of wooing the ladies.

"Who are they?" John asked beside Andrew's ear.

Andrew started violently. He hadn't heard John move to stand behind him in the beta's position of support. Silver pressed herself against his other side. This must be what she'd tried to warn him about. How had Tom known? On the heels of that thought came another: few others in the room knew who these people were. Maybe if he acted quickly, he could get this under control. He needed to do something at least before Raul locked his jaw with teeth too deep in flesh to tear out.

"Raul, go home and tell Madrid," Andrew said, raising his voice to carry, "that we have no need for Europeans here."

The room exploded, alphas and betas all coming to their feet, anger at Rory congealing in the air. Andrew concentrated on taking deep breaths and holding up his neutral mask.

"He is Madrid, Dare," Arturo said with a smirk. "He takes the idea of ties with North America seriously enough that he has come himself."

"Or the idea of a takeover," Andrew countered over the roar of everyone's voices, raising the noise to a new pitch. This was bad, very bad. He'd had no idea Raul had challenged since he left Spain. He'd always figured the man was dangerous, but now it seemed he had the position to back it up.

Raul said nothing through it all. He waited impassively for the storm to pass, arms crossed. Dammit, what did it take to shake the man? Was that confidence that the rest of his meta-phorical pack was even now circling around to box in the prey? Arturo glanced back and then smirked anew at Andrew. There was something else they were hiding. Andrew knew it.

Maybe somewhere in there, he really had forgotten to breathe, because Andrew's whole world stopped dead. Only he existed, him and the young woman who walked through the door. She looked about fifteen years old, wearing too much makeup, with her black hair left loose to tumble in waves over her shoulders. He didn't recognize her at first—maybe he didn't want to recognize her—but he knew. He knew.

He pulled away from Silver and took a stumbling step forward. At first, she didn't look at all like her mother. This girl's face was harder, wilder, sharper. She was much taller than her mother had been, height in her legs, like Andrew's own mother. But he could see Isabel's bones in her face, the line from deep brown eyes to the corner of her jaw to the curve of her chin.

"Felicia." The word came out mangled and husky. Andrew had to try twice to make it audible even to himself over the pounding of his own heart. "Felicia."

He ran. Arturo and Raul stepped out of the way and part of Andrew screamed that that wasn't right, after all the effort they'd put into keeping her from him. But that wasn't loud enough to be heard over his heart either. Felicia. She'd grown into a beautiful young woman, healthy and confident.

He reached her, she looked in his eyes, and she snarled. Short, but with so much contempt in the sound. Andrew tried not to hear it, tried not to have it be true. Contempt? He'd known they'd probably turned her against him. He'd known it, and seeing it in her face was still like a physical blow. All the times he'd imagined her grown, it had been smiling, as she smiled as a child. That smiling toddler was gone forever, as gone as Isabel. At least when he'd lost her, it had been an honest pain that faded as time passed. Straightforward. Having lost the child but not the person—that was a silver knife to the gut, twisted.

"Felicia—" He tried again, but this time she cut him off.

"You." Her lip lifted in another snarl, but she didn't give it voice this time. "It's good to finally meet you again, *Father*. Maybe you can explain to me why you were so cowardly as to stand back and let my mother *die* when you could have saved her. But you couldn't risk your precious skin, could you?"

Andrew stared at her for several seconds, trying to understand what she'd just said. Let Isabel die? He still had nightmares about the first sight he'd had of the house, pounding down the streets so hard he couldn't draw in enough air, following the smoke. Every breath had been filled with the smell of that fire, burning too far advanced, he'd known it. But still he ran and found the house with ravenous orange licking from every window, every door, devouring the beams around where the roof had collapsed.

He'd still have gone in. He remembered the moment with crystal clarity, seeing the house and knowing no one could be alive. But werewolves could heal, couldn't they? He had to go in and try.

Felicia had been sobbing wildly in his arms for the whole run. She hadn't understood what was going on, but she knew it was more frightening than anything she'd ever encountered before. At that moment, the moment when he'd looked at the house and made that calculation, she screamed with absolute terror. It reached Andrew. He held her against him and breathed in the scent of her hair, the scent of her, and he didn't go. He stayed as the second floor collapsed down and the firefighters arrived. He held his daughter as she screamed and screamed. His tears were silent.

"There was nothing anyone could have done," Andrew said. "We got there too late." He searched her face for some hint she was listening, but found only righteous anger.

Arturo murmured something to Raul. Andrew caught enough of the end to realize that it was a translation of his words. *"You were the first on the scene, Dare,"* Raul replied in Spanish. He smoothed and flipped Andrew's name with Spanish vowels. Andrew understood, his former fluency seeping to the surface, but emotion blocked out his ability to find words to answer.

Arturo joined in, a beat late, first with a translation of Raul for the audience, then words of his own. "How do we know you're not lying, to try to save your honor?" Andrew would have laughed, if his grip on control hadn't been so tenuous. Raul should have known better than to rely on Arturo for his little act. The man couldn't hide his true emotions to save his life. Arturo knew he was lying.

Andrew imagined shouting at them both, shouting that they'd raised his daughter on lies, even though he'd known that before. That had been different. Having her right in front of him, hearing the lies from her own mouth, was different. He imagined backhanding the smug look right off Arturo's face.

In the new, his wolf form should have felt miles away, but it seemed close enough to touch now. So easy, to shift and tear Raul into bleeding shreds. Not kill him. Just teach him to regret what he'd done.

But he couldn't. This was about more than him and Raul and Felicia. Whatever Rory's plan was in inviting these snakes into the Convocation, Andrew needed to thwart it. "Been losing your memory, Raul? Last time I saw you, you understood English perfectly well." The words came out flat, but better that than snarled.

Raul spread his hands, the picture of reasonability and confusion, exactly as if he hadn't understood. It came to Andrew in a flash: who knew what pieces of information people might drop around him if they thought he couldn't understand. Lady damn him, Andrew refused to let him play his games, play them on Andrew's people, but he couldn't attack Raul to prevent it.

"*Fuck you,*" Andrew said in Spanish. He remembered that much. But he needed to keep *control,* and it was slipping away from him each moment Raul stood watching him impassively as Felicia's snarl echoed in his ears. Raul needed to feel *pain.*

Silver's fingers closed on his wrist. "Andrew Dare," she said. "Everyone is watching. Your daughter is watching."

Andrew swallowed. She was right. He couldn't throw away the challenge he'd worked so hard for, and he couldn't become the fireside-tale monster they'd made of him to her. If he couldn't keep control, he had to leave. He turned and fled, seeing nothing but the big double door out to the porchlight-stained darkness outside.

23

Silver let Dare go. She wanted to follow so badly, but she could hardly see the world at the moment. She couldn't move through what she couldn't see. She had needed that name, needed her mate's name to truly reach him. But that name was tangled up in the memories it hurt to remember, the memories it drove her mad to remember. Pull on the name and the rest dragged behind. She pulled, she let go, and hid. The rest didn't overwhelm her, but they did hurt.

"Patience," Death said, in her mother's voice, dimly remembered from when she was a cub. "He could not hold to show his strength. Make a virtue of a necessity, and hold yourself."

So she held until the world seeped back in, and then she put her hand on the shoulder of the young man who had tried to warn them and let him lead her back to her cousin. She sat and let the words around her—accusations, speculations, insults, support—slide over her skin and away like harmless rain.

With Dare's world at a greater distance, she saw wild selves in greater focus, so she concentrated on reading their enemies' secrets in theirs. The alpha's wild self held too still and was light in patches to suit a forest's shadows. In a pack hunt, Silver suspected he would claim the kill by darting out for the last bite when the others had already chased it far and worn it down. The beta's dove-gray wild self kept too much behind the tame's legs for Silver to believe anything the tame's stance said about his confidence.

Dare's daughter's wild self pressed against the tame's legs, but bared its teeth defiantly. It was dark, darker than most other wild selves in the room, black with hints of russet underfur. It seemed fitting to Silver, considering how the course of the girl's life had been changed in flames, that her fur should look so burnt. She seemed to lose some of her confidence as the passion of her anger at Dare waned with his departure. She backed to her uncle's side and he slung a comforting arm around her shoulders.

The voice of Dare's old, wise ally cut through the voices when the rain of words had lost its initial force and settled into a pattern that seemed likely to hold for hours unless interrupted. "Perhaps we should officially adjourn for the night, so we may eat dinner and think developments over in peace."

Silver groped for his name, any name besides Dare's, as others filed out before her. The alpha who had replaced the one her cousin's human killed paused and gave her a thin-lipped smile of sympathy as she passed. In the stress of the moment, her wild self walked shoulder to shoulder with that of her beta. So not beta, but mate? Or perhaps both? That was a very difficult balance of dominance to hold. Silver chose to think about that rather than anything else, until her cousin tugged her up.

Once they were outside, on the path to the temporary den, Silver let herself run. Each jarring step traveled as pain up her shoulder, but the sensation grounded her. The night air was sharp with the chill, the way it had been sharp with sunlight before.

Inside, she found Dare curled up as much as a tame self could, on the ground beside the bed. The salt smell of tears draped him, though she couldn't see his face. There was hardly room for her in the small space he'd tucked himself, clinging to the false security of a tight den. But Silver joined him anyway, and he moved to let her in.

"Her whole world. Made of lies," he said after a long silence.

"I know." Silver looked at Death. She'd lost her names for the moment, and now she couldn't find the right words. Did the Lady herself have the right words for this situation? It hurt worse than her shoulder to see the agony those cats were putting him through. Death sat tall and said nothing.

"Did you see the way she looked—" His voice broke. "The way she looked at me?"

"I did." Silver chased words through her thoughts like one might chase a winter rabbit with the last of one's starving strength. They eluded her. So she stayed with Dare, and let her presence do what little it could.

Andrew lost track of time until Silver joined him. It felt like an hour, but if he was honest with himself, it had probably been about twenty minutes. His thoughts spiraled down, repeating themselves as they worked deeper into despair. What now? What little hope he'd had for reuniting with Felicia, crushed. And crushed by *her*. If he fought, he'd be fighting her, and he'd lose either way. He couldn't stand it.

But having Silver there reminded him the world held things other than him and his daughter, and it was only about fifteen more minutes before he drew in a shuddering breath and pushed to his feet.

They'd lied to his daughter? Fine. Their mistake was letting him see her. He'd tell her his side of the story over and over, whether she believed him or not.

He helped Silver up and finally noticed the way her eyes couldn't seem to focus on anything but him. Worse than usual. She'd called him Andrew, he remembered in a flash of clarity. The only other time she'd called him by his first name had been when she'd briefly allowed back her memories from before the silver-poisoning. Selene, she'd been. He doubted he could ever understand the depth of the effort it had taken her to do that, and now she'd done it for him again.

"Selene?" he asked, and cupped her cheek. "I'm so sorry."

The muscles pulled under his hand as she gave him a minimalist smile. "Not precisely. I didn't need all of her, just a name." She turned away, the "and I don't want to talk about it any more than that" as clear as if she'd spoken. "I think the others want to talk to you, if you're up to it."

Now that Andrew paid attention, the sounds and smells of a small army and food in the living room were clear. These cabins were terrible for holding overlapping scents, so he hadn't noticed the newcomers among the traces remaining from earlier in the day. Andrew considered staying in his room, but only for a moment. Hiding wouldn't help anything, even though his control seemed to shred into even finer pieces each time he tried to gather it. Madrid wouldn't be out there, he reminded himself. It smelled like just the Seattle contingent and Benjamin.

"You're hungry," Silver declared, and towed him out by the hand. "Everyone else is having dinner, after all."

Andrew might have laughed in other circumstances. That had always been his mother's solution to emotional upheaval in the pack. Silver had proved several times before that it worked, much better than he thought it should. A plate piled high with lukewarm burgers sat on the kitchen table, presumably stolen from the catered dinner at the hall. Everyone in the room had one in hand already. Susan had apparently made it back all right and been told the story, because she nodded to Andrew in awkward sympathy and took Edmond and her burger to her bedroom.

Laurence stood by the door. He must have been invited by someone, but Andrew could guess why whoever it had been had taken the initiative. Laurence held his shoulders hunched as if expecting an attack. Andrew knew Rory had been taking his frustrations out on his beta, but the fact that the man was unconsciously on guard for it even now was an even worse sign. The moment he saw Andrew notice him, he launched into an apology.

"Rory kept the delegation secret until the very last minute, and then he was always watching us, it seemed like. I had no idea who the girl was either, I swear on the Lady. She mostly kept quiet, out of the way. Let Ginnie follow her around. I should have broken away to come find you anyway—"

Andrew cut Laurence off with a gesture. "What's done is done."

He went and got a burger, made himself finish it before he said anything else. His next, he bothered to open the bun for condiments. "Raul would have come up with some other way to control you if necessary. That's how he works."

Silver stole the mustard for her burger before he could reach it. He managed a thin smile at the teasing. Dammit, of all the people in the Madrid pack, the one he least wanted to go up against was Raul. For all he'd lived with the pack for half a decade, he still had no idea what Raul wanted personally. His methods for getting what he wanted, sure. But his motivation, his likely endgame? Andrew had no idea.

"You know them well?" Benjamin asked. He had a plate balanced on his knees and was cutting his burger into pieces with a knife and fork.

"Mm." Andrew squirted mustard on his bun before he answered in more depth. He outlined what he knew of Arturo and Raul's personalities. Laurence nodded when he finished. It was a relief to have verification that the men hadn't changed too much since Andrew had known them.

Benjamin chewed in silence for a few seconds. "This has to be more than just revenge on Dare. It coincides so perfectly with when an ineffective North American alpha seems likely to be deposed by a pair of extremely effective ones."

Andrew had serious questions about his effectiveness at the moment, given how he'd let Madrid get to him, but he let that pass. Compared to Rory, half the alphas on the continent would be more effective, and he had Silver. "What does Europe care how strong North American alphas are?"

Benjamin laughed without much humor. He aligned his knife and fork on his empty plate and set it on a side table. "I remember when Roanoke first united. Rumor said the Europeans all but pissed themselves. In Europe, uniting packs and territory means an empire is being built. Empires come looking for their neighbors. European packs have tried to gain power and territory over here often enough before, no wonder they expect us to do the same. Roanoke left them alone for two generations, but now it looks like more than just Roanoke might end up united in North America."

"What, they're afraid of me pulling in Western packs?" Andrew scrubbed his face. "They must be pretty paranoid to think I could herd that set of cats anywhere."

"You underestimate yourself, Dare." Benjamin's lips turned up in a slight smile. "Madrid had a chance to observe you for several years, did he not? Perhaps he saw something of what the rest of us see in you. And now you have a partner."

Andrew stared at Benjamin. That was flattering, but he would have expected Benjamin to be more pragmatic. Perhaps the Europeans did fear a united North America, but the Western packs were too independent for that. After his time out here, Andrew knew them better than Benjamin did.

Andrew waved all the speculation away. "Whatever it is that scared them, we're never going to convince them an empire isn't our intention. You can't prove a negative."

Benjamin shrugged. "We'll have to just get rid of them. The easiest thing to do would be to have one of the Western alphas move to exclude Europeans from the Convocation, and send them home."

"Michelle would do it," John said, first few words hard to understand until he swallowed his mouthful. "If we asked her."

Andrew swallowed his first panicked denial. He wanted to

sound logical, not off-balance. He needed this with a desperation that made him feel almost shaky. He took a deep breath. "But that needs to wait until I've had time to talk to Felicia. Then we can kick them out."

"No." Benjamin didn't hesitate. "You think just because you tell her the truth, she'll smell it and believe you? She's had her relatives lying to her for years. She didn't disbelieve that, she's not going to believe you, no matter how you smell.

"And the more you push her, the more you ensure that she'll stay set against you." He held up two palms pressed flat against each other, and pushed until his muscles shook. Then he dropped one and let the other rebound forward with the sudden lack of pressure. "Don't push. Don't talk to her, don't let her see you. She'll be so confused, she'll seek you out, and then you'll have your best chance."

Andrew set his burger down and then clenched his hands. Easy for Benjamin to say. But this was the first chance he'd had in a decade, and even if it was only a false hope, it was a chance. She was here. He could *talk* to her. Even if it didn't work, he couldn't live with himself if he didn't at least make the attempt. If he waited like Benjamin said, she might be gone again, never to return. "She's my daughter. I have to try, Boston."

Laurence hesitated and then moved away from the door as Andrew pushed to his feet and strode to it. John placed himself in the way. "He's right, Dare. You're still dancing to their tune."

"I know!" Andrew realized he was shouting, but couldn't make himself stop. He had to make them understand. "And that doesn't matter. I *need* to do this. If you're going to get them kicked out, I have to do it *now*." He put his hand on John's shoulder, wrestled his volume under control. "Don't make this a fight, please."

A muscle jumped in John's clenched jaw. It seemed that had been the right tack, to request rather than attack so John could meet force with force. With the lightened resistance, some of the pressure eased off Andrew's chest. He could talk to her.

"I'm getting tired of this, Dare." Silver put her hand on her hip. The anger in her voice sounded more like a way to get his attention than a real emotion, but there was a hint of the real thing in her expression. "Just because you're hurting doesn't give you permission to demand we stand by while you gnaw off your own leg to get out of the trap. *Think*, stop reacting."

"No." Andrew whirled to face her. None of them understood! Some part of him knew it was the wrong thing to do, but he had to do something. If he didn't channel this raw emotion into action he'd explode. He'd managed to not attack Raul, so this was his only option remaining. "Lady's light, Silver. I need to do this."

"No, you don't." Silver grabbed a handful of his shirt to pull him closer and went on tiptoes. She locked eyes with him.

Andrew had measured the strength of her dominance before, but he'd never fought it. He didn't want to fight it now, knew he shouldn't be doing this, but now that it was right in front of him he couldn't seem to stop. He met Silver's gaze and strength, and she matched him every step of the way, until he was pouring so much effort into the struggle that a shift came close to the surface.

It did for Silver too, only she didn't have a shift. It was like a slow-motion landslide, danger you could watch happen, but never stop. Her back arched and her muscles tightened toward a seizure. Andrew broke the struggle instantly, caught her as her muscles released and she stumbled. The others jerked forward, but settled back when they saw Andrew had her.

"I'm sorry," he breathed into her neck. When her arm came around his back he felt a subtle shake to it. He repeated it over and over. "I didn't mean to hurt you, Silver." He realized now how apt her analogy had been: he was pushing away his friends so that he could have the space to hurt himself even worse.

"Just don't do it again," Silver said with a ragged laugh. She buried her face against the side of his neck, and lifted her fingers to lace into his hair. "Stay with me tonight, hm? I'm sure we can find something to do to pass the time, so the thoughts don't devour you."

She nipped him, and Andrew started. "But you're hurt," he protested, as the heat of her feminine scent right against him warred with his desperation. The two more or less canceled each other out, until Silver's hand wandered south, hidden from the others by how they were standing. The distraction would be so, so welcome if he gave himself up to it. But— Andrew tried to finish that sentence. It was difficult, since there were other things competing for his attention. They shouldn't, should they? But if Silver wanted to—

Silver laughed, husky. Andrew gave in and lifted her to carry her to the bedroom.

24

Susan put Edmond down once the voices in the living room quieted enough for him to fall asleep. She'd missed pieces of it here and there, but the walls were thin enough she'd gotten the gist to add to what John had told her when he and the others arrived from the hall in Andrew's wake.

She picked up her book and stared at the pages without comprehending the words for a little while after the voices stopped to make sure she wouldn't disrupt anything. She figured things were emotionally fraught as it was without adding her presence to the mix of people trying to talk Andrew down.

A giggle reached her through the wall of the adjoining bedroom. Susan almost laughed herself. That was another way to talk Andrew down. She pushed off the bed, checked Edmond, and let herself out.

The living room was empty. When she opened the front door,

the edge bumped into the back of someone sitting on the front step. "Oof," John said, tone suggesting it was more to identify himself than protest injury.

She turned sideways to slip out without opening the door any farther. He scooted over to give her room to sit beside him. She sat in silence for a while, until her thoughts had built up to a pressure she had to voice. "I can't even imagine what it must be like for him, seeing his daughter like that—" She frowned at the horizon, trying to follow the outline of pine branches between the cabins opposite them. The lack of moon made it hard to tell tree from sky. The division coalesced as her eyes adjusted. The despair in Andrew's voice when he'd insisted he needed to talk to his daughter made her throat squeeze even now.

"I think I can. But I'd rather not." John frowned out at the horizon too.

Susan looked over at him, and reached up to smooth a cowlick at his crown. The uncertain light from the weak porch bulb made his face look shadowed and older. "How old is Dare?" she asked.

John turned his head to meet her gaze in surprise. "What?"

Susan zipped her fingernail along the threads in the knee of her jeans. "I've been trying to do the math. It's hard to tell with the hair making him look older, but I'd have said he was early thirties or something. Felicia looks around fifteen, so that would be awfully young to be starting a family. You said he was a decade older than you. So he's really forty?" Of course it didn't matter how old Andrew had been when he'd had his daughter, but something in Susan wanted to understand him better now. Had the girl been the product of young love, or mature planning? Had she been an accident, like Edmond had been?

John looked away. For a long time it seemed like he wasn't going to answer, which was strange. What did it matter? Did he think she was prying into Andrew's private life? They were all watching part of it now, whether they liked it or not.

"So far as I know, he's in his early fifties. You'll have to ask him if you want the exact number."

Susan blinked. She hadn't thought he was *that* old. Her mind turned the fact over and over, trying to fit it and Andrew's appearance together and failing. Then the next connection sparked, and she subtracted ten years. She stared at John. "You told me you were thirty-two!" She frowned, searching her memory. Yes, she had seen his driver's license, when they'd gone to that bar on the second date. "I saw your license."

"I showed it to you on purpose." John let his hand fall to the wood of the step, tapped fingertips in his usual nervous fidget. "We have a guy who makes us IDs to match our appearance every decade or so."

"So you're—"

"Forty." Tap, tap. John wouldn't look at her.

Susan stared at a point in the gravel in front of her, tracing the line of a particularly white chunk against the darkness as she grappled with the idea. She'd never have imagined herself with someone that much older than her at this stage of her life, but then John didn't act that old. So did it matter, then? They were both adults. Fifteen years difference was hardly an eon. Susan almost laughed at herself. What was she doing, worrying about being lied to about eight years of age, when she'd been lied to at first about the very existence of supernatural creatures? Somehow, an age difference was something she could wrap her head around to get upset about.

Then it hit her: if Were aged slower, what about their son? How would he age? He was hitting all the milestones faster except the ones to do with talking. "Edmond—"

John looked up and took her hand. "He won't grow any different than you'd expect. It's about mid-twenties when things get out of synch. Tom's as young as he looks." He seemed so relieved to find one thing he could reassure her about Susan had to suppress a half-hysterical laugh.

"So Silver's—?" Susan suddenly felt desperate to know everything. How much was there left to stumble onto about these people? "How long do you guys live?"

"Silver's thirty-one— No. Thirty-two. Her brother was definitely three years younger than me and they had five years between them." A long pause. "We can live to maybe one eighty if we're lucky. Hard to tell. Most in previous generations fell to hunters long before that."

Susan considered that with sudden horror. If they aged so slowly, she'd be growing old while he was still— Enough. She pushed the thought away. Right now she had to worry about tomorrow's trial. She could worry about decades from now later.

"I didn't mean to hide that specifically." John's words tumbled out. Even though she'd decided to set the issue aside for now, Susan let the silence stretch to see what might slip out as he sweated. It had worked before, and Lord knew he deserved all that sweating and more for keeping this information from her.

"I wanted to pretend absolutely everything else was normal, when I first told you. More than just keeping you safe, I valued your outside perspective in my life. Then when Silver showed up, and everything started falling apart, I lost track of it, and there was so much everyone was telling you all the time, it got lost in the shuffle . . ."

"Later," Susan said, giving John a lopsided smile. "Apparently we have a little time."

A laugh drifted through the door, anchoring her even more closely in the here and now. "For now, fuck it," she told the trees. Fuck the age difference, fuck the fact she was a killer, fuck all of it for tonight. Andrew and Silver had the right idea.

She put her hands on John's cheeks to turn his head and kissed him. She hadn't meant to push quite so hard so quickly, but it had been a long time. Once she started, she couldn't stop the hunger from pressing her against him.

He didn't try to pull away from the kiss, but he didn't return it with the same fire. "Edmond," he protested weakly when she came up for air.

"He's sleeping right now. We can make Tom babysit, go to the car. Or the hall. Everyone's back at their cabins by now, aren't they?" Even as she made the suggestions, Susan could read in John's tense muscles that it was a lost cause. He'd probably find an excuse if they had the cabin to themselves, a babysitter for Edmond, and an engraved invitation.

"Susan—" John scooted away to the far end of the step so they were no longer touching. "Not here."

"Where?" Susan was too horny to sit still so she pushed herself up to pace, crunching on the gravel. "You said you loved me, John, but you won't touch me when there's anyone who might hear it or smell it. And given werewolf senses . . ." Susan wanted so badly to kick him in the balls at the moment. Was this how it was going to be? After all she'd done to try to join him in his life, that's all he could give her?

Her next breath caught on the way in. What if she was too dominant now? She didn't understand Were power dynamics at all. They'd never done any BDSM stuff in the bedroom, but Susan had no idea if that was what he wanted. She swallowed. He'd said he loved her after she'd killed Sacramento, but that didn't mean he was still attracted to her.

"Is it because of what I did?"

"No!" John pushed to his feet. "It's just—with everyone and their omega here, you know? It will be different when we get back home."

Susan scrubbed at her eyes before tears could surface. Sure it would. But it made as good a self-delusion as any of the others she was using to get herself through this. Maybe she could ask Silver for advice about Were sex. She trusted Silver to answer her honestly.

"All right," she said. John shoved his hands awkwardly into his pockets, lingered for a moment, and then strode off up the gravel road. Susan stayed and stared out at the night for a while, rather than go inside and listen too closely.

25

Dare woke when Silver slipped out of bed, but she told him to go back to sleep, he had plenty of time yet. After a moment, he did. She figured he was tired from exertions, first emotional, then physical. She ached a little herself, but in a pleasanter way than she had for days.

She sat out in front of the den and watched the sun rise. The scents on the wind were quiet, the background of a world not yet awake. Few others were stirring in their dens. The colors weren't quiet. They burst pink and orange over the trees and left saturated blue behind. They reminded her why, once upon a time at the beginning of all stories, the Lady and Death had chosen to walk this world and experience its heartache rather than live in the safety of her chill white and his cold black.

Boston came, to add the richness of his brown to the riot of the sky. He waited politely at a little distance until Silver moved to make room for him. They watched the sky together, companionable. "That was a kind thing you did for Dare," he said at length.

Silver sighed and brought her hair forward to finger-comb it. Time to order herself and face the day, looking neat and confident even if she wasn't sure she was. She smiled and laughed with the warmth remaining from the time they'd ignored the world last night. "I enjoyed it plenty too, I assure you."

Boston chuckled, rich as his skin. "I wasn't talking about that, puppy." He let his smile fade into a sigh of his own. "You knew that would happen if you got into a dominance contest, didn't you?"

Silver looked down at her toes. She wiggled them. At least all of those worked, even if her arm didn't. "I suspected it would." She'd expected someone would figure that out, if not Dare himself. Better Dare didn't, if she could manage it. He'd be angry she'd do that to herself, for him, but it had been her gift to give and she didn't regret it. She'd done it to give him the chance with his daughter Boston had promised. Dare's daughter meant so much to him; that was worth most anything.

"So it was a kind thing you did." Boston placed his hands on his thighs. "You know, I feel responsible for him sometimes. It's not logical, of course, but he met his wife at a party of mine, soon after he joined my pack. I'd thought it was a good idea then too, to try to form ties with the Europeans." He smiled, small. "I saw Dare's face when he first caught sight and scent of her. I knew he was done for even then."

Death prowled in from the trees, light dust speckling his fur here and there until he shook himself and was unbroken in his blackness once more. "He didn't know when first he saw you. Are you jealous, *chica*?" He'd used that woman's voice before, warm and accented, and Silver already knew which of Dare's ghosts it was. Her stomach flipped. What Death said was true. Her courtship with Dare had been very different. She was very different from the passionate woman the voice sounded like.

But then she thought back to last night. Here, Dare's past had come as close as it could, and it had been only the two of them together, neither of their ghosts between them.

"I don't fear the ghost of a voice," she murmured. "Dare holds that time too close sometimes, but not for his wife. For his daughter." Her lips thinned. "I can't have cubs of my own. My blood will always carry too much taint." She wanted to look at the scars, but her arm was held against her to save her shoulder, so she left it. She hugged herself with her good arm. "I don't understand why it hurts him so much, missing his daughter, but to see him in so much *pain*, and I can't do anything about it—I'd do anything to ease it for him, but I just don't know how—I hurt just watching him, and she's not even my daughter, I can't even have a child."

Boston switched his hand from his knee to hers and squeezed in wordless sympathy. "Thank you," he said at length.

"For what? Hurting too? It doesn't do him much good." Silver watched Death stalk a lizard's shadow through the grass. Her eyes stung, but if she didn't blink, maybe the tears wouldn't fall.

"Bringing him all the way back. This is a setback, but you know how far he's come with you. I brought him as far as I could, after she died, but he was a stubborn cat's bastard and dug in his feet."

Death's jaws closed with a chomp on his shadowy prey. "He would have decided to come back on his own eventually, I'm sure," Silver said. "You remember the story of how Death refused to collect voices as the Lady needed him to, at first?"

Boston pressed his thumb to his forehead. "I do. But I've

heard you've a talent for telling stories. Perhaps some evening, you could tell it for all of us." He blew out a sigh and pushed to his feet. "Come. We should eat before the meeting."

Susan and Silver's cousin joined them when they smelled the food, and the large gathering brought Dare out of bed soon after. "It's getting late. I thought you said we had plenty of time," he said, eyeing Silver as he brushed out hair damp from washing. The white streaks grew more distinct as he untangled them from the rest.

Silver's heart picked up speed as she doled out his food, but she refused to let her worries show in her face. He wouldn't like this, but that was his problem. "You have plenty of time because you're not coming this morning."

Dare sputtered something, but cut himself off. He stood tall and glowered at her instead, not speaking until he had control of himself again. "Why not?"

"Because you told me they get the trivial matters out of the way first. Today will be full of them, and it will only wear you down. I can sit and nod during border disputes without you. My cousin can give me advice on how to stand." She nodded to her cousin and he dipped his head respectfully in return.

Silver looked around and located the young man next. She knew his name, really she did— "Tom. You can guide me through any complicated things of this world I can't see." Better for her status if she used a low-ranked Were like an assistant rather than appearing to lean too heavily on her beta's strength.

Tom bounced to his feet and bowed extravagantly, hair falling into his eyes. As she'd suspected, he radiated delight at getting to participate. Dare growled and Tom subsided, pushing his excitement below the surface.

Dare came up beside her and put a hand on the back of her neck. His hand was shaking again. She'd made the right decision, then. Good. She'd worried about making him feel vulnerable in front of the others to no purpose, but she'd never let him try to sit still and listen to people whine all day when he was like this.

"You shouldn't have to deal with Seattle business on your own, Silver."

"I'll be fine." Silver took his hand away and kissed the inside of his wrist. "We're equal partners, aren't we? Either of us can handle business. Besides." She nodded to Boston. "This way your daughter will notice your absence, and start to get interested."

"Mm." Dare gathered up his food and stalked away to their room. Silver bit her lip. Had that been agreement, or had that been "Fine, once you leave I'll do whatever I want"? She had done that a few times herself.

"Susan." Silver went over to where the woman sat and petted her son's head. Susan looked up at her, and Silver considered her approach. As the woman's alpha she could order her, but that didn't seem right. She crouched to put herself at a more companionable height as she asked the favor. "Can you stay with him? So he doesn't have to be alone. And so he doesn't run out to find his daughter the minute we leave."

Something heavy thudded against a wall back where Dare had holed up. Silver winced. She'd been right.

Susan bounced her knee until Edmond laughed. "How am I supposed to stop him if he decides to leave? He's hardly going to listen to me."

"But he won't hurt you. Block his way so he can't move you without hurting you."

Susan's expression turned dubious, but she examined Silver's, probably to judge her honesty. She nodded at whatever she found there. "All right. I'll try."

Silver pressed fingertips to her temple. What else did she need to do before the meeting? That was the best she could think of to help Dare while she wasn't here. If there were things she should do to anticipate actions from their opponents, she couldn't think of any now.

"Silver," Boston said with a hint of a dry laugh in his tone. "You need to eat something."

Silver laughed in return. After everything else, she should follow her own frequent advice to Dare. She sat, and let her cousin heap food in front of her. She'd done what she could. With luck and the Lady's favor, today would be quiet, giving Dare time to recover. Silver didn't really believe it.

Susan settled on the dusty old couch to nurse Edmond and let him fall asleep against her. Andrew was still back in his room. Unless he knocked an Andrew-shaped hole in the back wall, *Looney Tunes* fashion, he wasn't going anywhere for the moment. She heard him pacing in a pattern of creaking boards as her arm grew tired from holding up her book around Edmond.

After about three-quarters of an hour, he came out and banged around the kitchen at length. He ended up with only a mug of coffee, which he sipped while staring out the kitchen window into the trees behind the cabin. Maybe there were rabbits or something out there to draw a Were's attention.

He finally turned one of the battered kitchen chairs to face her and flopped into it, resting his mug on one knee. "How'd you sleep?" His tone turned the simple question into almost an accusation. Susan stared at him. What was that supposed to mean? What business was it of his, anyway?

When he got her annoyed stare instead of an answer, Andrew sighed. "I'm sorry. Small talk's beyond me at this point, but I can't just sit here in silence. Isn't there something you could ask about? Were . . . baby naming traditions, or whatever the hell you want. Something to keep my mind off what Silver has to be dealing with." He drew in a careful breath. "Please."

"Okay," Susan said. That was fair enough. She cast her mind about, but now that she was looking, the many questions that had occurred to her lately had fled. Murphy's Law. There was only . . . but that hardly seemed polite. Then again, Andrew wanted to be distracted.

She hesitated another second or two, then launched into it. "Well. I was going to ask Silver because—you'll see. And I don't know if it's the kind of thing it's rude to ask." Andrew still looked amused, so she pushed onward before he became annoyed with the delay. "BDSM."

Andrew choked and had to cough a mouthful of coffee out of his lungs. As the spasm faded, Susan realized he was laughing. "I presume you know the definition of the term. What about it?" His lips curved with suppressed amusement.

"Is that what you guys want? You talk, and it's all about dominance and submission everywhere else. I mean, obviously you can do vanilla, but—" Susan held her breath. He wouldn't think she was hitting on him, would he? But if werewolves could smell half the stuff they seemed to be able to, he should know she was overwhelmingly embarrassed.

Andrew slumped back into a more comfortable sprawl and

chanced another drink of coffee. "Forbidden stuff is the most titillating, right? In general. That kind of clear hierarchy, complete control and obedience, that's usually forbidden in most humans' daily lives. You hide it, try to pretend it's not there. Us, it's not hidden. It's not as interesting to play it out in the bedroom too. If anything, healthy relationships have to be more about equality."

"So do couples have to be the same rank?" Susan leaned forward, intent.

Andrew grimaced. "It helps. But it's more—you figure out how you relate to each other, in private, separate from how you relate to the rest of the pack. It's not always the same. That's what Silver was getting at back when she told you to think before you raised your issue with John in front of his pack. Some things need to stay in private."

"So what *are* Were men into?"

Andrew snorted. "What are human men into?"

"Depends on the man," Susan said, because she knew that was the answer he expected. "But. You can make some generalizations. Tits. Blow jobs."

Andrew tipped his cup to her, acknowledging her point. "Chasing, maybe. Not quite like humans usually think of it, though. I don't know about other guys, but I've always hated the 'playing hard to get' thing. That's less about the excitement of the chase, and more about the woman's whims and her playing head games. The real thing is knowing she'll be waiting for you at the end of the chase, she's just making you work for it a little. Gets the blood up, makes you appreciate it. No one appreciates what they don't work hard to gain. But it goes both ways. Men and women."

"I can do that . . ." Susan murmured under her breath, then

mentally cursed when Andrew smiled. Damn them and their hearing. "But what can't I do? What's he missing, not settling down with some nice Were girl?"

Another laugh. "Not *that,* if that's what you're trying to ask. Not really that exciting once you've tried it together in wolf once or twice. And birth control doesn't work."

"I meant like, scents and stuff—" Susan pressed a hand to her cheek. Jesus Christ, she was burning up. She hadn't even thought of that, but now she couldn't get it out of her head.

"They help, I suppose. Reading your lover's reactions. It makes someone who can't smell a little clumsier, but it's not a huge difference."

Something about how he said that— "You've slept with human women?"

Andrew snorted. "I was practically a lone for nearly a decade. What do you think? Even pack Were have a pretty limited pool when they're not traveling. You were perfectly usual until John couldn't keep his mouth shut."

"So what's the usual for when there's a baby?" Susan tightened her grip on her son automatically, then made herself relax. No one was trying to take him away at the moment. "Or does that just not happen?"

"Not that often. Scent helps one avoid certain parts of the cycle, even if it's not perfect." Andrew's expression grew bland. Susan recognized it as the way he usually looked just before he imparted some detail he figured would freak her out. She braced herself accordingly. "Babies die. Less in this day and age, but it used to be easy to switch one in, and take the Were child to be raised properly."

Susan gritted her teeth. After all she'd gone through to get this information, she couldn't freak out when she didn't like a piece of it. "And whose dead child would you guys steal to put in its place? Or did you kill one specially?"

"Better that than having a Were be forced into their first shift in ignorance and fear. And the rest of us hunted thereafter." Andrew's words had the cadence of something repeated, as if from a myth or childhood cautionary tale.

Susan hugged Edmond as tightly as she could. "That's terrible."

"We're predators." Andrew sighed. "And survivors. You think wolves were the only shapeshifters that ever existed, or the only ones that managed to survive?" He rubbed a temple and then smoothed out the white lock there, tone softening. "Humans did things just as terrible in the bad old days of history. With birth control, it's not so much an issue now."

Edmond twisted like he might wake up, so Susan relaxed her clutch. "I'm sure you know why I was asking, anyway. He hasn't been interested lately, and if there's something I can do . . ."

"John," Andrew said, and took a generous swig of coffee, "has his muzzle planted as deep in his own ass as it will go. If I were you, I wouldn't waste any effort on trying to figure out what will pull him out of it."

"That's *not* helpful," Susan snapped, unconsciously channeling the way Silver had sounded earlier. To her surprise Andrew bowed his head in something like apology.

"But the effort's yours to waste. All right." Andrew stared meditatively into middle distance. "It might come with time. Silver and I have lived in such atypical Were social situations, it's a little easier to accept one more strangeness. John's too traditional for his own good, but he did tell you in the first place. He's getting there." He sipped his coffee again. "Or you could follow Benjamin's basic advice. Rile him up, avoid him, and see if he comes searching." He shrugged. "I really have no idea. It will come as no surprise when I say we're not exactly close."

Susan nodded. "Thank you anyway." He'd given her something to think about, at least, and maybe she'd done some good distracting him too. He no longer balanced on the chair as if he would explode back up into pacing at any moment. She exhaled in a low laugh. "So what about Were naming traditions?"

26

Dare was lucky to avoid sitting through this, Silver decided after the second item of Convocation business. Couldn't Western alphas deal with questions of territory on their own? Silver knew that while they could and did, the Convocation provided a more permanent settlement, rather than forever skirmishing and guarding the line. But she'd have thought the alphas would bring a proposed line to the Convocation and ask them to ratify it, not demand they decide the line's location.

Two alphas wrangled now, reciting long lists of dates when this part of the territory had been won or lost, or the line passed through a location the other claimed it had never touched before. Even Death seemed bored, lying on his side at full stretch, eyes half lidded. Most wild selves looked that way, whatever their tame selves' apparent attention.

The leader of the foreigners showed patience in both his

selves, though Dare's brother-in-law was the worst of all at hiding his boredom. Silver supposed she couldn't blame him. Territory wrangling could be of no interest to them; they had only been invited because it allowed everyone to keep an eye on them.

Dare's daughter's wild self paced. She kept staring at Silver, probably looking for her father. Silver ignored her pointedly. That was what they wanted, her interest piqued.

Then it came time to stand for the territory issue. Silver didn't know who had the right in the argument, but she did know who would. She looked at her cousin as each alpha in turn called out, "Under the Lady's light, who stands with me?" He shook his head on the first, nodded on the second, and Silver stood with three-quarters of the others.

Roanoke remained sitting, which Dare had explained was to be expected. When he stood, all his sub-alphas stood with him, which was too much power to be exercised lightly. With him sitting, the sub-alphas could stand or sit as they liked. Roanoke flashed a smirk as everyone returned to their seats, which was not expected.

"Roanoke has business," he said, and stood. Ears of wild selves across the room snapped to him. When they were readying for the Convocation, Dare had told her that Roanoke didn't bother bringing up trivial territory questions at the Convocation. They settled such things internally. "On behalf of another who can no longer speak for himself."

Silver concentrated on drawing in her next breath to keep her heart from racing out of control. He could only be talking about the former Sacramento, but by tradition, that shouldn't be happening today. Dare had said that originally, and her cousin and Boston had agreed this morning. Dare was supposed to be here for this part. She had confidence in her ability to get people to listen to her simple orders, but she knew this needed more than that. Dare would need to make his arguments with a singer's voice: the right pitch, the right sequence, to the right people, in the right order. Lady, she wasn't supposed to be defending Susan alone.

Tom hadn't gotten it, Silver could see that as she reached to dig her fingers into his wrist. "Get Dare and Susan," she said, low, as Roanoke drew himself up to declaim the rest of his little ploy.

"The former Sacramento was murdered. And not just murdered, but murdered by a human who not only lives, but is here among us, gathering more secrets with each passing moment. We must deal with her immediately, before she puts us in additional danger."

Tom had been moving slowly, perhaps from confusion at his orders, but he ran then. That left only Silver and her cousin. He put a steadying hand on the back of her shoulder. Silver considered knocking it away to avoid any appearance of weakness. But the touch helped, and besides, wouldn't reacting draw more attention than ignoring it?

"The accused deserves a chance to hear and respond to what is said before anyone stands in judgment. We will wait for her, Roanoke." Silver held her voice steady. Confident.

Roanoke opened his mouth, perhaps to dismiss her, but on seeing the nods of the other alphas, he frowned and sat himself. "For a few minutes," he allowed. He gestured his beta to collect food for him. The others seemed to take this as a general signal, and everyone pushed up to swarm around the food. Silver stayed where she was, the better to maintain the illusion of confidence. Dare would be here very soon. Wouldn't he? She looked at Death, trying to see an answer in his expression.

Death watched all of them, tongue lolling out in a silent laugh. "*Now* things get interesting."

Tom was in a terrible hurry, but Susan still made him wait while she loaded up Edmond's things. It wasn't like she could dump him at the nursery without any supplies.

Tom slammed into Andrew and Silver's bedroom and back out again. "Where's Dare?" he demanded, like she was hiding him for some nefarious purpose of her own.

"Out for a walk." Susan held up a forestalling hand and whatever Tom had been about to say was actually forestalled. This acting dominant thing really worked. Who'd have thought? "And I know Silver said to keep him here, but he seemed pretty damn serious, and he swore on both the Lady and Death he wasn't going to find his daughter or go anywhere near the meeting."

"On Death?" Tom looked confused, but he shook it off like a shaggy dog shaking off water. "It doesn't matter. You go to the Convocation, I'll track him." He took her wrist and almost yanked her off her feet, werewolf strength badly leashed. Outside, he took off into the trees. "Tell Silver I'll bring him back as fast as I can!" he called over his shoulder.

On the way to the nursery, Susan jogged as much as she could while carrying a baby and a full diaper bag. She dragged fingers through her disarranged hair as she left and ran for the hall, panting with the exercise at this altitude. They'd said her case wouldn't come up until tomorrow. Had it been moved forward? She hadn't put on makeup this morning, and the suit she'd brought was still in her suitcase. If Tom had told her what this was about, maybe she could have done something to make herself more presentable, dammit. She already had a red sunburned mask like a dumb tourist from yesterday. It stung in the current sunlight and wind.

This time, she went to the front of the hall. The door stood open, letting in a breeze, so she pushed right through rather than let anyone see her hesitating on the threshold.

She immediately regretted not taking the time to gather herself. It was one thing to look down at the room full of powerful people, but it was quite another to face it, knowing these people would be deciding her fate. Utilitarian banquet tables, scarred without their camouflaging tablecloths, were placed to form four sides of a very large square. There was no head or foot, just people along every side, with a small gap left to enter the center. Was that where she would have to stand?

People stared at her, talking inside their little groupings in murmurs. Susan crossed her arms and tried to apply what Tom had told her when looking down at them. Alpha, beta, and mate. Which was which? Scattered plates rested by elbows, many empty, though some held pastries that matched the selection on two sideboards along both long walls of the hall.

She found Silver near the center of one of the square's sides and hurried over to her and John. She didn't care if it embarrassed John, she seized his hand and held it as tightly as she could. He didn't try to stop her.

"Where's Dare?" Silver hissed. Outwardly, she looked calm, but her voice sounded like Susan felt.

"He went for a walk, I had no idea—" Susan swallowed to cut off her panicked babble. "Tom's tracking him right now."

John added his other hand on top of hers. "It will take some time for them to present their version of the story. Dare should be back in plenty of time for our turn to tell ours."

Susan nodded jerkily and sifted through her memories with shaking metaphorical fingers. She had lines memorized. She could hang on to that. They'd gone over what questions would probably be asked several times. She could do this. She took a deep breath. She could do this.

John moved a hand to her back, gave a nudge toward the empty center of the tables' square. Susan felt like every muscle in her body was shaking with nervousness, but she made it around to the gap and through without tripping.

"I stand to listen to what—" Susan turned to shoot John a panicked look. Who? Who was the one who'd actually made the accusation? When planning, they hadn't known for sure. *Roanoke,* John mouthed, or at least that's what it looked like. "Roanoke's business with me may be." No one gasped or whispered rude remarks, so that must have been the right answer. One obstacle down, who knew how many left to go.

"You murdered Sacramento," Roanoke said with a small sneer. She assumed it was Roanoke, since he was the one speaking and he had the muscle-bound football player look Dare had described to her. She turned to face him at his seat, but he entered the center of the square with her and lounged with his ass against the edge of a table.

"In defense of my pack." That did bring gasps. Susan closed her eyes for a moment to keep from flinching. She could feel the press of everyone's stares from every direction. How could anyone bear being in the center like this? Lines. She needed to keep to her lines.

"You can't have a pack, human. In fact, you shouldn't even be alive now, knowing about us." Roanoke prowled around the inside of the square, ending in front of Silver and John. Blocking them, Susan realized after a moment. Dammit, the man was playing with them! A cheap trick, but she could feel panic rising even so, now that she couldn't catch John's or Silver's eyes.

"The rules about humans exist for a reason," Roanoke said. "Can you imagine what danger we would be in, if they knew about us? They'd kill us, cage us, study us."

"But Sacramento was the one who—" Susan tried to break in with the next line before Roanoke warmed too much to his theme, but he continued right over top of her. Susan clenched her hands so she wouldn't break down and start screaming. If she let him bully her into that, she was the one who looked weak and emotional.

"Think of all those she might tell these secrets to, now she has them. And all those they might tell in turn."

The man had a powerful voice. Susan fought a rising tide of helplessness as Roanoke grandstanded on about the danger of humans. No. She hadn't been helpless when Sacramento had Silver in his hands. She wasn't helpless now.

"Sacramento was the one who—" Even shouting it didn't help. Susan gave up trying to talk through him. If she couldn't sound confident, she would have to look confident. Silver would think of something, and if not, Dare would be here soon. She concentrated on believing in that.

27

Silver listened to Roanoke's pretty speech and imagined having a wild self to slam his to the ground and hold her teeth in its neck until it whined in surrender.

Tom burst in and skidded to a stop next to her. "I found his trail, but it twists and turns so much, I could waste all day following it to him when he was just over the hill in the other direction, I didn't know what to do—" He paused long enough to take in Roanoke's rhetoric and swallowed convulsively. "Silver, I'm sorry."

"Just you now," Death said in her brother's voice. Just her now. Silver put her hand on Tom's shoulder to let him know she wasn't angry, but could spare no more attention. All right, just her. In a contest of shouting, there was no way she could best Roanoke. Some might say that was when you should try even harder, but Silver knew better than that.

That was when you *changed the rules*.

First, she removed her bad arm from the sling and tossed the sling aside. It ached sharply even with that small movement, but she'd need it in a moment. Roanoke was blocking the other alphas' view of her, so she climbed up behind him on the table. She stood tall, feet planted, her head now far above his.

She saw she had the others' attention. Silence splashed down with the suddenness of a flash flood, but for Roanoke's continuing irritating whine. She saw in the brace of his back muscles he knew she was there, but he didn't turn. Perhaps he was trying to show how little he considered her a threat. He hadn't realized she'd changed the rules yet, the fool.

Silver didn't hesitate as she pulled out her silver metal chain, a replacement for the one Sacramento's underling had destroyed. She'd worried before, but now it was time to run and pick up momentum and not stop for anything until you'd run right up and over the obstacle in front of you. This would work or it wouldn't, she had no time for worry.

She tangled the chain's end in her fingers on her bad side. She could curl them enough to keep it there and that was all she needed. Even now, she could see the others didn't understand. She always stank of silver metal, part of her essential scent. They didn't yet realize that this piece of silver was separate from that.

She looped the chain up and over Roanoke's head to rest around his neck like a real necklace. She kept it low, touching only fabric. For now. She rested a hand on either shoulder, so he knew the moment she pulled her hands back, the chain would be tight around his throat. Then, finally then, he stopped talking, shock at the smell of silver stilling him for a breath.

Then he lunged against the chain, clearly thinking to snap it too quickly to cause much pain. Silver knew better than that. She'd seen it tried. Roanoke should not have underestimated the amount of pain silver ground into one's skin could cause. He fell back, sobbing with the agony of the line now seared across his throat. Silver shook her good hand to settle the chain onto fabric again. For now. This time, Roanoke remained still.

Whispers chased each other around the room. Several alphas had half-stood while Silver wasn't paying attention, perhaps meaning to lunge at her and stop her. "Under the Lady's light, I have a story to tell you all," Silver said. The alphas slowly returned to their seats when she made no more threatening moves, fragile stalemate tightening around them all.

Silver closed her eyes. Worse than the agony she'd awakened in her shoulder already, this was going to hurt. But even if the memories left her flayed and bleeding, this was how it had to be. To protect Susan.

"There once was a small pack, stubborn and independent. A crippled Were came to their den one day and begged for shelter. Compassionate, they invited him in. He charmed them all with his politeness and gallantry. He stank of silver from old injuries, and there was something strange in him, but they dismissed it. Aren't we all a little strange, they said."

"What does this have to do with—" Roanoke blustered with his words though he didn't try to move this time. Silver tightened her fingers to just kiss his skin with the metal. He fell silent.

"Then, one night when everyone was in the den, he picked up one of the cubs to play with her and suddenly he had a silver knife at her throat. And he said that no one need be hurt, if they would sit quietly. He only wanted to talk to them, he said. And then the cubs would be safe. So they sat, and he bound them with silver.

"But he'd lied, because there is no honor in one like that. So he killed the cubs one by one with his silver knife in front of us—of them—" Silver's voice failed her, but her eyes found Death. Death sat still and tall, and she found strength in him, ignored the strangled gasps among the alphas. Seeing their horror would make it horrific all over again.

"He killed them because they were too young to receive his mercy, he said. It was mercy he offered the rest of them, he said. Pure and cleansed of their wild selves. So he poured the liquid fire into their blood to clean it, only it burned them all away too." *But for one,* her lips said, but she didn't give it voice. That wasn't the point of this story today.

"He said it was for mercy, but in his eyes, I saw a light. A light of joy. The pain of others was joy to him, the purest joy this world had to offer. He said it was for mercy, but oh, he liked it."

Silver paused. Her hands were starting to shake. Quickly, quickly, before the memories made her bleed out. "I've seen that light again. The former Sacramento had that light. It was a flicker compared to the flames of the one who tortured each of my former pack, but may Death cast into the void the voice of anyone who says I do not know that light when I see it. Does anyone say I do not know it?"

Everyone was too frozen to answer at first, but Boston bowed his head to her. Then Portland and Sacramento followed suit. Here and there, Silver saw someone press a thumb to their forehead, invoking the Lady.

"There is no snuffing out that light while the one who has it still lives." Silver made her voice ring. "Dare and I killed the one who tortured my former pack and Susan killed the one who tortured my current one, and may the Lady bathe me in Her light, I would do it again, and she would do it again. She protected all Were with that action, in her pack or out of it, and so is more true alpha than half of those sitting here. She should go free."

Sacramento's beta—or mate—shoved to her feet. "She is still a human!" The woman's voice was shrill, but it carried in the silence. "It doesn't matter what she *did*; because of what she *knows*, she must be executed to keep our secrets." She tore the "executed" from the air like a chunk from a deer's throat. Perhaps, seeing that her case was failing, she thought that any death would serve her wish for revenge.

"You think—" Susan forged her fear and desperation into action, as Silver had seen her do once before with a weapon in her hands. She spread her hands wide, taking up the center of the room, jerking attention to her rather than wavering under its pressure. "You think if I would *kill*, to save a *single* Were, that I would speak a word to another human that would harm all of you and my *son*?"

Susan didn't have Silver's skill with a story, but Silver realized her single sentence had the same effect as her weapon. One precisely aimed thought to knock everyone down.

A breath, another, and the whispers began again. But Silver didn't want people to talk themselves out of it, so she hurried to speak. "Susan is pack of my pack, bound with ties of family, and friendship, and love, the same as any of us here. That is why she fought to protect them. That is why she would never betray them with a careless word."

Silver would have liked to sweep her hand across the crowd, but she tilted her chin up instead. "Now, under the Lady's light, I say: who stands with us?"

Silver couldn't keep the shaking down as she waited. She

prayed to the Lady. Please, for Susan, let them stand. For what Susan had done for all of them, she did not deserve to be punished; she deserved a reward.

This time Sacramento began it, though Dare's other friends stood only a split second later. Madrid sat expressionless, only sign of his thoughts his crushing grip on Dare's brother-in-law's wrist. Madrid probably intended that pain to wash out the shock on the other man's face. Other North Americans followed Sacramento, more and more as each looked around at those who had stood before, until the last stood with frowns at how they had been shamed by the majority. Silver didn't care. Her knees tried to collapse, so great was her relief. But she was not quite done yet. There was Dare's challenge yet to think of.

Or was it just his anymore? After dealing with the former Sacramento, she'd let her fear of leadership go, but something in her sang at the thought of it now. She'd helped Susan to protect herself because she'd needed protecting, and it felt so *right*. Like this was what she'd been made for. And perhaps the Lady had made her that way.

"Seattle has business," Silver said. She braced her weight against Roanoke's back and ground her thumb against his burn when he seemed likely to try to take advantage of her weakness. The unexpectedness of a wound that could still pain him, however he might know intellectually that silver burns healed slowly, bought her a little more time.

"When the one who tortured me and my former pack was abroad, searching for me and his next victims, this coward called his enforcer home to protect the alpha, and the alpha alone. Is that not correct?" She found the beta's eyes, and his fierce triumph gave her the strength to stand straight again.

The beta stood. "That's correct. And not only that, when Dare broke with Roanoke rather than follow such a fucking stupid order, he kept all of us too close to the house." The beta clenched his hands, anger vibrating in every syllable. "That madman took Ginnie, because we didn't have enough warning. If we'd been in a proper guard pattern, we'd have smelled him from a mile away, but we were so close, he darted in and grabbed her before we could get to him."

Silver spared the time to send him a thin smile of thanks. "We will challenge for Roanoke at a time of your choosing." She jerked the chain and Roanoke snarled. It was a full, rolling noise, directed not only at her but undoubtedly at his beta as well.

"'We'? I'd be happy to beat the delusions of grandeur out of you, crazy pussy." Roanoke clenched his hands. As if that would scare her after what she'd seen, memories dragged bloody to the surface of her mind.

"Division of labor." A hysterical laugh bubbled up in Silver. "He's brawn, I'm beauty, and sometimes I let him share brains with me." Several of the others laughed, a punchy note to their tones as well. "Dare will meet you in the challenge fight at the time of your choosing. Under the Lady's light, does any dispute it?"

No one did. Silver let the chain fall free of her bad hand, gathered it into her good, and turned from Roanoke. She jumped down and the impact jarred her shoulder so shadows swallowed her vision. She hardly knew if she was still standing and which way was up or down until she felt Tom's hand under her arm, holding her up.

"Seattle! Ma'am. Please, wait." Roanoke's beta loped to her. Silver made Tom stop them both by moving her grip to his arm and squeezing. The beta went to his knees before her. "I no longer wish Roanoke as my alpha."

"I'll bet he doesn't. Not with the punishment he'll get for stepping out of line like that." Death used the former Sacramento's voice, heavy with the weight of all the punishments he'd probably inflicted in his lifetime.

Silver worried she'd fall if she took her hand from Tom's arm, but she couldn't ignore the beta. He was in this situation because he'd helped her, and helped Dare. She gritted her teeth, mentally told the shadows Death would rip them to shreds if they didn't behave, and put her hand on the beta's head. If he felt her weight behind it, how she needed the touch for balance, he said nothing. "Seattle welcomes you. My beta will tell you anything else you need to know." She nodded to her cousin, because she'd smelled his sudden tension, presumably fearing his status might be stolen.

Enough. Silver didn't want to deal with anyone else's temper, or soothe anyone else's misplaced fear. She wanted to get out of here, and curl up deep somewhere until the shadows could fade from her. She left the Convocation, leaning on Tom's strength, with her Were behind her. Silence lingered in their wake.

28

Andrew found Tom's scent on his backtrail as he returned to the cabins. Tom was supposed to be helping Silver. Why was he chasing after Andrew? Had something happened? Andrew took the rest of the path back to their cabin at a run.

Silver slammed out of the door as he arrived. The fabric of her shirt was bunched under her sling like it had been put back on in a hurry. "There you are," she snapped. Her hand was out like it rested on Death's head, which worried Andrew more than the anger in her voice. She talked to Death in public sometimes, but she never touched him. "I've arranged your challenge." She seemed to choose her path specifically to have to shove him out of her way. "Death and I are going for a walk," she shouted back over her shoulder.

Andrew stood half-turned, staring after her. What had happened? He had to lock his muscles to keep from running after her. She didn't take off often, but when Silver wanted to be alone, she wanted to be completely alone.

Tom hit the door a moment later and pounded down the path after her. Andrew caught him on the way past and got dragged along for a few stumbling steps. "No," he said, keeping the word as controlled as he needed to be himself. Venting his frustration with not knowing what was going on would only delay him finding out.

Tom stared at him. "But she's—"

"If anyone goes after her, it'll be me in an hour or so, if she hasn't come back by then. You are going to stay and tell me what in the Lady's name is going *on.*" The volume of Andrew's voice increased toward the end despite his best efforts.

Steps crunched on the gravel and they both turned to see Benjamin approaching at a jog. Tom gave a small sigh of relief and Andrew remembered to let go. "Rory suggested lunch early. So he can lick his wounds in private, presumably," Benjamin said. In contrast to Silver, he seemed triumphant.

Benjamin clapped Andrew on his shoulders. "She was amazing, Dare. You'd have sworn it was the Lady herself who stood there, putting Rory in his place." He pressed a thumb to his forehead.

Tom made the same gesture, more jerky with excitement. "She stood up behind him, right on the table, and with her white hair, and she was even using her bad hand, and—"

Andrew cut Tom off with a gesture, a suspicion forming. "Did anyone mention the Lady directly to Silver?"

Tom blinked at him. "It came up on the walk back. Why?"

Andrew twisted to look in the direction she'd gone again. Oh, Silver. Which had upset her more? The argument with Rory, or being compared to the Lady? Personally, he would have been

pissed to have whatever he'd accomplished attributed to someone who didn't even exist, but that was him. Silver believed, but
she'd always said that being unable to shift made her feel cut off
from the Lady. How must it feel to have people tell her that the
Lady's hand was on her when she could feel it no more than before? But he had no idea what she'd felt. Maybe he was wrong,
and she'd had a religious experience like everyone else.

Andrew forced himself back to trudging to the cabin. Even
now that he had more insight into what had happened, following
her still wouldn't help. "She says she feels barred from the Lady.
Since she lost her ability to shift, she can't feel Her presence."

Benjamin's expression tightened with worry immediately. Tom
looked confused. Benjamin squeezed Tom's shoulder. "Don't
mention it to her again," he said, in a tone of command.

Andrew opened the cabin door for them, grateful that Benjamin seemed ready to help him keep further mentions from Silver's ears. "So what happened, religious implications aside?"

Benjamin started the story once they were inside. The cabin
was cramped with everyone, including Laurence, crowded inside, but no one chimed in. Andrew started to sit on the couch,
but hearing about Rory's trick made him want to go stomp on
the man's neck so badly he ended up pacing. Benjamin didn't
seem surprised by it and kept on with the story.

Andrew ended up on the couch eventually, head in his hands.
Silver shouldn't have had to go through telling that story, not for
him. No wonder she'd wanted time alone.

"Here." Susan lowered a cheese and salami tray into his range
of vision and smiled weakly at him when he looked up. "I liber-
ated this from the kitchen on the way out, since our timing is
once more terrible for getting food."

Andrew accepted the tray and slid it onto the nearest end table. He wasn't hungry, but accepting the offer was the point, he supposed. Susan reeked of an impulse to help with nowhere to channel it. Andrew picked up a variegated yellow and white cheese slice and rolled it into a tube, then ate it slowly. There wasn't much he could do to help Silver at the moment, either.

Susan picked up a piece of salami, sat down on the couch, and started peeling off the outer edge. "Tell her thank you from me, would you?" she said all at once. "I could see how hard that was for her. I'd heard bits of the story, but never the whole thing. I can't even imagine—" She shook her head jerkily.

Andrew petted Susan's hair and ended with his hand on the back of her neck, as he would do to soothe a Were. He might once have suppressed the impulse as too canine, but Susan was honorary Were at this point. "I'll tell her," he promised.

Susan nodded under his hand and ate her salami skin. He could feel the moment when her muscles tensed and she must have realized consciously what her unconscious instincts allowed her to accept. She pulled away and went to stand by John. He hesitated before setting his hand in a more human gesture on the small of her back.

In the silence of no one having any idea what to say, Laurence moved away from the wall he'd been propping up. He knelt before the couch. "Sir . . ."

Andrew scrubbed his face with both hands. "Get up," he said. All this respect when he'd nearly screwed everything up and they weren't out of the woods yet. "I agree with Silver's judgment. What, you expect us to stake you out for the hunters after you supported us?"

He pushed to his feet and gave Laurence a hand up. "You'll

have to stay out of the Convocation, though. You screw up our numbers, and I'm sure Rory would jump on that."

Laurence dipped his head more deeply than necessary to acknowledge the order. "I'm single, though," he said with a light laugh. "Could be I'm here for the mixer."

Andrew snorted and smacked Laurence's shoulder. "Got a sudden hankering to hook up with a nineteen-year-old? I think Philadelphia brought one who must be at least twenty-two."

With Laurence settled for the moment, Andrew looked around at everyone else. Had he missed any other reassurances he should make as an alpha? He wished Silver was here to remind him. He couldn't leave Rory to stew for too long, or he'd risk losing the advantage that Silver had given them.

"I'll go talk to Rory and then find Silver," he said. If only he could have switched that order.

29

Silver couldn't walk away from her memories, but at least among the trees no one was talking to her about them. A raven passed at a distance, a black shape about his own business. Her bad arm started to hurt again just from the movement of each step, so she finally stopped and found a place to sit. The flat rock tipped as she settled her weight on it.

"That was rude of you." Death declined to lie down, remaining on his haunches, and Silver wondered if it was because he didn't want to get dirt on his fur. It would remove some of his mystique, to have the depthless black given definition by a powdering of brown.

"Dare knows I didn't mean anything by it." Silver flexed her good hand. She'd make it up to him later even if he didn't, but that was one of the many things she loved about Dare. He didn't chase when she didn't invite him to, as so many others did out of worry. At that moment, he'd been handy to be angry at, with their real opponents out of reach. But now as she calmed down, it became easier to remember that even without Dare's—their—challenge, without Dare's daughter, she would still have chosen to save Susan's life.

Even sitting, the pain in Silver's arm hadn't lessened. The others had bound it up again so it couldn't move, but it felt like they'd done it too quickly. She released her bad hand and carefully set it on her knee. She twitched her fingers and grinned, showing her teeth. Maybe her arm didn't work completely, but it had worked enough to get Roanoke where she wanted him.

And they'd said she looked like the Lady. She wondered if they were right. It had been so long since she'd felt the Lady's light in her core that the memory was crumbling into dust. Not enough of the feeling remained for Silver to form it into a woman in her mind. White-haired, certainly. But what more than that?

Of course, there was one here who knew exactly what the Lady looked like. Silver glanced at Death. He stared into the distance, more distance than Silver could ever comprehend. "Did I?"

"Did you what?"

Silver stared at Death outright now. He knew perfectly well what she meant. He never stalled that way, never cared enough to be bothered by a subject enough to avoid it. He was Death, after all. "Did I look at all like the Lady?"

Death bit her.

He sank his teeth into her bad hand and then loped off into the rocks, leaving her alone with the sharp pain. Tears beaded up in her eyes from the shock more than anything. When she examined the mark, she found he hadn't even drawn blood. It had been a nip for a disobedient cub.

But he'd bitten her! How could he? Then again, didn't Silver bear a great part of the blame, for pushing the question? Silver swallowed against a lump of guilt. He'd be back. She hoped. She'd apologize then. She hadn't meant to hurt him, barred from the Lady's presence same as her; she'd just wanted the answer so badly. If she held some part of the Lady in her own appearance, at least Silver could hold that close, with no other connection to Her.

And she had an answer, she supposed. She just wasn't quite sure what it was. Maybe the answer was that she didn't want the answer, something Silver was suddenly quite willing to accept.

Andrew felt like a coiled spring as he waited on the doorstep of Roanoke's cabin, sound of his knock fading. What if Rory had Madrid with him? What if Felicia was there? He could smell only ephemeral traces of the Spanish Were, but the wind was going the wrong way and they hadn't left any windows open. He watched out of the corner of his eye as the number of Were making their way back to cabins or eating outside the main building doubled. Everyone loved a show.

After all his anticipation, it was Ginnie who opened the door, and he could smell only Rory and his wife inside. The girl had shot up another inch since the last time he'd seen her. She gave him a wide grin that still seemed like it should be missing a few teeth, though that had been years ago. She must be nearly ten by now.

Her grin dimmed as she seemed to remember something.

"My dad's pretty mad at your mate," she said, confidentially. Andrew almost chuckled, punchy. An understatement, he suspected. "I wasn't there, I was here with Mom, but he said she used silver on him. Isn't that supposed to be evil?"

Andrew considered mentioning the irony of the fact that Rory had allied himself with foreigners who considered the use of silver on other Were to be quite necessary. Rory was undoubtedly listening. But Ginnie deserved better than to be a conduit between two fighting alphas. "She has to, sometimes. Since she's weak in other ways, she uses it to make sure people don't take advantage of her."

Ginnie drew herself up. "Good!" she declared. This time, Andrew allowed himself the chuckle. Rory was raising himself a little alpha. But of course the trouble had never been that he didn't do everything possible for his daughter, it was that he couldn't balance her with the rest of the Roanoke sub-packs. And that he got mean when he felt insecure in his power.

"I do need to talk to your father," Andrew said, pushing the moment of humor away. Ginnie stuck the tip of her tongue out at him and scampered back into the farthest bedroom, shutting the door behind her. Raised right in another way: she knew when to stay out of pack business.

Conscious of his audience, Andrew chose to stay in the doorway. Better to use the fact that this was occurring in front of everyone and their omega to his advantage. Rory would have a much harder time wiggling out of it if there were witnesses. "We have a challenge to settle, Roanoke."

Rory stepped from the other bedroom into the living room, a clone in both floor plan and furniture to Andrew's cabin, and stopped a few feet back from the threshold. He was hulking enough in the first place; he didn't need to push any closer to be physically intimidating. His lip lifted in a silent snarl. "How about now? Or are you too afraid you won't be able to shift fast enough in the new?"

"You disrupted the Convocation enough already by inviting Europeans to interfere in North American business." Andrew raised his voice a little, playing to the crowd. He'd be fighting Rory physically, but the more psychological support he could rob him of, the better. "I'm not going to break the rules even more by shifting and then fighting on Convocation ground. We can wait two days until it's ended, and then we'll fight."

Rory's gaze moved out past Andrew, probably judging reactions. "In two days," he said, voice just as ringing. He lifted his hand like he was thinking of offering to shake on it, but he must have read Andrew's expression because he dropped it again. Andrew didn't trust his control if he let Rory get in punching distance, never mind touched him.

"In the meantime, perhaps we could talk privately." Rory lowered his voice. He gestured for Andrew to precede him and stepped out of the cabin. Apparently he meant off in the woods. Andrew supposed that made sense, though they'd have a fair hike to make sure no one could hear.

Andrew drew a deep breath to try to read Rory's intentions. His muscles were all wound as tight as Andrew's felt and his scent was mostly composed of that sense of keeping a tight hold. On what, was the question. This stank, metaphorically. What could Rory possibly have to say to him? He knew Rory—he'd worked for the man for nearly a decade—and if there was one thing Rory trusted, it was his own physical strength. Fear of losing the challenge wouldn't be making him want to talk Andrew out of it. And what else would he possibly want to talk about?

Andrew backed up onto the path, and made no move to follow Rory. "Do I look stupid? Private with me and you and my in-laws, all ready to get a few licks in, three to one." That wasn't Raul's style, but it was Arturo's. Andrew's brother-in-law had trouble dealing sometimes, and took out his frustration by hitting whoever had upset him. Andrew suspected he'd fit that definition for the rest of his life now.

"Pussy," Rory snarled, then his face blanked as he perhaps realized that he'd just verified Andrew's guess by not being surprised by the idea.

"That's what I thought. Next time you want to talk, let me know and I'll bring along my beta— Oh, I forgot. And your beta too." Andrew threw Rory a sneer to drive home the last jab.

To keep the last word, he left Rory and strode for the main hall. His stomach was protesting loudly that it was lunchtime and a cheese slice wasn't cutting it. He didn't really feel like dealing with other alphas in the main room, but he could steal something from the kitchen. The only people back there should be a couple of the teens, heating and carrying out the food the catering people had dropped off. At most, two or three people would be in the kitchen, depending on whether a mate or beta was directing. He'd have to hope they'd belonged to a sympathetic pack.

After all the anticipation, a dark-skinned young woman of about twenty was the only one there. She had the look of Benjamin, and Andrew suspected she was one of his great-grandchildren, along as a single. She nodded at him and nudged a half-full foil pan of barbecued ribs along the counter. She picked up the full one next to it and disappeared through the double doors into the main room.

Andrew tucked into the ribs, getting sauce all over his hands. He was too hungry for neatness. A door opened, not the double doors he was watching, but the kitchen's back door behind him. He turned quickly.

Felicia stood in the doorway, squinting like she was waiting for her eyes to adjust. Andrew would have thought it would be easier this time. He'd seen her once already, after all. But the feeling of a physical blow was the same, no softer. She stood so confidently. He'd wondered what kind of young woman she'd grow into, and now he knew some of it, at least.

She seemed as frozen as him for that moment. It stretched even after her eyes had to be adjusted. So many things fought for Andrew's lips, "I love you" foremost among them. But with so many, they choked each other off. Benjamin had told him not to say anything. That thought fought its way to the surface. Andrew had to avoid anything of substance for now.

"Hello," he said. He licked the worst of the sauce from a couple fingers as he crossed to the gigantic sink and washed the rest off. Felicia didn't say anything, and it nearly killed him to have to turn his back and not be able to see her face after he spoke.

"I thought—" Felicia stopped. Andrew wondered if Benjamin was right, and she wanted to get more reaction from him before she continued. When he couldn't take it anymore he turned around anyway.

"Maybe we could talk." She looked at her hands.

"Okay." Andrew clamped down on his surge of hope. He couldn't take this small step as proof everything would be all right, but at least she'd reached out, hadn't she? She smelled suspicious of him, unsure, but at least she was here. "What do you want to talk about?"

"I—" Felicia looked much younger for a moment as confusion crossed her face. Andrew remembered that strange, wobbly stage when teens wavered from emotionally adult to childish and back like a boy's voice breaking. She must not have expected him to agree so easily.

"We could go outside." Less chance of someone coming back into the kitchen, and it would also give Felicia time to find her words. As Andrew approached Felicia to get past her to the door, he imagined grabbing her and pulling her into a crushing hug. He'd pet her hair, and it would be as soft as it was when she was a little girl. And he'd feel her, real and tangible and alive and his daughter. Isabel's daughter. He'd hug her and hug her and everything would be all right.

He didn't touch her, of course. He played the imaginary feeling of holding her tightly every single step, but he didn't touch her. She stared, a child's confusion regaining control of her face as he passed. He made it out into the glare of the sun and felt like he could breathe again despite the light and heat.

"Did your new mate really go through all that?" Felicia didn't speak until Andrew was yards away. The question actually sounded like a question rather than a rhetorical inflection in an ongoing speech, though the "new mate" came out with a disgusted flip. Now Andrew had the space to pay attention, he was impressed by her accent. It was already better than her mother's had been when he'd met her, and Isabel's English had never gotten that idiomatic.

He stopped and forced himself not to turn around. Make her

come to him. He had to remember that's what he was doing. "Yes."

"She's nothing like Mama."

How much of Isabel did Felicia really remember, and how much had she built from what her relatives had told her? And how much of a lie was that? Even concentrating on those thoughts, Andrew felt the flicker of an old guilt, as he'd felt in varying degrees with every woman after Isabel, before Silver. Perhaps even a little with Silver, until he'd talked to a hallucination of Death with Isabel's voice, and banished it. It didn't serve Isabel's memory or her voice, if you believed in that, to offer his utter loneliness like some kind of sacrifice at her altar. "Exactly," he told Felicia, and left it at that.

Felicia took a couple running steps to come even with Andrew. He moved to the side of the path to allow her to walk beside him without running into low pine branches, but still made himself not look at her. It was already bad enough, smelling her changed scent so very close to him. Or maybe it hadn't changed so much as his memory of her scent as a child had faded.

"So what is it they're supposed to have been lying to me about?" she said finally, sullen.

Andrew frowned at the line of a mountain peak at the horizon. "Your mother was dead before we even got there. Our house—the flames were climbing out of the windows. On one side wall you could still see the white paint, but then you turned the corner and the rest was just collapsed, the roof, the second floor, Isabel somewhere under that." Andrew swallowed against the remembered taste of smoke in this throat. "And what could I do with you? I couldn't set you down to cry in the street."

"Me?" Felicia stopped. Andrew kept going. His steps gave

him something to focus on, so he didn't fall apart. After a moment, she ran to catch up. "I was there? I remember something—but Uncle Arturo said I was with him. Everyone talked about it so much after, I must be remembering that."

Andrew snorted. "Arturo? Your uncle was a terrible babysitter. Extremely determined, but one wail and he'd fall to pieces, convinced he'd never be able to fix it and you'd cry forever."

Felicia laughed. A short, startled sound, but it was still a laugh. It was a beautiful laugh. The next moment her tone was even more sullen as if to make up for it. "There's only your word she was already dead."

"Let Raul get Arturo to repeat his rhetoric. There's no need for you to."

Silence, with a dangerous tinge. Andrew wondered if it meant that Felicia was planning to storm off. But she'd said she wanted to talk, and he'd been ready to hurt his friends for the chance to talk to her, so he needed to take advantage of this opportunity for as long as he had it. "I couldn't leave you crying in the street, and I couldn't leave you in a larger sense, Felicia." He gave her name the proper accent and vowels, as her mother would have, soft and smooth. "If I'd been killed, you would have been alone. Certain people," Andrew had to grit his teeth to keep that polite, "kept me from you later, but in that moment, I chose you over what would have made *me* feel better."

"Big talk, when you turned tail and left me after things went wrong for you in Barcelona. Couldn't manage to contact me again."

Andrew stopped short and turned. He couldn't not look at her any longer. She looked so hurt, it tore his heart and broke his

voice. Normally Andrew would have fought the religious metaphor the moment he noticed it creeping into his thoughts, but
he needed something, anything, to hang on to at the moment.
Whether he believed it or not, that solid part of his upbringing
was a comfort at this moment. He switched to Spanish to try to
evoke the same in her. In the heat of the moment, the forgotten
fluency surged back.

*"I fought, puppy. Fought the former Madrid and the pack
physically to reach you, called every day for weeks, months, once
I'd had to flee, sent you letters—I knew they wouldn't give them
to you at first, but I thought if I could wear them down . . ."* Andrew's throat closed and he couldn't continue. Intellectually, he
knew they'd burned every letter the same as they'd hung up on
every call, but some part of him must have hoped they'd let one
through, because he felt that hope die now. One more lie they'd
told her. Just one more. A part of all the others.

"Ask Arturo," he begged. *"Ask him and smell for his lie. He was
always a terrible liar. Ask him if I ever called, ever wrote."*

Felicia crossed her arms and hugged herself, folding in. *"How
am I supposed to know which of you to believe about any of this?
No one else was there at the time of the fire."* Her lips thinned in
an expression not quite a smile. *"Or is able to remember it, if I
was."*

"I was," Death said in Isabel's voice as he paced on Andrew's
other side. The stark shadows of the trees and rocks seemed almost to yearn for him and his true blackness as he passed. Andrew couldn't tell if Death meant his comment as himself, or if
he was pretending that Isabel spoke through him. Andrew knew
perfectly well she didn't—or wouldn't, if Death was real. Either

way, the last thing he wanted right now was Death distracting him and making him look crazy by staring at nothing.

"*What do I have to gain by lying to you? If I supposedly walked away then, why shouldn't I walk away now?*" Andrew said.

"*I don't know!*" Felicia shouted it to the hills more than to Andrew, hands clenched.

"*You've got her stumbling now, Dare. Finish her. Maybe she'll be too angry to accept you, but at least you'll have been right. Is being right worth it?*"

Andrew opened his mouth to shout at Death to shut up. He closed it with a snap, just in time. Raul would feast for a month on something like that. Dare talks to the air? He'd clap his hands with joy when he found out. Andrew had no doubt that as her alpha, he was practiced at getting everything Felicia knew out of her, whether she intended to share or not.

They started walking again in silence. Andrew had no idea where they were going anymore, except that they hadn't come up against the mountains yet. Still more trees stretched out in front of them. Finally, Felicia drew a deep breath like she'd come to some sort of decision. "Roanoke's planning to go after that human, you know. Take care of the problem simply and efficiently, as soon as possible. I heard him asking Uncle for help."

"What?" Andrew stared at her as he processed the non sequitur. Susan. In danger. He spun and sprinted back toward the cabins as Death laughed. How could he not have thought of it? He'd noticed Rory had been up to something when he'd threatened Andrew directly, but he should have considered others Rory might harm. Would Silver and the others think to keep Susan under watch now that she'd been cleared of the charges? Wouldn't John be sticking close to her generally?

"Wait!" Felicia must have been taken off guard by the strength of his reaction, because it took her several seconds to start running after him. "They're not going to do anything there. They'll take her somewhere. Maybe the place they've been meeting to plan while we've been here."

Andrew kept running, but his steps slowed. If Rory was going to move soon, where should he go? To the cabins, assuming they hadn't grabbed her yet, or to where Felicia suggested, assuming they had? If he went to the cabins, they'd have all the time they needed to kill her before he reached the next place. But if he went to the private spot and they weren't there yet, he could wait. Assuming Felicia was right about where they would go.

And assuming she wasn't leading him into a trap, the same as Rory had tried. That was two people in as many hours who had tried to lead him out into the woods alone. Andrew's stomach twisted nearly to nausea. He didn't want to even think it. If she was telling the truth, how could he refuse his daughter that way, when she was just beginning to reach out? How could he put Susan in that kind of danger? But. How could he ignore the instincts that screamed at him that this timing was too coincidental?

Felicia stopped and turned back to him. "Don't you trust me?" Her voice wavered.

Andrew drew in a deep breath. In the end, it came down to trusting each other. If they didn't, they could never reconcile. She'd reached out; so would he. "Show me where you think they'll take Susan."

Felicia nodded and set off parallel to the line of cabins for a while, running until the dark square lines of the structures through the trees had grown small. They reached a cluster of metal outbuildings surrounded by odds and ends of abandoned equipment. The buildings seemed even more utilitarian in comparison to the old-timey feel of all the wood back in the main ranch compound.

Andrew stopped the moment they were close enough to make out the door of the nearest outbuilding. He was a fool if he charged in without planning first. He lowered his voice to the barest whisper to speak to Felicia, who had followed his lead and slowed. "You said he was asking for help. Who else might be there with him?" He circled, nose to the wind, walking carefully to minimize the sound of his footsteps.

"Uncle. Madrid wasn't going to bother with a human."

It took Andrew a second to remember that Felicia meant Raul. It was so strange thinking of him as the alpha, not just the puppet master behind it all. As he got the right angle for the wind, he found Arturo's scent, but no one else's. Was Rory not here yet? But why would Arturo wait here for someone to arrive with Susan, rather than helping with the kidnapping? The danger would be in Susan breaking free or summoning help before they could silence her. It didn't take two Were to do the actual killing in private.

Something fell around Andrew's neck from behind. Behind. Downwind. Dammit! He hardly had time to see it before it tightened on his throat, but he knew from the feel what it was. A sturdy silver chain, with a silk sleeve to allow it to be held and minimize scarring.

He scrabbled at the chain instinctively, but he couldn't get any purchase. He kicked, jabbed back with his elbow. He felt the blows connect, but they didn't have enough force.

"Thank you, Felicia." Raul's voice came from behind Andrew as his vision grayed out. *"I knew he would listen to you."*

30

Andrew woke with a heart-pounding start, the stench of silver metal in his nose. Where was Silver? She was in danger. Slowly the differences between his current situation and that memory filtered in. He was chained in a seated position surrounded by the stink of silver metal, yes, but the man who'd killed Silver's pack was dead. They'd killed him together. A dead man couldn't capture Andrew again.

His enemies were the ones who'd caught him this time. At least that meant Silver was safer, if not completely safe. But his daughter had betrayed him. Worse than being in his enemies' power, that betrayal pulled Andrew's head under a tide of desperation. It had been a trap. Had the whole conversation been part of it, the reaching out only bait? Bait he couldn't resist, apparently. Dammit. Damn her.

Andrew drew a breath but couldn't seem to get any air. Her

contempt had been one thing. In contrast to this betrayal, it seemed almost neutral. Denying him a place in her life, certainly, but not delivering him to capture and undoubted torture. How much hate must she feel toward him, to countenance that?

He dragged himself from that downward spiral with a force of will and slowly lifted his head to take stock. The scent of silver metal fought with the tang of iron that was more rust than metal. They were inside a metal outbuilding, the one he'd approached with Felicia, Andrew presumed. The whole building was filled with rusty farm equipment, though organized in piles to provide generous walkways.

Raul stood against the bed of a broken-down old pickup, so weathered and dusty that it was impossible to tell the original color under indeterminate tan. His eyes rested on Andrew, lips quirked in amusement. He apparently wanted Andrew to have the chance to assess his situation, because he made no move on seeing him look up.

Arturo scrambled out from under a new ATV and wiped a pocketknife on a rag. Andrew couldn't figure out what he'd been doing, but oil smell seeped slowly into the air. Felicia perched on the ATV's seat, a beam from a window painting floating dust over her hair. She'd managed to hook her heels on the edge of the seat with the rest of her, knees to her chest. Her expression was tight with distress, but Andrew couldn't bring himself to believe it. She'd brought him here. She had to have known what she was bringing him to. Damn her. Damn himself for believing her.

Andrew's wrists were chained behind his back to the axle of some rusty two-wheeled contraption with a curved metal comb along the length of it. When Andrew tried to move to a more comfortable position, several of the teeth poked him in the back. His ankles were chained to the far side of the wheel beside him. He bucked to see how heavy it was. It moved about an inch to the side, so not too heavy, but seated with his legs stretched out, he couldn't move it more than that.

Raul's smile widened fractionally when the contraption jittered with Andrew's efforts. Andrew flexed his wrists, but he already knew what was binding him. More of the silk-covered silver chains. Didn't want the prisoner breaking them, but didn't want to scar him too badly either. They were popular all over Europe.

"If you wanted to talk privately, you could have just asked nicely," Andrew said. He wondered if Raul would bother with the charade of Arturo's translations, but Raul just snorted.

Arturo strode toward him, face darkening, then stopped, blocked by Raul's extended arm. "I wished to discuss a bargain with you." Raul's grammar was as good as Felicia's, but his accent was much thicker. He used it with flair, like a foreign soap opera star.

"Let me go and my mate, beta, and allies don't break every bone in your bodies before they escort you to the airport?" Andrew used the edged humor to drive back the burn of helplessness at being chained up, but Arturo's rolling growl promised later pain.

Arturo stomped to the edge of the room and picked up a worn pile of rope. He snapped a length taut between his hands, and then started coiling it into his hand with sharp, deliberate movements. In a North American, it might have been meaningless tidying, but Andrew knew better. That was exactly how Arturo would have coiled a whip.

"Pledge that you won't attempt to take over Roanoke, or any

other pack, and we'll give Felicia here the choice whether she wants to stay." Raul took a few steps toward Andrew, hands spread. "Can't ask for more than that, no?"

Andrew watched shock flash onto Felicia's face. It appeared so sincere. He wanted to believe that she hadn't been in on that part, but he couldn't allow himself that. His daughter had chosen where she stood.

But even knowing that, Andrew wanted to shout yes. For Felicia, he'd do almost anything. Even knowing all the reasons why Roanoke needed a strong leader, if he thought it would free her from that pack of cats in Spain, he'd swear it off in a heartbeat. But he kept the word locked inside. Felicia had more than proved she'd make that choice exactly the way Madrid wanted.

If he made that pledge, he'd be giving up everything he worked for, and gaining nothing but the certainty that his daughter was no longer his.

"*Madrid . . .*" Felicia slid down from the ATV. "*You never said—*"

Raul silenced her with a jerk of his hand. "*Go. You should get back before they notice all of us are gone at once.*"

Betrayal seeped across her face, and Andrew smiled internally. Good. Let Raul have the fun of dealing with a teen who thought she'd been wronged.

Arturo set his rope down and put his hand on the back of Felicia's neck, comforting. He murmured something in her ear as they walked to the door, too low to catch. Andrew wondered if he was assuring her it was all going according to plan, just as she'd agreed to. He tried to catch one last glimpse of her face, but she didn't look at him as she darted out of the building.

Arturo waited until the door clanged shut and then slammed a savage kick into Andrew's stomach. Andrew folded with it as much as he could, though it still hurt. The metal teeth stabbed into his back again. This was what he'd expected right at the start of the hunt. Had they been holding back in front of his daughter?

Raul seemed to see Andrew's thoughts in his face and smiled. "Do you think she would have felt sympathy for you, if she saw this? I guess you'll never know."

Arturo switched angles and dislocated one of Andrew's knees with the next kick. Andrew locked his jaw so he didn't make a sound. At least with his back against the axle they couldn't discover the weakness there by chance. He clung grimly to that thought as he jerked his leg into a flare of agony so the joint would heal right.

"Well?" Raul asked Andrew. "Do you accept my offer?"

Andrew drew in a deep breath and snarled in contempt, the same as Felicia had on seeing him. "You're shaking under a bush, anticipating I'll take the course *you* would take. I'm no empire-builder, whatever you seem to think. But my daughter has already made her choice. No deal, Raul." He drew the name out, disrespectful and as American as he could make it.

"You always were a fool, Dare." Raul shrugged and turned to the door. "Spend some time with your brother-in-law. Reconsider your position a little."

Andrew clenched and unclenched his hands where they couldn't see. He'd been in the hands of a master torturer before, when the man who killed Silver's pack had captured him. Arturo didn't rate in comparison. He had to keep reminding himself of that. "You forget I have a pack who will soon be tracking me."

"You've also been making a habit of missing Convocation sessions. Why should they look for you yet?"

Andrew kept his face blank with an effort. Raul was correct, but damned if he'd let the man see it. Timing was the key. Maybe they wouldn't notice his absence for a couple hours, but Silver was smart enough to know something was wrong after that. What was a few hours of beating?

Raul drew a cell phone from his pocket. The way he turned his back and stepped a few feet away when Andrew could hear perfectly well made it even more obvious that he wanted to be overheard. *"You're safe to join us now. Bring everyone in."*

He closed the phone with a snap. "Some company, should you get tired of each other. *Have fun.*"

Andrew closed his eyes against a feeling of falling. Of course Raul had brought more of his pack. Why have just one goon to do your dirty work when you could have half a dozen? They must have been on the next flight in after Raul's, carrying Raul's silver weapons and waiting out of scent range until needed. Andrew had no doubt the group would include those in charge of Raul's punishments. A few hours with them would be a whole different beast.

And it was Felicia who had led him here. Maybe she would have felt sympathy, seeing him being hurt, but maybe she so believed in Raul's plans she would have set it aside anyway.

Still, doubt lingered, and with it hope. Maybe that reaching out had been based on some germ of something true. The opportunity to speak with her still seemed almost worth it, Andrew reflected as Arturo slammed a fist into his jaw. Maybe that would change when the others arrived.

31

Silver was surprised by how abandoned she felt when she arrived back at the temporary den and found Dare still wasn't
among the people there. She was the one who had run off in the
first place, after all. She couldn't expect him to sit there, waiting
for her. She checked their bedroom, in case the scents had gotten confused, but his scent was even staler there. He hadn't been
in there since the morning.

She reached for Death's ruff to steady herself with the touch,
but of course he'd run off earlier. Silver clenched her teeth as her
heart started to pound at the empty feeling. Death had business
of his own. He was never with her every second. Silver tossed
the bedding aside in frustration, as if Dare could ever hide underneath.

"You could wait for Dare. Pine a little, maybe. You have the
coloration for pining." Death nosed the tumbled bedding out of

the way so he could stride past to investigate some flicker of a shadow in the corner.

"Shut up." Silver made her tone extra sharp to camouflage her relief. Death was arrogant enough as it was.

She strode away in search of Susan and the baby. She didn't need Death anyway. She'd distract herself so she didn't wallow or pine. Susan didn't know enough about the Lady to look at her sideways for any resemblance.

Silver's cousin caught her halfway to Susan's room. He put out a hand to curve beside her arm, giving the feeling of touch without the reality. "Silver, I hate to ask it—but the lunch break's over, and I can't for the Lady's love find Dare. Someone has to attend the afternoon session for Seattle. It can't just be the beta."

Silver's stomach soured. She hadn't realized quite how much time had passed. That made it even more worrisome that Dare wasn't here. Look at how much trouble they'd had making him put his duties aside this morning. There was no way he'd just forget and wander off now. "Someone needs to track him."

"I'll put Tom on it." Her cousin ushered Silver outside. He sounded like he was just saying it to shut her up, so Silver smacked his shoulder, hard. Tom was too young to be much of a tracker yet. They needed someone experienced.

"I know Dare, and this isn't like him." Either her tone or the smack must have convinced her cousin, because he growled under his breath and stopped trying to herd her to the Convocation.

"Maybe it's not. But you have to admit, you've never seen him halfway to berserk dealing with his daughter before, have you?" Her cousin raised his arm in anticipation of another blow.

Silver did lift her hand, but she let it fall. Was he right? Yes, she'd never before seen Dare act the way he had yesterday, but he'd still been the man she loved. She knew that temper was a part of him, the same as he did. "I'm the one who runs and hides," she said on a weak laugh. "Not him."

"When the session finishes for dinner, I'll look for him myself. What danger can he get into in a couple hours? Roanoke and Madrid will be right there where we can keep an eye on them." Her cousin hesitated, then drew her into a sideways hug, her good shoulder against his chest. "I'm sorry he's dragged you into his shit."

"I'll hit you again," Silver warned him, but on a ragged laugh.

He laughed again, the sound a vibration against her side. "I'm sorry you both got dragged into this by Madrid and Roanoke. Better?"

"Mm," Silver agreed. However much she hated to admit it, her cousin had a point. As long as Roanoke and the others were in sight, she couldn't imagine what danger Dare could be in around here.

Susan woke to Edmond crying. She sat up in semidarkness and her novel slid off her chest to crunch its pages on the floor. Her light-based time sense was off, south of home, but it seemed later than it should be. It had been nearly dinnertime when she put Edmond down and tried to read a little. She'd expected the Were back with food soon.

Susan flicked on the lights and checked her watch as she picked Edmond up. Seven already? Damn, the baby would never sleep tonight! She'd only planned to read and let Edmond nap until the others got back. John had said they usually broke at five, sometimes earlier when an issue was settled without time to finish another. The cabin was silent except for her son. Where were they? She laid Edmond down and changed his diaper with practiced motions as she tried to think what might have kept everyone, that they wouldn't have sent someone back to get her.

The door slammed. "I told you! I told you something was wrong!" Silver's voice filled the whole cabin. It wasn't hard, given the size of the place. Susan winced and Edmond began wailing again. She carried him out to join the others.

Susan had apparently missed John's response while dealing with their son, as when she opened the door to their bedroom, Silver was shouting at him again. "If we'd started earlier, maybe the trail wouldn't have been destroyed. I don't care if you break Convocation rules and shift, we need to find him." Silver swept her hand in a broad gesture, glowering at John. She looked worn and thin. The planes of her face couldn't have gotten sharper since lunchtime, but some combination of her flush with pale skin made it look that way.

Susan immediately counted noses to find the missing man. John, Tom, the guy from Roanoke . . . Andrew? Andrew was missing? Edmond's crying wound down to whining and sniffling that grated on Susan's suddenly raw nerves. Someone who could make Andrew disappear had to be a heavy freaking hitter. Susan trusted Silver if she thought it had to be the result of foul play rather than Andrew's mood.

"It does Dare no good if I get myself shot as a wolf or coyote around here!" John's voice was even, though Susan could see his tension in the wrinkles his fingers created in his shirt at the elbows of his crossed arms. "It's not just a Convocation rule. We've had plenty of injuries in past years from trigger-happy ranchers. Who knows, maybe that's what happened to him. Another wolf showing up at that scene would cause even more trouble."

Silver drew in a breath for another outburst and Susan stepped into the pause. Maybe she could short-circuit some of the yelling before Edmond started screaming too. "What do you mean, the trail's been destroyed?"

"I thought I found where he entered the woods, but someone drove over the place on an ATV leaking oil. I remember hearing it during the meeting this afternoon. Some kid trespassing from the highway, I assume. I can only smell so much in human, and it stirred everything up. Without even a starting point, we can't try to find where the trail picks up again."

Edmond tried to squirm out of her arms, awake enough now that he wanted to be crawling around. She set him down, watching him carefully for whatever unknown materials he might find on the floor, despite several earlier baby-proofing sweeps. "Who saw him last?" Silence greeted her at that, and she looked up. John looked blank.

Susan laughed, a little punchy from the tension in the room. These Were really did need a human around sometimes. "Humans have figured out a strategy or two for finding people when you can't magically track them by scent. You ask around. Who saw him? What direction was he going? Did he talk about a destination he had in mind?"

John nodded, slow at first, then sharply, perhaps as the implications of the strategy dawned on him. "When he left here, he was going to talk to Roanoke. But Roanoke's not going to tell us a thing."

That was a good point. Susan stooped to turn Edmond around

and set him crawling away from the space under the couch. Who knew what was hiding back there. The pause shook an idea free and her heart sped with a sudden surge of excitement. "Roanoke has a daughter, though. I've met her. Tom. You're friends with her, right? Would you be willing to come call her away from her parents innocently for a while?"

Tom bounced to his feet from his seat on the rock bench in front of the fireplace. "I've known Ginnie since she was like that." He pointed to Edmond, now pulling himself up on his father's pant leg. Tom was out the door before Susan could say anything else.

Edmond wobbled and thumped back on his bottom and John scooped him up. He looked down at the baby and back to Susan, as if he'd just realized he couldn't go around intimidating fearsome Were for information with a baby squirming in his arms.

Susan took a step over to put her hand on his arm. "More flies with honey than scary Were threatening to beat the information out of them, I think. Let me try first?" She meant that to be a statement, but it came out as a question. She strengthened her tone at the last minute, trying to make it like Silver and Dare talked to each other: equals asking for ideas, not an underling asking for permission.

John looked disgruntled, but he only tightened his grip on the baby. "I'll watch Edmond," he said. Susan decided now wasn't the time to push him about his tone. She'd gotten what she wanted.

"I can't just wait here!" Silver burst out with the words as if in answer to some long argument. Maybe they were, just one that Susan couldn't hear.

Susan took Silver's good hand and laced their fingers together. Andrew grounded Silver in this world, she'd seen that, the same way Silver helped ground Andrew from his temper. Maybe Silver needed someone else to do that for her for a while. The desperation did fade a little from her expression at Susan's touch. "Come on. The more of us there are, the more people we can talk to," Susan told her.

Silver nodded and dropped Susan's hand to make it easier for them to make it out the door. Tom, who had been waiting impatiently outside, bounded ahead and Silver followed him.

"What about me?" The guy from Roanoke caught Susan on the step. He looked like he was trying to prove he could be intimidating too, but his slight frame made it impossible for him to pull it off the way John could.

Susan hesitated. Andrew and Silver apparently trusted this guy enough to let him stay with them in the cabin. "Can you ask about Andrew without giving it away that he's missing under mysterious circumstances?" Susan used her best Were authority voice.

The man's head dropped, perhaps in response to the voice, and he nodded. Just because he thought he could be subtle didn't mean that everyone couldn't see through him, but at least he'd be thinking about it. Susan pointed to the cabin across the way. "Roanoke's down at the other end. Work your way up asking whoever you run into if they've seen Andrew. If we don't get anything from Roanoke, we'll work down."

When Susan reached the Roanoke cabin with Tom and Silver, Tom gestured them back. "Gimme a second," he said, and strode confidently up to the front door. He knocked and gifted the woman who answered with his best grin. Susan remembered seeing her associated with Roanoke at the Convocation table, so maybe she was his mate. "Is Ginnie around? I found an owl—I think it might be a Great Horned—out in the woods a little way and I thought she might be interested." Tom pointed out past the last of the cabins. "I'll make sure she doesn't go any farther than that." The woman eyed him, but sighed after a moment, and stepped aside for her daughter to burst out in excitement.

Tom swooped her up and carried her piggy-back. "Do they taste good?" she asked.

"It would probably scratch you with its talons. Besides, you can hardly eat one if you don't have a wolf form, can you, purse dog?" Tom headed off the path back into the trees and Susan and Silver followed. Neither of the Were seemed to notice, but Susan slowed for a few beats to let her eyes adjust when they left the light pooled around the main ranch buildings.

Ginnie bopped Tom soundly on the shoulder for the apparent insult. "I'm not stupid! What good is it, then?"

"To watch it hunt." Tom slowed and let Ginnie slide down to her feet.

Susan figured this was her moment. She lengthened her last few strides to catch up to the pair. Silver hung back, looking a little out of her depth. "Before you go, I wondered if you could help me, Ginnie."

Ginnie chewed on her lip as she frowned at Susan. Her hand sought Tom's. Probably deciding whether she should talk to the human again. "Daddy told Felicia that he was going to take care of you himself," she confided in a burst. "I think he really doesn't like you."

Susan's heart stuttered into a pounding race and Silver made a noise that was probably a swallowed growl. The girl might not guess the meaning of that, but knowing Were as she did, Susan could. Jesus Christ. But she was with both Tom and Silver, who

were more than capable of protecting her. Better to be out helping Andrew than hiding whimpering at the cabin.

The question was, which tack should she use with the girl?
Frame her question as something her parents would want her to
answer, or something she could use to rebel against them? Or
better yet, reference someone else she liked. Andrew had to have
known her, and Susan had noticed that he was pretty good with
kids when he wasn't paying attention. "That's okay, a lot of Were
aren't used to dealing with humans," she told Ginnie. "But it's not
really to help me, it's to help Andrew. You guys are friends, right?"

Ginnie grinned and stood a little on tiptoe to seem taller.
"Mr. Dare knows that I'm really smart." She stuck out her tongue
at Tom, who looked properly chastised for his earlier remark.

Susan smiled at Ginnie encouragingly. "When did you last
see him?"

"He came to talk to Daddy after lunch. They're going to fight in
two days." Ginnie tugged on Tom's hand and looked anxiously up
at him. "My daddy's going to win, right? Since he's so powerful?"

"Even if Dare wins, he'll be a really good alpha. You and your
family won't have to worry." Tom covered her hand with both of
his, but Ginnie still looked dubious.

"Where'd he go after he talked to your daddy?" Susan held her
breath. Here was where things might break down. They'd known
Andrew was going to go talk to Roanoke, and he had. But where
had he gone next?

"To the kitchen, I think. Daddy called him a bad name and
Mr. Dare went in that direction. Felicia thought it would be the
kitchen, anyway. We were playing Go Fish, only it had some other
weird name in Spanish. Daddy told Felicia how what Mr. Dare

did didn't matter, he was going to take care of the human—I mean, you—and she snuck out without finishing the game because she wanted to talk to Mr. Dare. She wouldn't let me come with her, either." The girl frowned with remembered frustration.

Tom caught Susan's eyes and she nodded. That's what they'd needed. If they interrogated the girl for too long, she'd get suspicious, or her parents would later. "That owl's gonna fly away," he said, and took off running, Ginnie laughing beside him.

Silver started immediately in the direction of the hall, but Susan didn't move. Something was niggling at her, trying to break through the stress of knowing Roanoke might be after her. But that was the thing. Was he really? "Why would Roanoke tell Andrew's daughter anything about a random human? Why would she care? She must have given herself a crick in her neck, she was looking down her nose so hard when we met. Ginnie said he told Felicia specifically he was taking care of me."

Silver slowed, brows drawing down in thought. "The question is not why Roanoke would do anything. The question is why Madrid would tell him to." She flexed her hand in an ear-scritching motion beside her hip.

Susan eyed the gesture, then decided she didn't want to think about it. Easier that way. She exhaled in absent amusement at Silver's words. None of the Were seemed to think much of Roanoke. "The first thing Felicia apparently did after being told the plan for me was to go looking for Andrew. So let's assume Madrid wanted Andrew to know about that plan—or for Andrew to *think* Roanoke was planning something."

Silver sent Susan a sideways twisted smile. "If he heard about that kind of plan, he'd want to protect you." She shook her head and started moving again with purpose. "We need to find Dare's daughter. All of this is speculation for now. If Madrid is up to something and she knows anything about it, we'll get it out of her." She snorted, not a kind sound. "Yes, even if means resorting to that."

Susan couldn't help but stare at the air and wonder what "that" was. Was Silver falling apart worse than usual with Andrew gone? Or was it that she wasn't hiding her craziness as much as usual? Susan hoped it was the latter, but it still made picking up the line of conversation like nothing had happened painfully awkward. "Can you track Felicia's scent, or do I need to go back and grab John?"

Silver shook her head. "If she left the main area with Dare, her trail would have been destroyed, the same as his. But she should be back. I saw her with her alpha at the Convocation." She stumbled. "Lady! Dare's brother-in-law came in late. I didn't even think about it, because he was so submissive to Madrid. He wouldn't have been doing anything on his own, but if he had orders—" She stumbled again on a gnarled root in the path as she tried to break into a jog. The ground out here was treacherous in the dark, at least for Susan. She noticed that except for those moments of distraction, Silver seemed to pick a path just fine.

"The jarring can't be good for your shoulder. Slow down." Susan put a hand on Silver's back this time. Silver wasn't the only one who needed grounding at the moment. The uglier their conclusions grew, the more her stomach twisted. What could the two of them do about whatever Madrid had done? He wouldn't kill Andrew immediately, would he? Hadn't that been half the point of her trial for killing Sacramento, that Were tried to avoid killing as much as possible? Or was that just North American Were?

"Let's try the hall first." That was easy enough for Susan to find even with human sight in the darkness, so she took the lead along the path to the big hulking shape against the horizon. "I know a place where we can check nearly everywhere at once." She had to tug Silver onto the side path to the back entrance when she headed automatically for the front doors.

They got halfway up the stairs to the loft when Silver hissed at Susan to stop. "We're not the only ones with the idea of keeping an eye on who's here."

Susan flattened herself to the side of the stairs so Silver could pass her, since that was obviously what the woman wanted. "Don't let her past," Silver whispered to her as she squeezed by.

Mindful of Silver's request, Susan stayed at the head of the stairs rather than follow her into the cable-snarl of the loft. Her eyes adjusted slowly back from the bright fluorescent lights of the kitchen and she finally spotted the dark-haired teen crouched against the railing. Felicia. Susan hoped that Silver was right, and they'd get information out of her, rather than scare her into silence.

32

Silver took a moment to just breathe before she spoke. Too many of her emotions threatened to wrest control of her words from her. She wanted to scream in rage at Dare's daughter for the way she'd hurt a father who loved her. She wanted to beg her for help in finding him. She wanted to scold her like a mother for all her many mistakes. Susan was the mother here, though. She'd proved that with her skillful handling of Roanoke's girl.

But Silver at least knew screaming or scolding was not the way to go. The girl's wild self huddled beside her hip, tail and nose tucked in like no one would notice it if nothing disturbed the sooty line of its flank. The girl looked at Silver and then away again, like she too hoped that Silver might go away if she didn't acknowledge her.

"You'll need her name if you want to command her," Death said. He nosed at the girl's wild self, forcing it to uncurl to avoid the harassment. It edged away and tucked its head back again. "I don't think she'll respond well to 'Hey you, girl.'"

Silver reached deep, a quest for the name before she even began the quest for information. "Felicia." She knew it sounded strange, coming all in a relieved burst, but it got the girl to look up again.

"What?" Felicia said, sullen and challenging. Her wild self started to shake very slightly.

In that word, Silver found the steady ground that she needed to choose words of her own. Young or not, Dare's daughter was enough of an adult to be paralyzed by what her conscience told her when it clashed with what others did. Silver could smell the panicked confusion on her. She needed to give that attack of conscience a firm push. "You know where my mate is. You know it's not honorable that your pack captured him by playing on his need to protect." That had been Susan's realization, but Silver saw it hit home when she used it.

"Did you know that it was a trap? Did you really believe that Roanoke would bother to mention his plans for a meaningless human to you? Or were you delighted to help them, delighted to punish your father for crimes he never committed, except in the minds of your relatives?"

"I didn't know!" A growl started in Felicia's throat, but she suppressed it and kept her words to a soft intensity, perhaps conscious of ears below. "I just wanted to talk to him. I didn't care what Roanoke did or didn't do with a stupid human." She glared at Susan. "But I thought Father should at least know. I didn't know Madrid meant to— And then he—" She trailed off into angry words in a language Silver didn't know. It took her several moments to realize that was the problem, not that Felicia was speaking of things too tied up in this world for Silver to understand.

"And then Madrid what?" she prompted.

"Treated me like I was just—something to trade! For Madrid's political shit." For a moment, Dare showed strongly in Felicia's face and voice. Silver couldn't pin it down, but some spark of temper had been passed on.

"That's what alphas do when they seek power for power's sake, not to fulfill their instinct to protect people. No matter how they start, they always end up sacrificing people for the power in the end." Silver took a deep breath. She couldn't push her too hard, no matter that this was the most important question yet. "Do you know where Dare is? What they're doing to him?"

Felicia bit her lip until the skin bleached white in a line beneath her teeth. "Yes. I know where. Madrid called in the rest of the pack that came over and they're holding him until he agrees to give up trying to be alpha in exchange for Madrid giving me the choice to stay." She hugged herself. "Father didn't even *consider* it. And he claimed he hadn't wanted to leave me behind—"

Silver grabbed Felicia's wrist and yanked her to her feet. Her patience only extended so far when a crisis of conscience began to turn into whining. "Of course he didn't consider it, because he's not Lady-darkened *stupid*." She dropped the girl's wrist and took her chin in the same firm grip. "Look me in the eye and tell me you'd consider staying for even one heartbeat. Or would you do exactly as Madrid planned?"

Felicia hit her wrist, but Silver ignored the pain and held on. The girl wasn't hitting seriously yet. "Lady! That's what he said. Why does everyone assume that about me?"

Silver smiled, showing teeth, and channeled the tone Death

had used so often with her. "Prove us wrong, girl." She switched her grip to the girl's wrist again and dragged her downwards, nodding to Susan on the way. "We have to gather help before we go, if Madrid called in his pack. More than just the Seattle pack."

"Planning on making another scene?" Susan threw her a tight smile as they descended. At the foot of the stairs, Felicia hesitated, but jerked into movement again as if Susan had shoved her from behind.

"If they're going to impose their religious imaginings on me I suppose I might as well." Silver didn't look at Death, who was loping along beside them, but from the corner of her eye she saw him bare his teeth in edged approval.

Most of dinner was cleared away, but a good number of the Were lingered in the main room, talking over drinks. Silver scanned the crowd, finding Boston first, and then Portland. Allies, good. She took a beat longer to make doubly sure neither Roanoke nor Madrid hid in a shadowed corner, then exhaled in relief.

Felicia balked again, and Silver let her feel her strength by nearly jerking the girl off her feet. Dare didn't have time for this. "Alphas," she said in a ringing voice. "In the Lady's name, I need your assistance."

Silence rippled unevenly through the room and Silver waited until it was complete. A few young ones slipped outside in the pause, undoubtedly to spread the news of something interesting happening. Silver would have to work quickly in case they found Roanoke.

She lifted Felicia's wrist high. "One of Madrid's own pack has honor enough to reveal that Madrid has captured my mate, to avenge what they imagine to be his crimes." The girl swallowed hard and then straightened to hold her own hand high, forcing confidence into her body. Silver sent her silent thanks. "We need to stop them."

"Lady-damned Europeans!" Portland strode to the front of the crowd, clenched hands the only physical sign of the rage that vibrated in her voice. "We need to drag them out of our territory by force." A tide of voices rose behind hers.

"Just wait," Death said, his voice low against the alphas' rising volume, but catching Silver's attention all the same.

"I agree completely." At first, Roanoke couldn't manage silence the way Silver had, but he crossed his arms and intimidated it out of those standing nearest the entrance where he had just appeared. "I take full responsibility for the way they tricked me with their talk of a new, more peaceful relationship between us. Normally I'd lead the force to take them down, but in light of my mistakes, I leave that to another."

Silver had one split, frozen second before the room erupted to realize what Roanoke had just done. He'd thrown a kill into the middle of starving lones and stepped back to watch them tear each other to bits over it. After all, who asked questions about the thrower when the prize was so fat and juicy?

She thought it had been loud before, but now she could hardly think for everyone trying to shout everyone else down and claim the position of authority. Roanoke smirked, but no one seemed to even notice besides Silver and Susan. The human drew closer to her in automatic reaction to the noise. Silver wanted to sink to the ground and put her hands over her ears.

She caught Portland's eyes instead, and the other woman looked as helpless as Silver felt. Portland too was silent, not proud enough to put her personal advancement before saving Dare like the others.

"We don't have time for this." Silver drew a deep breath and beckoned Portland to join them. The woman slipped between the intervening Were, using her short stature to advantage in some places, and her elbows in others. Boston started the same journey from another direction, using the weight of his presence to make people move aside, though it didn't stop them arguing.

"*I* could lead this clusterfuck better than them," Susan muttered, and used a parody of an alpha's tone. "All of you. Together. Go that direction."

"Not a bad idea," Silver said as she calculated a path to the exit. The Were might laugh at a human trying to take charge, but then again someone outside all existing hierarchies might be what they needed. At least the attempt might distract them from their own personal ambitions long enough for them to remember the important things about the situation.

Silver leaned close to Susan. "Can I leave it in your hands? I'll go ahead and stall them." She dragged Felicia toward the exit.

Susan followed. "Silver, no! Where are you going?"

"Just to stall. Nothing dangerous." Silver tipped her chin to her bad arm, since her hand was full. "What could I do against them otherwise?" And why would she want to attack them straight on, when looking weak until backup arrived was much better tactics?

Susan didn't look convinced, but Portland's arrival distracted her. Silver seized the opening to escape, dragging Felicia out. She heard Susan give a human growl of frustration, but she didn't chase. "I guess we do this without Silver. These alphas have their mates with them, right? Any way we could enlist their help in making people shut up?" The wash of argument cut off the rest of Susan's suggestion to Portland.

In the chill air outside, the girl started struggling again. It still seemed like half a struggle against her conscience, because she was close enough to full-grown that Silver could never have held her if she was really trying to get away. Death nipped mockingly at her wild self's heels. The wild self bristled up its ruff, the motion exposing variations of sooty black so different from Death's absence of color.

Silver released the girl and gave her half a breath to rub her wrist before she tilted her chin toward the starlit trees. "You need to lead us." She realized she'd slipped a moment later. Her and Death, she'd meant, but perhaps the girl thought "us" meant her and Felicia. Felicia's eyes didn't search for someone else, in any case.

Felicia bit her lip and started loping along the slight dip of a trail through the pines. Silver would have demanded greater speed, but this pace jarred her bad shoulder enough as it was. She set her teeth against the pain. No point getting to Dare a few minutes sooner if she was useless when she arrived.

"I didn't mean for any of this to happen," Felicia burst out.

Silver shushed Felicia and frowned ahead as far as she could when pine branches blocked one's line of sight here and there. She couldn't smell anything, but if they were upwind, they might still be close enough to their goal for sound to carry. She wanted these people to see her, but not with much time to think.

"It's a ways yet. I'll warn you before we get too close," Felicia muttered, bristling at the shushing.

"I believe you didn't mean it to." Silver picked up the thread of the conversation and pressed her lips together to prevent a smile at the girl's look of surprise. She'd expected a scolding, not sympathy, Silver bet. Well, Silver wasn't done yet. "That doesn't excuse you from doing something about it now, however." She released the smile when Felicia's surprise turned to sullenness. "Or did you think you would get to just stand back?"

"I'm just fifteen," Felicia told the ground.

"You're old enough for the Lady to have released your wild self. You bear the mark of Her trust. That's old enough to make choices of your own." Silver took a few running steps, gritting her teeth against the pain, to draw even with the girl and look at her in profile. Dark waves of her hair, dark fur of her wild self, against the stars and silhouettes of the horizon. Darkness and fire in her life, same as there had been in Silver's, but that didn't excuse her from running forward.

"But how am I supposed to know who to believe?" Felicia kicked a rock savagely from their path. "Of course my father's story casts him in the best light."

"So ask someone else." Silver squinted ahead. When would they be able to see where Dare was being held? Would she be able to recognize it, or would it be one of the things from this world that slipped away from her?

"No one else was there." Felicia's tone dripped with the scorn only the young could muster.

"Not about what happened. Ask someone else whether your father lies. Ask a lot of people whether your father lies. So many that it's impossible all of them could be trying to protect him. Then ask them if your alpha lies. Then, when you know who's a liar and who isn't, return to what they each said about what happened."

"Well, of course you think your mate's not the liar!" Felicia took several running steps ahead and Silver let her keep the lead. It hurt too much to keep catching up.

"Am I one of the people you're going to ask, then?" Silver

paused a moment, but didn't make the girl say it. "My mate is an honorable man, or I would not be mated to him. But if you're already trying to deny it without asking anyone, I think you must have some idea of what people will say."

"People say all kinds of things." Felicia kicked another rock.

"Watch what they do, then. Who do they support? People lie less often with their actions."

Felicia's answer to that was stubborn silence. They stayed that way for several minutes until Felicia held up a hand for Silver to stop. She scented into the wind, and then picked her path based on the direction she found. Silver set her feet more carefully. Even though they were approaching from downwind, she couldn't smell Dare yet. Getting closer, but not close enough.

33

Even when the three other Spaniards arrived with their whips, they inflicted pain no worse than anything Andrew had felt before. Bearable. It helped he knew their methods. You couldn't really brace for this sort of thing, but it removed some of the fear. He watched the hallucination of Death laugh at him, and thought about Felicia. When she went back to Spain, what then? Someday she'd be an adult, and if he could find her location, his in-laws could no longer deny him the ability to contact her. But maybe she'd deny him that herself.

Bearable became less so through repetition. Andrew's world narrowed with each lash, graying at the edges. They couldn't kill him. And the others would come looking eventually. Silver would know something was wrong, would bring them. Raul would have to slink home to Europe and take his imaginary fears of empires with him.

Then, a pause. Andrew's head cleared in a rush, giving him a breath of clarity between the end of his healing, and the start of the fog of exhaustion it created. Standard procedure, he recalled. Let the victim heal up before you started in again.

Andrew had better take advantage of the time, then. He couldn't return blows, but he had words, and he knew Arturo better than the other three. Knew where his buttons should be, if memory was any guide. "So what do you think, Arturo? Seeing your alpha use your niece this way?" The other Spaniards probably knew English too, but Andrew used it anyway for the illusion of privacy between the two of them.

Arturo had been prowling at the sidelines while the others worked, and now he froze. "What way?"

"As a bargaining chip. To save you all from whatever imaginary monster Raul believes in. You think he brought her to meet me after all this time for *her* sake?" Even though the words were true, it still was a wrench for Andrew to say them. That's all this had been. An elaborate trap. He'd known it, he'd thought he could beat it, and he'd failed. "Allowing Raul to do that is the best you can take care of Isabel's daughter?"

Arturo charged forward. He slammed a kick into Andrew's stomach that left him without air. He hardly had time to think, never mind draw another breath before Arturo was on him again. Dammit, he hadn't meant to make the man snap. What if Arturo just kept going and killed him?

The other Spaniards seemed to have come to the same realization. One tried to drag Arturo off and got a punch to the jaw for his trouble. Another came at Arturo from the other side. *"Madrid said he was to live."*

"But we're running out of time. What does it matter if we kill

him? Roanoke will still slowly fall apart under that weak alpha, whether he allies with us or not," Arturo snarled.

"You think killing me will make Felicia ever forget she had a North American father?" Andrew panted the words, but Arturo understood him. He growled and threw himself at Andrew, blows growing wilder. The harder he fought, the more the others restrained him. Andrew closed his eyes for a moment.

If he taunted Arturo too much, he might break free and kill Andrew, but if Arturo had the chance to calm down, he might find an opportunity to do it anyway later when the others stopped watching him. Andrew didn't see he had any choice but to try to push his brother-in-law so far the others locked him out of the building. "Everyone thinks better of the dead. Look at how you remember your sister. And are you sure you want to kill me so soon after I talked to Felicia about your lies? It looks pretty bad."

Arturo yanked forward in the others' grip and snarled in Andrew's face. *"Should have killed you when she brought you home, disgusting North American mongrel."*

"No daughter of Isabel's is going to let you control her life any more than your sister did, I can tell you that."

This time, Arturo ripped a hand free and tried to snap Andrew's neck. He didn't have the angle or the grip, but he got a handful of hair and wrenched Andrew's neck muscles to screaming. Andrew sobbed for his next breath.

"A perilously thin path to walk, love," Isabel's voice said from Death's mouth. "Are you sure of what he'll do, sure that they'll stop him? Really sure?"

Andrew closed his eyes so he couldn't see Death. No, he wasn't sure. But what choice did he have?

"Stop." Raul strode in. He didn't even have to touch Arturo;

he just looked at the man and he collapsed to hang in the other Spaniards' holds. *"He's the berserker, not you. Don't let him play you like that."*

Raul banished them all to the other side of the room with a gesture. He stood considering Andrew. Andrew pushed himself straighter, the bruises from Arturo healing slowly, but healing. He wasn't prey down and ready to be eaten yet.

The longer Raul waited, the more Andrew's abused stomach tried to twist itself into nausea. Raul had something good; he could read it in the man's whole body.

"It comes to this, Dare." Raul smiled, smiled like Andrew had rarely seen him smile before. "I have your daughter. Perhaps you didn't like my earlier deal, but we both know you're kidding yourself. You'd do anything to keep her safe, and I have her." Raul tightened his fingers into a fist, crushing.

Andrew's next inhalation sounded a lot like a sob, though he tried to smooth it out. No. No. He couldn't let Raul control him this way, but Felicia—how could any parent not do anything they could for their child? Wasn't that what the whole of civilization was built on? Protection of your kin, your mate, your people, your children. Most of all, your children.

Hearing that sobbing breath, Raul's smile grew smaller and more concentrated in its malice. "You will not be alpha. Understand?"

Andrew looked around, trying to find something, anything, to focus on until his emotions eased enough to think straight. He stopped on Arturo's face. His brother-in-law looked surprised. Taken aback by Raul's threat—but not worried. Not angry, when Andrew had recent proof how fiercely protective he was of his niece. He didn't believe Raul would hurt her, Andrew realized.

But then Raul must have helped raise her. He'd clearly use her without a second thought. But perhaps he wouldn't *hurt* her, according to his skewed definitions of hurt. "You won't hurt her. She's part of your pack." Andrew hated the way his voice broke, but he couldn't stop it.

Raul released his fist, tapped the middle of that palm thoughtfully. Andrew saw tension ripple through his muscles. "All right. I'll never understand why you always choose the hardest road, Dare."

He strode to a duffel full of equipment his pack members had brought, and drew out a knife. Over the stink of his blood and other weapons, Andrew didn't realize its nature until the silver plating glinted just so in the light. "Even if you agreed now, you could always change your mind later. But no one will accept a cripple as an alpha. Think of it this way, at least you and your mate will match. What do you think? Hamstrings?"

Raul crouched beside Andrew. He couldn't stop himself from jerking away, dragging the piece of equipment a few inches. No, please. He'd been so worried about his back injury, this new threat slammed him into the ground. Not able to walk, forever, because cuts made with silver never healed.

"Or maybe one eye." Raul lifted the knife, tipped it in the direction of Andrew's right, then left.

Each breath came faster, but Andrew's lungs were burning anyway. He jerked desperately against the chains. No. No. He searched the room for support, for a sign of help arriving, but found only the set faces of the Spaniards. If they thought their alpha was going too far, they didn't make any move to stop him.

"Silver kept going," Death said softly in his usual male voice, just a drift of shadow in a corner. "You could too, if you needed to."

A beat later, and Andrew could no longer make out the line of a wolf in the shadow, but the words sank in regardless, removing the edge of unreasoning panic. He could. If he had to. It wouldn't be easy, but he had a shining example to guide his way. Knowing that, now was the time to fight. Words once more.

"All this, for a North American alphaship? Are you really that worried?" Andrew's voice was breathy, but steady this time. There had to be something he could find to use against Raul, even if he had to repeatedly snap his teeth on empty air. "Or is it specifically me? Is this revenge, for Isabel? For her choosing me, instead of one of you?"

Raul just smiled and switched his pointing knife back to the other eye. Nothing. Andrew wasn't connecting. Dammit! "Felicia, then. More than just keeping me from the alphaship, you're breaking down any hope of reconciliation. Why is it so important to you that I can't touch her?"

Raul's lip curled. "When Isabel died, you'd have taken her home with you, wouldn't you? Raised her human." He spat the last word. "This whole continent—you interbreed, adopt their culture, call it civilization. Like it makes you better than those of us who keep traditions alive."

Andrew stared. Raul's words had the resonance of years. Years he must have been watching Andrew after he arrived in Madrid, keeping it all locked away. Andrew couldn't even imagine the kind of iron will that had allowed him to do it, or the energy it must have taken not to collapse in on himself from the constant bitterness.

"Humans own this world. They design the game, they award the prizes. To turn your back on that is also to wither away in isolation. Hybrid vigor, Raul. No lineage ever survived through purity." Andrew made the words crisp to hold his fear at bay. It didn't really work.

"Humans don't fuck apes." Raul strode away, his back to Andrew, like he needed time to pull his usual blankness back over his face. "They're making you their dogs. Breeding you into toy poodles who would starve if set free in the wilderness."

"They breed pit pulls too. Abuse them until they only know how to attack, and have to be put down when discovered. Only humans don't have to breed that into European packs, you're doing it all on your own." Andrew snarled at Raul, the sound calculated to show his disdain. "You preach avoiding humanity, but I don't see you joining Alaska to run like a true wolf. You like your house: saves misery in the winter. Your car: lets you hold a bigger territory. Your phone: lets you control your pack. You'll take what suits you from the humans."

"*She's mine, Dare.*" The smoothness of the Spanish words after the choppiness of Andrew's English syllables emphasized Raul's soft point. Andrew must have scored some hit if Raul was retreating to that position. But did it really matter where he retreated, while he still held the silver knife?

Death huffed from the side like he was exasperated with Andrew ignoring him to watch Raul. He came to stand before the man and sat tall on his haunches, instantly taking possession of the space. "When a child is grown, a parent lets them go," Isabel's voice said. "Parents' lives are enriched by, not defined by, what their children do. Parents' lives are defined by what they do. Leave your child's actions for her own definition."

"She's not grown," Andrew whispered. Still a child yet, so very young.

"You think as an adult you'll have any more chance with her?" Raul sneered.

Death shook his head, ears flattening dangerously. "She's grown enough to have a life of her own. Live yours, Dare."

Someone rapped a knuckle against the door and Raul straightened, grip on the knife loosening. He set the knife on the side of the pickup's bed, where Andrew could see it, but it wouldn't be obvious to someone in the doorway. "Think about it," he told Andrew, and went outside to confer with his guard.

Silver stopped with Felicia when the twisted scents of several Were finally resolved. Dare, Madrid and his beta, as well as three strangers. Two against five were much worse odds than she'd anticipated. Madrid stood with one of the strangers before the door, discussing something in low tones. Some diffuse hint of an intruder's scent, she suspected. They'd pinpoint her location soon.

"Can you—" Silver turned, voice low, to find Felicia gone. She'd melted off somewhere downwind. Silver didn't have the luxury of time to follow her trail. Besides, if the girl wanted to disappear, she wasn't an ally Silver wanted.

"Did you really expect her to help?" Death asked, making an act of incredulity. "Be too busy wringing her hands in indecision on the sidelines to help your enemies either, perhaps, but certainly no help to you."

Silver let the doubt twist around her stomach for a single moment as she stood in the darkness, staring at where Dare was being held. Had she really been trying to win Felicia over, or trying to make the girl feel guilty for what she'd done to Dare? She hadn't thought about it, just prodded at the girl as Death did to her. But sometimes that was the wrong strategy. Had she let her frustration with the whining get in the way of what the girl actually needed to hear—or didn't need to hear?

When that single moment had passed, Silver gathered herself. It didn't matter now. If she'd proved herself unable to lead quite as well as Dare did, she still had herself to rely on.

"Madrid!" she called as she strode forward. The stranger with Madrid whistled for another the moment he spotted her. The first placed himself opposite her while the new one strode off into the trees, searching for her backup. If only she had it. Maybe he'd bump into Felicia and she'd distract him for a while whether she meant to or not.

"Oh, it's the mate." Madrid took a few steps forward and narrowed his eyes, doing his own search for anyone else around her. "A better tracker than I'd expected."

Silver flashed him a slash of a smile, plenty of teeth. "*My* trail's very easy to follow, however. The others will be along very soon." The trick to bluffing was believing it yourself, Silver reminded herself. She'd do most anything for Dare, that was true. She just had to pretend to herself that doing this would do him any good. "I don't want his daughter tangled up in this, for his sake. Take her and go, before the rest of the alphas get here."

"Please," Madrid said. He gestured his underling aside and met Silver halfway as she forced herself to walk forward in a show of confidence. "If they knew what you were doing, they'd never have let you come alone. If you didn't tell them, they'll never follow you. Try again."

"You underestimate the number and strength of allies Dare and I have." Silver would have liked to cross her arms, but she didn't dare clasp her bad one, for fear the pain would flare up and seep into her scent.

"Oh, I'm sure Roanoke did his job." Madrid's manner warmed with satisfaction, though Silver tried to hide her flicker of anger at the mention of Roanoke's actions. "Pathetic, the way he has to grasp after even what little power he has." He inclined his head to her, correct to the exact degree for the respect due an alpha, and all the more mocking for it. "So it's you and me, Seattle. What can I do for you?"

"Roanoke's trick won't last forever." Silver spat the words at him and realized too late that it made her sound insecure.

Madrid didn't even bother to answer that. "I was surprised that Dare finally moved on from his wife to someone pre-broken. The emotional cripple is drawn to the physical cripple?" He tapped his chin in an exaggerated thinking motion. "Does it make him feel better, to have someone he can smother with constant protection, since he failed to protect Isabel?"

Silver dropped her head to hide the confidence seeping back into her. Did the fool really see her stand as co-alpha, see her defend Susan, and still consider her broken? He deserved what he was going to get for underestimating her. She let silence be her answer, to make Madrid think his verbal blow had connected.

"Let me see him." Silver passed Madrid, giving him a wide enough berth his underling didn't stir. Madrid smiled at the apparent evidence of her fear. Inside, the last stranger had a hand on Madrid's beta's shoulder, holding him back from Dare, who had his head down. Silver hoped he was conserving strength, not that he was so hurt as to have given up.

Dare's head snapped up as she approached and his eyes widened. "Silver, no! What are you—?"

Silver ignored the words and examined him. He smelled like sweat and old pain and too many healed injuries. His whole body conveyed the tension of not looking in a particular direction. Silver didn't look that way either yet, but she noted it. She knelt, leaned in to kiss him, and rested her hand on his leg. He flexed his knee so she could feel it. If he could move his legs, his back injury had not been reopened. Good. She set her cheek against his chest, which left her facing the direction his tension pointed.

A silver knife, set to one side. She wondered if it came with a promise of its purpose. It didn't entirely explain the intensity of his attention, but she didn't need the details. She had her own associations with silver knives.

"What are you doing here?" Dare asked again as she sat back. His gaze flickered behind her and then back again. He was looking for their allies too. Well, they'd be coming. Silver trusted Susan for that.

He gave a ragged laugh. "We've got to stop meeting like this."

Silver squeezed his knee. "Getting you out of trouble again." His ankles were bound with silver, covered so those without her peculiarities could touch it. With the binding right there, she couldn't not try to remove it.

The underling left the beta to jerk Silver up by her arm. He said something Silver didn't understand, and Dare translated it, mocking it by flattening the intonation. "He says 'none of that now, cat.'"

"You've seen him." Madrid held his arm out toward the exit. "Now we need to leave him to consider his options and come to his senses alone." He snapped his fingers at the beta, too. Perhaps he wasn't allowed to be alone with Dare. His expression suggested he shouldn't be.

Silver tried to put everything she didn't want to say in front of Madrid into her last glance at Dare—she loved him, and she was going to do whatever was necessary to get him out of this—but she wasn't sure how successful she was.

She kept her head down, took a few steps as if following Madrid quietly, then grabbed the knife. She had it in her hand before he had fully turned. He lunged for her, probably to wrest it from her grasp, but she laid the flat against her cheek and smiled like Death. That stopped Madrid, made his eyes widen.

He smiled to cover his discomfort. "A nice party trick. I saw you touch silver at the Convocation, and it still looks strange. But tricks won't help you." He held his hand out mockingly for the weapon.

Silver suppressed a smile. If he insisted. She reached out to lay the flat of the blade on his palm instead. He jerked back.

"Keep it, then. I have others." Raul threw a meaningful glance back to Andrew and led her outside. Hints of discomfort remained in his movements. The more off-balance he was, the better, though she couldn't see how it helped at the moment. She couldn't take on five even with a knife.

He led her a little ways off, two underlings following at a discreet distance. "What do you want from us, Madrid?" Silver asked. She let the knife fall to her side and looked out at the horizon, but watched him from the corner of her eye. She didn't have to play-act much confusion. "If you planned to kill him, you would have."

"Dare needs to understand his position," Madrid said, discomfort smoothing away. "And why he wants to do exactly what

I say." He caught her sideways observation and smiled. "Don't worry. I have no doubt he will."

"No amount of torture—" Silver clenched her hand tighter to keep her voice even. Dare would never give in. This man was twice the fool if he thought he would.

Madrid held up his palms for her to stop, expression pained. "Please. I have no need for torture. He'll do it because he knows I control his daughter."

Silver ignored the insulting lie about torture—she'd seen how hurt Dare was—and looked back toward where Dare was held, doubt squeezing off her breath like something tangible. Oh, she could see Dare giving in to that. She didn't want to, but she could see that. Of all the things that mattered to Dare, his daughter was one of the most important.

She turned into the wind, not caring if Madrid saw her do it. Where were the others? She should smell a hint of them following by now. Had Susan been unable to talk the alphas into laying aside their arguments? It had been a lot to dump on the human. She knew almost nothing about Were culture, after all, so she couldn't necessarily formulate her arguments to convince them. But Portland and Boston were there with her. What was taking them so long?

After all she had tried to learn about how to get others to trust her, how to lead, it came down to her alone in the end. Well, fine. She could do plenty without relying on anyone but Death. "You speak of him making decisions, but I'm sure he can hardly be thinking at all, bound and hurting. Why not let him go, and I will stay with you as a surety." If they thought she was broken, they wouldn't bind her tightly or watch her closely. She need only bide her time, and then she'd be free too.

Madrid's brows rose. His surprise took longer to smooth away this time. "You can stand less than him, little broken alpha."

Silver lifted her chin. She could hear in his voice it wasn't working. Somehow, she had to convince him. Lady, lend her strength. "You said no torture, didn't you? If you want Dare to think, give him space to think. If you think those thoughts need something to motivate them, I assure you he cares no less about me than his daughter." She reversed the blade, offered him the handle.

A slight figure resolved itself from the side of the den, moving for the entrance while Madrid and his underlings were distracted. Felicia. Silver saw the girl look at her, probably listening to the desperation in her tone. Silver stood firm and pretended she didn't notice. She didn't need the girl's help. She could rely on herself and Death. After a moment, the girl slipped inside the den. The underling at the entrance let her pass with barely a nod, he was so interested in watching the show.

Madrid smiled, a flash of teeth, and took the knife. He laid it against her cheek in imitation of her earlier gesture and turned it just enough that the edge pressed into her skin without breaking it. "Try again, little broken alpha. No one's coming, and we have all the time in the world."

34

Susan wanted to scream. She would have, too, if she'd thought it would do any good. She remembered how Silver's grandstanding had worked at her trial. But those who had nominated themselves to lead the expedition to deal with the Europeans were competing through volume. Susan noticed their rhetoric had all become very general—defeat the Europeans, not rescue Dare. Because that would be time sensitive, and Lord knew they were wasting a lot of that.

At least everyone besides the major players had calmed down. Three men Portland had labeled Reno, Billings, and Charleston shouted at each other in the center of the space created by dragging the banquet tables to rest along the walls. They looked inches from a shoving match or possibly a bloody battle breaking out.

The front doors opened a crack and Tom slipped in. "I dropped off Ginnie," he told Susan at normal volume after glancing at all the shouting going on. He probably figured, same as Susan, that no one would be bothering to listen to them. "What's going on?"

"Silver went after Andrew on her own, and those assholes are still fighting." Susan bit off the words, and gestured at the knot of shouters. She smiled thinly when Tom's brow creased with anger. "Look, would you be willing to go get John and offer to watch Edmond so he can come help? I don't know what he can do—" Susan glanced at the shouting Were. "But he can't hurt, I suppose."

Tom nodded enthusiastically and reversed course to bound out the door into the night. Susan remained standing uncertainly near the front doors. The blast of night air introduced by Tom's passage made her shiver.

"And you think leading one measly little pack qualifies you to direct the Roanoke pack's united might?" Charleston's rich brown skin stood out, though lighter than Boston's. He had some paunch, but it did nothing to diminish his appearance of sheer power.

"And your qualifications are what, following? At least the Western packs are independent, not boot-lickers." The taller Reno gestured in Charleston's face, each sweep coming within inches of hitting him.

Boston touched Charleston's shoulder. "We have a direction, and time is of the essence—"

Charleston held up a hand, forestalling Boston. In contrast to the barely restrained violence of his following finger-jab at Reno, the gesture was almost respectful. Susan snorted to herself. It didn't matter if people respected Boston if they didn't listen to him.

Billings pushed between the other two men, maybe planning to play the role of authority figure separating two squabbling children. Reno spun him out of the way by his elbow, sending him almost crashing into Portland, who was slipping through the crowd around the fight.

Portland pulled back into the crowd and spoke to another woman, gesturing with clear exasperation to the three arguing Were. Susan couldn't see what she was saying, but she could imagine the gist. The woman shook her head and crossed her arms, apparently planning to wait until the fight played out.

At least people listened to Portland. Those Susan had tried to talk to earlier just stared at her blankly.

Susan bit her lip. She was failing Silver and Andrew, but she didn't know what to do. If even Boston couldn't talk them down, what was she supposed to do as a single human, formerly accused of murder?

Susan drew in a breath as a realization struck her. She'd been just a single human when Sacramento threatened everyone before. No one had helped her then. She'd go after Andrew. She'd see if John would come with her, but even if he wouldn't, she'd be a single ally more than Andrew and Silver had before. Screw werewolf noses—she could call up satellite photos on her phone and see if the ranch had any other buildings. She doubted they were just holding Andrew randomly in the middle of the woods. She could go check them out, call 911, and have help follow her GPS location once she found the right one. The Spanish Were wouldn't be expecting that, she was sure.

Portland had worked her way back around nearly to the front doors and Susan closed the few steps between them. "Fuck the others, I'm leaving now," she said in a low voice. The nearest

Were turned, responding to what Susan would have called the fundamental human instinct to eavesdrop on something they thought someone was hiding from them.

Susan didn't wait for Portland to answer before she pushed the front doors open. The blast of night air hit her full in the face and she shivered. Fuck them. She could do this herself.

Running footsteps followed her, and Portland drew level with her a beat later. "I'll help with the trail," was all she said. Susan nodded. Two allies. Even better.

Boston didn't have to run to catch up. He lengthened his strides instead, making his approach quieter. "You have something of the Lady's light of your own, girl," he said, his voice a quiet rumble.

John arrived a moment later, panting. He must have seen her leaving the hall from the cabins and sprinted the whole way. "Tom said Silver went off after Dare on her own again?"

A bubble of hysterical laughter formed in Susan's chest at the parental mix of fear, anger, and exasperation in John's tone on "again" but she swallowed it down. "We're going after her." With or without him. Susan didn't bother trying to be authoritative in her tone, just put in her absolute certainty of that. He dropped his head in acknowledgement, didn't comment, and fell in behind her.

Susan heard more leaving the hall and following behind her, but she didn't turn around. She didn't want them to see the tears beading up in her eyes. She could hardly believe it. Had she really been the one to succeed in leading the Were?

It seemed so.

———

The building's walls made it impossible to pick out words in Silver's conversation with Raul, but Andrew strained to hear it anyway. What did she think she was doing, putting herself in danger?

Andrew jerked his wrists against the silk-covered chains. No one was left inside to watch him. If he could escape now . . . But the chain wouldn't break, and he couldn't move the piece of farm equipment more than another half inch. His muscles screamed as he bucked again. Why had Silver come? This was his burden to bear, his mistakes to suffer for.

The door creaked and Andrew froze. Felicia slipped inside, head down and hair hiding her face. It reminded him of how Nate's daughter had looked. Was Felicia really so ashamed of him? Andrew tried to find words, but after all that had happened, he couldn't. If only. If only things had been different with her. But they weren't different, and he needed to accept that.

Felicia circled around the wheel beside Andrew. He couldn't turn his head far enough to follow her, but her shoes scuffed like she'd crouched behind the axle at his back. "*Why would she offer herself in your place?*" she whispered in Spanish, as if speaking to herself.

Andrew choked. Silver was—Lady! "Silver! Don't you dare!" he shouted at the top of his lungs, bucking the wheels desperately.

"*Why would you walk into a trap for a human just because she called herself a member of your pack?*" Felicia whispered into the panting space when Andrew had to rest from the effort of lifting the metal.

"Because it's the right thing to do," Andrew snapped. He couldn't explain it any better, and at the moment he didn't feel like trying. If only Silver and Raul would move closer so he could hear what was going on.

"*Actions,*" Felicia murmured, and then drew in a jagged breath. Her fingers touched Andrew's wrist and he froze. Hope surged into life, painful in its jaggedness. Had she chosen him over Raul after all? Had what he'd said gotten through?

She placed her hand full on his arm, the first they'd touched since she was three years old, Andrew realized. "I'm sorry." Then her fingers fumbled at the small lock and a key clunked. She hissed with discomfort at the nearness of the silver and Andrew's wrists dropped free.

A thousand phrases crowded on Andrew—thank yous, scoldings for her actions before, pleas for her to continue to help him. He squashed them all. The surge of hope had left a realization in its wake. He couldn't let himself be manipulated like that, cast down by Raul and swooping high at the slightest crumb of encouragement only to be inevitably cast down again. Felicia would choose what she would choose. He had to let her go and live his life as if she could take care of herself, if he was to lead anyone.

"Thank you," he said, without quite looking at her. She nodded, not quite looking at him, either, as she slipped to the door. She let herself out quietly and closed it behind her. She would keep the others from seeing him, but not stay and help, apparently.

Andrew retrieved the key, bent, and freed his feet. He shrugged off the mess the whip had made of his shirt, then pushed himself up and strode for the door. At least, he tried to stride. His head swam. While sitting down, he hadn't realized just how little energy he had left. He slowed down, stopped. He couldn't fight five at once, even if he had Silver's help, even completely healthy.

Andrew checked the building's walls, but even with his new range of movement, he couldn't find any good options. The windows were small and high, and the large sliding door in front of the pickup was locked with a heavy-duty padlock, leaving only the small door that would take him out directly into the jaws of Raul and the other Spaniards.

Fine, then. He'd have to even the odds another way. He stooped and picked up one of the abandoned chains.

He kicked the metal wall near where he'd been chained and then positioned himself right beside the door. The dull thud should hopefully sound like he'd dragged himself and the wheeled contraption somewhere he shouldn't. Sure enough, a moment later the door opened and he looped the chain over Arturo's neck and snapped it taut. How did he like the feel of his own teeth turned back on him? The Spaniard's silent, choking struggles filled Andrew with a dimly familiar tide of savage satisfaction. If Arturo died, he'd die paying for what he'd done. There was a heady rightness to that.

Arturo threw himself back, smashing Andrew against the metal wall. Again, and again. Andrew nearly lost his grip as his head clanged off the metal and his vision grayed out for a moment. If he lost consciousness, Arturo would kill him for sure. At least he would have died fighting.

But Arturo was steadily losing strength. Andrew gritted his teeth and hung on even though he couldn't see properly. Arturo must have been having the same problem because he staggered and seemed to lose his sense of direction, but he still slammed Andrew against the metal again. The wall gave beneath Andrew's back—not the wall, the door. The door swung open and the two of them tumbled onto the concrete path beyond. Andrew rolled them so he was on top and used the angle to pull the chain even tighter. Slowly, Arturo stilled, unconscious.

"Planning to tear out his throat when you're done?" Death padded up to Arturo's head. He used a voice Andrew hadn't heard for a decade, the voice of Barcelona's beta, the voice of the first man he'd ever killed. Killed in a berserker rage for revenge, an action that wrenched his life onto a different path.

Andrew let the chain drop. He could snap Arturo's neck now, so easy. He even took a grip on the man's hair as he panted raggedly and his vision came back. So much pain Arturo had caused Andrew and those he loved.

But Andrew liked the path he was on now. He didn't need to walk old ground again. He let Arturo's head down. Death would have no voices tonight.

Death snorted. "He and his packmates used their voices mostly to repeat the thoughts of others. They're of no special value to me anyway."

"I see you have the situation well in hand." Benjamin's voice, close by.

Andrew jerked his head up, finally seeing what he and Arturo had fallen outside into. Every adult Were from the Convocation seemed to be there. As he watched, they finished spreading themselves into a semicircle, trapping Raul and his three remaining pack members against the outbuilding. Susan was also in the center, shaking, but standing tall between Raul and Silver. Raul had his empty hands up, his expression at its blandest and least threatening. A beta pushed out through the crowd, holding Raul's knife out at a slight distance, as if it was offal being taken for disposal.

Andrew pushed to his feet. How much had they all seen? The tense silence told him they'd seen plenty.

If they were silent, he might as well take what advantage he could from it. Andrew held out his arms so the shadows of bruises where he'd struggled against the bonds and the fading welts from the whips were obvious. Everyone would know that if those hadn't healed, his energy had gone to much worse injuries. "This is what Europeans do!"

The continued silence left nothing to hide the panting harshness in Andrew's voice. He'd wanted the rhetoric to ring, but he'd have to make do. "When they don't get their way, they try to take it by force. Madrid told me that if I didn't follow his orders, he'd take my eye with silver." Andrew drew a line over his eye with a fingertip, waited for the gasps to die down.

"That's the European way. In North America, we want nothing of the European way, do we?"

"No!" Someone growled, and others joined in. Hands seized Raul and the others. Andrew looked for Felicia at the edges of the crowd, but people bunched in too close. He yanked his attention back to Raul.

Silver strode to Andrew, naked relief peeking through her controlled expression. Her hand on his back made him want to collapse and curl up with her for days. But no rest for an alpha.

She glared at the assembled Were. "It took you all long enough to realize how you were being manipulated. I thought you weren't coming."

Andrew looked down at Silver. What had he missed? His confusion must have been obvious because Silver stepped away to sweep her good arm to the crowd. "Roanoke was kind enough to blame himself for what happened and step down from leading the expedition to deal with the Europeans. A new leader had then to be discussed, apparently at length." Silver's tone was so acid, Andrew caught several alphas flinching. He searched the crowd, but couldn't find a sign of Rory. No surprise he didn't want to be around to reap the consequences of his trick.

"Until the human showed them for the cowards they are," Benjamin said, on a low rumble of laughter. Susan lifted her chin higher, proud. And no wonder. She'd gotten them moving? Andrew needed to hear that story.

But Susan shouldn't have had to do anything in the first place. Disgust welled up until Andrew couldn't control the snarl that escaped. "So Rory played every single one of you, and you let him? Just ran, nose down to the trail he'd laid right into the hunters' arms?"

No one answered, but the words were tumbling out of Andrew, so he probably wouldn't have heard them anyway. "This! This is why we need to be united. I don't care under whom, as long as he or she is competent, but we can't live apart, letting threats pick us off one by one. The Lady granted us our wolf sides, and wolves hunt in packs. Together, we survive. Alone, we die. Look at how easy we are for the Europeans to fracture! One comment and we're completely useless. We cannot keep on this way!"

Andrew's words might have been rough, but the silence that followed them rang. He wasn't even quite sure what he'd done, except that all his pent-up frustration with the Western packs' willful stupidity and politics had bubbled up at once. He'd spoken without thinking. What was he supposed to do now?

"Well said, Roanoke." Benjamin went to one knee. Andrew drew in a ragged breath. As always, Boston was wiser than he. Perhaps he and Silver could depose Rory without a challenge if enough of the Roanoke sub-alphas supported them now, especially since Rory was still nowhere to be seen.

"You wish the Butcher of Barcelona for your Roanoke? A man so emotional he followed his daughter right into our trap?" Raul didn't smirk, didn't allow satisfaction into his voice, but Andrew heard it all the same. The man was so calm, you'd never have known his enemies had him surrounded.

"Oh, but you cured me of that, Madrid." Andrew strove for the same calm in his voice. "I carried a three-year-old's voice in my memory. That girl is gone. My daughter is Spanish now, you showed me that. I would protect her, the same as I would protect any of my pack, but I will not be controlled by anyone using her."

"And he does not lead alone." Silver shook her hair back and lifted her chin high, gaze straight ahead in an implicit offer to anyone who wanted to meet it and test her dominance. "What wounds one does not wound the other. This is the value of a pair."

"And he is a Butcher no more. You all saw. He chose not to kill." Benjamin brought his other knee down, spread his right palm flat on the ground, and leaned forward until his head nearly touched the ground too. Andrew wanted to wince. That was overplaying it a bit. He hadn't earned that degree of respect. Silver smelled similarly embarrassed by the gesture, but she slid her arm over his back again, a united front.

Each of Roanoke's sub-alphas went to their knees, some slower than others. Charleston glared before he dipped his head, which Andrew marked, but others went further, as Benjamin had done. Andrew started to breathe again when no one shouted in challenge or objection.

"Lady! You're each as crazy as the other, but Lady knows we seem to have need of that." Michelle sank to her knee and Andrew lost the calm he'd gained. He'd never dreamed one of the

Western packs would bow to Roanoke by choice, not in the deepest heat of his rhetoric about a united pack.

Sacramento knelt next. She jerked her beta down beside her, hard enough the woman cried out when her knees hit the ground. "Owe you both one," she murmured. The angle of her head partially hid her smile, but that made the visible corner of her lips seem even more sharply amused. "C'mon, boys. The women are showing you up."

Slowly, Denver knelt. Salt Lake followed, then Billings. Andrew's light-headedness pounded with each beat of his heart as one by one the remaining Western alphas and their betas and everyone knelt until no one was left standing but the Spaniards and those holding them.

Silver's hand spasmed where it was tucked into the waistband of his jeans. Andrew could guess her worry, very similar to his own. Somehow, outside of all expectation, they had this power. Now what did they do with it?

At least the problem in front of them was obvious enough. First things first. "Bring him." Andrew snapped his fingers to Raul and pointed to the ground in front of himself and Silver. When the man stood before him, Laurence and a beta holding either elbow, Andrew pressed a flat palm toward the ground, an intentional parody of a human gesture for a dog to sit.

Raul started to snarl and struggle, but the two Were forced him to his knees after a few moments of effort. Andrew didn't have the emotional energy left to enjoy the sight. "Someone take a picture. I think there might be a few interested to know that Madrid lost to us uncouth barbarians out here in North America. Barcelona, perhaps. I'll get you the number."

Several phones came out, and repeated flashes of light caught Raul's profile as his eyes widened with fear. Andrew had just enough energy to rejoice in *that*. Barcelona would be *delighted* to hear that his major rival for territory looked so weak. Andrew didn't know if Raul would lose his pack once they saw the picture too, but he'd have the fight of his life on his hands. Couldn't happen to a better man.

"Take them to the Phoenix airport." Andrew jerked his thumb vaguely south and Raul's guards let him shove to his feet. "Guard them until they're on the first direct flight overseas, I don't care where. They can manage transfers on someone else's territory."

People pushed to their feet, coalescing into a tough barrier between Raul and any thoughts he might have of making a run for it. Someone jerked a groggy Arturo to his feet and herded him in with the others. Together, they all headed back toward the ranch. Silver's breathing was ragged as she walked with him. Her shoulder must be in agony from the jarring of her path over uneven ground. Their success didn't seem real to him, as much a hallucination as Death. He and Silver were Roanoke—of all of North America?

Arturo twisted to look back and was roughly jerked back on his path. *"What about the girl?"* he demanded of Raul, voice rough from a still-healing throat, apparently trusting to the language barrier to keep the comment somewhat private. *"You plan to leave her behind? Throw her to the North Americans to appease them?"* The other Spaniards looked from Arturo to Raul and back again, restive.

"I intend nothing of the sort," Raul snapped, lacking some of his usual cool. He raised his voice to play to the crowd. "You can't keep your daughter here against her will, Dare. That would

be dishonorable." He used his accent to twist the last word mockingly.

Andrew stopped and searched the clearing around the buildings and the trees beyond one more time. There, in the shadow of the outbuilding. A darted movement. Felicia, but running away. If she'd been close enough to hear what was happening and she was running, that choice was clear enough. Part of him demanded that he go and find her, comfort her, but that was a very small part now. Other people needed him first. She wouldn't die of a little delay.

"She'll have exactly the choice you never intended to give her," Andrew said. He raised his voice, not for the other alphas, but to carry to Felicia. "If she wants to stay, she's welcome to join any pack she likes or go roaming. If she wants to go, she can approach anyone. They'll get her on a plane back to Spain and I'll pay them for the ticket."

"*Felicia!*" Raul stopped and shouted it to the woods. "*Hurry up.*" Raul tried again with her name while everyone waited in charged silence, and his pack grew more restless. Raul snarled at them. "*She'll follow.* No one would choose to stay in a pack with such mongrels."

Laurence prodded him to get moving again. Raul made a show of walking cooperatively only to lunge at Andrew. Rage twisted his expression to a degree Andrew had never seen in him before. "*You've earned your death—*" he spat in Spanish. Laurence wrestled him back, and he fought him every inch of the way, his calm manipulation apparently subsumed under the thought of what awaited him at home.

More Were joined the effort, throwing Raul to the ground. A kick landed in his side, then another.

Silver growled. "There's no need for that."

Andrew was glad she'd said something, much as he would have loved to mete out a little punishment himself. A lot of punishment himself. But intellectually, he knew she was right. They had to take the high road. Were pulled Raul up and pushed him on his way with no further blows. As they walked, the trees grew sparser around the trail and people started to spread out to the grass on either side, talking excitedly in little groups.

Something slammed into him from the side.

Andrew struggled for breath from the impact as he skidded along the grass. Silver cried out, and Raul laughed.

Andrew got one arm up defensively as he pushed to his knees through pure instinct. He didn't have time to process what had just happened before his attacker rushed him again, on four feet. Andrew caught the wolf's teeth on his arm, keeping them from his throat. Rory! Rory was attacking him, already in wolf. Blood dripped as Rory forced Andrew's arm back toward his throat, teeth sinking deeper and deeper. Andrew had to clench his own teeth to hold back a gasp from the pain.

Of course Rory wouldn't give up his pack without a fight. Dammit, Andrew should have expected that. Andrew dug the fingers of his free hand through fur into the tender skin of Rory's throat. He gouged until the man choked and relaxed his grip enough for Andrew to rip free and stumble back and up to his feet. He was at an incredible disadvantage, stuck in human while Rory was in wolf. The cat's bastard must have been off in the woods for quite a while, giving him the time he needed to change in the new.

"If you want anyone to follow you if you win, give me time to *shift*," Andrew snarled. He probably should have also expected Rory wouldn't care about an honorable challenge when his power was on the line. Growls rippled around them both, other Were reacting to Rory's dishonor. In a real challenge, opponents faced each other in human before shifting at the same time. But Rory had drawn blood, marking the challenge fight officially joined. No one could stop it now, or they would have committed an offense worse than Rory's.

Andrew's arm seeped blood steadily. Not good. Not only did it mean he was dangerously low on energy, despite the boost adrenaline had given him, it meant more was dripping away even as he stood still.

Rory ignored his words and lunged again. Andrew could hardly have shifted completely between an enemy's lunges in the full, never mind in the new, so he dodged, and dodged again. But sooner or later Rory was going to trap him against one of the pines surrounding them and then Andrew would be at the mercy of his teeth, with none of his own to answer.

Andrew's vision smeared and he stumbled against a tree trunk of his own choice to hold himself up. He snarled again, to show Rory he wasn't going to give in, whatever dirty, cheating tricks the coward pulled. Andrew had defeated and humiliated *Raul,* a man whose cleverness made Rory look like a Pomeranian in comparison. Andrew wasn't going to lie down because Rory's teeth were currently sharper. Never.

No amount of rage or confidence could give him a wolf's teeth, but maybe they could help him shift. Andrew focused on every short-sighted, cowardly, selfish, and dishonorable thing Rory had ever done, and braced to block Rory's next lunge while he scrabbled for the shift. He just had to hold Rory off long enough, feel angry enough that the shift came quickly in the new. But the shift was still so damned far away . . .

But Rory's next lunge didn't come. Andrew refocused on his surroundings to find John blocking Rory's path, soon joined by Benjamin, and others. "You'll wait until he shifts," Benjamin snapped, contempt draped over every word.

Rory growled, and prowled on the other side of the wall of people, but didn't try to shoulder through. Andrew dragged off his remaining clothing and reached for the shift through the buzzing, grayed-out feeling of adrenaline that was almost gone.

And then he had it, and the transition was almost easy. Or maybe not easy, but filled with a rightness that got Andrew on four feet within a minute. This was what he'd come here for, to challenge Rory. All for this, and he wouldn't fail.

The shift scabbed the wounds on his arm—now foreleg—and Andrew took the fight to Rory as the others stepped back. He lunged and they both went to their hind legs, each grappling for a grip on the other's neck as they growled. Andrew broke away first, when Rory's greater strength began to tell. He was faster, better suited to quick lunges in and then out again.

The pain and the growls and the hovering fog of exhaustion made it hard to think, but something about the fight didn't feel right. Andrew danced back and once more Rory's snap missed him by inches. A realization hit Andrew as hard as Rory had at the beginning of the fight: Rory had gone soft. Andrew had been his enforcer for nearly a decade. When in that time had Rory fought a battle of his own? Not once.

"More fool he," said a wolf-shaped shadow between the feet of the spectators. Andrew caught only a glancing glimpse of Death before he focused on Rory again, but he felt almost like laughing. Rory *was* a fool. A fool who probably still believed in his greater strength.

The realization gave Andrew a burst of energy, and he used it to act the opposite. On his next stride, he dragged his leg, just enough for Rory to notice the limp. Andrew bet Rory was too arrogant to think twice or question an opening like that . . . Rory lunged for him like he was certain he was about to finish him off, but Andrew twisted and closed this teeth around Rory's throat, good and deep, ready to go deeper. Soft, slow, and predictable. Fool.

Rory still tried to shake him off, and fresh blood filled Andrew's mouth. As Rory realized how close to death he was if he didn't stop moving, Andrew changed his grip to bear Rory to the ground. Rage vibrated in Rory's muscles, but he slowly relaxed, ceding the fight.

Andrew let him go and stepped carefully back. He was shaking a little himself, and his legs felt like they might collapse any minute. He'd done it. Won Roanoke. Won it twice over.

Now he had to shift back, of course. He couldn't have his first official act as alpha be to collapse, panting, still in wolf. Euphoria made him light-headed, brought a laugh nearly bubbling up. He knew it would hurt, but for a few moments he just didn't care. He'd won! Andrew pushed back into human before good sense could reassert itself.

Muscles and bones always screamed protests in the new, but this time they were injured, and exhaustion dragged the process almost too long to stand. But Andrew made it, shaking with the relief of being fully back in human. He pushed to his feet immediately, telling himself the movement couldn't be as bad as shifting. It wasn't, but the way his head pounded, graying out his vision, wasn't exactly good. He made it up and tried desperately not to sway. He concentrated on looking like surveying the

Were ranged around them was his true purpose for standing still, not that he was unable to walk.

People fidgeted, like they weren't quite sure whether to kneel again, as they would after a normal challenge fight. Rory's wife had joined the group, and she pushed to the front now with Ginnie held on her hip. Sarah had smoothed most other signs of anxiety from her body, but if she was holding her ten-year-old like that, she couldn't be calm. Humans weren't usually strong enough for that, so Were avoided the gesture in case they slipped up in public. "It seems we have a new alpha, Ginnie," Sarah said softly, as if wrapping up a previous conversation. Andrew inclined his head to her.

With only a slight scrabbling in warning, teeth sank deep into Andrew's calf. He yelped with shock and staggered. Did Rory *want* to be killed? That was how challenges sometimes ended in Europe, when someone refused to concede when bested.

"That's what you want your daughter to remember?" Andrew's voice came out rough, but there was nothing for it. "Her father's dishonor? I would value her opinion a little higher than that, if I were you. Trust me, I would know."

"Daddy?" Ginnie's voice startled Andrew, focused as he was on Rory's teeth in his leg. "Why are you cheating?"

Rory slowly released his hold and backed up, shaking his head in a canine gesture that still evoked the one in human: *no, no, no!* Silver darted in and placed herself solidly beside Andrew, arm across his back. The relief was so great, Andrew's vision went blurry for a moment before he adjusted his stance so he could lean on Silver but not collapse on her. She accepted all the weight he put on her without showing a sign of it.

"Since Rory has made such great friends, I think he should

join them. Put him on the plane with Madrid." The pleasure of saying it gave Andrew's voice a little more strength.

Rory's body language sharpened with sudden fear and Raul snorted from where he was being held. The Madrid pack would not welcome Rory into their territory, Andrew was certain. He'd have to find his own way in Europe once he was on the ground.

Sarah set her daughter down and tugged Ginnie with her to her knees. "Roanoke, please. For Virginia's sake. Exile us if you must, but not to Europe. That's no place to raise a child."

Andrew cursed mentally. Of course she'd follow him. He should have considered that. "I said him, Sarah, not you and the girl." Dammit, why did she have to force his hand? He didn't want to appear weak by backing down, but in a rather ironic mirror to Raul, he'd try to save any child he could from Europe's culture of violence. "There's no reason you have to go with him," he said heavily. He gestured for her to rise.

Sarah rose and placed a protective hand on Ginnie's back as the girl clung to her waist. "He's a good father, a good husband, whatever his other faults."

The certainty and loyalty were so strong in her voice Silver inclined her head in respect. Andrew exhaled in a rush. That made his only possible choice clear enough. If it made him look weak, so be it. "Ottawa." He waited until the alpha stepped forward from the crowd. "I'm sending Rory and his family back with you. Find them somewhere to live beyond your border, in northern Quebec maybe, and make sure *he* stays there." Andrew underscored the last pronoun with a snarl—Rory's family was welcome to leave the wilderness to visit other packs. Rory was not.

Sarah half-sobbed with relief and strode to Rory to bury her hand in the fur of his ruff as if seeking comfort. Because Silver had done it to him so often, Andrew noticed how that touch also nudged Rory toward Ottawa and out of his presence. Good for her.

Andrew could only hope Sarah would take advantage of her ability to leave sometimes, and that he hadn't just ruined Ginnie's childhood by exiling her without a pack. His chest tightened at the thought, but there was another young life he would have to trust to her own inner strength.

Andrew looped an arm over Silver's shoulders as another point of support. Her loose hair made his grip slip until he pushed it aside. A moment later he realized someone had just said something to him. What had it been? No matter how he tried, he couldn't find any memory of the actual words. "Later," he said. Apparently that answer made sense, because the alpha stepped back.

He drew a deep breath. Time to make a fast exit as gracefully as possible. "Other decisions will have to wait until morning. I need to consider who would be best suited to any positions that need filling." The murmurs seemed positive, so Andrew pushed forward along the path back to the cabins. His vision narrowed to the ground immediately in front of his feet long before they reached the buildings and the gravel grew tinged with light from each cabin they passed. After the small eternity to reach the cabins, the walk among them was almost too much. Why had he picked the farthest, again?

John opened the door for him when they reached the cabin. "So you'll be moving back East?"

Andrew and Silver couldn't fit through the door very well

side by side so he nudged her on ahead. Of course John was impatient. He wanted to know if he'd get his pack back. Well, he could wait like everyone else—

The floor slammed into Andrew's hands. He caught most of his weight short of a full faceplant, but he let himself down to sort it all out in his head. He'd fallen, obviously. It must have been the lip of the doorframe. In another moment of delayed memory, he recalled the feeling of his foot catching.

"Lady above, how'd he get this bad?" John helped Andrew to a sitting position before pulling him farther inside. "I thought he smelled hurt, sure, but . . ."

Andrew would have protested the indignity, but he heard Silver burst into tears. The last thing he wanted to do was worry her. This would pass in a moment. "Love. Love, I'm fine." He tried to push away from John and reach for her. Things . . . tilted, and next thing he knew, John was holding his shoulders again.

"Shut the door," John snapped. "Boston, are you sure you need to be here?"

Andrew couldn't see Benjamin from where he was sitting, but he heard the low warmth of the man's laugh after the door clicked closed. "I'm familiar with the concept of those in power falling to pieces in private once in a while. My loyalty to Roanoke won't be shaken, beta."

John hesitated for a second, but he must have come to some decision. "Help me with him," was all he said.

The next time things made sense, Andrew was on his bed and Silver was climbing in to press herself against him as if trying to find every single point that one body could physically intersect another. She was crying more quietly now, a tang of salt and dampness against Andrew's skin. "I'm sorry," he murmured. For worrying her, for getting caught, for having such terrible in-laws, and probably more he couldn't think of.

"No," Silver said, distinctly but emphatically into his chest. "Don't you dare."

Andrew huffed a laugh and let his mind drift.

35

Silver woke to the feeling of cold where once there had been warmth on one side. Dare slept on at her other side. Death stood close enough that it made her wonder: had he been sleeping beside her? She couldn't quite tell, though a feeling lingered of being tucked between two sources of warmth rather than just one from Dare. Silver decided to pretend she hadn't noticed.

She rolled over and found Dare's wild self at his feet. She buried her hands in its fur, searching for any lingering injury. The scars on his back looked only as bad as they always had. Rest and plenty to eat would help the hollow and pale look of his tame self's face.

Silver could have stayed there a lot longer, watching Dare's face as he slept, but a need to relieve herself drove her up. Dare didn't even stir, a mark of how hurt he was. When she was done, hunger had also awakened, and Silver foraged for food as the light warmed and strengthened with dawn.

Silver slipped outside to eat and breathe in the fresh air, sweet with a day's promise. She found a place to sit out of easy hearing but not sight of the dens. Death curled comfortably just far enough away he could not be said to be at her feet. She could come to like these mountains with time, she decided. Not the trees, too sharp and sparse, but the slopes had a beauty when considered from a distance.

Thank the Lady Dare had been all right. And somehow they'd won everything they'd been fighting for and more. Thinking about it still made her head hurt. When had it gone from being impossible to being inevitable, like running downhill? She hadn't been trying to win anyone over, and she suspected Dare hadn't either, they'd just done what they thought was right. Perhaps that was the point—they'd done what needed to be done because it needed doing, and the other alphas had seen that.

Felicia's scent, filled with suspicion and anxiety, curled into Silver's nose long before the girl herself appeared. Her dark hair was tumbled like she'd snatched only naps last night, curled up somewhere. "Hello," Silver said, and then ate in silence. She was too wrung out to even wonder what the girl might want.

Felicia found a seat on a rock a short distance away. Not within reach, but not so far she had to raise her voice. "I still don't understand why he left me," she said finally into the small sounds of wind through branches and over grass, the world waking.

"Have you ever heard the story of how the Lady had to first leave her children?" Silver suspected Felicia had, and the girl nodded, but she didn't object. Good. Sometimes you had to hear a story all over again to find a new meaning.

"It was the humans. In the beginning, their gods walked among them as the Lady did among us. But the humans breed too quickly. Their gods could not resolve so many conflicting desires when they were so easy to petition in person. So the human gods withdrew, forcing their followers to find their own strength or truly work for the help they needed.

"But the Lady's children were few. Lost in Her love for them, She paid no attention to what the humans did, or to the human gods. The humans grew greedy, as humans do. Perhaps they wanted to take what we had, or perhaps they were simply envious, and wanted to make sure that if they were abandoned by their gods, so too were we."

Felicia hugged herself. Thinking of abandonment, perhaps.

"In those days, we lived forever. Only fire could destroy us, because fire destroys everything created so creation can begin anew. But we did not know this, did not understand how a life could end. When the humans came with fire, we would have all fallen before them if not for Death. He took the first of us before the humans arrived, and taught us of mortality so we understood the threat the humans brought. We fought back. We were not all killed, but we could no longer live forever.

"And so to punish Death for his betrayal in harming us, the Lady had to take his voice, leaving him to use those of the souls he brought back to Her. And to punish Herself for failing to protect us, She had to leave us, so that She no longer attracted the humans' envy to us with Her light."

Silver paused until Felicia looked up in confusion, and she caught the girl's eyes. They were a little wide, still frightened. "But we didn't understand. We saw that we could die, and we saw that the Lady had left us. Some of us cursed Her name, and vowed to renounce Her as She had renounced us.

"And some clung to the belief that She would return someday, if we were somehow . . . good enough. But She never did. Because it didn't matter what She wanted, She was caught by circumstance. It did not change Her love for us—in fact, it made it stronger. But sometimes . . ." Silver tried to find the right words.

"Things fall apart," Death said, the cadence of his voice heavy too. "To quote a human."

Silver repeated Death's words. "And sometimes you build anew. Not the same, but still something."

Felicia shook her head, like her wild self would to dislodge a burr from its ruff. Silver could only hope her story was like that burr, refusing to let go. "That isn't how I heard the story," Felicia said.

Silver shrugged. "Maybe the story changed. Maybe the listener did." She pushed to her feet. "You must be hungry. Come in for some breakfast? Dare isn't awake yet. "

Felicia shied back. "I'll find something."

"You have to decide soon." Silver wanted to reach out to the girl, but she turned the gesture into combing her fingers through her hair. "You can't stay here in the woods alone forever."

"But I don't have to decide yet." Felicia twisted fingers into her hair too, bringing it over her shoulder in a tail. Then she turned and it all tumbled back out again. She loped away.

"No, not quite yet," Silver said, and went back to the den. She left her breakfast on the rock. She could get more inside, and the girl would be hungry by now.

Andrew snapped into full wakefulness with a surge of panic. Where was Silver? Her scent around him, diffuse as it was, started his heart slowing before his mind worked out what had happened. He must have been too exhausted to wake briefly when she got up as he usually did. She was still safe.

And she'd left him breakfast. The smell of food reminded Andrew he was ravenous, and he groped for the bags on the nightstand. He assumed it was Silver who'd left them because the leftover sandwich fixings were still separate: a loaf of bread and packages of cheese and lunchmeat. Andrew didn't bother with assembly himself, just ate the first package of ham slices all together in a single stack. Bread could wait.

Silver slipped out of the bathroom, still nude from the shower. Water glistened on her pale skin where she'd missed it with the towel she was currently using on her hair. She caught him appreciating and grinned as she dropped the towel.

Andrew tossed the empty lunchmeat package aside and stretched, testing how much he'd healed. He stuck with just appreciation for the moment. "Where's your sling, love?" He held out his hand and Silver sighed. She turned back to the bathroom, giving him another good view, and returned with the sling as well as her shirt and bra.

Andrew pushed himself up and Silver sat down beside him. Getting her dressed without jarring her shoulder too much required a lot of concentration. When he finished, Andrew demolished the rest of the food in double- and triple-stacked sandwiches while Silver watched with amusement.

With the edge of his hunger gone, Andrew slid an arm around her waist and rested his cheek against her neck. Back to business, he supposed. With a night of rest behind him, food in his stomach, and breathing in Silver's scent, things didn't seem quite so overwhelming.

He laughed, a low breath of sound. "So we're alphas of all of North America now."

Silver laughed too. "It seems someone should be."

Andrew thought back to another conversation, sitting close on another bed. Then, Silver hadn't wanted to lead. "You'll be a good alpha."

Silver brought up her good hand to pet his hair. "As will you. If you won't doubt yourself, I won't doubt myself. Deal?"

Andrew kissed her neck. He was the luckiest Were alive, to have her to share the burden with. "Deal. Who should we make our beta?"

Silver cupped his jaw with her palm. "Where are we going to live?"

Andrew laughed. "One thing at a time!"

Silver smacked the side of his head lightly. "It's related. Are we going to settle somewhere with an enforcer, like you used to be? Are we going to do the traveling ourselves? It changes what our beta would need to be good at."

Andrew started to answer and caught himself, trying to consider more carefully. Just because Rory had used an enforcer didn't make the position a sign of weakness. "If it were just me," he said at length, "I'd say I'd have to travel. The Western packs aren't going to be comfortable for a long time, if ever. I think it will help if the alphas show up personally to deal with their problems."

"I agree." Silver's words had the smell of sincerity, but her muscles tensed in anticipation. "When you were enforcer, you still had a home, didn't you? Even if you didn't get to spend much time there."

"Sort of. I had Laurence clear out the apartment and put my

stuff into storage when I had to stay out West." Andrew frowned, casting about for a mundane detail in the midst of all that had happened recently. He'd paid the last bill for the unit, hadn't he? There was nothing there he'd particularly cry over losing, but he liked some of the furniture. "I'm not tied there, though. We can base the pack anywhere we want. I can't think of a time when a Roanoke actually lived in Roanoke the city."

When Silver didn't say anything else, Andrew smoothed a hand down her side. "What's wrong?"

"I think we should keep our home in Seattle. Or somewhere in the West. You said yourself, we won't be there much. The original Roanoke sub-packs are used to working together, and listening to a distant alpha. The others would benefit more from the gesture of having the alphas settle nearby." She hiccupped in her next breath. "And I am tied there, I think. The scents I grew up with, and being near my cousin—"

"Shhh," Andrew murmured, tightening his arm around her soothingly even as he thought. She did have a very good political point, anything else aside. Being closer to the Western packs would be very good PR. In the East, he had Benjamin. If Andrew could talk him into it, he'd make an excellent . . . neither enforcer nor beta seemed quite the word that Andrew wanted. Leader, perhaps, for the other sub-alphas. Someone to provide an example to channel them in the right direction. "I think it's a good idea. I presume your cousin will want his pack back, though. We probably can't stay in Seattle itself."

"I don't know." Silver relaxed against Andrew now, exhaling on a laughing note. "I think he's rather taken to being a beta. And he's still got to come to terms with Susan before he goes back to being alpha."

"We'll have to ask him privately first." Andrew turned the idea this way and that, and found it stood up. John had been good as a beta here, and as long as he wasn't resentful, he'd make a good choice. "While we're away he'll have a lot of autonomy anyway. I could hand Rory's home pack over to Laurence, let him take them to Richmond or something."

Silver patted Andrew's knee and then scooted to the edge of the bed. "That was easy." She paused for his laugh, and dodged his grab after her. "You should eat some more."

Andrew's stomach growled, reminding him of how quickly calories burned away while healing. He sighed and slid his feet to the floor. "I should. We might as well let in some of the people who want to talk to us while I do, though." No rest for the alphas.

36

It may have been all over but for the shouting, but there seemed to Susan to be an awful lot of shouting to be done. Or talking, at least. A parade of people tromped in and out of the cabin starting the moment Andrew was up and dressed. They didn't even wait for him to finish breakfast. He ate continuously and Silver grazed as they talked to each person. Susan was glad she'd gotten her breakfast earlier before the Were demolished all of it.

Even without formal meetings the nursery was still operating, so Susan dropped Edmond off. Once she was back on the gravel path outside of that cabin, she found that she didn't actually know what she was planning to do with her free time. She'd been acquitted, Silver and Andrew had what they wanted, and the bad guys were exiled. Shouldn't she be breaking out the champagne instead of feeling so strange?

John came out of the Seattle cabin as she returned. He was

much more polished this morning, the well-groomed man she'd met at a trade conference rather than the Were who looked like he'd forgotten to comb his hair half the time. Susan wasn't sure she liked the change. Too much water had passed under the bridge since they'd been the people at that conference.

"Susan!" John put a hand behind her back, not touching, but urging her to the side. Even without that, the awkward way he shoved his hands into his pockets suggested he wanted to talk. "Dare—Roanoke says that he wants me as beta for all of the Roanoke pack, if I'm willing to give up alphaship of Seattle."

Susan massaged her temple. Just when she thought she understood most of the Were's hierarchy. "So who would be alpha of Seattle, then?"

John shook his head with a sheepish grin. "The Roanoke has a home pack. Kind of his White House staff, I guess you could say? If I agree, Silver and Dare will stay, and the old Seattle pack will become the Roanoke home pack."

"And what do you want to do?" Susan searched his face. Did this sudden polish mean he wanted to go back to being alpha? He'd said the responsibility weighed on him, but maybe he thought it would be different under Andrew. She hadn't liked John as alpha, but she didn't want to hold him back. More than his refusal to touch her in public, she hated the feeling that it was a symptom of him feeling she was holding him back. If she kept him from being alpha, that would be even worse.

"I'm not sure. Roanoke's a charismatic guy. You could make the argument that beta of all the Roanoke pack is a higher rank than alpha of one small pack." John shoved his hands deeper into his pockets. "There's Edmond to consider . . ."

Susan's stomach clenched. There it was. It was almost a relief to have it out in the open. "And me. An alpha with a human mate. Or wife." She held up her left hand and rubbed her thumb against the empty ring finger. "Because Christ, John, if you're not taking that into account, you should be." The words kept coming, buoyed on the high of finally saying them. She didn't even care about the way John tensed his shoulders against them.

"I've seen the way Andrew and Silver balance each other. Whole greater than the sum of the parts. She evens out his temper, and he grounds her in reality. They'll be better alphas together than they ever would alone. In the same way, if you were alpha, I'd want to balance you, not diminish you. But you have to *let me*, John."

John finally brought a hand out of his pocket to brush a wisp of hair away from her face. "I love you, Susan. With all my heart— every tone of my voice, as we would say. I only ever wanted to protect you from the others . . ."

"Fuck them!" None of the people walking by or talking on the front steps of the other cabins looked at them, but Susan could feel their attention like they were in wolf form with ears to swivel. Susan gestured widely. Let them have a show. "Fuck all the other Were. My son is Were, the man I love is Were, I have friends among the Were. I killed to protect Were. I led them when they couldn't lead themselves. I should be a fucking adopted Were by now for what I've done for all 'the others.'"

Boston came out and shut the Seattle cabin door with a soft click. He did them the courtesy of looking at them directly as he wandered over. "A woman who knows what she wants. Also another very Were quality."

Susan stared at Boston in surprise, and he nodded to her, paternally encouraging. That tipped her over, turning frustration fully into the high of not caring what happened. She dragged John into the middle of the path where the most people could see them. She laced fingers into his hair, mussing up the stupid groomed lines, and pulled his lips onto hers. She pulled up every drop of frustrated arousal she'd been shoving down, concentrated by their dry spell into something that flared up and all but took over her body. She arched to mold herself against him, holding tight to keep him there as she kissed him hungrily. Let the others see this. Let the others smell what she was feeling now.

And John kissed her back. It took a second longer for his hands to find her back, but he kissed her so hard it fanned the flames even higher, spreading them outwards from their low point of origin. When they came up for air, he looked bemused, but finally, *finally* not ashamed. "Like I said before, I have a lot to learn. Better I learn it as a beta."

"Good." Susan drew in a husky breath. Chasing, Andrew had said. Maybe they'd try some of that. She pulled away from him with a laugh, skipped a few steps backward and waited.

John stared at her in confusion and didn't move. Susan opened her arms. "Well? Aren't you coming?" She waited until he was nearly close enough to touch and skipped back again. She saw his realization in the spread of a smile across his face. She ran, and this time he followed with a loud bark of a laugh. Susan headed for the stables. It seemed like a good place to be alone.

37

Packing for the return trip two days later was mostly a matter of throwing things into suitcases and then throwing the suitcases into rental cars, but with every pack doing it at once, things got chaotic. Barred from heavy lifting by his newly confirmed beta, Andrew found himself in the position of watching it all happen rather than participating.

Andrew squinted at the mountains as he stood with his shoulder against the corner of the cabin. Late afternoon sunlight was still strong enough to give a slight warp to the air. He realized he was searching for something only when his eyes passed over the same sweep of trees a third time. No sign of Felicia, of course.

But then by now he didn't really expect there to be. He'd put a pack with her clothes, her passport, and some cash out in a clearing, and had Tom guard it from a distance. He said she'd taken it. With that, she could go anywhere she wanted, and she'd hardly starve when she could hunt in wolf.

Andrew rubbed his thumb absently over his opposite knuckles. He'd been sixteen when he first set off roaming. Felicia wasn't that much younger. She'd be fine.

John shut the side door of the van after buckling in his son. Susan passed him on her way back from ferrying the diaper bag to the trunk. His initial hesitation made the motion not quite smooth, but he patted her ass anyway. They both laughed, and Susan knocked her hip into him before heading back into the cabin for another bag.

"Finally," Silver murmured into Andrew's ear after coming up behind him. He suppressed his laugh but not his smile.

"We need to leave soon if we're going to make the flight." John stopped respectfully in front of them. He followed Andrew's glance out into the trees and huffed in exasperated sympathy. "You put the printout of the flight itinerary in with the stuff you left for her, didn't you? If she wants to show up, she knows her deadline."

Susan slipped by with her last bag and squeaked when she was out of sight behind the van. It had sounded surprised to Andrew, not fearful, but John's head snapped around and he strode over. "I thought it was still too close to the new moon for you guys to want to be wolves," Susan said in annoyance.

Someone being in wolf was strange enough to send Andrew jogging after John. When he rounded the side of the van, Susan was accepting a familiar pack from a black wolf. Susan grimaced at the wolf slobber on the strap, and tucked it at the top of their pile of luggage.

He'd never seen his daughter's wolf form before, Andrew realized. Her scent made it clear that's who it was. He had no idea where the color had come from. Something recessive in Isabel's family, probably. He'd seen a few black wolf forms in Spain. His family was all gray. She had her mother's shape, though, lean and built for speed.

"Are you coming with us?" Andrew's heart thudded as he nodded to her pack, now shut away in the van. He didn't kid himself that she'd love him now and everything would be wonderful. But if she came with them, maybe he'd have time to win her over with more than just words.

Felicia tipped her head up to look at him, gave a canine snort, and went to stand imperiously by the van's side door. John opened it for her. She hopped gracefully in and flopped across the whole back row of seats.

"Silver, you can take the front. I'll—" Silver waved away any need for Andrew to even finish the sentence. They had a lot of them packed into the van as it was, so someone would have to take the backseat. John was driving, and Andrew didn't want to force Tom or especially Susan to share with Felicia.

Felicia eyed him and squished herself against the side of the van so no part of her would possibly touch him. He buckled in and looked out the window as Susan and Tom arranged themselves on either side of the car seat in the middle row.

Andrew watched the pines with great concentration as they pulled out of the ranch and onto the highway leading to the airport. He heard Felicia move, probably trying to curl comfortably in the small space she'd allowed herself, then move again.

After the third movement, her head slid onto his lap. She made a grumbling, growling sort of sound and finally relaxed. Andrew watched the hills and ruffled her ears. "Welcome to North America, puppy."

Turn the page for a preview of

Reflected

Rhiannon Held

Available in February 2014 from
Tom Doherty Associates

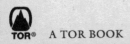

TOR® A TOR BOOK

1

Felicia ran full tilt, tongue lolling out as she panted. She'd let Tom catch her soon but not quite yet. She skidded in a U-turn, showering a bush with dirt and needles kicked up by her paws. Up ahead, near where they'd left their clothes, erosion had carved the descending path into a bare, hardened slide. Exposed roots provided improvised steps only here and there. It was much harder to navigate on four feet, without hands to grab at branches, but Felicia cleared most of it in one soaring jump and skidded down the rest.

At the bottom, she turned back in time to see the sandy-colored werewolf trip and slide down nose first. Tom rolled into it, ending on his back with his legs in the air. He gave Felicia an upside-down canine grin. Felicia snorted. Dignity? What was that? His fur tended to stand up every which way anyway, so the additional disarranging hardly made a difference.

Even without dignity, he was good-looking as a man and had an intriguing scent in both forms. Felicia twitched her tail as he righted himself and crouched low over his forepaws in an invitation to wrestle. Felicia waited to make sure he was watching her, then shifted back to human. No one cared about nudity, but watching the exact moment of shifting was very intimate. She knew he'd look away if he had warning. She wanted him to see her shift.

The Lady was near full, so the shift was as easy as diving into water from the bank above. When she finished and straightened, fully in human, his face showed he realized what she'd done. He turned his head belatedly.

Felicia crossed her arms under her breasts and waited. Even though it was June, it was late enough in the day that only slices of direct sunlight peeked through the trees, leaving much of her body in cool shadow. Seattle hadn't managed to muster much of a real summer the three years she'd lived there. She supposed at least they were better than the summers near Washington, D.C., where her father's home pack had been based before he'd expanded their territory to the rest of the country.

Tom shifted after an awkward moment. Felicia watched unapologetically. The twist of muscles from wolf to human had a real grace this close to the full.

"Felicia . . ." Tom pushed himself to human feet, his cheeks flushed with embarrassment. He held his ground, but only barely, as she walked up to him, rolling her hips. "What are you doing? We were just playing."

Felicia placed her hand on his shoulder and went to her tiptoes to breathe his scent from the curve of his neck. His light hair was too shaggy in human to stick up, but it tried anyway, making him look perpetually rumpled. His attraction was clear to smell, and it fed Felicia's own. She was tired of all this waiting. "You don't smell like just playing." She nipped at his ear and he shivered.

"That's not fair." Tom pushed her to the length of his arm. "I can't help that. But your father would kill me—"

Felicia caressed his wrist until he had to release the pressure holding her back if he wanted to avoid the touch. "What, I have to be celibate forever because I'm the alpha's daughter? How is *that* fair?"

Tom huffed. "It's not just that—" This time, when Felicia touched him, palm against his chest, he didn't push her away. He was still lankier than she thought of as her type, but he'd definitely filled out some muscles since she'd first met him. She wanted to caress them, sternum to navel and lower, trace the delicious curve of his hip bone, but she stopped herself.

He didn't push her away, but he didn't pull her closer, either. Felicia's stomach wobbled. Was he making excuses because he wasn't actually interested? She'd smelled attraction, but every Were knew that was sometimes physically unavoidable. Just because you smelled it didn't mean the other person wanted to act on it.

Felicia shook out her hair, wishing the black waves would curve smoothly together rather than always curling against each in an unruly mass. She looked down at her side, checking the smooth curve to her hip. There were other young men she could invite to a game of chase—*had* played that game with. They thought she was pretty enough. But Tom had never thrown himself at her. If she was honest with herself, she'd have to admit she could never really tell what he was thinking under the silly exterior.

Well, fine. If she was going to get herself rejected, she might as well get herself rejected for really trying. "I'm eighteen. Even the humans think that's legal. I can make my own decisions." Felicia balanced against his chest to whisper in his ear. "But if you're so scared of my father you can't get it up, I'd totally understand—"

Tom jerked back, but only to give himself room to claim her lips in a fierce kiss. His hands came up to her back and ass, yanking her tight against him. Felicia arched her body within the hold and gripped those glorious hips. Thank the Lady. She hadn't misread him. He did want her.

When they came up for air, he glanced at the lowering sun. "You know this close to the full the rest of the pack will probably be coming out here to hunt once they get off work," he said, resigned laughter in his voice.

"We have plenty of time. That just makes it more exciting." Felicia braced herself for another round of objections—why did Tom care so much what other people thought?—but he just grinned mischievously. He freed one hand and ghosted fingertips down her spine. The sensation was surprising, not quite ticklish, but something that made her back muscles arch without thinking. She gasped and shivered all over.

Tom rocked back a step, grinned wider, then danced out of her reach. "Better capture me quick, then." He dropped to rest fingertips on the ground as he shifted back to wolf.

Felicia shifted as quickly as she could to follow. Wouldn't want to give him *too* much of a head start, though she didn't want to capture him immediately either. That was the best part of sex, catching someone who was delighted to be caught.

Tom raced off through the thickest part of the underbrush,

and Felicia dashed after, jumping branches and crashing through ferns. Rather than going for distance and speed as they had in their earlier running, he captured the intensity of this chase by using the obstacles to keep them tangled close. When he darted one way, she darted the other, trying to cut him off, but he countered her every move until she panted with canine laughter.

Time for a new strategy, Felicia decided. She sprinted in a straight line away from him and hunkered down behind a downed tree's upturned roots. She pressed herself flat to the ground and watched between hanging clods of dirt as he followed her trail, slowly and suspiciously.

She surged out of her hiding place and bowled him over, both of them nipping at each other's fur as they rolled around in the dirt and pine needles. She knew perfectly well he'd been expecting that, but she didn't mind. She got on top of him and he surrendered with a flop of his head to lie stretched out flat on his side. She scrabbled back just enough to give herself room to shift to human to smirk at him. She'd captured him fair and square.

Tom shifted back and pushed to his feet, head bowed. Too late, Felicia caught the grin he was hiding. He lunged away, but she was fast enough to get a tight grip on his ankle. "Dirty cheat!" She was breathing almost too hard to get the laughing words out.

"You didn't think I'd make it easy on you—" Tom lost the rest of his words in the wheeze as she yanked his foot out from under him and he fell on his ass. She grabbed his calf and then the opposite thigh as she climbed up his body, knees on either side. No way was she taking her hands off him now.

"Gotcha." Teasingly, Felicia stopped short, straddling his thighs rather than his hips, and slipped her fingers along his length. She began by mimicking the ghosting pressure he'd used on her, growing more and more insistent. He moaned, whatever smart answer he'd been planning lost for good. She used her free hand on herself, rocking her hips as she tapped into the familiar delicious rhythm.

Tom touched her upper arms and drew her up until she was leaning over him and he could draw her nipple into his mouth. Felicia was about to prompt him, but his own experimental graze of teeth against it made her gasp and he increased the pressure until she almost couldn't stand it.

When she moved down his body again, she stopped at his hips and guided him into her. His hands settled on her hips as she wriggled, finding the perfect angle. Then the rhythm, slowly increasing. Felicia abandoned herself to it.

Tom might have seemed silly, but he was really good with his hands. And tongue. Like any first time together, it took some experimenting to find just the right pressure, just the right rhythm, but when they collapsed to tuck against each other, Felicia had no complaints. That had been *nice*.

Languid contentment pooled in her limbs. Even when the sweat drying on her skin started to chill her, Felicia didn't want to move.

Tom slid his arm over her waist, probably feeling the same chill. "Wow," he commented, tone warm rather than teasing.

"What, you thought I was as innocent as Father wishes I was? My first was back in Madrid, before I even met Father properly." Felicia tried to burrow against him for more warmth, but it was a losing battle. She finally surrendered and sat up. Tom stood first to help her up and then draped his arm over her shoulders as they wandered back up to the trail in search of their clothes.

They'd stashed their bags with their clothes in a tree a couple yards off the trail. Even if Felicia hadn't remembered where, the werewolf scents layered on human-made fabric stood out sharply among the growing things. Tom knocked their packs down, and they both rummaged. Felicia wished she'd thought to bring a brush. Her hair was probably a sight.

Cars had been coming intermittently up the winding road that bordered the Roanoke pack's hunting land, heading for the houses buried in the trees farther up the hill. Now one engine rumble slowed, changed direction, and stopped. A slammed door from close by made it clear someone had turned in.

"Lady!" Tom hurriedly dumped all his clothes into a pile rather than pulling out each piece in order. "Roanoke Dare is going to kill me."

Rather than jump to conclusions, Felicia waited it out until a few moments later a breeze came at the right angle to bring the newcomers' scents. "Father's not with them. It's just Silver and the beta."

Tom frowned. "Roanoke Silver, you mean." He threw her an apologetic grimace. "Sorry, Felicia, but your stepmother's just as scary."

"She's not my stepmother." Felicia immediately regretted the snap to her tone, but it was true, wasn't it? Fine, her father could have anyone he wanted as a mate, but that didn't give her any connection to Felicia. "They're not married. She's not my anything."

"She's still one of your alphas." Tom froze, underwear in his hands, as voices reached them.

"Go ahead. I'll be up by the stream," Silver said, presumably to John, the beta. Her white hair showed in flashes here and there through the trees farther down the trail. Felicia suppressed an instinctive urge to look back over her shoulder. The stream beyond them wouldn't have moved in the last few minutes.

Sudden laughter bubbled up in her. What were they worrying so much for, anyway? She was an adult; she could make her own choices. What did it matter if Silver found out? She'd had enough rest to regather her energy since the last shift, so she shifted to wolf and snatched Tom's jeans out of his hands. She stopped a few yards away, her turn to bend over her forelegs, and growled an invitation for him to try to get them.

Tom frowned without the humor she'd hoped for and grabbed for one pant leg. She took off, as fast as she could go on four legs. A beat later she heard Tom's growl, from a wolf throat this time. No surprise. No way he could keep up with her on two legs.

Since she was trying to avoid the beta and Silver as well as evade Tom, Felicia headed off the trail quickly, straight to the edge of the property. She ducked under the pathetic barbed-wire fence that marked the property line but couldn't really keep anyone out. It snagged a fluff of fur in retaliation.

Across a shallow ditch, pavement sliced through the trees. She hadn't realized she'd been heading for the road, but it had probably been inevitable. The pack's hunting lands weren't that big. Tom crashed through the underbrush behind her, and she danced onto the road to keep out of his reach, grinning as she dragged his jeans along the ground. She backed onto the grassy rise on the other side until her tail brushed the fence, and she waggled the pants back and forth.

Tom tumbled under the fence and into the ditch, righted himself, and glared at her. After a moment and with a visible sigh, he bounded after her.

Then everything went wrong all at once.

Felicia registered the purr of a sports car barreling down the hill barely a heartbeat before the car itself flashed past. Tom gave a sickening canine shriek, the car thumped, skidded, swerved, and the engine growled away at even greater speed.

Felicia hurled herself back down onto the pavement. Tom. What had happened to Tom? Was he all right? Lady, please let him be all right.

Silver looked at Death when she heard Tom's scream, even as she pounded into as much of a run as she could get from her human legs. He seemed amused, no more, as he effortlessly matched his pace to hers, the advantage of four wolf legs. The low growl of some great beast, perhaps the cause of Tom's misfortune, disappeared down the mountain.

Something Silver couldn't see caught at her legs, tried to scratch and trip her. Thorns, her eyes told her, reaching malevolently for her skin, but she knew better than to trust her eyes. They suffered from the shadows that poisoning had brought to her mind. The deeper the shadows, the more unexpected the truth beneath. To help Tom, she needed to find that truth.

Two hands would have helped, but Silver did the best she could with one after tucking her scarred and useless arm more securely, hand in pocket. If the thorns caught that, she would bleed before she was done. She tore the plants up at the roots with her good hand and half slid down a hillside to reach Tom.

More shadows there—rushing water, tumbled to white over rocks, foaming up around the flat place where Tom lay. Water that Silver knew wasn't water. In her worry for Tom, the harder she tried to see something else, the more the rushing sound filled her ears. Felicia waded out into the current from the other side, red-tinted black fur remaining pristine and dry as she reached Tom and whined over him in shock.

"I'd hurry," Death said, using her brother's voice. Good advice, like her brother would have given, even though it wasn't him speaking.

Silver nodded and darted out to Tom. Water that violent meant danger. The sooner she dragged Tom out of it, the better. Felicia looked up from trying to nose Tom out of his protective curl around his injuries, so they could see the damage. Silver stroked his tame self's hair, sandy like the wild self's fur, and eased it to lie more comfortably, trapped beneath the wild self. Blood from both mixed on her hand and Felicia's ruff and in the water.

Felicia kept whining and Silver wished she could make the sound properly with her human throat. Finally, Tom's wild self relaxed enough for her to roll him over to see the wounds. The torn and abraded skin wasn't knitting, which meant his healing had more important things to do, like repairing smashed organs. They needed to get him out of the river to help.

Not river. *Path*. Having a plan focused her, and Silver found that understanding with a bubble-pop of relief. They needed to get him off the path. Felicia must have been thinking along similar lines, because she crouched and began to switch her wild self for tame with hands useful for carrying.

"No," Death snapped.

"No!" Silver held out her hand to stop Felicia before she even quite understood what Death was reacting to. Another growl approached from up the mountain, more uneven in tone than the beast that had hurt Tom. Felicia, surprised by Silver's order, settled back onto four feet as a human arrived and stepped out of her vehicle. A vehicle, not a beast.

"Oh, my God! Your poor dog!" The human woman smelled of children, though she had none with her at the moment. She jogged up and leaned over Tom, slippery black hair fanning down to hang over her shoulders.

Silver smoothed Tom's ears, trying to imagine he was a pet, not a Were she was desperate to get away from human eyes so further healing at werewolf speed would not raise alarms. "If we can just move him out of the way, my friend's around, we'll—"

The woman gasped in objection. "That'll take too long. I'll give you a ride down the hill, the—" She said a word Silver didn't understand but could guess at. One who healed pets, not humans. The last thing Tom needed, though he could have used a Were doctor. "—we use, she's really great. I'm sure she can do something for him."

Silver looked again at Tom's wounds. Which was the greater risk? Going along to the pet doctor, hoping that Tom's healing, without additional sleep or food, would stop short of the torn skin, leaving something to at least explain the blood? Or would it be better to knock the woman down, run for it?

And how would they take Tom with them if they did run? Felicia couldn't help carry him as her wild self, couldn't switch to her tame in front of the human. Silver couldn't drag him one-armed without showing strength greater than a human woman should have. She seemed to have no choice but to pray to the Lady the doctor would see nothing more than a pet with wolf ancestry.

"Thank you," she told the woman, accepting. She helped the human lift Tom into her vehicle and glanced back to see Felicia standing in the path, stock-still and smelling of anger at Silver's choice. Silver squashed exasperation she had no time for. Even if Felicia had a better idea, circumstances didn't allow her to share it, so better she put her effort into making this one succeed.

"Run, girl," Death said in a woman's accented voice that belonged to Felicia's and her father's past, not Silver's. Silver saw what he meant immediately. If Felicia ran off, Silver could justify coming back to find her later, after treating Tom. Meanwhile, Felicia could warn John what was going on.

But of course Felicia couldn't see Death. She stayed where she was, and the human woman turned back to her. "C'mon, boy," she crooned in a voice for a pet or a baby. "There's room in the back for you too." She got a grip in Felicia's ruff.

Too late. Silver would have to bring her other "pet" too. She almost called Felicia by her real name, but of course that wasn't a pet name. Silver wanted to snarl a curse. Names were hard enough for her to remember as it was. Glaring at Felicia's wild self, she remembered a thought she'd had on first meeting the girl: so much of her childhood had been shaped by flames.

"Smoke," Silver snapped, using an alpha's command in her tone before Felicia could decide to fight free of the human. "Come." She took over the woman's grip on Felicia's ruff, pushed her into the vehicle, and climbed up after. She smoothed Tom's fur along his head, one of the few places free of blood, and wondered what in the Lady's name she was going to do once they reached their destination and the only one who could speak was the one whose sight was obscured by shadows.

The human woman chattered in a bright tone as they traveled down the hill, but Silver could smell the stink of her worry. She seemed to think Silver would fall apart if she wasn't distracted. Silver would have preferred silence, though if the woman could have gotten Felicia to stop staring at Silver with wide, frightened eyes, Silver would have hugged her. She needed to *think*.

"I'd do it now, if I were you," Death said. He used what Silver thought of as "his" voice, though of course he had none of his own since the Lady had taken his from him. This voice must have belonged to someone long dead.

Silver pressed the heel of her hand between her eyes. Even if she could have said "do what?" out loud to Death with the human listening, he would have just laughed. She knew what he meant. She could see past the shadows, but the pain that caused had been worth it only once before.

She checked Tom again first, to stall. He was still unconscious, and the tears across his side seeped slowly and did not heal. Silver had no food for him, to give him more energy to heal, so perhaps the doctor would find something to explain all the blood after all.

But there would still be questions. Her name, the location of her home, payment. Silver knew she couldn't give the kind of answers the humans would want without one of her pack members with her. Unless she did what Death had already decided she must do. Lady, wasn't there any other choice?

She supposed not.